BLACKMAILED DOWN THE AISLE

LOUISE FULLER

To my parents.
For taking me to the library.
A lot.
Thank you.

CHAPTER ONE

THE PARTY WAS loud and hot and crowded.

Everywhere people were dancing, laughing, punching the air. Everyone was having fun. Everyone except Daisy Maddox. Leaning against the wall, her blonde hair lit up by the flashing strobe lights, she stood slightly apart, gazing critically across the room.

Nowhere in the world was as vibrant as Manhattan at midnight. And nowhere was more glamorous than Fleming Tower, the lean, gleaming skyscraper of steel and glass owned by her brother David's boss, Rollo Fleming, billionaire property tycoon and the party's host.

Daisy sighed softly. It was a great party.

As long as you were a guest!

Stifling a yawn, she glanced down at her uniform. If, like her, you were handing out glasses of champagne, then it was just another shift at work. And being a waitress sucked—no matter how cool the venue. Or how attractive the guests.

She glanced over at the young man who had been hovering at her elbow all evening.

Skinny, dark and charming, he was exactly her type. Ordinarily she might have flirted a little, but tonight she was struggling even to remember he was there.

'Come on!' He smiled at her hopefully. 'One little glass won't hurt.'

Behind his back, Joanne, another of the waitresses, rolled her eyes.

Daisy breathed out slowly. Six months ago she'd arrived at David's apartment, hoping to make it big on Broadway. Only just like the rest of her life nothing had gone to plan, and her dreams had got lost in a depressing loop of auditions and rejections. But all those years at drama school hadn't been entirely wasted, she thought wearily as, setting her expression to one of disappointment, she gave him a small, regretful smile.

'It's sweet of you, Tim. But I can't. Like I told you earlier. I don't drink when I'm working.' She glanced pointedly down at her uniform, but he wasn't taking no for an answer.

'It's not Tim—it's Tom. Come on. It's just one glass. I promise I won't tell.' He grinned encouragingly. 'It's not like the big boss man is here to catch you.'

Rollo Fleming. The 'big boss man.' Picturing his cool, handsome face—the one that gazed so disdainfully out from the Fleming Organisation's website—Daisy felt her heart thump nervously. It was true. Despite the fact that the party was in *his* building, for *his* staff, Rollo had declined to attend.

Of course, there had been the usual rumours he would turn up unannounced. Someone even claimed to have seen him in the foyer. But Daisy knew for sure that he wasn't coming. Rollo Fleming was in Washington on business, and by the time he returned the party would be wrapped up. Finished. Over.

And not just the party, she thought, glancing furtively at the clock on the wall.

'So do you work for him?'

Startled, she turned and saw that Joanne was looking curiously at Tom.

He nodded. 'Yeah, for about a year now.'

'Really?' Joanne's eyes widened. 'He is seriously hot. What's he like?'

Her question was directed at Tom, but Daisy had to bite her tongue to stop herself from replying. Hours scouring the internet had turned her into the world's leading authority on Rollo Fleming. Not that there was much to know. He rarely gave interviews and, aside from being photographed

with a string of breathtakingly beautiful models and socialites, his private life was largely undocumented.

Tom shrugged, and a mixture of awe and admiration
crossed his face. 'I don't have that much to do with him personally. But when it comes to business he's definitely got
the Midas touch. *And* he gets all the hottest babes.'

He frowned.

'He's kinda scary too though. I mean, he works insanely
hard and he's a total control freak. He knows everything
that's going on—and I mean every tiny detail. And he's
obsessed with honesty…' He paused, frowning. 'I was in a
meeting with him once and there was a problem. Someone
tried to cover it up and he was… Let's just say you wouldn't
want to get on the wrong side of him.'

Daisy felt her stomach twist.

Tom's words confirmed everything David had already
told her. Rollo Fleming was a ruthless workaholic and a
commitment-phobic philanderer. Basically a supercharged
version of Nick, her ex, and exactly the kind of man she
loathed.

Looking up, her heart gave a jolt—not at the memory of
her latest failed relationship but at the time showing on the
clock. Her shift was nearly over. On any other evening she
would have been relieved, but tonight was different. Tonight
was the first and hopefully the last time she would have to
choose between breaking a promise and breaking the law.

'Are you okay?' Joanne nudged her arm. 'You look like
you're going to be sick.'

Daisy swallowed. She felt as if she was too. Just thinking
about what she was about to do was making the contents of
her stomach curdle.

She smiled weakly. 'I know it's the city that never sleeps,
but sometimes I wish New York would have an early night!'

'Look…' Glancing around, Joanne lowered her voice.
'Why don't you go home? I can finish up here.'

Daisy shook her head. 'I'm just tired. And I don't want to leave you in the lurch—'

'You're not!' Joanne frowned. 'So stop pretending you feel okay.'

Daisy hesitated. She hated lying to Joanne, particularly when her friend was being so kind. But she could hardly tell her the truth. She was only just coming to terms with it herself.

Stomach tightening, she thought back to the moment four days ago when she'd arrived back at David's apartment to find him in tears. After much coaxing he'd finally confessed that he had a gambling problem. *Only it was way more than a problem.* It turned out he'd been gambling and losing money for months, and his debt had spiralled out of control.

Daisy shivered. Her parents had drummed into them the importance of living within their means. But David's debt was the least of his problems. Dropping off some papers in Rollo Fleming's office earlier that day, he had noticed a watch on the floor. Only it hadn't been just *any* watch. It had been an exclusive designer watch. And he hadn't just noticed it. He'd picked it up and pocketed it, imagining that he'd be able to sell it and thus clear his debt.

Back home, he'd realised what he'd done and broken down completely. Which was why Daisy had ended up promising to return it for him.

The thought jogged her back into real time. Looking up, she grimaced. 'I do feel a bit odd. Maybe I will go now. Thanks, Jo. You're a star.'

Joanne nodded. 'Yes, I am. But don't be too grateful. I need you to cover for me on Tuesday.' Her face softened. 'Cam's taking me out to dinner. It's our six-month anni-versary.'

That was what she wanted to be doing, Daisy thought dully as she negotiated a path between the drunken partygoers into the deserted hallway. Going on an anniversary date with a boyfriend.

But, of course, that would require a boyfriend.

And five weeks ago Nick had decided that he needed some space.

Space!

Glumly, she stopped in front of the lifts.

Romeo never told Juliet he needed 'space.'

Antony hadn't said, 'It's not you, it's me,' to Cleopatra.

She stared at her reflection in the gleaming steel doors.

All men were unreliable and selfish or, more likely, she was just an extremely poor judge of character. Either way, she'd had enough. For the foreseeable future she was going to enjoy being single.

Reaching into the large pocket at the front of her apron, she pulled out a laminated card and stared down at her brother's face. Thank goodness for David. He was always there for her—helping her rehearse for auditions, even finding her this waitressing job.

Swiping the card, she felt her breath twitch in her throat as the light turned green and the doors slid open smoothly.

She owed David big time.

And now she had a chance to pay him back.

Her fingers trembled. But could she do it. Could she actually go through with it?

She hesitated. But only for a moment.

David was waiting downstairs for her in the lobby and the thought of his face, his relief as she walked towards him, propelled her forward.

Inside the lift, panicky thoughts fluttered inside her head, darting back and forth like startled birds, but then the doors were opening and, heart pounding, she stepped into a dimly lit corridor.

David had told her which office belonged to Rollo and, her heels clicking lightly on the polished wood floor, she walked across the reception area and came to a standstill in front of a plain wooden door. For a moment she stared at it in silence. There was no nameplate—nothing to differentiate it from any of the other doors—and for a moment she wondered why. It seemed a strangely modest touch from a man worth billions who made no secret of the fact that he considered himself not just a businessman but an empire builder.

But then, did a man like Rollo Fleming really *need* any introduction? Particularly in the gleaming glass tower that bore his name.

It felt like she was about to enter the lion's den. But, lifting her chin, she braced her shoulders. The lion wasn't at home. And by the time he returned, she would be long gone.

Breathing in sharply, she swiped the card and pushed open the door.

Everything was silent and dark. But through the window all the familiar landmarks were lit up against the night sky, and she gazed at it in wonder. Rollo Fleming must have the best view in New York. But every moment spent in his office increased her risk of being caught and, galvanised by that thought, she stepped forward unthinkingly.

'Ouch!'

Her knee collided sharply with something hard in the darkness, but her pain was quickly forgotten as she felt whatever it was she'd walked into start to move. Heart pounding, she reached out, groping blindly, trying to stop whatever it was from falling. But it was too late, and the next moment there was a thump that echoed round the empty office like cannon fire.

'Good one, Daisy!' she muttered into the taut, strained silence that followed. 'Why don't you just set off some fireworks while you're at it?'

Gritting her teeth, she reached down and gingerly rubbed her knee—and then suddenly froze as from the other side of the door she heard the clear and unmistakable sound of footsteps approaching.

They slowed and stopped, and her heart began to beat with such force that she thought it would burst through her ribcage, and then she scrunched up her eyes as the door swung open and light flooded the room.

For the longest moment she waited—hoping, praying like a child that if she couldn't see whoever it was, they wouldn't be able to see her. But her hope was swiftly extinguished as a voice—cool, curt and very, very male—interrupted the tense silence.

'I've had a long and disappointing day, so I hope, for your sake, that you have a good explanation for this intrusion—'

Opening her eyes, Daisy blinked. The words had sent a ripple of dread down her spine, but that was nothing compared to the dismay she felt as she gazed up at the face of the man standing in front of the open door.

Rollo Fleming was supposed be in Washington.

On business.

But, unless she was hallucinating, neither of those facts were true.

The shock should have felled her and it would have done so, had she not been so distracted by the reality of his beauty.

On a screen, or in a magazine, Rollo Fleming was movie star handsome. In the flesh, however, his good looks were multiplied by ten, compounded by an intense mix of masculinity and power that made heat break out over her skin.

Not that he was her type, she thought hurriedly. He was too blonde, too poised, too calculating. It must just be the shock that was making her want to look at him. And keep on looking.

Golden-skinned, with a sharp clean-lined jaw and close-cropped blonde hair, he looked more like a Roman gladiator than a billionaire property tycoon. Only the very dark and obviously very expensive single-breasted suit gave any hint that he was worth more than the GDP of some small countries.

He looked at her directly then, and she felt his gaze like cool water hitting the back of her throat. His eyes were extraordinary—clear, glittering green, like shards of broken glass. But it was the beautiful full-lipped curve of his mouth that tugged the most at her senses. It was a mouth she could imagine softening into the sexiest smile—

Her heart jerked.

Only it wasn't smiling now. Instead it was set in a straight, forbidding line that perfectly matched the rigid hostility of his body blocking the doorway. Nervously she glanced around the office, looking for another means of escape. But despite it being the size of a small barn, there were no other exits. Just a lot of cool designer-looking furniture.

She was trapped.

Her pulse shivered. This wasn't supposed to be happening. She hadn't come here for confrontation or explanation. But now there was no choice but to improvise.

'I—I can explain,' she stammered.

'Then I suggest you begin.'

He stood like an actor on stage, his spotlit face impassive, but there was a dangerous undertone in his voice that made her heartbeat accelerate unevenly.

'Just keep it short and simple. Like I said, I've had a long day… *Daisy.*'

He spoke her name softly, almost like an endearment, so that it was a moment before her brain registered the fact that he knew who she was. As she glanced up, eyes widening in shock, he shook his head dismissively, his gaze dropping to the laminated badge pinned to her blouse.

'So it *is* your name. I thought you'd stolen that from some poor hapless waitress downstairs.'

There was no mistaking the flicker of scorn in his eyes,

and her hand rose protectively to cover the badge even as his accusation stung her out of her fear and shock.

'I didn't. My name really is Daisy and, for your information, I *am* one of those *poor hapless waitresses*. That's why I'm here.'

Her eyes locked with his. Pushing her hands into the pocket of her apron, her fingers brushed against David's security card, and she felt a sudden fierce urgency to protect her brother.

'I was working at the party downstairs and I was going to get some more napkins from the kitchens,' she lied. 'But I pressed the wrong button in the lift.'

For a moment Rollo stared at her coldly, then without turning he pushed the door shut.

In less than three seconds he had crossed the room, and as he stopped in front of her, her body tensed with panic.

'I told you to keep it short and simple. Clearly what I should have said was tell the truth.' His eyes hardened. 'Please don't insult me by trying to pretend you "pressed the wrong button…"'

Daisy felt the walls of the huge office shrink inwards. In his dark suit, his broad shoulders blocking the light, Rollo Fleming dominated the space around them. But she couldn't allow him to dominate *her*. If she did, then the truth would come out and David's life would be ruined.

She tried to let out her breath without his noticing.

'You're not the only one who's had a long day,' she retorted. 'I've been on my feet for hours and I'm tired too. Which is why I made a mistake.'

He shook his head.

'I don't class breaking and entering as a "mistake." And I'll think you'll find most juries agree with me.' His face was hard, anger harshening the fine features. 'So stop prevaricating and tell me why you're sneaking about in my office at quarter to one in the morning.'

'I didn't know it was your office.' She forced herself to meet his face. 'How could I? I don't even know who you are.'

His expression shifted into one of pure disbelief.

'You're working downstairs and you don't know who I am?'

Daisy glowered at him. His derisive tone, coupled with his arrogant and irritatingly correct assumption that she would know who he was, made her see red.

'I work for lots of people,' she said stubbornly. 'I don't remember all their names and faces.'

Watching his mouth tighten, she felt a stab of satisfaction at having punctured his pride.

There was a long, abrasive silence and then he shrugged. 'Which is no doubt why you're just a waitress.'

Her cheeks flooded with heat, his sneer stinging like a slap.

Just a waitress!

'Don't patronise me—' she began furiously.

'Then don't lie to me,' he said softly.

She glared past him, face flushed. 'Fine. So I know who you are! So what? It makes no difference to me—'

'Then you are either exceptionally foolish or dangerously foolhardy, because this is *my* building, and *my* office. *And you shouldn't be in it.*'

His voice scraped against her skin, sending flickers of fear in every direction.

Watching her face turn pale, Rollo felt his stomach twist.

Beneath her bravado she was scared—maybe she *wasn't* the hardened criminal he'd taken her to be.

But she *was* still guilty.

Guilty of knowing the power of her beauty and guilty of exploiting it to deceive and disarm. He stared at her critically, noting the slight tilt of her chin, the wash of colour on the flawless cheekbones. He'd known women like her before. One in particular, who had thought nothing of lying and manipulating those around her, causing havoc and devastation even as she played the victim.

Daisy had made the biggest mistake of her life if she thought her charms would work on him and, eyes narrowing, he let the silence lengthen until finally, with a mixture of defiance and almost exaggerated casualness, she said, 'I was curious. I just wanted to have a look around.'

'I see.' He loaded his words with sarcasm. 'And yet you didn't put on the lights? You must have truly extraordinary night vision.'

Daisy bit her tongue. Already she hated that sneer, the way his eyebrows lifted, and the glitter in that mocking green gaze. Of course, she'd imagined what would happen if she got caught. But in her head she had pictured some bumbling security guard. She certainly hadn't expected to be grilled by Rollo Fleming himself. The watch's owner and a man who was demanding an honesty she couldn't give.

'I didn't put the lights on because I thought somebody would see,' she said quickly.

He was standing too close; the heat and scent of his body was messing with her head so that speaking in sentences was suddenly a struggle.

'I know this floor is off limits, but I've worked here a couple of times and I wanted to see…'

She paused. *What could she have possibly—believably—wanted to see in an unlit office?*

Blood pounding in her ears, she stared desperately past him at the lit-up skyscrapers—and then her gaze locked on to the Empire State Building.

'The city. At night,' she said, her breath juddering in relief. 'Everyone says the view from up here is amazing, so I thought I'd come and look.'

He stared at her for so long and so hard that she had to clench the muscles in her legs to stop them from giving way.

'How?'

She blinked. 'What?'

'Not *what. How?* How did you get up to this level? Catering staff only have clearance for the floor they're working on.'

Daisy swallowed. *Keep it simple*, she told herself. 'I don't know,' she lied again. 'I just pressed some buttons.'

Her head was starting to ache, and there was no way she could keep this up for much longer. It was time for a dignified retreat. David would understand, and together they could think of another less humiliating way to return Rollo Fleming's watch to him.

She breathed out, fighting for calm. 'Look, Mr Fleming, I'm really sorry I came up here, okay? It was a bad idea—a mistake—and I promise I will never do anything like it again. So if you could just forget I was ever here, I'd be really grateful.'

There was a taut silence as his gaze held hers.

'Daisy. Pretty name…' he said quietly.

She could sense he was battling to control his temper.

'Old-fashioned. Sweet. Decent.'

He smiled—a chilling smile that sent a shiver down her backbone.

'It's a pity you don't live up to it.'

She felt her body still. 'I don't know what you mean,' she said carefully.

He shook his head. 'Then let me explain. I've had a long day…'

Pausing, he felt his shoulders stiffen. Not just long. It had been a day of frustration and failure. The deal was generous—he'd offered way more than the market value of the building—and yet once again James Dunmore had rejected it out of hand. And he still didn't really understand why.

His lips pressed together. Or rather he *did* understand; he just didn't know what to do about it. Dunmore didn't approve of him, or his reputation for ruthlessness and womanising and so he wouldn't sell. Rollo breathed out slowly. But he *wanted* that building—had wanted it for seventeen years—and he wasn't about to give up now.

If only he could somehow persuade Dunmore that he'd changed…

He felt his pulse quicken. It made him feel tense, thwarted, just thinking about it. And now, as if he didn't have enough to deal with, this woman, Daisy, was trying to hustle him.

So call Security, he told himself irritably.

There was no reason for *him* to deal with this.

But, looking up at Daisy, he felt his body twitch.

Except there was.

A beautiful, brown-eyed reason, with a body that made that completely uninspiring uniform look both chic and sexy. His eyes rested on her face. Aside from a faint smudge of pink on her lips, she was make-up-free. But then beauty like hers needed no enhancement. Everything from the soft curves of her mouth to the huge espresso-coloured eyes was designed to seduce.

She had attempted to pull her long blonde hair into some kind of low ponytail, but it was coming loose, and to his annoyance he found himself wanting to loosen it more. Could almost imagine what it would feel like between his fingers, the weight of it in his hands, and how it would fall forward when they kissed, the silken strands brushing his face—

Abruptly he lifted his head, his eyes glinting.

'As I was saying, I've had a long, difficult day—'

'Then why don't I just get out of your way?' Heart lurching like a ship at sea, Daisy edged backwards. 'I probably should get back to work anyhow.'

She glanced past him, every fibre in her body focused

on reaching the door and freedom, and then her stomach lurched too as he shook his head slowly,

'I don't think so.'

His hand coiled around her wrist, his touch searing her skin. 'You're not going anywhere until you tell me the truth.'

'Let go of me.' She tugged her arm, trying not to give in to the cold, slippery panic curling around her heart like an eel. 'I *have* told you the truth!'

'Enough!'

His voice was sharp and final, like a guillotine falling, and she felt his grip tighten.

'You have done nothing but lie since you opened your mouth. Now, most men might fall for this eyelash-fluttering, little-girl-lost routine, but I'm not most men. So save your pouting and tell me what you're doing here.'

'I'm not pouting.' She jerked her arm free. Stuffing her hands back into her apron, she tightened her fingers involuntarily around the swipe card. 'And most men—most reasonable, decent men—wouldn't be interrogating me about an honest mistake.'

He laughed without humour. 'Honest? I doubt you know the meaning of the word.'

Her hands curled into fists. 'Just because you're some big shot property tycoon, it doesn't give you the right to play judge, jury and executioner. I'm not on trial here.'

'No. But you will be.' He stared at her speculatively. 'At a rough guess facing charges of trespass, unlawful entry, intent to rob—'

'*I* didn't come here to rob anyone,' Daisy snapped. 'If you must know, I came here to—'

Breaking off, she stared at him in horror. Around her the tension in the room had soared, so that suddenly she felt as though the walls and the windows might implode.

His gaze was fixed and unblinking. 'To what?'

She stared at him mutely, frozen, horrified by how close

she'd come to betraying David—and then in the beat of her heart she darted past him. But he was too quick, and before her brain had even registered him moving, his arm was curving around her waist and pulling her against the hard muscles of his chest.

It was like an electric shock. For a moment she forgot everything. Everything except the fierce, prickling heat surging through her body, warming her blood and melting her bones, so that in another second she knew her legs would buckle beneath her.

'Let go of me.' Angry, outraged—more by her body's inappropriate response than his restricting grip—she started to punch his arm, but he simply ignored the blows, jerking her closer.

'Stop it,' he said coldly. 'You're not helping yourself.'

'You're hurting me.'

'Then stop fighting me.'

His arm curled tighter, so that his stomach was pressing against her spine. But despite his anger, and even though she could feel his strength, she was surprised to find she wasn't afraid of him physically.

Only there was no time to ponder why that should be the case as he said sharply, 'What's in your hand?'

Instantly all her efforts were concentrated on clenching her fist as tightly as possible. But it was a short, unequal fight, and she watched helplessly as, uncurling her fingers, he prised the security card from her hand.

'Thank you,' he said softly, and abruptly he loosened his grip and jerked her round to face him.

She gazed at him dazedly. Her pulse was racing, her blood thundering like an incoming tide. She felt her stomach tighten painfully as his eyes flickered over the card.

'Where did you get this?'

For a moment she considered telling him the truth. But one look at his face was all it took to convince her that that course of action would not only be foolish but hazardous. He was furious. Beyond furious. He was enraged.

'It was on the floor.'

'Of course it was!'

The jeer in his voice sliced through her skin like a knife, so that she had to swallow against the pain. The air was thickening around her and she was finding it hard to breathe. His anger was overwhelming her. She couldn't fight the way he did—didn't have that desire to win whatever the consequences. Whatever the cost...

'I...I... It must... Someone must have dropped it.'

Rollo shook his head dismissively.

He could deal with her lies. He could even understand why she was lying. But he couldn't deal with all the other lies that were crowding into his head. Lies from the past. Conversations between his parents. His mother darting between stories, swapping truths—

Suddenly he just wanted it over. Wanted her out of his office and out of his life.

Lip curling, he glanced to where she stood, wide-eyed, the pulse in her throat jerking unevenly.

'I know this looks bad,' she said haltingly. 'But I wasn't doing anything wrong. You have to believe me—'

'I think we both know it's a little late for that,' he said savagely.

He didn't trust her, and for good reason. Life had taught him at an early age that there was nothing more disingenuous or dangerous than a cornered woman.

But this one wasn't his problem.

'I'm tired,' he said bluntly. 'And this conversation is over.'

He reached into his jacket and pulled out his phone.

'What do you mean? Who are you calling? No. Please—'

He felt his stomach soar upwards, snagged by the desperation in her voice even as anger swept over him like lava. Was she really going to keep this up? This pretence that she'd come up here to see the view.

'I gave you a chance to tell the truth. That you came here to steal from me—'

'But I didn't.' Her voice was husky with emotion. 'I admit I lied to you. But I swear I'm not a thief.'

He held her gaze. It would be easy to believe her. She sounded so convincing. But then he remembered how she had fought him for the swipe card, with fire—not fear—in her eyes, and glancing at her face he could see tautness— the nervous dread of a skater standing on thin ice, waiting to hear it crack.

But *why*? What was there left to dread?

His shoulders tensed. And then, as his gaze dropped down to the short black apron, he saw her face freeze. He felt a dizzying anger like vertigo. Slowly he moved in front of her, his powerful body blocking her exit.

'Prove it. Empty out your pockets,' he said tersely. 'Unless you want me to do it for you.'

She shrank away from him, eyes widening with unmistakable guilt, her face pale with shock and uncertainty. 'Are you threatening me?'

'I don't know,' he said, his voice soft, light, his face sculptured with menace. 'Do you feel threatened?'

Daisy swallowed. Yes. She did. And not just threatened. Trapped. But how could she do what he asked? If he saw the watch—*his watch*—there was zero chance of her getting out of the office, let alone the building.

'I can explain…' But her words faltered as she realised that she couldn't.

Rollo stared at her in silence. A sudden vivid memory of his mother saying exactly the same words slid into his head, and he let them echo and fade until he was able to speak.

'I'm sure you can. But I think I've had enough bedtime stories for one evening.'

His words sent a chill through her.

'Don't worry though. I'm sure someone else will find them far more entertaining.' He paused, a cold smile curling his lips. 'Like my security team. We can go and talk to them right now. They're downstairs with David—your brother. Waiting to take you both to the police station.'

CHAPTER TWO

DAISY STARED AT him in horror. His words were burning inside her head, so hot and bright she couldn't think straight. Finally she forced herself to speak.

'What's David got to do with any of this?'

But even as the question left her lips, she knew there was no point in pretending any more. There was only one possible explanation for why her brother was with Security.

Rollo knew everything.

The thought made her feel dizzy and she took a quick, shallow breath, trying not to give in to the damp chill sweeping over her skin.

'You know about…? That David…?'

'That your brother stole my watch?'

His gaze held hers, the derision in his voice making her cheeks burn.

'I knew the day he stole it. My office has security cameras. Your brother was caught on film.'

He paused and, looking up, she saw the glittering contempt in his eyes, felt her stomach cramp with fear. He'd known right from the start—before she'd even steeled herself to step into the lift. He'd simply been watching, waiting…

Waiting for her to realise that fact.

All her carefully laid plans had been for nothing. Suddenly she was struggling to hold it together.

'Please—'

Her voice sounded all wrong, high and breathless, not at all like her voice. But maybe that was because she was no longer Daisy Maddox but some anonymous criminal. The thought made fear crystallise on her skin like ice.

'Please don't do this. I know it looks bad. But if you'll just give me five minutes—'

His eyes narrowed. 'I think you've wasted more than enough of my time already.'

'But you don't know the full story,' she protested.

'Story? More like fantasy!' He shook his head. 'Save it for your lawyers. They'll be *paid* to listen to your lies. I'm not.'

His derisive words punched through her panic. The man was a monster! Didn't he understand what breaking into his office had cost her?

Suddenly her whole body was rigid and vibrating with anger. 'I might have known someone like you would bring it all back to money,' she snapped.

'Someone like me?' His voice was chillingly cold. 'You mean a law-abiding citizen?'

She glowered at him. 'I mean someone without a heart.'

His eyes glinted threateningly beneath the lights. 'I don't need a heart to recognise a thief.'

'David's not a thief.' Her head jerked up.

'So he didn't steal my watch?'

'No—I mean yes. But it was a mistake—'

'I'm sure the prisons are littered with people all saying the same.'

'No, you don't understand—'

'And I don't want to.' He frowned at her impatiently. 'Your brother's motives are of no interest to me. I'm only concerned with his guilt.' His gaze didn't flicker. 'And yours.'

Daisy stared at him open-mouthed.

'*My* guilt!'

His lip curled up impatiently.

'Look, I may not have a heart, but I do have a brain and I'm not stupid. You didn't come up here by accident, or to look at the view. You came to see what else you could steal—'

'*No.*' Her voice echoed around the empty office. 'I did not.'

'Yes, you did.' The finality in his voice sent a warning chill through her. 'As whatever you've got stashed in those pockets will no doubt demonstrate when we get downstairs.'

She gazed at him dumbly. Something had just hit her. A way to corroborate her story. Desperately she fumbled inside her apron and pulled out the watch.

'I didn't break in here to steal from you,' she said breathlessly. 'I came to bring this back.'

If she'd been expecting flags and a parade, she would have been disappointed. Rollo barely glanced at the watch. Instead his eyes were fixed on her face.

'That proves nothing. Or rather, given that it contradicts everything you've just said, it merely confirms that you're a liar as well as a thief!'

Her hands were trembling. She felt almost giddy with anger. 'I'm not a thief.'

He shrugged. 'Unlike some people, I prefer to tell *and* hear the truth.'

'In that case you're a bully.'

'Is that right?' His shoulders rose and tensed.

'Yes, it is. Ever since you walked through that door you've done nothing but make threats and try to intimidate me.'

A muscle flickered in his cheek, and then slowly he held out his phone.

'So call the police,' he said softly. 'Go on. Call them.'

Her pulse gave a jerk. She had effectively backed herself into a corner, and he knew it. But watching his green eyes gleam triumphantly, his smug assumption that she would back down, flipped a switch inside her head. Stepping forward, she snatched the phone from his hand.

'Fine. I will,' she snarled. 'At least that way I won't have to spend any more time with you.'

'Don't be so bloody childish.'

There was a tension in his voice she hadn't heard before.

'I'm not being childish,' she snapped. 'You're going to call them anyhow, so what does it matter?'

Their eyes locked—hers furiously defiant, his cool, opaque, dispassionate—and then her mouth curved scornfully.

'Oh, I get it. *You* wanted to do it. So who's being childish now?'

There was a small, tight silence.

Rollo took a slow, deep breath. His chest felt hot and taut. Her stubbornness was infuriating, and yet part of him couldn't help admiring her. She was just so determined to keep fighting him—even to the point of making this crazy kamikaze gesture.

Glancing from her face to her tightly curled hands, he sighed. 'You don't want to do that, Daisy,' he said at last.

'You don't know *what* I want. You don't know anything about me or David.'

He met her gaze. 'So tell me.'

Daisy stared at him in silence. Why was he offering her a chance to talk now? More than anything she wanted to hurl it back in his face. But already her anger was fading and picturing her brother waiting, wordless with terror downstairs, she took a shallow breath and lowered the phone.

'Why?' she said sulkily. 'So you can use it against him.'

His eyes narrowed. 'That depends on what you tell me. To date, all I know about your brother—aside from his penchant for expensive watches—is that he works in Acquisition and Development. And he's tall and twitchy—'

'He's not twitchy. He's just a bit nervous.' She spoke defensively and instantly wished she hadn't as he turned his penetrating, unsettling green gaze on her face.

'Guilty people often are.'

There was no short or easy way to refute that statement, so instead she satisfied herself with giving him an icy glare.

'He's not some criminal mastermind. He's shy, and he finds it difficult to make friends with people.'

'He might find it easier if he didn't steal from them,' he said smoothly.

'It was a mistake.' Her voice rose with exasperation.

'So you keep saying. But a mistake is when you forget to charge your phone. Not when you purposely steal something that doesn't belong to you. That's called theft.'

'Not always.' She looked him straight in the eye, her shoulders set high and pushed back as though for battle. 'Sometimes it's called "charging market rent."'

Rollo gritted his teeth. Not in response to her confrontational remark but because he knew that this time she was telling the truth. David Maddox was clearly not a criminal mastermind. Which was why he'd requested a background check instead of just firing him.

It had taken less than half a day for a file to land on his desk, and the research had been thorough—health records, academic results and employment history. And one line noting the existence of a twin sister who also happened to work for the Fleming Organisation's hospitality team.

Glancing across at her face, he felt his breath suddenly light and loose in his chest; he felt weightless, off balance, as though he'd been drinking. That was all she'd been. A line in a report. A name without a face.

But no words could ever have conveyed Daisy's beauty and spirit. Or the way her eyes softened when she talked about her brother. Or that tiny crease she got on her forehead when she was digging in her heels.

His fingers twitched and suddenly, more than anything, he wanted to reach out and touch the curve of her cheek, then carry on touching, his fingers sliding over the soft skin of her throat, then lower still, to the swelling curves of her breasts and waist—

He felt his body jerk to life—muscles tightening, groin hardening.

Sitting watching the camera footage of her breaking into his office, he'd thought she was beautiful but greedy—a woman who didn't believe the rules applied to her. And it had angered him so much that for reasons he didn't want to examine, he'd broken with protocol and convinced his security team to let him deal with her personally.

Only now here she was, clutching his phone like an amulet to ward off evil, and he couldn't seem to hold on to his anger. At least not the vindictive, punitive kind. Instead— and he really couldn't explain why—he felt wound up, and almost irritated by her reckless stupidity.

Had she really thought she could get away with it?

Then she was not only foolhardy but utterly deluded; there was no way he would ever have fallen for her lies.

Except that he would have done.

His muscles tensed as the truth hit him square in the chest: if he hadn't watched her breaking in he would have believed every word, trusted each hesitant glance. She would have had him eating out of her hand.

The thought should have repelled him, but instead he felt his pulse accelerate, the blood humming inside his head, as slowly, miraculously he realised that maybe—just maybe— he had found a way to change James Dunmore's mind.

Gazing blandly over at her, he shrugged. 'Obviously I'd love to hear your views on social housing some other time, but right now I think we should talk about *you.*'

There was a startled pause. She stared at him suspiciously. 'Why?'

He shrugged. 'I'm curious. What do you do when you're not breaking into offices?' he said softly.

'Why do you care?' she snapped. 'You've clearly made

up your mind that David and I are some of kind of Bonnie and Clyde. Nothing I say is going to change that.'

'Try me,' he said lazily. 'I can't say for sure that it'll change anything. But what have you got to lose?'

Holding her breath, Daisy watched in mute fascination as he reached up and undid the top button of his shirt, tugging the dark green tie loose to reveal a triangle of sleek golden skin.

Angry, Rollo Fleming was formidable, but she was just starting to realise that anger was not the most effective weapon in his armoury. His charm was far more lethal. And when the chill and distance left his voice he was at his most dangerous.

'You said earlier you weren't interested,' she said stiffly.

'And you said earlier I didn't have a heart.'

His gaze rested on her face—cool, unblinking, unreadable—and her own heart skipped a beat.

'So what are you saying?'

'I'm giving you an opportunity to redeem yourself. And David, of course.'

Rollo could see she was tempted by his words. He could read the conflict in her eyes, her distrust of him battling with her impulse to protect her brother. He waited, knowing the value of both silence and patience, until finally she sighed.

'There's not much to say. I'm twenty-five. I live with my brother, who's my twin. And I'm a waitress.' Her eyes flared. '*Just a waitress.* But not through choice. I'm actually an actress, only I'm between jobs at the moment.'

There was a sharp, complicated silence.

'That's it.' She looked up defensively. 'I told you there wasn't much.'

Rollo studied her in silence. There was a flush of colour on her cheeks and her eyes were daring him to prove her right.

'Depends on your definition of "much",' he said smoothly. 'A half-point swing in my commodities portfolio could cost me millions of dollars.'

Daisy stared at him warily. Something was happening around her, silent and unseen.

She narrowed her eyes. 'What do you want?'

The corners of his mouth curved upwards into a tiny satisfied smile.

'Let's just say that I think I've found a way for all of us to move on from this unfortunate incident.'

A fresh fear rose up inside her. 'I'm not going to have sex with you, if that's what you mean. I'd rather sell my kidneys!'

'I believe the norm is only one.' He stared at her impassively, his green gaze colder and harder than any emerald. 'And don't flatter yourself, Ms Maddox. I like a woman in handcuffs as much as the next man, but not when the only reason she's wearing them is because she's been arrested.'

She bit her tongue. 'So what *do* you want, then?'

He scrutinised her for a long moment, almost as though he were trying to see through her or past her. It made her feel taut, trapped—vulnerable, a deer gazing into the headlights of an oncoming car.

Finally he smiled—a smile that tore the breath out of her.

'I want you to be my wife,' he said softly.

There was a moment of pure, absolute silence.

She gazed at him in shock, trying to catch up. The last few hours had proved unequivocally that Rollo was a cold-blooded megalomaniac, but now it appeared he was also utterly and irrefutably insane.

'I'm sorry.' She shook her head slowly. 'I think I must have misheard you. I thought you said—'

'That I want you to be my wife.' His eyes flickered over her stunned expression. 'You heard correctly.'

Breathing out unsteadily, she lifted her hand to her fore-head, as though to ward off the insanity of his suggestion.

'What are you talking about?' she managed.

It must be some kind of trick or trap—another way to make her look stupid and feel small. She stared wildly round the room, hoping to find some explanation. But turning back to meet his gaze she felt a shudder of alarm ripple over her skin.

He was being serious!

She stared at him incredulously.

'You barely know me. And we hate each other. Why would you want to marry me?'

He paid no attention. 'Why don't you sit down and we can talk about it properly?'

He was just like a politician, she thought desperately. Answering a question with a question. Ignoring what he couldn't answer or didn't want to discuss.

She opened her mouth to protest but he was already walking past her, and as she watched him take a seat be-hind the huge glass-topped desk she felt her ribs expand. He looked calm, relaxed, as though he often proposed marriage to young women who broke into his office in the early hours of the morning. But his eyes were alert and predatory, like a wolf watching a lamb stumble around in its lair.

'Come on. Sit down. I don't bite.'

It wasn't an invitation. It wasn't even an order. It was a dare.

She lifted her chin.

'Fine. But I can't see what difference talking will make. Nobody marries a complete stranger.'

Sinking into the soft leather, she felt the tiredness of the last few hours rise up beneath her skin in a wave as, loung-ing back in his seat, he stared past her, in a way that sug-gested he was pondering some deep philosophical question.

'Is that true? Plenty of brides all over the world only meet their husband on their wedding days.'

'Yes. If they're having an arranged marriage.' She glowered at him.

'But we are.' He smiled a smile that made her wish that his chair would open up and swallow him whole. 'And *I'm* arranging it.'

Daisy felt her skin grow warm; her head was spinning. 'Don't be ridiculous. You're not arranging anything,' she snapped. 'Look, you can't want to marry me, so why are you pretending you do?' She stared at him doubtfully. 'Is it your idea of a joke? Some way to punish me for…?'

Looking up at him, she felt her words falter in her mouth. For an endless moment he studied her in silence and then, leaning forward, he fixed his eyes on hers with an intentness that seared her skin.

'If I wanted to punish you, I'd think of something a lot more…*diverting.*'

Her stomach clenched, and a tingling excitement swept through her like fire through a forest as he smiled slowly.

'For both of us.'

A hot shiver ran up her spine and she stared at him mutely, her body stilling even as chaos raged inside. Her heart was beating too fast and too loud, and a dark ache was swirling over her skin like a riptide. In an effort to break the spell of his gaze, she pressed her nails hard into the palms of her hands.

'You can't just tell someone you're marrying them,' she said carefully. 'It doesn't work like that.'

The tension in the room quivered, as though she had somehow pressed her foot onto an accelerator pedal, and her eyes flickered involuntarily across to where Rollo sat, examining her with detached curiosity.

'It does if you want your brother to keep his job. And, more important, to stay out of prison.'

She was out of her seat and leaning across his desk before she had even realised she was moving, her whole body shaking with shock and anger.

'You unspeakable pig!' Her voice rose. 'That's blackmail—'

'Yes, it is.'

He wasn't even embarrassed! Furiously, she glanced around for something blunt and heavy.

'Why are you getting so bent out of shape about this?' He stared at her calmly.

'Why? *Why?* Maybe because it's weird and wrong.' Heat was blistering her skin. She couldn't keep the shake out of her voice. 'You're cynically exploiting this situation for your own ends.'

He frowned. 'You're being melodramatic. You and I marrying will be mutually beneficial. As to the morality of blackmailing a thief and a liar, I'm not sure we have time to tackle that right now, so why don't you just calm down and sit down?'

He lifted his arms behind his head and stretched out his shoulders.

'Sit down,' he said again, and this time there was no mistaking the authority in his voice. 'I didn't explain myself properly. I need to marry you, but in essence you'll just be playing the part of my wife.'

She felt a rush of hope. 'You mean like in an advert or something? For your business?' He stared at her in silence.

'No. Not like an advert. We're going to have to marry legally.'

Daisy searched his face, looking for answers, for a way to escape the certainty in his voice. 'Why can't we just pretend?'

He shook his head slowly. 'That won't work. It can't just *look* like we're married. It has to be legal.'

'But no one needs a wife that badly,' she said almost viciously. 'Not at two o'clock in the morning.'

He shrugged. 'I do.'

'But why?'

'That doesn't concern you.' The certainty in his voice had hardened to granite.

She stared at him, sensing that somewhere a door was closing, a key was turning. Soon there would be no way out of this mess.

She felt her temper flare. 'Fine. But I'm not marrying anyone—especially you—unless you tell me why you need a wife.'

It wasn't just curiosity. She needed to assert herself. Needed him to know that she wasn't just some puppet on a string.

She folded her arms in front of her chest. 'I don't need details. Just keep it short and simple.'

She held her breath as his eyes narrowed into knifepoints, and she knew he was gauging how much he needed to tell her. Finally he shrugged and met her gaze, cool and back in control again.

'I'm trying to close a deal. For a building I want to buy. The owner is old-fashioned…sentimental. He'll only sell to someone he trusts. Someone he believes shares his values. I need him to trust me and for that to happen he needs to see my warmer, softer side. Marriage is the simplest way to demonstrate that to him.'

She breathed out slowly. There was a kind of warped logic to his argument.

'But surely I can't be your only solution? What if you hadn't found me in your office? What would you do then?'

His eyes were watching hers. 'But I did find you. And you're perfect.'

Her heart thudded against her ribs and she felt her cheeks grow warm. 'I—I am?'

Rollo felt his groin grow hard, his body responding not only to her tentative question but to the flush of colour in her cheeks, the pulse jerking at the base of her throat. She was like a flint striking, sparking against him, catching fire.

And fire burned.

Ignoring the twitch of lust in his groin, he breathed out slowly. 'Yes. You're single. And you're an actress. But primarily, and most important, I can trust you to be compliant.'

Daisy knew she had gone white.

'Compliant?' Her hands were trembling.

'Out-of-work actresses are ten a penny. But I need someone I can depend on. And as your brother's freedom and future are in my hands I'm confident I can rely completely on your discretion.'

He sounded so calm and controlled that she thought she might throw up. Was this how people got to the top in business? By turning every situation to their advantage no matter what the collateral damage?

'But, of course, if you'd rather take your chances with the police...'

He let his sentence drift off as Daisy stared past him. She felt bruised, battered and beaten.

'How long would it be for?' she said dully.

'A year. Then we'd go our separate ways and the slate would be wiped clean.'

She flinched inside. He made it sound so simple. The perfectly packaged, one-use-only relationship. An entirely disposable marriage. And maybe it was that simple for him, for clearly his brain worked in an entirely different way from hers.

Her heart contracted. But it was so different from the marriage she'd always imagined. Given her failed romantic history, she knew she was more likely to win a starring role on Broadway, but what she wanted was a relationship based on love and trust and honesty. Just like her parents'.

Only that was the polar opposite of what she and Rollo would have if she agreed to this stupid fake marriage.

The thought made her feel utterly alone.

Pushing back her shoulders, she lifted her head, a flare of defiance sparking inside her. 'And you're okay with that?' she asked flatly. 'It's how you always imagined your marriage?'

Leaning back, Rollo swivelled his chair to face the window. He knew that her question was more or less rhetorical. But the blood was beating in his veins with swift, hot, unreasonable fury.

For a moment he gazed out across the city, silently battling the sickening panic and feeling of helplessness stirred up by their conversation. The short, expurgated answer was *no*—it wasn't the way he'd imagined his marriage. Not because it would be fake and devoid of feeling, but because he had never once imagined being married at all.

Why would he? He knew for a fact that people weren't capable of being satisfied with just one partner. And he certainly didn't believe marriage represented love or devotion.

His mother's behaviour had proved that to him over and over again, slowly destroying their family and his father in the process.

But marriage to Daisy would be altogether different, he reassured himself. It would be carefully controlled *by him* and there would be no risk of pain or humiliation, for that would require an emotional dependency that would be absent from their relationship. In fact, their lives need only really intertwine in public.

Feeling calmer, he turned to face her.

'I can't say I've expended much mental energy on the matter. Personally, I've never seen the point of making such an emotionally charged and unrealistic commitment to somebody.'

Daisy glared at him. 'How romantic! Do you say that to *all* the women you date or just the ones you blackmail?'

He stared at her impassively, but his eyes had darkened in a way that made the breath jam in her throat.

'I never promise anything to anyone I date,' he said, his eyes lingering on her face. 'But you don't need to worry on their account. They want what I want. They're independent women who enjoy having sex. *With me.* And I can assure you they're perfectly satisfied with the arrangement.'

Daisy caught her breath.

'I'll just have to take your word for that,' she said tautly. 'And, just so we're clear, if I do become your wife, I'll play my part in public but our relationship will not extend to the bedroom. You can *satisfy* yourself in private.'

Watching the hard flare of anger in his eyes, she felt a sudden spasm of hope. Rollo might have arrogantly assumed he could conjure up a marriage between two strangers—strangers who despised one another—but clearly he hadn't thought everything through.

So maybe it still wasn't too late to change his mind.

Folding her arms in front of her chest, she tried to replicate the cool, flat expression that was back in place on his face.

'Look, I know you don't want to hear this, but are you really sure we can pull this off? Think about it. We're complete strangers. And we're never going to have sex. So just how are we going to fool everyone into thinking we're some loved-up couple who can't keep their hands off one another?'

She felt her stomach twist. It was a perfect description of her dream relationship. The one she had tried so hard—and failed—to create with each and every one of her boyfriends.

'I don't think that'll be a problem.'

His words bumped into her thoughts and her pulse jerked

as abruptly he got to his feet, his body disturbingly, powerfully muscular and male in the confines of his office.

'Then I think you're being really naive,' she said with more confidence than she felt as he walked slowly around the desk towards her. 'I could probably pull it off. In public at least. But I'm a trained actress. What you're asking is not as easy as it looks. Think of all those films that bomb at the box office because the two leads don't have any chemistry—'

She broke off as he stopped in front of her and held out his hand.

'We need to leave,' he said quietly. 'The security teams will be changing shift soon, and I think we've both answered enough awkward questions already tonight.'

Ignoring his hand, she stood up—but instantly she regretted it, for suddenly they were facing one another, only inches apart. Gazing up at him, she felt her skin grow tight and hot.

'What were we talking about?' he said softly. 'Oh, yes. Our chemistry.'

'It's just not there,' she said hastily, trying not to breathe in the clean, masculine smell of his body. 'And, believe me, you can't just manufacture it for the cameras. It has to be real.'

Rollo let a silence build between them. He wondered if she realised that her body was contradicting her words. That her cheeks were flushed, her lips parted invitingly.

Scrutinising her face, he frowned. 'Well, this thing won't work unless we can convince people.' His eyes narrowed. 'I wonder… How would we test it? If this was a *real* acting job, I mean.'

Her eyes froze midblink. 'I suppose we'd do an audition.'

Taking a step closer, he smiled a small, dispassionate smile. 'What a good idea…' he murmured.

And slowly he lowered his head and kissed her on the lips.

For a fraction of a second he felt her tense against him, and then her mouth softened under his and she was kissing him back...

Daisy curled her fingers into the fabric of his shirt. She knew she should be repelled by his touch. He was her enemy, a bully and a blackmailer. But instead she felt her body catch fire as he deepened the kiss, his mouth suddenly fierce against hers.

A shock—sharp, raw and electric—ran over her skin and her body jerked against his, her hands coming up to grip his arms, her nails cutting into the muscle. She felt him respond, heard the quickening of his breath, felt her own breath stalling in her throat as he arched her body, tipping her head up to meet his—

And then suddenly he lifted his mouth and breathed out softly.

'What was it you said? Oh, that's right. It has to be *real*.' His lips curved upwards and he stroked a strand of hair away from her face. 'I'd say that was pretty damn real.'

There was no mistaking the gleam of satisfaction in his eyes.

Daisy stared at him dazedly. Her heart was slamming into her ribcage. With shock and more than a little embarrassment she realised that her fingers were still wrapped around his arm and slowly, cautiously, not wanting to draw attention to the fact, she lifted her hand.

He watched her calmly. 'So... Last chance. What's it to be? Me? Or the police?'

Daisy flinched. The bluntness of his question was like a punch to the jaw. If it had been just her, she wouldn't have hesitated. She would have turned him down right there and then. He was ruthless and cold-blooded. The relationship he was suggesting would be a travesty of everything she believed. Why, then, was she considering marrying a man she hated with whom she would share nothing but a lie?

Because it wasn't just about her. There were other people to consider. Not just David but her parents too.

Before she could change her mind, she met his gaze and said quickly, 'You.'

He smiled a small triumphant smile that made panic trickle over her skin, cold and damp like rain. She was too ashamed of herself to care. Too ashamed that her decision had been made not solely out of love and loyalty but because being with Rollo would mean that, just for a while, she could forget Daisy Maddox and her hopeless dreams of true love. Because right now finding the right man was a whole lot scarier than the thought of faking it with the wrong one.

'Good. Then we should leave.'

'I want to see David—'

He shook his head. 'Another time. He needs to go home.' His eyes met hers—clear, green, assessing. 'And you need to come with me. To the Upper East Side,' he said lazily. 'Your home for the next twelve months.'

Home! The word sounded so warm and friendly. Daisy bit her lip. It seemed unlikely, but maybe Rollo really did have a softer, warmer side. And silently she prayed that he did. Otherwise she was going to spend the next twelve months feeling like an inmate at the world's most exclusive prison.

CHAPTER THREE

I AM SO not ready for this, Daisy thought as just over an hour later she followed Rollo into the hallway of his penthouse on Park Avenue.

Everything was moving so fast.

Waiting in the lift, she'd half thought that the whole crazy plan might just dissolve in the face of reality. But Rollo had overseen all the arrangements with a quiet, indisputable authority. David had been escorted home and told to take a few days' leave. Daisy's absence had been explained by a hastily concocted plan involving a last-minute callback for a part at a theatre in Philadelphia.

Within minutes of agreeing to become his wife it felt as though time had sped up exponentially, so that one moment she'd been standing in his office and the next she'd been sitting in a sleek black limousine, moving smoothly through traffic towards the Upper East Side.

She might have started to panic sooner, only she had been so distracted by how it had felt when he'd kissed her that she had barely registered the journey. Instead she had simply sat in silence, replaying the moment when his lips had touched hers.

Gazing up, she felt her heartbeat slow. In his office she had just been grateful that Rollo had not called the police. But now that her panic had gone and she was standing in a hallway roughly the same size as David's entire apartment she felt the same mixture of shock and doubt as an astronaut crash-landing on a strange alien planet.

It didn't feel real. It certainly didn't feel like her life anymore.

In front of her a huge chandelier made of crystal droplets

cascaded down like a waterfall into the centre of the marble floor, while on the far side of the hallway a staircase wide enough for a car rose gracefully up to a galleried landing. But what drew her attention most were the three vast contemporary canvases on the walls.

Gazing at the one nearest, she frowned. It looked familiar…

'It's a Pollock. One of his earlier works.'

Her pulse jolted forward like a startled deer. Engrossed by her new surroundings, she had completely forgotten that Rollo was there. But her shock was quickly supplanted as his words registered on her brain.

A Pollock! Rollo owned an actual Jackson Pollock.

The thought blew her mind.

Theoretically, she knew he was rich, but this was a real work of art—the sort that fetched millions at auction. And it was in his hallway.

Hoping she didn't look as gauche as she felt, she nodded nonchalantly. 'David loves his paintings.'

'Personally I find them a little busy. But these…' he gestured casually towards the walls '…weren't my choice anyway. My curator picked them. He thinks they have the greatest potential to rise in value.'

Tearing her eyes away from the paintings, Daisy frowned. 'And that's what matters, is it? That they make you money? Not that they give you pleasure?'

His eyes roamed lazily over her face in a way that made her squirm inside. 'I find they're usually one and the same thing. Shall we go in?'

Staring past him stonily, she took a shallow breath and nodded slowly.

Moments later, she felt her jaw drop as she walked into the open-plan living area.

The room was enormous.

But it wasn't just the size of it that made her eyes widen.

It was the opulence oozing from every corner. Glancing sideways, she noticed a beautiful oil painting of a woman gazing dazedly upwards at a colonnaded ruin. She looked mythical, possibly Greek or Roman. Maybe she had just stumbled across the place where the gods lived. If so, Daisy knew exactly how she felt.

'Welcome to your new home,' Rollo said softly. 'I won't give you the guided tour now, but this is obviously the living room and the kitchen is over there. In case you get hungry in the night.'

She could feel him watching her, gauging her reaction, but she barely noticed. Eyes flitting nervously around the room, she was trying to remember exactly why she'd agreed to move in with him.

It had seemed to make sense earlier. Move in, spend some time getting to know one another and then announce their engagement.

But what the hell had she been thinking? She couldn't imagine living in this apartment, let alone living in it with Rollo, pretending to be his wife.

As though reading her thoughts, he shrugged his jacket off and, throwing it carelessly onto a huge cream leather sofa, met her gaze.

'You'll get used to it.'

'Will I?'

She glanced around nervously. Everything was so big and bright. As usual, after the end of a shift, she had changed into her own clothes. But her comfortable jeans and baggy sweatshirt made her feel as though she had shrunk. If she stayed, she might disappear altogether.

'I should imagine so—' he paused, his expression coolly assessing '—if you want to keep your brother out of prison.'

It was like a sudden icy shower.

Instantly her fear and doubt evaporated, replaced by a blinding flash of anger. 'You really are a bastard,' she said shakily. 'Why would you even say that? I've said I'll do this and I will. Just leave David out of it.'

Her muscles were quivering. He'd just blackmailed her into being his wife. That wasn't normal and he knew it. Hell, he'd even admitted it back in his office. So why was he acting as though she was overreacting? As though she was making a big deal out of nothing?

She shook her head.

'I don't understand you. Doesn't this bother you in any way? That we're going to have to lie? And keep on lying to so many people? And not just tell lies but live a lie too?'

He raised his eyebrows in the way that she now knew preceded one of his hateful, mocking remarks.

'You've spent all evening lying to me, Daisy. A few more months won't make that much difference.'

Their eyes clashed. She swallowed hard, feeling trapped, hating him for the way he twisted everything to make her sound like the villain.

'Don't you have *any* compassion?'

'Generally, yes. Specifically for you, no. You brought this upon yourself. You and your brother, that is. Besides, quite frankly, lies or no lies, I find it difficult to believe that living in a triplex apartment in Manhattan is going to be that much of a hardship for you.'

'If you say so,' she said stiffly.

It was clear she was wasting her time. She might be struggling with the decision they had made, but clearly Rollo was immune to the concept of guilt. And she couldn't keep challenging him all night. Not without anger anyway, and her anger was fading, the adrenaline draining away like bathwater, so that she was suddenly too tired to argue.

'Do you mind if I sit down?' Without waiting for a reply she dropped onto the nearest sofa, stifling a yawn. 'Is there anything else? If not, I'd like to have a hot shower and go to bed.'

Bed!

Rollo felt the word tug at his senses like a kite on a string. It was just three little letters…a place to sleep. But spoken by Daisy in that husky voice it seemed to hint at tangled sheets and bodies moving slowly in the half-light.

Glancing over to where she sat, leaning back against the cushions, he felt his body stiffen in immediate painful response. She was looking up at him with those dark espresso-coloured eyes—eyes that somehow managed to look sleepy yet seductive at the same time.

He gritted his teeth. In his office he'd thought she was beautiful, but now, dressed casually, her legs curling against the leather of the sofa, she looked sexier than any woman he'd ever seen.

Maybe it was the curve of her bottom beneath the tight denim, or the glimpse of bare skin where her oversized sweatshirt was slipping off her shoulder.

The bare skin she would soon be soaping upstairs in the shower.

The thought of her standing naked, water dribbling over her body, was so tantalising that he could suddenly hardly breathe and, swallowing hard, he turned to where a faint pinkish glow through the windows indicated that night was turning to day.

Daisy's desirability was undeniable. But this was a once-in-a-lifetime chance to get what he wanted from James Dunmore. He must be careful not to get distracted by her beauty and her sexual allure.

Clearing his throat, he shook his head. 'No. There's nothing. Everything else can wait…' he glanced round '…until morning,' he finished slowly.

Daisy was asleep, lying on her side, one arm curled under her head like a cat. For a moment he watched her in silence, seeing her as though for the first time—a younger, more vulnerable Daisy. Someone who needed protecting.

The thought needled him, lodging beneath his ribs like a thorn. Why wasn't anyone looking out for her? Her family, her brother, her parents? It made him feel angry all over again only in a different way—angry that she was there on his sofa. That somehow she was now his responsibility.

Responsibility. The word snagged in his throat like a fish bone. Feeling responsible hadn't been part of the equation when he'd come up with the idea of marrying Daisy. It made him feel tense, with its implication of commitment, that somehow there was a bond between them.

Frowning, he ran a hand wearily over his jaw, feeling the scrape of stubble against his fingertips. But was it really such a big deal? All business transactions needed a bond to function. And that was all this was. A transaction. All the rest was just tiredness making him paranoid.

Sighing, he leaned forward, picked up his jacket and gently draped it over her shoulder. She shifted in her sleep, murmuring, fingers splaying apart, and he held his breath. But she didn't wake and finally, after one last look, he turned and walked slowly away.

Waking, it took Daisy a moment to realise where she was. Drowsily she twisted over, sensing daylight, wondering why she had forgotten to draw the curtains in her bedroom. And then her eyes snapped open and instantly her body stilled as she remembered exactly where she was. And why.

Heart beating fast, she lay rigid, the breath trapped in her throat, her limbs stiff, until her muscles began to ache and finally she forced herself to sit up. She gazed warily around the huge living room. There was no sign of Rollo, but her relief was tempered with a slight sense of uneasiness for she could still sense his presence.

Glancing down, she instantly realised why. Someone, presumably Rollo, had covered her with his jacket while she was asleep. Tentatively she picked it up, and inhaled the clean citrus scent of his cologne from the fabric.

The thought of his cool green eyes watching her while she slept made her feel edgy, exposed. He was the enemy, and yet he had seen her at her most vulnerable. It was unsettling. Almost as unsettling as the idea that he had tried to make her comfortable. It seemed a strangely caring gesture from a man who was entirely lacking in empathy.

Her phone vibrated inside her pocket and, pulling it out, she forgot all about Rollo. It was a text from David, along with two earlier messages she had missed.

Scrolling down, she read them slowly, a lump swelling in her throat as she realised how completely her brother trusted her. Not only had he believed her explanation for why he was being allowed to keep his job, but he was almost unbearably grateful to Rollo for being so *'understanding, compassionate, forgiving...'*

Remembering her hurried phone call to him from the limo, she sighed. It hadn't been her most convincing performance, only David had been too exhausted and relieved to notice the strain in her voice or question the credibility of her story. But she knew he might not be so easily persuaded the next time so she'd agreed with Rollo that it would be better not to speak to him in person again for a couple of days.

Leaning forward, Daisy tried to ease the sudden thickness in her throat. She loved her brother. Only right now and for the first time ever, she was glad not to have to hear his voice.

Of course, she was relieved and happy that her brother's life was back on track. He would keep his job and with his debt almost cleared, he could put everything behind him. But a small, whining voice inside her head kept on asking the same question.

What about me? What about my life?

Her stomach gave a low, protesting rumble, as though it

was objecting to her selfishness, and sliding her phone back into her pocket she took a deep, calming breath.

What was done was done. And what was more it had been *her* choice, not David's, to go along with Rollo's crazy suggestion. David knew nothing about it and there was no way she was going to tell him either. She knew her brother—he would want her to call the whole thing off or, more likely, she would convince him to let her carry on and the guilt would destroy him.

Far better just to let him think that everything was back to normal. And then, at some unspecified point in the future, she would tell him and her parents, her friends—the whole world, in fact—about her 'relationship' with Rollo. The thought made her breath hitch higher in her throat.

David was her twin. They told one another everything. Lying to him, and about something so personal and important, was going to be difficult—especially when the shock of it was still so new to her.

Her stomach grumbled again more loudly.

But right now, though, there were more pressing matters to address. Like the fact that if she didn't eat soon, she would probably keel over. She needed some food, and then maybe she might take a look around her new 'home.'

And standing up, she went in search of the kitchen.

Later, having eaten, she walked slowly through the apartment, trying to shift the feeling that she was a guest at best, an intruder at worst. Her family's house was large and comfortable, if a little shabby. But with each step here she felt increasingly out of place.

In daylight the apartment was breathtakingly beautiful. Pale wood floors added warmth to the clean white walls and stark, architectural furniture, and huge windows offered striking views of Central Park and the city. The size and the stillness were dazzling, and without Rollo's reaction to consider she simply stood and gazed in speechless silence.

But it was the outdoor space that left her groping for adjectives. Impressive, stunning, jaw-dropping… None did justice to the tile-covered terrace that stretched uninterrupted towards the skyline. Nor could she find a word to capture the impossible luxury of the infinity pool, its mirror-like surface reflecting nothing but sky and the odd passing aeroplane.

And yet, aside from marvelling at the opulence, Daisy found herself oddly unmoved by the apartment. It felt more like a hotel than a home. There were no personal effects to suggest anyone actually *lived* there. Certainly no sign that Rollo was the owner. It could have belonged to anyone. Or no one.

In which case who was she marrying? Daisy thought nervously.

Stepping into yet another stylish room, she stopped in the doorway. There was something different about it. It was still grand. But it had a sense of being 'used' that the other rooms lacked.

Hesitantly, her legs quivering with tension, she walked over to the desk. There was a striking silver bowl on top of the smooth dark wood. Breathing in, she reached out and touched it with a hand that trembled in time to the beating of her heart as, finally, her brain caught up with her feet.

It was an office. Rollo's office.

Now she really *did* feel like she was snooping! Her muscles twitched involuntarily and, despite having only just eaten, she felt a pit open up in the bottom of her stomach.

It was his private space.

'That didn't take long.'

And his voice.

Her fingers jerked back and, muscles tensing, she turned slowly to where Rollo stood watching her, his shoulder pressed against the door frame.

Her heart had stopped beating and for a moment she

stared at him in silence, the only sound her breath fluttering in her throat like a moth against a lampshade.

Even in an entire apartment filled with works of art there was nothing that could compete with the flawless symmetry of his face. But it wasn't his face that was making her legs tremble like blancmange. It was the fact that he was wearing a pair of black running shorts.

Just a pair of black running shorts.

Clearly he'd been to the gym; his hair was damp and a towel hung loosely around his neck. Or maybe he always walked around like that, she thought desperately, heat wrapping round her throat and her shoulders like a heavy scarf.

Any ordinary seminaked person would have been unnerved or embarrassed when confronted by someone fully clothed. Rollo, however, seemed not to care. But then why should he? Her gaze roamed furtively over the smooth muscles of his arms and chest. He was gorgeously, unashamedly male and he knew it.

Tearing her eyes away from the hard definition of his taut, golden stomach, and her imagination from what lay beneath the shorts, she looked up at him warily. 'What didn't take long?'

He didn't reply. Instead his dark green gaze fixed on her face as he stepped into the room. His body filled the doorway so that Daisy had a sudden vivid flashback to the night before.

'You didn't. Stealing the family silver and it's only day one.'

His voice was so quiet, the tone so conversational, she might have thought he was joking. But nothing could disguise the cool contempt in his eyes.

'I should warn you the paintings are a lot heavier than they look, even when they're rolled up.'

Breathing in sharply, she felt her cheeks grow cold, then hot. 'I wasn't stealing anything—'

'Of course you weren't. Let me guess.' He interrupted, his mouth curling into a sneer. 'You just wanted to *have a look*?'

Her temper flared. 'Yes. I did. And why shouldn't I? I live here, and at some point in the future I'm going to be your wife. So, yes, I was having a look.' She stared at him pointedly. 'Although, frankly, I think I've seen a lot more than I wanted to.'

There was a sudden strained silence.

'Is that right?'

The sudden harnessed tension in his voice made her stomach shrivel with panic, but she lifted her chin.

'Yes. Yes, it is.'

She wanted it to be true. Wanted to prove that she was immune to him. Wanted to make a dent in that armour-plated arrogance. But almost instantly she regretted her words as, eyes narrowing, he began slowly walking towards her.

She took a hurried step back. 'What are you doing?'

Her eyes widened… Her voice was high and panicky. But he was still moving forward and frantically she held out her hands.

'Stop. Stop it!'

Finally, thankfully, he did so. Only now they were close enough to touch—so close she could feel the heat of his skin. *Too* close, she realised. Too late. With no physical distance between them there was nowhere to hide from that beautiful sculptured body. Or the seductive curving lips. Lips that had kissed her with a fierce, sensual passion she had never experienced before, rendering her both helpless and hungry.

And now that hunger was rising inside her, dark and treacherous as a storm tide, pulling her under.

'Stop what?'

His voice—cool, blade sharp—sliced through her brain.

'All the name-calling, the snide remarks.' Her own voice was shaking and she hated herself for sounding so weak.

Hated her body for responding when it should be rejecting

him. But she hated him more for taking over her life. Breathing in sharply, she folded her arms. Only how was anyone going to believe they were in love if there was only hate?

'This is not going to work,' she said as firmly as she could manage. 'Us, I mean. I know in theory it sounded like it could, but—'

Her words vaporised on her lips as his eyes slammed into hers.

'Let me remind you of why you might want to make it work in practice. It's the only way you and your brother are avoiding criminal records.'

Her chest was hard and tight; her throat felt as if it was closing up.

'But I can't live like this for the next twelve months.'

'I don't care.'

She stared at him, her body trembling not with desire now but with anger.

'Oh, I know you don't care!' She glowered at him, furious responses whirling inside her head like sparks from a Catherine wheel. 'You don't care about me or my feelings. You made that clear from the moment we first met—and, yes, I know I was breaking into your office, so you can spare me the part about how I brought it on myself,' she snapped.

His face was hard and impenetrable, like a castle wall, eyes narrowed like arrow slits.

'I'm warning you, Daisy, I've had just about enough of—'

His voice was like a whip crack, but she wasn't going to let him intimidate her.

'Of what? Of me being a human being? With feelings? You can't call me names and—'

'Call you *names*!' He shook his head incredulously.

'Yes. Call. Me. Names.' She punctuated each word clearly and firmly, like Morse code. 'You do it all the time. And it's not fair—'

'Fair?' His face hardened like water turning to ice. 'I've been more than fair. I could have just handed you and your brother over to the police, but I didn't.'

She gave a small strangled laugh. 'That's your idea of being fair? Blackmailing me to be your wife? You weren't being fair—just self-serving.'

The skin across his cheekbones grew tauter, his eyes glittering like splinters of glass.

'I see it more as a strategic response to a business opportunity.'

His words should hardly have surprised her, let alone upset her—after all she'd agreed to this relationship partly to avoid anything emotional and meaningful. And yet the knowledge that she was just a means to an end still smarted.

'It's a wonder you even have a business if you put this little effort and commitment into all your other deals,' she said stiffly. 'Let me tell you something, *Rollo*, you might not care about me, or my feelings, but you *do* care about this deal. You must, or why else would I be here? But I'm an actress—not a miracle worker. And no one—certainly no one sane and rational—will ever believe our marriage is real if you carry on behaving like this.'

Surely he could understand what she was trying to say. That normal people in a normal relationship needed a level of trust and respect for one another to make it work.

She sighed. 'I know you think it doesn't matter how I feel. That I deserve it even. But it *does* matter because I can't just ignore all the nasty things you say in private and then act all lovey-dovey in public.'

'Why not? Surely that's what acting is.'

His dismissive statement grated over her skin like a serrated knife.

'What, like business is just people signing bits of paper?' She shook her head dismissively, her brown eyes flashing with scorn. 'I'm an actress. So trust me when I say that if you want an audience to believe in your performance, you can't just pretend. You have to believe too. It's not enough just to say you want me to be your wife. You're going to have to *act* a little yourself. And *commit* to the part.'

She exhaled slowly.

'So, even though you don't like me or approve of me, can you just stop sitting in judgement of me and my brother? Otherwise we're not going to be able to pull this off.'

His gaze rested on her face. 'You broke into my office and he stole my watch. Doesn't that give me some right to judge?'

'No. It doesn't,' she said with spirit. 'All you know about David is that he's tall, twitchy and took your watch.' Picturing her brother, she felt her hands start to tremble. 'But you don't know the real David. The David I know. He's never done anything like this, ever. He's the most law-abiding person you'll ever meet. And the sweetest.'

Watching her eyes soften as she defended her brother, Rollo felt a tightness in his chest. There was something about Daisy and her devotion to her brother that touched him. Something he'd consciously chosen never to imagine. Only now it was here—inside his head, inside his home.

And it made him feel jaded and hollow, so that for a moment it was as though they'd traded places and he was the one creeping through a darkened office. Only he was intruding on something far more personal and private than an empty building.

She might not know truth from fiction, but her love for David was real and pure and unassailable.

His shoulders tightened, muscles setting.

Unassailable and undermining.

He clenched his jaw. Forget drugs and alcohol. Love was a far greater threat to health and happiness; it turned perfectly rational people into fools and strength into weakness.

Love betrayed those it should protect and protected those who betrayed others.

He knew that from personal experience. His father's total and unswerving love for his mother had been rewarded not with loyalty but defection. Worse, he had watched his mother weep, felt her pain as his own, only to realise that what he'd taken for misery had actually been self-pity and frustration. Only there had been no way of knowing that until it was too late. When all that had been left was a letter on the kitchen table.

It was why he'd sworn never to make the same mistake as his father. And why, when opportunity presented itself, he was choosing to 'marry' Daisy—a woman he didn't and would never love.

Jaw tightening, Rollo stared past her, his guarded expression giving no hint of the turmoil inside his head.

'If he's so law-abiding and sweet, why did he steal my watch?'

Daisy blinked. Her palms were suddenly damp. It was a reasonable question, and she wanted to tell him the truth. Only how much should she tell? The little she knew about Rollo didn't exactly encourage her to expect a sympathetic reaction. But, glancing up at his set, still face, she realised it was a risk she was going to have to take.

'He needed the money. He's been gambling online. And losing. A lot.'

Saying it out loud, she felt shock again. The same stomach-plunging mix of terror and denial she'd felt when David had finally broken down and told her the truth. Remembering the sharpness of his breath, the fluttering panic in his eyes as she'd tried to calm him down, she felt her vision blur and her stomach cramp around a hard, cold lump of misery.

'I think it was fun at first,' she said quietly. 'Something to do when he couldn't sleep. And then suddenly he had this huge, horrible debt.'

She could feel the misery spreading out and over her, like dark clouds blotting out the sun.

'And now?'

She looked up.

'He didn't sell the watch, so is he still in debt?' He was staring at her impassively—watching, waiting—but for the first time since they'd met, she felt he wasn't judging her.

'I paid most of it off with my savings,' she admitted. 'I did a few commercials last summer. They're not really acting, but they pay well.'

He nodded. 'And has he spoken to anyone about his problem? Other than you, I mean. Friends, maybe? Your parents?'

She shook her head. How could she explain about her parents? About their marriage, their life together. About how it was what *she* wanted to have. Maybe not their diner, the Love Shack—she'd had enough waitressing to last her a lifetime—but they were so supportive and happy. She and David would never do anything to jeopardise that happiness.

'He didn't—we don't want them to know. They'd only worry. Besides...' she added, meeting his gaze '...I—we can sort it out.'

Rollo studied her face. Wrong, he thought silently. This kind of problem could never be sorted out without professional help. Addicts rarely believed that they had a problem, no matter what pain and chaos they caused to those around them. And sometimes even when they did, it made little if any difference to their behaviour.

'So when did he tell you?' he said at last. 'About the gambling.'

She swallowed. 'The same day he stole your watch.'

He was silent a moment, considering her answer. Then he said quietly, 'Selfish of him, don't you think?'

Her head jerked up. But what had she expected? Had she really believed Rollo would understand? Or care.

Rollo Fleming.

A man who thought nothing of exploiting another man's moment of weakness or a woman's affection for her brother. She felt sick, her stomach lurching. She had betrayed her brother's confidence, and for nothing.

She glared at him. 'He's not selfish—' she began.

But he cut in.

'He's your twin. He must have known that you'd step up and sort it out for him.'

He held up his hand as she started to protest.

'I'm not judging him, Daisy. But addicts don't think like other people. They lie and deny and prevaricate and make excuses. It's part of their sickness.'

She watched his face carefully. It sounded as if he knew what he was talking about and she wanted to ask him how. Or maybe who. But his expression was distant, discouraging, as though he knew that she was trying to figure out the meaning behind his remark.

She nodded mutely.

He met her gaze. 'David is sick. He needs care and support.'

His eyes were cool and untroubled, but his expression had shifted into something she hadn't expected to see; it was oddly gentle...almost like sympathy.

'Which is why I'm going to arrange for him to receive professional help at a clinic.'

Daisy's heart stopped. Unsteadily she pushed back her hair, trying to make sense of his words. 'Why?' she said finally. 'Why would you do that?'

Why, indeed?

Rollo gazed at her taut face. The fine cheekbones and delicate jaw were offset perfectly by her pale, almost-luminous skin. She was very beautiful. But that wasn't the reason he was going to help her brother.

He didn't approve of what David had done. Theft was still theft. Nor did he agree with how Daisy had behaved. But he understood their motives better now.

He shrugged. 'Despite what you think, Daisy, I'm not a complete monster. He needs treatment. As his employer, I feel some responsibility for his welfare. But there is one condition.'

His voice was quiet but she heard the warning note—felt it echo inside her and through her head to the corners of the room.

'I'll take care of David but I won't be messed around. You might not be on my payroll, but you work for me now, and I expect…' He paused, his eyes pulling her gaze upwards like a tractor's headlight beam. 'I demand honesty from my staff.'

Forcing herself to meet his eyes, she gave him a small, tight smile. 'I understand. And thank you for helping David. It's very kind of you.'

He nodded. 'Leave it with me.'

Pulling out his phone, he glanced at the screen and frowned.

'Right. I'm going to go and change.' He paused again. 'Which reminds me—you need to go shopping.'

The change of subject caught her off guard.

'I do?'

His gaze held hers. 'There's a charity fashion show a week from tomorrow. I think it should be our first public appearance. We'll be ready by then.'

Daisy flinched inwardly. He wasn't asking, but telling her, and his cool statement was yet another reminder of the fact that she was dealing with a man who always got what he wanted, one way or another.

He stared at her calmly. 'It won't be too formal or intimate, and you'll be visible but anonymous, so it will be the perfect moment to introduce you as my girlfriend. But you'll need something to wear. Kenny, my driver, knows which stores to go to. Just choose whatever you like and charge it to my accounts.'

'That's very generous.' She frowned. 'But I don't expect you to buy my clothes. Besides, I have quite a few back at David's,' she said, trying to make a joke.

But he didn't laugh. Instead he stared at her, for so long and so intently that she wasn't sure if he'd actually heard her. But then, finally, he smiled coldly.

'I'm sure your clothing was adequate for your life before, but trust me—you'll feel more comfortable in something a little more *appropriate.*'

Adequate! Appropriate!

Hands curling into fists, Daisy gazed at him in angry disbelief.

Moments earlier she had felt…if not close to Rollo, then at least more relaxed with him. Now though, she was remembering just how much she loathed him.

He was so unspeakably arrogant and autocratic.

'Shouldn't it be up to *me* to decide what is appropriate?' she said tightly.

'Ordinarily, yes. But that was before you agreed to become my wife.'

He took a step closer and she felt her shoulders tense, priming her for his next move.

'You told me earlier that I needed to commit. And I have…'

He paused and her skin seemed to catch fire as, reaching out, he stroked the curve of her cheek gently.

'But in return you need to stop fighting me. That's only fair, isn't it?'

The rhythm of his fingers was making her breathing slow so that she felt as though she were suffocating.

'So when I politely suggest you go shopping, you go shopping,' he said softly. 'Or next time, I might not ask so nicely.'

And, leaving her furiously mouthing words after him, he turned and sauntered out of the room.

CHAPTER FOUR

'So…' ROLLO PAUSED and glanced over to where Daisy sat, slumped in one of the apartment's huge leather armchairs. 'You prefer coffee to tea, red wine to white and you hate whisky.'

He waited, letting a long silence pass, battling with an irritation that had become familiar to him over the last twenty-four hours.

'And…?' he prompted finally as she continued to stare across the living room, her gaze fixed determinedly on the view of downtown New York.

Turning, she screwed up her face as though concentrating. 'You like red wine too.' She hesitated. 'And you prefer your coffee white.'

He gritted his teeth. 'No. Black.'

Ordinarily he would have already drunk several cups of espresso. But right now he could do with something stronger.

They'd started early—cross-examining each other again and again until the answers felt automatic. Or that had been the plan. A muscle tightened in his jaw. Only instead of knuckling down, Daisy was acting like a teenager doing a detention.

'Oh, yeah. I remember now.' Stifling a yawn, she met his gaze, her brown eyes challenging him. 'Sorry.'

She didn't seem sorry. On the contrary, she sounded both unrepentant and bored.

Watching her shoulders slump in an exaggerated gesture of exhaustion, Rollo gritted his teeth but didn't reply. Instead, leaning back against the leather of the armchair, he studied her in silence, trying to decide just how to manage this new, modified version of Daisy.

Since yesterday, when he'd more or less ordered her to go shopping, she had stopped fighting him openly, choosing instead to treat him with the sort of forced politeness normally reserved for teachers or dull acquaintances.

It was driving him mad.

Yet, despite his irritation, there was something about her that got under his skin. He could feel himself responding to her defiance, her stubbornness...her beauty. Shifting against the cushions, he felt his pulse twitch. She *was* beautiful, but it was more than that. He'd dated a lot of women—models, actresses, socialites—all of them as beautiful and desirable as Daisy. And yet none of them had ever made him feel this way—so off balance, as though his calm, disciplined world had been tipped upside down. As though his life were not his own.

Which, of course, it wasn't any more.

Running his hand through his short, blonde hair, Rollo pressed his fingers into the base of his skull, where an ache was starting to form. In truth, it wouldn't be *his* life for the next twelve months—until after his marriage had ended in a quick, uncontested divorce. A marriage that hadn't even happened yet.

He breathed in sharply. Having always vowed to stay single, the fact that he was not only going to be married but divorced too blew his mind.

But there was no other way. He wanted that building, and he was going to keep his promise to his father—no matter what the cost to his sexual and mental health.

He frowned. Usually in life, and in business, he got what he wanted through a combination of persistence and money. But he'd been trying to buy this building for nearly ten years, and James Dunmore had made it clear that money wasn't the issue. He would only do business with a man who shared his values—a man who truly believed that family and marriage was the cornerstone of life.

It was easy for Dunmore to believe—*he* wasn't the one having to put his life on hold. Nor was he having to co-habit with a stubborn, sexy minx like Daisy Maddox, he thought irritably. Everything would be so much simpler and smoother if she were like every other woman he'd ever met. Eager, accommodating, flirty. But the woman he'd picked to be his first—his only—wife seemed determined to challenge him at every opportunity.

Even when he kissed her.

Especially when he kissed her.

His breath swelled in his throat, and just like that he could remember how it had felt when her lips had touched his. How she'd come alive in his arms, her body melting into his, hands tangling through his hair, her feverish response matching his desperate desire—

He let out a shallow breath. It was an image he needed little effort to remember, having spent the night replaying it inside his head, his frustration magnified by the fact that the cause of his discomfort was on the other side of the wall, no doubt sleeping peacefully.

Unable to sleep himself, he had lain in the darkness, trying to piece together the fragments of nakedness that she had inadvertently revealed to him. The pale length of her neck and throat, gleaming beneath the harsh lights in his office, the curve of her bare shoulder when she had fallen asleep on the sofa. To that he'd added the scab on her knee she'd got breaking into his office—glimpsed as she'd slid past him on the landing in the T-shirt she wore as a nightie.

He'd picked at those memories until just before dawn when, finally, he had fallen asleep.

Feeling her gaze on the side of his face, he pushed aside the burn of frustration in his groin and forced himself to concentrate instead on the thankfully fully clothed Daisy sitting opposite him.

'This is boring for both of us,' he said slowly. 'But the

more committed you are to getting it right, the quicker we can move on.'

Daisy's brown eyes focused on Rollo's face. He was speaking to her as though she were a child. She felt her cheeks grow hot.

She shrugged. 'So I forgot? Big deal. It's not like anyone's going to be testing us.'

Last night, after his snooty remarks about her clothing, she had expended so much energy on hating him that she had instantly fallen into a heavy, dreamless sleep. Waking, she had felt calmer, determined to find a better way of managing him. Given that so far every confrontation had ended badly—*for her*—she'd resolved not to lose her temper. But it was going to be a hard challenge if he carried on being so aggravating.

'I'm an actress,' she said stiffly. 'I know what I have to do to get into character.'

'Then stop sulking and do it. It was you, after all, who told me that I had to commit to the role. Perhaps you should follow your own advice.'

He gave her a patronising smile that made her want to smother him with one of the sofa cushions. But instead she took a shallow breath and in her calmest voice said, 'It just feels so soulless and scripted. Couldn't we just hang out together and talk? That way we'd still get to know each other, only it would be more...' she searched for the right word '...more *organic*.'

It was a reasonable request. More reasonable, say, than demanding someone replace their entire wardrobe of clothes. But clearly being reasonable was not a concept that was familiar to Rollo.

Fuming silently, she watched him shake his head.

'Testing each other is the quickest way to learn this stuff. Then we can go out and start putting it all into practice. In public.'

The thought of actually appearing in public as his girl-friend made panic skim across her skin like a stone. She glanced across to where he sat, lounging lazily in an arm-chair. Even dressed casually, in a faded T-shirt and jeans, he radiated both superiority and authority—the sort of undefin-able power that went hand in hand with being an alpha male.

Her breath crowded in her throat as his gaze wandered casually over her face, down over the long white hippyish dress she had bought on holiday with David last year.

But what about *her*? She hardly qualified as a member of the elite. She had no job, no money and right now a future that didn't even really belong to her. Changing her clothes wasn't about to change any of those facts.

She lifted her chin. But why should she change, any-way? She wasn't ashamed of who she was or where she came from.

'Good,' she said, with something of her usual spirit. 'The sooner we can get on with this charade, the sooner it will all be over. I just wish it didn't feel so much like school.' She sighed. 'It reminds me of cramming for exams.'

'It does?' he said slowly, giving her one of his cool, blank looks. 'Interesting. I wouldn't have had you down as the swotty type.'

His green eyes were locked on to hers, taunting her. She opened her mouth to protest and then closed it again. It would be so gratifying to tell him that she'd been an A-grade student. That the library had been her second home. But she didn't think there was much chance of convincing him.

Mostly because it wasn't true.

'I suppose you were the top of the class?' She felt her cheeks grow warm as he surveyed her steadily.

'If you mean I worked hard, then, yes. But I made sure I had plenty of energy left for…*extracurricular activities*.'

He gave her a slow, suggestive smile that curled like smoke around her throat. Her heart was banging high up in her ribs and, swallowing, she forced down the traitorous heat rising up inside her.

'Fascinating though it is to hear about your school days, we should probably press on,' she said stiffly. 'I might just get a glass of water first.'

And, standing up, she stalked across the room and into the kitchen.

Rollo watched her leave, his groin hardening as his gaze locked on to the swaying hips beneath her flimsy dress. Clearly, despite having gone shopping, she was determined to wear her own clothes when they were at home.

He shook his head, exasperated by her need to make a stand, and yet part of him—the part of him that would have dug in his heels in exactly the same way—couldn't help admiring her.

That didn't mean there wasn't plenty of room for improvement, he thought caustically. Not least in her laissez-faire attitude to the business of becoming his wife. Maybe it was time to remind her of what was at stake here...

In the kitchen, Daisy stared blankly at the gleaming white cupboards. Her mind was tumbling, but that was nothing to the chaos of her body. Her legs felt shaky and a dark, dragging ache like a bruise was spreading out inside her.

Why did he have this effect on her? Or rather, why *still*? Back in his office, she'd put it down to a combination of adrenaline and heightened emotion. So why was it happening *now*?

Taking a glass from one of the cupboards, she turned on the tap, watching the water splash into the stainless steel sink. If only she could slip away down the plughole too, she thought dully, filling her glass. If only she could escape so effortlessly.

But who was she escaping from? Rollo or herself?

'There's bottled water in the fridge, if you'd prefer. Still and sparkling.'

She tensed, her heartbeat stalling in her chest.

Not him. Not here and definitely not now. She wasn't ready.

She'd been hoping for a few much-needed moments alone to pull herself together, to talk some sense into what supposedly passed as her brain. But of course, as with everything else in her life since Rollo had walked into it, her hopes were subject to his will.

Turning, she felt her breath catch fire in her throat. He was standing in front of her, closer than she'd thought he would be...so close she could see the flecks of bronze in his eyes.

He was too close for comfort.

Only time would show if it was too close for her self-control.

She smiled tightly. 'No, I'm fine with tap.'

He stared at her unblinkingly and she felt her pulse plateau. He was stupidly handsome, and being so close to him was making her stupid. Why else would she feel so frantic to kiss him? Her cheeks were hot and, desperate to stop the woman in her responding to his blatant masculinity, she switched into waitress mode.

'I'm sorry, I didn't ask. Did you want anything?' She couldn't resist. 'White coffee? Sorry, I mean black.'

There was a short, quivering silence and then, tilting his head, he gave her a long, steady look. He shook his head. 'No, thanks. I'm trying to cut back.' The corners of his eyes creased. 'Just in case you didn't notice—that was unscripted.'

She looked up at him uncertainly. His mood seemed to have lightened and she could feel herself responding, her tension easing, so that for one off-balance moment she wanted to smile. And to see him smile back.

Except that if he smiled she was scared of what might happen. A smile might seem innocuous. Like tiptoeing onto a frozen lake. But at some point the ice would crack and suddenly she would be out of her depth.

Feeling his eyes on her face, she looked up and met his gaze coolly. At least she hoped she looked cool. She certainly didn't want him guessing her real thoughts.

'I'm not trying to be difficult,' she said slowly. 'Truly. But you're treating this—*us*—like some kind of equation. We can't pull this off by just joining all the dots. We need to try and make our relationship feel as natural as possible. And that's not going to happen if we just sit here parroting facts to one another.'

It had to be the strangest conversation she had ever had. Only in some ways, wasn't it liberating to be able to talk so openly about what she wanted? About what it would take to make their relationship work? With all her previous boyfriends she'd just tried to second-guess everything and failed. Spectacularly. But because she wasn't in love with Rollo, and never would be, she didn't care about speaking her mind.

Half expecting him to argue with her, she was surprised when instead, he nodded.

'That makes sense.'

He sounded interested—friendly, even—and as something like panic bubbled up inside her she realised too late that being near him had been a lot easier when all she had felt was hostility.

Particularly given that he clearly *deserved* her hostility.

Or she'd thought he had.

But as his eyes drifted gently over her skin like a haze of summer heat she realised that his charm was something she hadn't allowed herself to imagine. And, glancing up into his face, watching his beautiful hard features soften, she knew why: it was too dangerous! Especially when that almost smile was making it impossible for her to think rationally, so that suddenly she felt unsure of herself, unsure of how she should respond.

He was lounging against the worktop, his eyes watching her intently in a way that she didn't fully understand. All she knew was that it made her feel hot and helplessly wound up.

'We can make this work, Daisy.'

She nodded, panic muting her.

'It's very new for both of us. Try and think of it as just another job.'

Frowning, she found her voice. 'But it's not like that at all. When I'm acting I learn my lines and get into character. But only when I'm on stage. I don't act like Lady Macbeth at home.'

His gaze was steady and unblinking. 'That's a relief,' he said softly.

His voice sent goosebumps over her skin and she felt a sharp, gnawing heat inside, like the first flames of a forest fire. She knew she had blushed and she wanted to look away, but she couldn't move. Instead she held her breath, heart hammering, trying to quiet the turmoil in her body.

Breathing out, she said quickly, 'It's just… We're supposed to be madly in love.'

Something shifted in the room—a loosening of tension like the wind dropping. For a moment they stared at one another, and then his hand came up, his fingers smoothing over her cheeks, his touch firm yet tender.

'Supposed to be, yes.' His hand dropped and he took a step back, his green eyes shadowed and still.

She swallowed, her breath cartwheeling inside her chest. 'So we need some…' She paused.

She'd been about to say *romance*, or *passion*. But passion was clearly a complication she didn't need to introduce into their relationship. Not if her body's intense but dangerous response to him was anything to go by. And, as for romance, she wasn't sure he actually understood the meaning of the word.

She frowned. 'We need to have some fun.'

His mouth curved. 'Fun?'

Daisy gazed at him. Was that an alien concept to him too?

'Yes. *Fun*. We need fun. Not facts. Let's get out of here and go somewhere we can talk and chill.'

For a moment she thought he wasn't going to answer. That maybe he hadn't even been listening.

'I see…'

The change in him was barely discernible. His voice was perfectly calm and even, but she could sense an indecision in him that she had never seen before.

'I keep a box at the Met Opera.' He pulled out his phone. 'I don't actually know what's on, but I'm sure you'll enjoy it and it's completely private. I'll get my PA to notify the theatre.'

She stared at him numbly. Clearly he hadn't been listening. Or why would he suggest a night at the opera? It was hardly the most laid-back way to spend an evening—nor would they even be able to talk. It was probably just somewhere he took whatever woman he happened to be seeing at the time.

Pushing aside the niggle of pain that thought caused, she glared at him coldly. 'I wouldn't want you to put yourself out. Besides, I don't like opera.'

His eyes jerked up to hers, their expression so cold and hostile that instantly her muscles tautened for flight.

There was a long hiss of silence.

Rollo stared at her coldly. Anger was blanking his brain, so that for a moment he couldn't speak—and besides, he needed the time to bank down his fury. Not just with Daisy for her rudeness, but with himself for trying to meet her halfway.

For being weak.

Keeping his eyes unfocused, he stared past her until finally he could trust his voice.

'In that case, I'll leave you to get on with learning your lines.'

It took her a moment to understand what he was saying. 'What do you mean? Are you going somewhere?'

'To the office.'

She felt his words scoop out a hollow at the bottom of her stomach.

'The office? But I thought you wanted to—'

'Then you made a mistake. As I did.' A muscle flickered at his jawline. 'But on the plus side, at least we really *are* getting to know each other.'

He turned and crossed the room in three long strides.

Daisy let out a short jerky breath. She wasn't quite sure what had just happened. But the emptiness of the room was doing something strange to her body—making her pulse race too fast so that suddenly she needed to do something with her hands.

Picking up her glass, she rinsed it out and started drying it furiously.

His words were rolling round her head like marbles in a jar. What kind of person upped and went to work in the middle of an argument? And then abruptly the marbles stilled.

Going to the office? But why the hell was he going into the office? It was Sunday.

Slumped behind his desk, Rollo stared bleakly out of the window at the city he called home. To the left was the past: the building where he'd grown up—the building he'd been trying to buy from James Dunmore for all of his adult life. To the right lay his future: the penthouse where he was living with Daisy. And, whichever way he looked at it, he needed one in order to acquire the other.

He wasn't regretting his decision to coerce Daisy into being his wife so much as reassessing it. Having overridden her objections, he had thought it would be just as easy to maintain her cooperation.

But, remembering her expression when he'd offered to take her to the opera, he felt a twist of anger low in his stomach. He should have just told her how it was going to be. Instead, driven by some inexplicable need to make their relationship more natural, more spontaneous, he'd let down his guard.

Let himself be manipulated, more like.

He gritted his teeth. A long time ago, he had sworn never to make himself vulnerable like that. Never to become his father—a man who had spent a lifetime trying and failing to please one woman.

Only he'd broken his own rules.

And there was nobody to blame but himself.

Daisy might be all soft brown eyes and seductive curves, but she was also a nightmare on legs. Devious. Wilful. Utterly untrustworthy. And that assessment didn't even take into account her ability as an actress to slip between multiple personas—one minute, a warrior queen, standing her ground in his office, the next, falling asleep on his sofa like an overtired child.

But was he marrying all of them or one of them?

A small draught swept across his shoulders and he heard the door to his office open softly. Around him the air seemed to ripple and tighten, and he knew without even looking round that it was Daisy.

The light through the window lit up her face and he was struck again by her luminous beauty. But not enough to break the uneasy silence that was filling his office.

'Your doorman let me in,' she said finally.

Her voice was brittle, like an eggshell, and she gave him a small, tight smile.

'He recognised me from the other night.'

He nodded.

She bit her lip. 'I can go if you want...' Her voice trailed off.

He watched her hovering in the doorway. A different Daisy again—not defiant or afraid so much as apprehensive.

'Why are you here?' There was no inflection in his voice.

'It's almost three o'clock.'

He heard her swallow.

'You didn't eat much breakfast.'

Her face was still.

'And then you didn't come back for lunch. So I brought you some food.'

Hesitantly she held up a brown paper bag.

Her eyes were searching his face and he realised that she was worried—worried about *him*—and shock spread slowly over his chest like a bruise.

'It's pizza. Four cheeses with extra olives. And a margherita.' She breathed out. 'I remembered.'

She made a small, shapeless gesture with her hand and set the bag down on the floor. Edging backwards, she said quickly, 'Anyway, I'll just leave it here and if you feel hungry later—'

'Did they use pecorino or Parmigiana?'

Daisy stopped. Her pulse quivered.

'Pecorino.'

'Light or heavy on the sauce?'

She swallowed.

'Light.'

'Okay.'

He was studying her face, his green eyes utterly unreadable. She held her breath until finally he held out his hand.

'Do you want to eat here or in the boardroom?'

In the end they decided to stay in his office, sitting at either end of the sofa with the pizza boxes between them.

'I've never had four cheeses before,' she said, nibbling a string of mozzarella into her mouth. 'I thought it would be too—'

'Cheesy?'

She almost smiled. '*No*. Too dairy! But it's actually not.'

They talked randomly. Nothing personal. Just about food and New York. But all the tension of the past two days seemed to have vanished. Finally he picked up the empty boxes, folded them in half and slid them back into the bag.

'I think that's probably the best pizza I've ever eaten. Where did you get it?'

Daisy felt a spasm of happiness shoot through her. It felt so much lighter, looser between them—normal, almost.

'Oh, there's this really great family-run pizzeria near David's apartment.'

Rollo frowned. 'Your brother's apartment? That's a bit of a trip from here.'

'I suppose so. But I was out walking anyway.'

She glanced past him, colour rising on her face.

After Rollo had left she had been too angry and thwarted and confused to sit down. Instead she had paced round the apartment like an animal at the zoo. But pacing and anger were hard to sustain, and after an hour or so, her strides had started to shorten, her anger fading, until finally she'd stopped walking and sat down.

She'd felt miserable. And guilty. No doubt Rollo had thought that arranging an evening at the opera—just the two of them in a private box—would be the perfect way to spend some time alone together. And, remembering that moment of uncharacteristic irresolution before he'd spoken, she'd felt her stomach drop.

It had been a peace offering.

Only she had thrown it back in his face.

Worse, she'd been so busy resenting him that she'd focused entirely on why their relationship should fail when she should have been finding ways to make it work.

She shifted uncomfortably on the sofa.

'I always go for a walk when I'm upset. You know, when I need to think.' Her eyes flickered past him. 'It's just all of this—us—it's harder than I thought. And I think it's going to get harder when I have to start lying to people. Not strangers…I mean my parents and David. But that's my problem, not yours—'

'That makes it my problem too.'

He was silent a moment, then he said quietly, 'Are you worried they won't approve of me?'

Her eyes widened with disbelief. 'No, I'm worried they *will*. They're going to be so happy for me—and I don't deserve it. It makes me feel cruel.'

'You're not cruel.' His face searched her face, eyes softening a fraction. 'You're here for your brother. That makes you loyal. And strong. It takes a lot of courage to do what you're doing.'

Was that a compliment? She stared at him, confused. 'Or stupidity.'

'I don't think you're stupid.'

She grimaced. 'You never read my school reports. "Could do better" was a fairly universal theme.'

'That's got more to do with your attitude than your aptitude.'

His voice was oddly gentle and, looking up, she saw he was leaning slightly forward, his expression carefully casual.

'Maybe a little.' She smiled weakly. 'But David's the smart one. He's, like, a genius at maths and science. But he paints amazingly too—and he loves the opera—' Her heartbeat gave a guilty little lurch.

'Perhaps I should have invited him.'

She shivered, half choked on her breath, cleared her

throat. 'About that—' She shifted uncomfortably on the sofa. 'What I said to you about opera. It was rude and unnecessary and I'm sorry.'

There was a fraction of a pause and then she felt his gaze sweep over her like a searchlight.

'I'm guessing you had a bad experience with *The Ring Cycle*.'

She gazed at him blankly. 'The what?'

'*Der Ring des Nibelungen* by Wagner. Lasts about fifteen hours. I thought it might be why you hate opera.'

She shuddered. 'Is that what we were going to watch?'

Shaking his head, he smiled—a smile so sweet, so irresistible, that Daisy instantly forgot all her misery and confusion.

'No. I wouldn't inflict that on my worst enemy.'

'Well, speaking as your worst enemy, I'm very grateful,' she said lightly.

His smile faded. 'You're not my worst enemy.'

Daisy gazed up at him. His eyes were focused on her face, so clear and green and deep that suddenly she wanted to dive in and drown in them.

'But you hate me...' For some reason she didn't understand her voice was shaking, the words dancing away from her like leaves on the wind.

Leaning towards her, he lifted his hand and touched her cheek. 'I don't hate you,' he said softly.

Her heart was somersaulting in her chest. It was lucky she was sitting down, because she could feel that gravity had stopped working and if she were standing up, she would simply have floated away.

His hand was tracing the line of her jaw, his thumb gently stroking the skin. She sat still and mute, hypnotised both by the tenderness of his touch and his fierce, shimmering gaze. Around her the walls were tilting inwards, spinning slowly.

Throat drying, she took a quick, jagged breath like a gasp. 'I don't hate you either.'

Suddenly she couldn't be so close to him and not touch him back and, reaching out, she put a hand on his arm. His skin felt smooth and warm, like carved wood. But it was his mouth—that beautiful, curving mouth—that made her body quiver, a hot, humid tension building inside her like a summer storm.

She breathed out softly. 'I didn't bring any dessert.'

His eyes locked on to hers and they stared at one another in silence. And then he dropped his gaze and, glancing down at his wrist, said quietly, 'It's late. We should head home.'

As they stood in the corridor, waiting for the lift, Daisy felt his gaze on the side of her face. 'What is it? Did you forget something?'

He shook his head. 'No.'

He paused and she felt that tension again—that indecision.

'Thanks for the pizza. It was fun.' Frowning, he cleared his throat. 'I just want you to know that I didn't suggest we go to the opera just because I have a box.'

She nodded dumbly.

There was clearly more to his words than their literal meaning, and part of her badly wanted to question him further. But instead she simply reached out and took his hand. 'And I want you to know that you don't have to worry. We can make this work.'

She felt his surprise and braced herself, expecting him to pull away. But after a moment his fingers tightened around hers, and as they stepped into the lift together she breathed out softly.

It might not be happy-ever-after, but it was a truce of sorts.

CHAPTER FIVE

'GOOD MORNING, MS MADDOX. I'm Kate and I'll be your personal therapist this morning.'

Looking up, Daisy smiled apprehensively at the slim young woman standing in front of her. Back at home she'd had manicures and the occasional facial. But the Tahara Sanctuary was one of New York's most exclusive spas. Everything oozed sophistication and exclusivity. In fact, it was so exclusive that she had an entire relaxation suite just to herself.

An hour and a half later Daisy was starting to understand why wealthy people always looked so relaxed. After a salt-and-mint-oil exfoliation and a cleansing herbal bath, she was now enjoying her first ever full-body massage and could feel her stresses dissolving beneath Kate's expert touch.

Stifling a yawn, Daisy closed her eyes as from somewhere across the room she heard a soft tap at the door. There was a slight shift in the atmosphere, the cool air mixing with the fragranced heat of the room, and then her body tensed.

An electric prickle rippled over her skin as she heard Kate say eagerly, 'Oh, Mr Fleming. How lovely to see you again.'

Her eyes snapped open, and the next moment her heart lurched sideways as she heard a familiar deep voice say casually, 'It's nice to see you too, Kate.'

Pulse hammering against her skin, Daisy held her breath, painfully aware she was naked except for a pair of panties and a towel folded across her bottom and thighs.

Since suspending hostilities with Rollo, over a week ago, she'd actually begun to enjoy herself. In part, it was because she'd stopped feeling that being happy was somehow a betrayal of David. And in part because her new A-list life was quite hard to resist. But the main reason was that, oddly, being with Rollo was by far the easiest relationship she'd ever had.

Not just because he'd kept his word and had stopped picking on her. Or because he was smart, sophisticated and stupidly handsome—although that helped. Truthfully, it was the first time she'd ever really felt free to be herself with a man. With Rollo, she didn't have to worry about her heart or the future. She could just sit back and enjoy the ride.

Although that theory had seemed a lot more convincing when she wasn't lying almost naked on a bed in front of him.

Something cool slipped over her neck and down her bare back, and she knew as surely as if she was looking at him that he was watching her. Pushing away an almost overwhelming impulse to yank the towel up over her body and hide from his scrutiny, she said as casually as she could manage, 'I didn't know you were going to pop in.'

There. She'd done it. It wasn't a ticker-tape parade, but they were now officially a couple. It felt strange, but exciting. Of course, Rollo's personal household staff had seen them together but somehow having Kate there made it feel more real.

'Oh, you know me, darling. Always acting on impulse. I hope I haven't disturbed you.'

The teasing note in his voice as much as the unfamiliar term of endearment made her pulse twitch and her heart pound. She lifted her head slowly.

He was standing beside her, his beautiful sculpted face lit up with mockery and amusement, and nervously she wondered why he was there.

Hoping she looked less flustered than she felt, she shook her head and smiled. 'Not at all.'

'Excellent—well, you're in good hands.'

Next to her, Daisy felt rather than saw the young therapist blush. Rollo's eyes, however, were fixed so intently on hers that for a moment it felt as if they were alone.

With an effort, she dragged her gaze towards Kate and smiled. 'Very good hands. I feel completely relaxed.'

'That's good. I know you've been a little stressed lately.'

He *should* know, she thought with a flash of irritation, since he was the prime cause of the stress. But, gritting her teeth, she said crisply, 'A little. But there's been quite a lot going on.'

'A lot of our clients suffer from stress-related conditions,' Kate said earnestly. 'Muscle pain, breathlessness, headaches, insomnia—it can even cause loss of libido.'

'Is that right?' Rollo said softly. 'We can't have that, can we...*darling*?'

The heat and the perfumed air were filling his head. But that wasn't why his brain was working at half speed.

What was he doing here? he wondered dazedly.

But watching Daisy's pupils widen, the black swallowing the brown, he felt his body throb with desire and knew that the answer to his question was lying in front of him.

He was supposed to be on a conference call. Only on his way back to the office he'd glanced out of the window and noticed a pizza delivery scooter—bright red, with a big cooler box clamped behind the seat. Instantly he'd thought of Daisy, and before he'd known what he was doing he'd told his driver to divert to the spa.

But he'd needed to see her, he reassured himself. To tell her about the party at the gallery and give her time to get used to the idea. After all, tonight would be their first public outing.

Feeling calmer, he smiled lazily down at her. 'Maybe I need to help you relax more. Perhaps I could learn how to massage.'

Daisy froze. There was something in his voice that made her breath dissolve in her throat.

Summoning up a careless smile, she said quickly, 'That's so sweet of you. But you don't need to do anything, *darling*. Kate's taking care of me.'

Rollo stared down at her assessingly. 'Yes, she is,' he murmured. 'But then Kate doesn't know you like I do. She doesn't know your weaknesses.'

His eyes roamed over her naked back.

'In fact, you know what? I think I've got this, Kate,' she heard him say quietly, and then she tensed, her body straining like a sail in a high wind, as across the room she heard the door open and click shut.

'I don't think this—' she began. But her protesting words dried up in her mouth as she felt his warm hand slide gently down her back.

Suddenly it was as though she was unravelling, his fingers untying every nerve, loosening her resistance and her willpower.

She watched dazedly as he reached down and picked up an open jar.

'Mandarin butter. Sounds delicious.' Scanning the label, he smiled slowly, so that her heart began to bang violently against her ribs.

'Apparently it releases the body into a state of euphoria. What's not to like?' he murmured as his fingers splayed out over her shoulders and heat flared over her skin like a gunpowder trail catching fire.

Daisy shivered, the bruising ache in her pelvis muting the alarm bells inside her head. His hands were gentle and firm, their warmth melting the butter. But it wasn't only the butter that was melting. A liquid heat was seeping through her body, her insides were growing hot and tight, and her muscles were tensing around the ache that was spreading out with a slowness that made her want to moan out loud.

Her heart started to pound. *Don't just lie here. Get up. Tell him to leave. Tell him to stop touching you*, she told herself desperately.

But, like someone in shock, she could only lower her head, her limbs growing heavier, blood thickening and slowing like treacle, her skin twitching restlessly beneath his touch. Her eyes fluttered and closed.

He didn't need to learn how to massage, she thought dizzily, a shiver passing down her spine as his hands rippled over her body. He already knew exactly how to touch. And where...

Staring down at the pale curve of Daisy's back, Rollo watched the pulse throbbing beneath her skin like a trapped moth and felt his body grow hard—painfully hard.

He'd expected her to be having some kind of beauty treatment. It was a spa, after all. But he hadn't expected to find her on a bed, her naked body barely covered. Glancing down, he rested his gaze on the jutting sweep of her bottom, pushing against the towel, and lust ripped through him like a train.

She was so beautiful—and he wanted her so badly.

Unable to stop himself, he lengthened his strokes, caressing lower and lower still—until, with the breath twisting in his throat, he pressed his thumbs into the cleft at the base of her spine, his groin tightening as he felt her body shudder and arch upwards.

'Rollo!'

Her voice—raw, husky, shivering with desire—broke into his passion-clogged brain like a thunderclap.

What the hell was he playing at?

He'd been on the verge of pulling her into his arms and letting his hands and mouth roam freely over that satin-soft skin.

His heart jolted forward. His blood was humming, his body taut, straining with desire like some hormonal teenage boy, and there was nobody to blame but himself. From the moment in his office when she'd looked up at him, dazed but defiant, he'd wanted her. And, as with every other woman in his life, he'd assumed that he was in control. That he could contain the chaos she'd unleashed inside him.

But when he'd walked into the spa the sexual tension between them had been like a brutal punch to the face. Seeing her on that bed had knocked everything out of his head except the need to touch her. A need so primal and intense that he'd been incapable of doing anything but respond to it.

His pulse shivered and, fighting against the excruciating sting of frustration in his groin, he ran a finger lightly up over her spine to the base of her neck. Pushing aside the loose knot of blonde hair, he watched as her eyelashes fluttered open.

'I think that might be enough euphoria for one day. Unless, of course, you'd like me to do your front, as well?'

His eyes rested on her face, his gaze so intent, so intimate that suddenly she felt a teasing heat tiptoe over her body like a ballerina en pointe.

She stared at him mutely—dazed, almost drugged by the shivering heat spilling over her skin.

Remembering how she had moaned his name, she felt her cheeks grow hot. Had he heard? Did he know the effect he'd had on her?

Meeting his cool, assessing gaze, she felt her stomach tense.

Of course he did!

Which was why she should never have let him touch her. Only it was too late to start having regrets now.

Aware that he was still watching her, and hoping he hadn't guessed quite how much her body had revelled in his touch, she gritted her teeth and gave him a quick, tight smile.

'I think I'll pass.' She glanced pointedly past him to the

door. 'Kate will be coming back any moment. She's going to give me a facial.'

According to Kate, it would help clear her skin of toxins. Her chest squeezed tight. If only it would also purge her body of this stupid and inappropriate physical attraction she appeared to have for Rollo. Not that anything was going to happen, she told herself firmly. She might have agreed to call a truce, but that didn't mean she was going to have sex with him.

Sleeping with Rollo would be a mistake—and she'd already made quite enough of those. Maybe if their situation had been different, she might have considered exploring the chemistry between them. But she could hardly ignore the fact that he was blackmailing her. And, besides, she wasn't about to do anything to jeopardise the entente cordiale between them.

Logic demanded that she override her hormones. It would be a lot easier though if her brain and body both felt the same way about him.

Or better still felt nothing at all.

Suddenly she was desperate to leave—to escape Rollo's unsettling presence and the spiralling tensions in the room—and, reaching down, cheeks burning, she snatched the towel, pulling it swiftly up to cover her naked breasts.

'Actually, I should probably go and look for her. Would you mind passing me my robe?'

He held it out to her, his fingers curling loosely in the soft fabric, and her heart started to beat faster as she remembered how freely and recently those same hands had roved over her body.

His green eyes lightened with amusement as she pushed her arms into the sleeves, trying to cover herself up as quickly as possible.

'Relax,' he said softly. 'I'm not in the habit of jumping women. Besides, I've got a meeting with my head of finance—and, much as I'd love to give it a miss, I can't just turn my back on work. Otherwise…' pausing, he gave her a slow, curling smile '…I might not have a business left for when we finally convince Dunmore to sell to me?'

Sliding off the bed, disconcerted by his sudden, blunt reminder of why she was in his life, Daisy tried to match his smile. 'Okay. Then I'll see you later.'

He frowned. 'Actually, a little earlier than that. There's been a change of plan. That's why I dropped in.'

His eyes rested calmly on her face and Daisy was jolted back into reality. Of course, there had been a reason for his visit. Hard-headed businessmen like Rollo didn't do random or impulsive.

Ignoring the prickling disappointment inside her chest, she met his gaze. 'Why earlier?' she said stiffly.

'We're going out tonight,' he said coolly. 'To a gallery. I meant to say something before, only I got a little distracted.'

She nodded. But her brain was seething with resentment. He was so autocratic—taking it for granted that she had no plans, or none that couldn't be rearranged to suit his agenda.

'The limo will pick us up at seven. That should give you plenty of time to get ready.'

He spoke with the same brisk detachment he used for discussing the logistics of his day with his driver, Kenny, and he was walking towards the door before she finally managed to speak.

'Tonight?'

He nodded. 'It's an exhibition. I'm a patron at the gallery and they're having a party.'

Daisy stared at him in horror. 'But what about my parents and David? They don't know anything about us.'

'That won't change. It's a small, private gallery. Local paparazzi will pick it up, but I doubt it'll make the national news.'

She lifted her chin. 'But you said we wouldn't be ready for another week—'

His eyes drifted mockingly over her flushed cheeks. 'I think we're ready. Don't you?'

She met his gaze. Her skin was still tingling from the heat of his touch, her body quivering like a city after an earthquake, and she knew that she must look dazed, feverish. *Turned on.* So, yes, they were ready.

Not that it mattered either way, she thought as the door closed behind him. Judging by Rollo's expression, she was going to be at that party—ready or not.

Only another two minutes and it would be showtime!

Glancing furtively at the screen on her phone, Daisy felt a familiar rush of nerves—the mixture of excitement tinged with fear and dread that preceded every first night. Tasting the adrenaline in her mouth, she shuddered involuntarily.

'Are you cold?'

She jerked her head around and glanced up at Rollo. She had almost forgotten he was there—which seemed incredible, given that she was sitting next to him in *his* limousine. But it was always the same before any performance: she had to lose herself in the fear, let the panic swamp her, before she faced her audience.

She shook her head. 'No. It's just nerves. I always get them—' Suddenly aware that Rollo was unlikely to be interested in her stage fright, she broke off.

But instead of turning away, he stared at her levelly. 'You're scared?'

'Yes.' She sighed. 'But I need to be.' Seeing his gaze sharpen, she felt colour suffuse her cheeks. 'I know it sounds crazy.'

'It's not crazy. It's biology.' Reaching out, he laid his hand over hers. 'Fear is important. It warns us of danger.'

Her heart squeezed. If that was the case, then why wasn't

she pushing his hand away? Or climbing into the boot? Or anywhere Rollo wasn't?

Glancing over, she felt her breath dissolve in her throat. Up close in the limo, his beauty was almost intimidating. He was so perfect, so glamorous, with that fringe of eyelashes grazing the curve of his cheekbones. His dark suit accentuated his broad shoulders and lean torso, and above a pale yellow shirt his eyes were as green and intoxicating as absinthe.

Smiling perfunctorily, she turned to the window—away from the dazzling symmetry of his face.

It was so confusing. He was the bad guy—the villain. She wasn't supposed to like him. And it had been easy not to like him when he'd been brutal and ruthless. But it was harder when he held her hand so gently. Hard too, to pretend that she wasn't enjoying being half of a beautiful couple.

She breathed out. Everything was so much simpler when they fought. At least then her feelings were straightforward. Now, though, she felt increasingly unsure of herself—particularly when she was sitting so close to him.

His fingers slipped around her wrist. 'Your pulse is racing,' he said softly.

'It's because I'm not breathing properly,' she said quickly. 'I need more oxygen.'

His eyes gleamed. 'A science lesson on the way to an art gallery? What's next? Spelling? Long division?'

She had to stop her mouth from curving up at the corners. 'It's just biology. And I'm sure you don't need me to teach you anything about *that*.'

His eyes locked on to hers. 'I bet you say that to all the men.'

'Actually, no,' she said crisply. 'Only you.'

After she'd come so close to losing control at the spa, she was trying to keep her distance. But it was difficult with the hard length of his thigh pressing against hers.

He smiled. 'So you're nervous. What can I do to help?'

She gazed at him in exasperation. '*You?* What could *you* do? You're the reason I'm nervous.'

His fingers stilled against her skin and there was a thick beat of silence. Staring past him, Daisy swallowed. Her cheeks felt hot. She was tingling all over.

'I make you nervous?'

'Not you,' she managed finally. 'This. Us.' Even to her ears her denial sounded unconvincing, and she felt her face grow hotter. 'I mean, us being out together in public. It makes me nervous. You, I can handle.'

Her heart was pounding. Who was she trying to kid? She might just as well say she could handle an escaped lion.

She met his gaze defiantly and instantly wished she hadn't, for he was watching her lazily, a hint of a smile tugging at the curve of his mouth.

'Is that right?'

Colour spread like spilt wine over her throat and collarbone, but thankfully there was no time to come up with a sensible answer because the car was pulling up outside a pale grey building. Suddenly there was a jostle of photographers, and flashbulbs exploded against the windows of the limo.

Inside the gallery everything was cool and quiet. A pianist was playing some familiar jazz tunes, and immaculately groomed men and women were drifting around in pairs and groups, stopping to sip champagne and gaze at the paintings.

Or rather they had been looking at the paintings.

Daisy felt her whole body grow rigid.

Now they all seemed to be gazing at her and Rollo.

'Relax. You look beautiful.'

His voice was soft, and she felt his fingers tighten around hers as she glanced down at her dark blue dress.

'Maybe it's too much?'

His gaze flickered over her bare shoulders. 'Any less and

I don't think I could be held responsible for my actions.' He smiled. 'Don't worry about everyone else. They're just curious. They don't bite.'

'You make them sound like goats,' she muttered.

He laughed out loud. 'Now you come to mention it, there is a certain resemblance.'

At the start of the evening Daisy had been anxious that she would feel out of place. Many of the guests were recognisable from television and the newspapers. But it was surprisingly easy to feel confident with Rollo's arm wrapped loosely around her waist. What was harder was remembering that she was there as part of some elaborate deception.

Not that anyone else would have known that was what she was thinking. She smiled and nodded and made small talk. But she was barely aware of anything except the steady pressure of his hand, and of how her body was responding to it, to him, to his charm and the sound of his voice.

Her pulse jumped. Surely that was a *good* thing. After all, she was supposed to be acting as though she was hopelessly in love with him. *So act*, she told herself firmly. And, leaning in towards him, she let her arm brush against the hard muscles of his chest.

'Shall we go and have a look around?' she said softly.

Despite never really having understood art, she found the paintings both interesting and beautiful. One in particular was mesmerising: a rippling wave of green and red and black done in oils.

'Striking, isn't it?'

A slim, elderly woman was standing beside her, gazing critically at the canvas.

Daisy nodded. 'They're all incredible. This is the one I'd buy though.'

But only in her dreams. According to the catalogue, the painting cost more than she'd earned last year.

Next to her, the woman who'd spoken held out her hand. 'Bobbie Bayard.'

Daisy blinked. 'Daisy Maddox.'

'Which Maddox? Farming or finance?'

Daisy gazed at her in confusion.

'Neither.'

It was Rollo. Sliding his hand into Daisy's, he leaned forward and kissed the silver-haired woman on both cheeks.

'She's not from one of the old families, Bobbie, so you can stop digging.'

'Good.' Bobbie beamed. 'The old families are like me. Obsolete and withering away.'

Rollo shook his head. 'Ignore her,' he said to Daisy. 'She's not even close to withering. She was sitting in the front row at New York Fashion Week just three days ago. And she's got a sixth sense when it comes to picking up-and-coming artists.'

'I think I might have just met my match. Your girl's got a good eye.' Glancing approvingly at Daisy, Bobbie moved on to the next picture.

Your girl. Rollo's girl.

An electric current snaked across Daisy's skin. Looking up, she blinked. His eyes were fixed on her face, so dark and green and intent that she felt a cool, juddering shiver slip down her spine, like water dropping over rocks.

'So why do you like it?' he said finally.

Feeling her heart start to thump, she glanced back at the painting. 'I don't know. It makes me feel like I'm drowning. But not in a bad way. More like I don't have to fight any more.'

It made her feel oddly vulnerable, revealing something to Rollo so spontaneously.

'Then maybe you shouldn't,' he said quietly. 'Fight it, I mean.'

She gazed up at him mutely. The chatter and laughter

around them faded away and suddenly she had the same sensation she'd had at the spa—that it was just the two of them, alone.

Rollo stared at her steadily, watching her eyes widen and soften. 'Maybe you should just give in…'

'So tell me, Rollo, just exactly how did you two meet?'

It was Bobbie. Head spinning, he turned as she looped her arm through his.

'That's a good question.'

He stared at her dazedly, trying to remember, his brain grasping for the right answer—the answer he and Daisy had agreed on. But it wasn't there, and he felt a blinding white-out of panic, his mind blank of everything except the moment he'd caught Daisy in his office. The one memory he couldn't actually use.

'I—I'm not sure,' he said slowly. 'Was it at work?'

Beside him he could feel eyes on his face. Only they weren't just Daisy's eyes any more. Around him he could feel the room shifting and shrinking, and he knew that soon the questions would get harder and everything would be so much worse.

'Yes, it was.' Daisy's voice was quiet but firm.

Glancing up, he saw she was smiling calmly at Bobbie, and some of the pressure eased inside his head.

'Rollo is trying to be discreet because he knows I don't like telling people I'm a waitress. But that's what I was doing the night we met. I'd done something stupid and he found a way to make it okay. But the weird thing was we'd already met.'

He stared at her. She was improvising her way back to their story, her eyes prompting him so that he heard himself say easily, 'Yes. We had. At a play. You see, Daisy's actually an actress.'

Rolling her eyes, Daisy shook her head. 'I trained to be an actress. And, yes, I was in a play. An awful play that was so off-Broadway it might as well have been in Pennsylvania. But Rollo was in the audience.'

'It wasn't that bad,' he said quietly.

Looking up at him, Daisy felt her insides tighten. His eyes were fierce, almost protective, and her breath stuttered in her throat as she forced herself to remember that he hadn't even been at that theatre. Had never seen her act.

'It's okay. You don't have to—'

'I'm not.'

He held her gaze and she stared at him in silence, hypnotised, her heart thudding, fear colliding with fascination.

'You were good. Better than good. You made people believe.'

Later, watching him talk to one of the artists, Daisy sifted through his words, twisting and rearranging them. Maybe he had meant what he said. But how could he when he had never seen her act? She glanced across the room. If anyone was good at acting, it was Rollo. Everybody believed in him, and more than anything they wanted him to believe in them.

But, of course, they did, she thought helplessly. Even surrounded by A-listers, he was movie star handsome, his charisma and poise matters of fact. Not just something to be switched on for an audience.

Suddenly he looked up and met her gaze head-on. Her pulse leapfrogged over itself as she watched him make his excuses and saunter across the room.

'Seen enough?'

For one horrible moment she thought he was referring to himself. Then her brain clicked up a gear and she realised he was talking about the paintings.

She shrugged. 'I think so. But I'm happy to stay if you want.'

Gently he reached out and tipped up her chin. 'What I want is to be alone with you,' he said softly.

And then he smiled—a smile that warmed her skin like sunlight—and pulling her closer, he kissed her.

Around them the murmur of conversation slowed and quietened, but Daisy barely noticed. Eyes closing, stomach flipping over in helpless response to his probing tongue, she was only aware of the heat of his mouth and the hard length of his body pressing against her quivering belly. Hands curling into his shirt, she dragged him closer, kissing him back as her stomach muscles tensed around the tight, aching heat that was balling inside her.

It's just a job, she told herself dazedly. *You're a professional actress playing a role and this is all part of the performance.*

But as her hands rose and splayed against his chest somewhere in the back of her brain she knew that whatever was happening it was no longer just for show. It felt real—dangerously real...

Only there was no time to process that thought. She felt him shift against her, breaking the kiss. And, opening her eyes, she saw herself reflected in his gaze—small and still and stunned.

For a fraction of a second she thought she saw something flicker across his face. But she was too busy trying to hide her own reaction to really be sure, and then he was drawing her against him, guiding her towards the door.

Back at his apartment, the lights had been turned down, and in the living room there was a bottle of champagne chilling in an ice bucket.

Catching sight of her expression, Rollo raised an eyebrow. 'I wasn't sure how tonight would go. Champagne seemed like a good idea either way. Here.'

Popping the cork, he filled two glasses and handed one to Daisy.

'To us.'

'To us,' she echoed, her heart twitching as she remembered the kiss they'd shared in the gallery. 'So you're pleased with how it went?' she said tentatively, dropping her bag onto the sofa.

'Definitely. I think we aced it. Which reminds me…'

His eyes flickered past her and, turning, she saw a large, flat parcel wrapped in brown paper.

'I have something for you. A present.'

Stunned, speechless, she stared at the parcel in silence until finally, with a hint of impatience, Rollo said, 'Aren't you going to open it?''

'Y-yes. Of course,' she stammered.

Putting down her glass, she tugged clumsily at the paper and gasped. It was the painting from the gallery.

She gazed at it speechlessly. 'I don't—'

He frowned. 'You don't like it?'

'N-no, I do. I love it. But I can't possibly accept it—' Not when she knew how much it cost. Only it seemed illmannered to mention money.

He shrugged. 'Why not? You like it and I want to give it to you.'

She swallowed. He made it sound so easy. So tempting. Looking up, she breathed out slowly, lost in the deep green of his gaze.

'Then, thank you.' Her heart felt suddenly light and gauzy, as though it might fly away at any moment. 'That doesn't seem like nearly enough. But I don't know what else to say.'

Rollo stared at her in silence.

Since leaving Daisy at the spa he hadn't been able to stop thinking about her. Or, more precisely, about having sex with her. And now that they were finally alone, it felt like the best idea he'd ever had. Not only would it create an intimacy that might conceivably add credibility to their 'relationship,' but it would also solve the aching physical frustration that had plagued him since he'd kissed her in his office nearly two weeks ago.

It was true she shared many of his mother's flaws, only there was one crucial difference. Alice Fleming's power had lain in her emotional hold over him. She'd been his mother and he had loved her. But he didn't love Daisy. So where was the risk?

The air seemed to swell around them.

Slowly he reached out and cupped her chin with his hand. 'Then don't say anything,' he murmured.

Her whole body was trembling, bones melting, blood beating inside her like a warning drum. Only then his eyes focused hungrily on her mouth and suddenly nothing mattered except the gathering storm rising inside her.

Standing up on her toes, she ran her tongue slowly across his lips.

He tasted of champagne and ice.

And danger.

Delicious. Intoxicating. It was the perfect cocktail.

Her head was swimming and she took a soft, swift breath like a gasp, her hands fluttering against his shirt.

'Kiss me,' she said hoarsely. 'Kiss me now.'

Rollo stared at her, his body in turmoil, the beat of his blood slowing to a pulsing adagio. Her eyes were shimmering; her face was soft and still and utterly irresistible.

He had no choice and, leaning forward, he kissed her fiercely. Instantly he was lost in the heat and softness of her lips, and as her fingers curled round his arms—gripping, tugging, tearing at his shirt—he felt his body harden with such speed and intensity that he almost blacked out.

'Daisy, wait—'

Lifting his mouth from hers, trying to slow down the pace, he groaned against her lips, his face taut with concentration.

'Slow down, sweetheart—' He was fighting to get his

words out. 'Or I won't be able to hold on until we get upstairs.'

He felt her body tense against him, and a flicker of apprehension, bright and jagged like lightning, cut through the dark clouds of passion fogging his brain.

'Why do we need to go upstairs?'

He breathed out unsteadily. 'I just thought it would be more private.'

The word, with its whispered hints of closed doors and darkened bedrooms, scraped over his skin and suddenly he didn't care where they were. Staring down into her face, he only cared about the warmth and the sweetness of her body against his.

'But we can do whatever you want,' he said hoarsely. 'Wherever you want...'

CHAPTER SIX

'*WHATEVER YOU WANT...wherever you want...*'

Daisy felt her body still, her mind snagging on an image of Rollo pulling off his shirt, his green eyes softening as he drew her closer to the hard contours of his chest—

The floor tilted and it was as though she was free-falling. The rush of desire and longing was so intense that she could hardly stand.

She wanted him.

But even as she acknowledged the truth of that statement she felt the sharp tug of the parachute pulling her back.

But what would happen if she gave in to that craving?

'No.' Stumbling backwards, she shook her head, her heart beating faster. 'We can't. We shouldn't. It's not right.'

Rollo stared at her in silence, the sudden distance in her voice jarring his senses. What was she talking about? *Can't. Shouldn't. Not right.*

His confusion hardened into irritation. 'I fail to see why,' he said slowly. 'We're both adults who want to have sex.'

Daisy flinched, but held his gaze. He was right. On both counts. But evidently two rights made a wrong, for—whatever her body might be telling her to the contrary—she knew it would be a disaster if they ended up in bed together. And Rollo knew it as well as she did. He just didn't like being told so.

She pushed against his chest. 'That may be reason enough for you. But there's a little more to it for me than just lust and being over the age of consent.'

'Like what? Love and romance?'

The sudden chill in his eyes as much as the harshness in his voice made her breath stutter in her throat.

'I'm a businessman—not a fourteen-year-old girl. We *are* getting married though. Won't that do?'

She jerked her hands away, the pulse at the base of her neck beating wildly. She could feel his hostility, see it in the set of his shoulders, but she didn't care. Nothing mattered except wiping that sneer off his irritatingly handsome face.

'It might have done *if* I wanted to have sex with you. But I don't.'

He shook his head, his lip curling into a sneer. 'So you're *still* a liar. Only now you're a tease, as well!'

Her fingernails cut into the palms of her hands. 'And you're back to calling me names.'

His eyes narrowed. 'I'll stop calling you names when you stop deserving them. I think that's fair, don't you?'

She felt anger—dark and fast—swirl and rush over her like floodwater. It was true, she had wanted him in the heat of the moment—she still did, judging by the pulsing ache in her pelvis. But his conceited assumption that she would fall at his feet, or rather into his bed, rankled with her.

'I don't care what you think.' She glowered at him. 'It was only a kiss. And just because I kiss a man it doesn't mean I automatically want to have sex with him.' Her hands curled into small, tight fists. 'Especially when the only reason I'm kissing him is for my job.'

He didn't reply at once—just stared at her in silence, his face cold and set like a bronze mask.

'Your job!' His derisive smile stung her skin. 'So that was a spot of overtime, was it?'

'No. That was a mistake!'

Her whole body trembled with fury. For a moment she couldn't speak. She was too busy hating him and his snide remarks.

'I thought you understood it was fake—just like we're faking the rest of this relationship.' She glared at him. 'But, of course, I completely forgot about your overinflated ego.'

Throwing her hands up in exasperation, she turned and walked swiftly towards the kitchen.

Rollo stared after her in silence, anger rolling beneath his skin like molten lava.

She was lying to his face. He didn't care how much she claimed otherwise. He'd felt her respond. He knew that kiss had been real.

More than real.

It had been hot and raw and urgent.

Only now she was trying to twist the facts—pretending *he'd* misinterpreted *her* behaviour and that *he* was the unreasonable one.

His mouth thinned. Daisy was more like his mother than he could ever have imagined. Honesty hadn't come naturally to Alice Fleming either. Instead she too had leapfrogged from story to story, lashing out with accusations when cornered.

Heart pounding, he stalked angrily across the living room into the kitchen.

Glancing over to where she stood, he felt his chest grow hot and tight. Above the disdainful curve of that temptingly soft pink mouth, her dark brown eyes shimmered beneath the lights. Another man might have lost his way in the perfection of that face. But, growing up with his restless, manipulative mother, he'd learnt early that beauty was only skin-deep.

'You need to worry less about the size of my ego and more about the gaps in your memory,' he snarled.

Daisy turned to face him. 'What are you talking about?'

'We had an agreement—*have* an agreement—about honesty.'

Honesty! Looking into his eyes, she saw the simmering fury, the thwarted authority, and felt her body start to shake. This wasn't about honesty. It was about pride. His stupid male pride.

Squaring her shoulders, she leaned against the worktop and scowled. '*You're* the one with a faulty memory, Rollo. I told you our relationship wouldn't include sex.'

His eyes blazed. 'And yet you asked me to kiss you.' His voice rose. '*You* asked *me* to kiss you!'

He swore beneath his breath, his eyes fierce with passion.

'Why are you being like this? I know you want me, Daisy. And I want you. Like I've never wanted any woman—ever. I can't sleep. I can't work. It's driving me crazy—'

As he broke off Daisy felt a treacherous warmth slide over her skin, the pull of his words strong and relentless like a riptide. And then abruptly she shivered. *Of course he wanted her.* She'd rejected him. Men like Rollo didn't like to be thwarted.

'You want me because you can't have me,' she said flatly. 'That's all.'

There was a long, gritty silence.

Finally he drew in a breath. 'That doesn't explain why you kissed me.'

She couldn't speak—didn't want to reply. But he waited and waited, and she knew from the uncompromising set of his jaw that he was going to keep on waiting until she gave him an answer.

Not just an answer but the truth.

Looking down, she swallowed. 'I kissed you because for one utterly senseless moment, part of me—the stupid, weak, irrational part I despise—wanted to have sex with you,' she said at last.

There was a fraction of a pause, then he said quietly, 'What about the rest?'

She frowned. 'The rest?'

Glancing up, she felt her pulse stumble. She'd supposed he would be gloating, but there was no sign of triumph. Instead his jaw was taut and his eyes were searching her face.

'You know—the smart, strong, rational part you admire.'

With shock, she realised he was attempting to make a joke. But she didn't laugh. She couldn't even smile. She felt too exposed, too vulnerable.

Shrugging, she stared past him. 'Our relationship is complicated enough, Rollo. Sex would just make it even more muddled.'

His eyes on her face were clear and unflinching. 'I disagree. Sex is simple. It's people who make it complicated. They expect too much. But you and I, we don't have to worry about that.'

She stared over at him, dry-mouthed, recognising the truth in his words. For she'd done it herself—confused sex with intimacy and love, and been left feeling foolish and crushed. And he was right: that wouldn't happen with them. There wouldn't be any expectations or disappointment or pain.

'Do you know how rare that is, Daisy? We can't let this moment pass.'

His face was expressionless, but something in his voice made her body twitch in response.

It would just be sex.

Pure, primal passion.

As though reading her thoughts, his eyes rested on her face.

'I know you feel it,' he said softly. 'I feel it too…because I want what you want.'

She shivered, tasting his words in her mouth.

'What do you want?'

Her voice was hoarse, her breath burning inside her chest as hesitantly he reached out and touched her throat, resting his hand softly against her pulse, so that her heart began to beat hard and slow.

'I want this…'

He lifted his fingers and pressed them lightly against her mouth.

'And this.'

Breathing out unsteadily, he stepped closer. With fingers that were both gentle and firm he loosened her ponytail, catching hold of the long, blonde hair. For one infinitesimal moment they stared at one another in silence. And then heat rushed through her as he tugged her head back, his pupils flaring.

'And this.'

He brought his mouth down hard on hers, his hand tightening in her hair, fingers grasping her scalp. Pulse racing, blood thickening, she leaned into him, her body melting against his as he deepened the kiss. She felt dizzy, desperate, her mind devoid of anything but the firmness of his lips and the need to feel him—his body, his skin.

She ran her hands over his shirt, her eyes widening as he pushed her fingers aside and undid the buttons, peeling the crisp fabric slowly away from his skin. She stared at him in silence. He was so beautiful...so golden and smooth and flawless. Gently, hesitantly, she touched his stomach, tracing the definition of muscle with her finger.

Instantly he sucked in a breath and, looking up, she saw that his face was stiff with concentration, his body taut, muscles tense.

'Are you sure?'

His voice was thick and constricted. She could hear the effort it was taking him to pause, to ask the question.

'I want you to be sure.'

Daisy stared at him dazedly, her pulse fluttering, her whole body vibrating with heat and need and emotion.

'I am. I'm sure. I want this.' She swallowed, the ache inside her throbbing in time to her heartbeat. 'I want you.'

His face was still, his eyes dark pinpoints.

'And I want you too.'

Reaching out, he slid his hands gently over her collarbone

and shoulders, pushing the straps of her dress down so that suddenly she was shivering, the cold air shocking her skin.

Rollo felt his groin tighten, hot tension flowering inside him.

She was wearing no bra.

He stared at her in silence, his gaze blunted by her beauty.

Then, wordlessly, he cupped her breasts in his hand, thumbs grazing the nipples. Slowly he bent his head and licked the tips, the blood beating wildly inside his chest as he felt them harden beneath his tongue, heard her soft moan. Then, lifting his mouth, he found her lips and, easing them open, he deepened the kiss, his hands pushing the dress down over her hips, the silken fabric brushing over his fingers as it slipped to the floor.

Daisy shuddered. His mouth was on her face, her throat, her collarbone, ceaseless and insistent. His fingers were sliding over her skin, sending shivers of heat in every direction, touching every nerve so that she moved restlessly against him.

'Rollo…'

She could hear the longing, the pleading in her own voice, but she didn't care. Nothing mattered except his touch.

Only she wanted more…

She needed more.

Looping her arm around his neck, she pressed against him, sweetness spreading inside her as she felt his body rise and swell. She was tugging at his belt, the button, the zip, her blood beating inside her.

With a rough groan, Rollo pulled back. His heart was pounding, his body groaning in protest. He wanted Daisy with an intensity that he'd never felt for any woman. But he also wanted to demonstrate his power over her.

And over himself.

He needed to prove that he would never surrender to any

woman—not even, perhaps especially not, to one as beautiful and seductive as Daisy.

His heart thumped, his mouth seeking hers again as he lifted her onto the worktop. Pulling her legs apart, he gently pushed aside the flimsy fabric of her panties, his breath stilling in his throat as she melted against his fingertips, her thighs clenching around his hand.

'Let it go,' he whispered against her mouth.

Daisy shuddered. Her whole body was dissolving beneath the teasing torment of his fingers. But it was not enough. Not enough to purge her body of the relentless aching tightness inside her. And, raising her hips, she rocked against him, a quivering pulse spilling over her hot, damp skin.

'Don't stop,' she gasped. 'Don't stop—'

And then her muscles tensed and she was arching upwards, shuddering, unravelling, her hands grasping at his arms, her mind blank of everything but the heat and the hardness of his hand cupping her body…

Glancing down at the sweet vintage-style dress she was wearing, Daisy frowned. Was it too flippant for a 'philanthropic benefit luncheon'? Possibly. But there was no time to change. The limousine would be arriving soon and they couldn't be late. Rollo was one of the guest speakers.

Rollo.

Her muscles clenched, and suddenly she felt as though she were suffocating. Just thinking his name gave her a head rush. But clearly Rollo didn't feel the same way for despite what had happened in the kitchen, he seemed in no rush whatsoever to consummate their relationship.

She bit her lip. In fact, the only hint of the passionate moment they'd shared had been later as they made their way towards their respective bedrooms when he'd hesitated, then pulled her against him, kissing her fiercely as if he couldn't help himself.

Lying alone in her bed, her body hot and twitching beneath the cool sheets, she had finally fallen asleep, her mind aching and exhausted with trying to make sense of his behaviour.

Waking, she had hoped they could talk. But, having both overslept, there had been no time to chat or enjoy a leisurely breakfast. Instead he'd been polite but strangely detached, given how intimate and uninhibited they had been just hours earlier. Remembering just how uninhibited she had been, Daisy felt her cheeks grow hot.

It was all very confusing, and more than a little embarrassing.

Glancing at her reflection, she breathed out slowly. She'd think about it later. Right now she had a job to do, and with one last twirl she turned and walked back into the bedroom.

'You look nice.'

Her breath jammed in her throat, her eyes widening with shock. Rollo was standing in the doorway to her room, watching her calmly. As usual his expression was utterly indecipherable. He might have just been elected mayor of New York, or just as easily have lost all his money on the stock market. It was impossible to tell.

She stared at him accusingly. 'You scared me.'

'Sorry. I did knock.'

'I didn't hear you,' she said quickly. 'I was just changing my shoes. I thought I'd wear heels.'

'I like them.' His eyes dropped to the black patent court heels and then roamed lazily over her dress. 'I like all of it. You look beautiful.'

Her face grew hot and tight, and she was suddenly unbearably conscious of her body's response to his precision-cut attention.

'Good. That's great,' she said mechanically and, picking up her phone, she glanced pointedly at the screen. 'We should go. Otherwise we'll be late.'

But he didn't move. Instead he shifted against the door frame, his green eyes fixed on her face.

'Actually, we won't. I cancelled.'

It was a first. The first time he'd ever put his private life before work. And certainly the first time a woman had been at the top of his agenda.

What made his behaviour as baffling as it was unsettling was that he hadn't even planned on doing it. It had just happened.

Sitting at his desk, he'd truly believed he would be attending the luncheon—right up to the moment when his subconscious had overridden his conscious brain and he'd picked up the phone and told his assistant to make his apologies.

But, planned or not, it was clear from his uncharacteristic behaviour that, despite his trying to treat his relationship with Daisy like any other business arrangement, she had brought chaos to his world. And now his life was full of precedents.

Including this self-inflicted discomfort in his groin.

Theoretically, last night had seemed like the perfect opportunity to demonstrate to Daisy that *he* was the one pulling the strings. Now, though, he could see that his logic might have been flawed. Not only was his body aching with frustration, but the satisfaction he'd felt at having made his point had been pretty much eclipsed by confusion over what it was he'd actually proved to Daisy—or himself.

Glancing up, he found her watching him warily.

'You don't seem very pleased,' he remarked.

Her eyes darted past him. 'I thought you were giving a speech?'

He shrugged. 'I was. But there are always far too many speakers at those lunches. Besides…'

He lengthened the word so that it pressed against her skin like a cold knife.

'I'd rather just speak to you.'

Her heart gave a thump.

'Okay.'

A cold feeling was settling in the pit of her stomach and her eyes focused longingly on the door.

'I thought we weren't going to fight any more.'

Hearing the hesitation in her voice, he frowned. 'Talking doesn't have to mean fighting.'

Except that up to now it had.

He felt a stab of frustration. But why was he trying to coax her anyway? He should just *tell* her she was having lunch with him. Only suddenly—incredibly—he found himself wanting it to be her choice. For some inexplicable reason that seemed more important than getting his own way.

He held her gaze. 'Have lunch with me. Please. I promise we won't fight. I just want to talk.'

Daisy stared at him. He looked serious and sincere. And very handsome. Feeling the knot of tension inside her loosen a fraction, she nodded slowly.

'I'd like that very much.'

Twenty minutes later the limousine pulled up outside a small restaurant with a flaking green-painted facade somewhere in East Harlem.

Glancing up at the name above the door, Daisy felt her body stiffen with shock. She'd heard of Bova's, but she'd never imagined eating there. Surely this couldn't be it? It was supposed to be the most exclusive restaurant in New York, but this place looked as though it might close down before they finished their meal.

She bit her lip. 'Is this that restaurant where even celebrities can't get a table?'

He hesitated, as though he was making some kind of decision. Then finally he nodded slowly. 'It is. But I happen to know the owner.' He held out his hand. 'Come on. Let's eat.'

Inside, the restaurant was even smaller than it had looked from the street. There were only seven tables, and all of them bar one were full.

'I hope you like Italian,' Rollo said as they sat down. 'Other than pizza, I mean.'

His mouth curved and, looking up, she saw his eyes were light and teasing, and a ripple of happiness went through her like an electric current.

She smiled. 'I love it,' she said truthfully. 'Especially the desserts.'

He seemed pleased.

'Then you must have the cannoli. It's sublime.' He frowned. 'I should have said—they don't have a menu here. If you're a regular, they know what you like and they cook it for you.'

Lifting his head, he paused as a waiter approached the table, and she felt a prickle of awe and envy as he switched into rapid and clearly fluent Italian.

Turning back to face her, he frowned. 'I hope you don't mind, but I took the liberty of ordering for you. I wouldn't know where to start with most people, but you're different. I know you as well as I know myself.'

His eyes on hers were very green.

Daisy blinked. 'Really?'

'Well, I should. That's the reason we've spent so much time getting our stories straight.'

He gave her a quick, dazzling smile and she nodded mechanically. Had she really imagined that he thought she was special in some way? Heart banging in her throat, she picked up her glass, hoping to hide her confusion.

'I'm sure it'll be delicious.'

Her heart was still pounding in her chest and, desperate to disguise the effect of his words, she gave him what she hoped was a cool smile.

'I'm actually really excited. I don't eat out much. I never

have. I think it's probably because of working so much at the diner with Mum and Dad.'

His eyes gleamed. 'Don't knock the Love Shack.'

She screwed up her face. 'I'm not. It's great—and they're great. And they love what they do, and they love each other, and that's why it's the Love Shack.'

She stopped abruptly. Her voice was too high and forced. But right now was not a good time to discuss her parents—particularly their *perfect* marriage. Not when she was sitting opposite her soon-to-be fake husband.

Desperate to change the subject, she glanced round the restaurant. 'It's not what I expected.' She frowned. 'It's so small and…'

'Ordinary?' he suggested. His expression was unreadable but his eyes were watching her carefully.

She nodded. 'It feels like someone's dining room.' Her eyes flickered over the faces of the other diners, widening as they stopped on a dark-haired man wearing a polo shirt. 'Isn't that…?'

Rollo held his finger up to his lips. 'It is. And that is his equally famous wife. They live in Tribeca. They come here twice a month.'

'They do?'

Hearing her surprise, he shrugged. 'The food here is the best in the city.'

She nodded, her pulse quickening. She believed him. But for the last few days, her life had been spent learning his life, and she knew that there was something more beneath his words. She could feel it in the way he rearranged his glass, hear it in the hair-fine tension in his voice.

'So, do you come here regularly too?'

He nodded. 'Probably a couple of times a week most weeks.'

As the waiter returned, bringing olives and water, Daisy stared down at her cutlery, his words scraping against her skin like fingernails on a blackboard. A couple of times *a week*! How many women was that a year?

She frowned, feeling some of her happiness oozing away.

But why was she counting? Rollo's private life was none of her business. She didn't have to care about his past. Or worry about being the latest in an ever-growing line of women that he brought to the same restaurant.

That was the upside to this whole crazy situation, and the beauty of their relationship. She could stay detached, unemotional, immune.

Or that was what was supposed to happen.

She caught her breath, shocked to discover that wasn't how she was feeling at all. Instead a thin curl of misery was coiling around her brain.

'You're very quiet.'

Rollo's voice bumped into her thoughts.

'I was just thinking.' She gave him a small, tight smile. 'Trying to work something out. A sum.'

He stared at her in a way that made her heart skid forward.

'A sum! You're not going to suggest we go halves on the bill, are you?'

'No! Although I don't see why I shouldn't. I'm not Orphan Annie, you know. I do have some money.'

He ignored her. 'So, what are you trying to work out?'

'It doesn't matter.' Her voice sounded more desperate than she'd intended and, picking up her glass, she took a sip of water. 'Truly. It was nothing.'

There was a brief silence. His eyes were level with hers and she forced herself to keep looking at him as he gazed at her thoughtfully.

'Okay,' he said after a moment. 'But promise me that if whatever it is becomes a problem, even if it's not really your problem, you'll tell me. So I can help.'

It was Daisy's turn to stay silent. He thought she was

worrying about David's debt, and it had sounded almost as if he cared. As if he actually wanted to help.

The blood was humming in her ears and her heart was suddenly beating too fast and too loud. She glanced across at him, her eyes scanning his face. But had he meant it? Or was he just being in character? Saying what a doting boyfriend would say to the woman he loved?

She looked up at him with a smile that betrayed none of her confusion. 'Okay. I promise.'

'Good. I've ordered a Chianti with our food. Is that okay?'

She blinked, caught off guard by the change of subject and by the sudden realisation that they were talking normally—almost like they were a real couple.

'Of course.'

'They do an excellent Montespertoli here.'

'I'll take your word for it. I don't really know much about wine. David buys it and I just drink it.'

He grinned. 'I have much the same arrangement with my sommelier.'

'You have your own sommelier?'

'Of course,' he said, feigning astonishment. 'Doesn't everyone?'

She laughed. 'Of course! In fact, I need to check in with mine—make sure he approves of your choice.'

His eyes were glittering. 'Trust me, I've made the right choice.'

She felt her breath explode inside her chest. Obviously he was talking about the wine or the food or maybe both. But her head was spinning, her heart speeding like a getaway car, and she knew that more than anything she wanted him to be talking about *her*.

When finally she felt that she could trust her voice, she tilted her head and said, 'So, how do you know it's the right wine?'

'Wine? Is that what we're talking about?'

His eyes rested on her face and she felt her colour rise. But, holding his gaze, she nodded.

'Come on. I really want to know. I promise not to tell my sommelier if you don't tell yours.'

Laughing softly, he leaned forward over the table, so that suddenly she was conscious of the solidity of his shoulders and the symmetry of his face.

'Okay… Well, if, say, the food has lots of flavour it would need to be partnered with something rich and smooth and sexy—'

She swallowed; her mouth felt suddenly dry, her throat like sandpaper. He might have been talking about himself. She felt an ache, sharp and intense like hunger. Only she knew it wasn't the sort of hunger that could be satisfied by food.

'Basically, you just need to trust your instincts.' Pausing, he glanced over her shoulder. 'Ah, excellent. I'm starving.'

Watching the waiters put their plates on the table, Daisy felt her appetite return.

As Rollo had promised, the meal was delicious. Tiny baby clams stuffed with breadcrumbs to start, followed by ravioli with pear and ricotta. The main course was osso buco—veal shanks in white wine and lemon.

Pressing her napkin against her lips, Daisy laid her knife and fork down on her empty plate. 'That was perfect.'

'I'm glad you liked it.'

His eyes across the table gave nothing away and, taking a deep breath, she said carefully, 'I can see why you bring all your dates here.'

He didn't answer. Around them, the air seemed to grow thicker, and she felt a nervous shudder run down her spine.

'I don't bring *all* my dates here,' he said quietly. 'In fact, you're the first *date* I've ever brought here.'

Daisy felt her heart punch against her chest.

'But you said you come twice a week, most weeks.'

'And I do. On my own.'

She swallowed. Men like Rollo didn't dine alone.

'I don't understand.'

He shrugged. His face looked shuttered, remote.

'It's like a home to me. I've been coming here ever since I was thirteen. The owner, Joe, his father, Vinnie, gave me my first job.'

He smiled—only it was a smile that made something inside her shift and crack open.

'What did you do?' she said hoarsely.

'I washed dishes at first. Then I was a waiter. *Just* a waiter,' he amended, his eyes meeting hers. 'They wouldn't trust me in the kitchen.'

She nodded. 'Very wise.' She tried a smile of her own. 'I've seen you incinerating toast. I definitely wouldn't trust you with veal.'

He smiled again, but this time it touched his eyes and she felt a rush of happiness and surprise—for when had she started wanting to make him happy?

'Would you like that cannoli?' He was back in control, his hand half-raised towards the waiter.

Groaning, she shook her head. 'Yes. But I can't. I would love a coffee though.'

The coffee arrived, together with a small dark green box.

Daisy made a face. 'Are those chocolates?'

He nodded. 'But they're very small. Go on.' Smiling a little, he pushed the box towards her. 'Have one, otherwise I'll never hear the end of it.'

Sighing, she picked it up and pulled off the lid. 'They'd better be small,' she grumbled, 'otherwise you'll never...'

Her voice trailed off.

It wasn't chocolates. Instead, nestling on top of pale green paper was a beautiful diamond-and-emerald ring.

She stared at it—stunned, mesmerised.

'I hope you don't mind. I asked Joe to help out.'

He gestured to where a large dark-haired man stood beaming.

She looked up, groping for the right words—any words, in fact. But her mind seemed to have stopped functioning.

'Yes—I mean, no…I don't mind,' she managed finally. 'Oh, Rollo, it's beautiful. I love it.'

'Here. Let me.'

She watched him slip the ring onto her finger, his hands warm and solid against hers.

'So, will you marry me?'

His voice was soft. For a split second she forgot it wasn't real. Forgot it was all just part of their performance. Then slowly, she nodded. 'Yes, I will.' She hesitated. 'But why here? Why now?'

He shrugged. 'Why wait? I want everyone to know that you're going to be my wife.'

He hadn't planned on giving her the ring until later. But last night everything had changed. Finally she'd been honest with him, admitting her desire in the most blatant of terms. Saying that she wanted sex, that she wanted him.

It had been like a starter pistol going off in his head.

Suddenly proposing had seemed like the obvious next step. And with Daisy wearing his ring their 'marriage' was a step closer to being real—a step closer to the moment when James Dunmore would finally sell to him.

Back in the limousine, Daisy couldn't stop looking at her finger.

'Relax. It's not going anywhere.'

She looked up. Rollo was watching her meditatively.

'I know. I just like looking at it.' Holding out her hand, she twisted the ring from side to side. If being seen with Rollo in public had been like putting on a parachute, this was like jumping out of the plane. Now it really was real. She was his fiancée.

'I suppose I should tell my parents and David.'

'I suppose so.' His eyebrows raised mockingly. 'But let's just have a couple of hours to get used to it ourselves.'

The next moment an electric thrill snaked over her skin as his fingertips brushed against hers.

'If it needs to be altered, tell me.'

She nodded. 'I will. I don't want it falling off.'

'Neither do I. It's got to go back to the jewellers in a year.'

Staring fixedly at the ring, Daisy felt her stomach plummet like a broken kite.

A moment ago she'd felt like Cinderella. Now though, she realised she was actually Sleeping Beauty—only the Prince hadn't woken her with a kiss. He'd tipped her out of bed and onto the floor.

Her head was pounding.

So what if he had? She knew it wasn't a real proposal. They weren't in love; their entire relationship was a sham. They were only together to convince Dunmore to sell his building to Rollo.

But for some reason none of that seemed to matter right now. She still felt like a failure. Just as she had when Nick had broken up with her. And before him, Jamie.

She'd thought they'd loved each other. She'd been wrong. And they'd been wrong for her. Only it had still been devastating to accept—particularly when all she really wanted was that effortless understanding with someone that her parents shared.

But it was supposed to be different with Rollo. With him she had thought she could relax and not worry about getting hurt.

Her heart twisted.

Except that apparently she'd got that wrong too.

Slowly she withdrew her hand and pressed it against her forehead.

'What's the matter?'

'Nothing. Just a headache. I expect it's drinking wine at lunchtime. I probably just need to have a lie-down.'

Rollo stared at her in silence. *A headache?*

Angrily, he looked down at the ring on her finger, its glittering facets like so many mocking faces. Back at the restaurant it had felt so real. The food, the conversation… He'd even told her about working there—something he'd never shared with anyone. But now she was lying to him. *Again*, he thought, with an almost unbearable sting of swift, startled astonishment.

'Perhaps you could just tell the truth.' Shaking his head, he stared down into her wide, shocked eyes. 'That you're upset about having to return the ring. Surely you didn't think you were going to *keep* it?'

For a moment she was too shocked to speak. Then slowly she felt a shivering hot anger slide over her skin.

'Yes, I did. And I thought you would give me half the apartment too,' she said curtly. 'No, Rollo, of course I didn't think that. I hadn't even thought about a ring at all until you gave me this one. Why would I? You said you were going to go public with the engagement in a couple of months.'

His lip curled. 'So I changed my mind? I thought women liked spontaneity.'

She glared at him. 'And I'm just a woman? How romantic!'

He stared at her in exasperation. 'It's not meant to be romantic. This is a business arrangement.'

'Fine! Then I don't need this. Here!'

Reaching down, she tugged the ring off her finger and held it out to him.

He ignored her hand, his face hardening. She was impossible. Irrational. Ungrateful. He could have thrown her and her brother to the wolves, but instead he'd given her a second chance, just like his father.

Leaning forward, he thumped on the window behind the chauffeur's head.

'What are you doing?' Daisy was looking at him, her eyes wide with shock.

'I'm getting out. I need some fresh air.'

'But you can't just walk away. We need to talk.'

Her anger was giving way to confusion and fear.

But as the car slid smoothly to a halt he yanked open the door, an expression on his face that she couldn't decipher.

'There's no point,' he said flatly. 'I really don't think we have anything more to say to one another.' And then, before she had a chance to reply, he was on the pavement, vanishing into the crowds as the car started to move forward again.

CHAPTER SEVEN

BACK AT THE APARTMENT, Daisy stared blankly around the living room, the tears she'd managed to hold back in the limousine burning her eyes.

What had he meant by nothing left to say?

But, recalling the flat finality of his tone, she felt her chest tighten and she knew what he'd meant.

He meant it was over.

And now her brother was going to pay the price.

Her mind began to race; her breath came fast and jerky, as though she'd been running.

She needed to warn David. She needed to be the one to tell him about the deal she'd made and wrecked. Her stomach shrank. And about what would happen next...

Panic crawled over her skin and, heart pounding, she walked dazedly upstairs. She would pack and then she would leave.

But if she left, there would be no going back. Shouldn't she at least try and talk to Rollo again?

But as she pictured his cool, expressionless face, her hands began to shake, and abruptly she sat down on the bed.

Rollo couldn't have made it clearer that he had nothing to say to her.

She lifted her chin, felt her heartbeat steadying. Then she would just have to do the talking—even if it was only to say goodbye.

He might be about to unleash hell, but she wasn't a coward. And, although she knew she'd made mistakes, she wasn't going to make herself look guiltier than she was by running away.

If only her hands would stop shaking.

Glancing down to where they lay in her lap, she caught sight of the ring and, stomach cramping, she slowly pulled it off her finger and laid it on the bedside table. She didn't need it anymore and, whatever Rollo might think, she didn't want it either. Even looking at it made her feel sick and helpless.

But staying to face him was her choice. And that meant she *wasn't* helpless, and whatever happened next, she needed to remember that. Now though, it was time to pack. Not because she expected him back anytime soon—it was, after all, a working day—but because she simply couldn't sit and wait for him. She needed to do something.

Heart heaving, she found her suitcase and began to fill it, barely registering what she was putting in, her arms and hands acting by themselves. Finally it was done. But as she fumbled with the zip, the air seemed to ripple around her and there was a sudden shift in the light. Looking up, she felt her throat close over tightly.

Rollo was blocking the doorway. The same doorway where he'd stood just a few hours earlier, when she'd tried to read his mood. Only this time she didn't need to try. His mood was unmistakable. He was utterly, shatteringly furious.

'Y-you're back,' she stammered, her stomach plummeting beneath his blank-eyed hostility. 'I wasn't expecting you.'

Rollo gritted his teeth, his gaze shifting from her face to the suitcase lying on the bed, and suddenly his whole body tightened and he was breathing too fast.

Packing her bags had been one of his mother's favourite tricks too.

Only for show though. He knew that because when she finally had left for real she'd taken no suitcase. She hadn't needed one. Of course she'd taken what mattered. But she'd left everything else behind.

Including her son.

And the note justifying her actions.

He felt sick. Anger and pain sliced through him but, pushing down his nausea, he met Daisy's gaze, his eyes narrowing with contempt.

'Clearly.'

'I didn't mean—'

'Save it. I know what you meant. And even if I didn't, the suitcase is a bit of a giveaway.'

'I—I wasn't running away. I was waiting. For you.'

'Of course.' His lip curled into a sneer. 'You're an actress. Your USP is making an entrance and an exit. But it works best with an audience.'

Rage was pounding inside his head.

He'd actually started to think she might be different. That maybe he'd misjudged her. Only he'd been wrong. Not just wrong, but obtuse. Forgetting all the lessons he'd learned from childhood, he'd let himself be fooled by Daisy's beauty and sexual allure.

Only he wasn't a little boy any more. He was a man—the owner of a global property company worth billions, who'd worked hard to build his business. Harder still to keep his life free of the sort of emotional tension and uncertainty he hated.

Which was why he'd brought their engagement forward.

It had been a unilateral decision, and as such a clear reminder to Daisy that *he* was in charge. And, of course, the first solid proof he could give Dunmore that he was a changed man—a man in love and committed to one woman.

Deep down though, what really mattered—what he had needed to know, to see and feel for himself—was that Daisy could be open and honest. When she'd finally not only admitted her desire but responded so feverishly to his touch it had been the assurance he'd needed to accelerate their relationship.

Only watching her open the ring box, he'd found himself in the extraordinary position of feeling nervous about how she would react. Worse, in the limousine she'd lied *again*, and he'd felt the same shifting unease, the same devastating, unbearable insecurity that had blighted his childhood.

And now she'd packed her bags.

His gaze shifted to her face, eyes hardening.

'I'd like to say I'm surprised or disappointed. But, given your character, it's all quite tragically predictable.'

Daisy flinched inwardly at his words but she forced her eyes up to meet his. 'You can insult me all you like. I don't care. I only stayed to tell you that I'm going to see David, so if you could—'

He cut across her.

'How thoughtful. The caring sister. He *will* be pleased.'

Meeting his cool, expressionless gaze, she felt misery clutch low at her stomach. So this was how it was going to be. He was going to play with her, punish her as he'd wanted to do right from the start—before he'd decided she was more use to him as a 'wife.'

'I know you're angry, Rollo, but this isn't all about you. Or us.'

He shook his head, fury spiralling inside him, his heartbeat slamming into his ribs. Had what happened last night and in the restaurant really affected her so little?

He gritted his teeth. The answer to that question was packed and ready to go.

'But, let me guess, it is about you.' His voice was rising. 'And your brother.'

She breathed out unsteadily, trying to ignore his contempt and animosity.

'It was only ever about David, and you knew that. Look, I can't stop you calling the police. But I want to be there with him when they turn up.'

He gave a humourless laugh.

'You really are a drama queen, aren't you?' He gestured towards her suitcase. 'And how you love your props.'

'It's not a prop,' she snapped, a flicker of anger catching fire inside her. 'How else I am supposed to pack my things?'

'You don't need to pack. This is all just for show. Like everything else you do.'

Her head jerked up, eyes darkening with outrage.

'Like everything we both do, you mean. You are such a hypocrite. Our entire relationship is a soap opera of *your* making, and you've got the nerve to accuse *me* of being a drama queen.'

'This is not my idea of a relationship,' he snarled.

'Well, it certainly isn't mine.' She bit the words out between her teeth. 'It's more like living in a war zone.'

'Then maybe you should stop turning everything into a fight.'

'Me! What about you? You're the one who threw a tantrum in the middle of Madison Avenue, storming off like some three-year-old.'

It was true. He had behaved childishly. But it was her fault. He might have a reputation as an ice-cold negotiator, but with Daisy his temper hovered between volatile and volcanic. It was an admission that did nothing to defuse his anger with her—or himself. In fact, it just seemed to wind him up more tightly than ever.

He stared at her coldly.

'Oh but you throwing the ring I gave you back in my face—that was just so mature.'

'I wasn't trying to be mature,' she snapped. 'I was upset.'

'You weren't upset. You were gutted. As soon as you saw the ring you thought you were going to get to keep it.'

He saw the sudden startled flinch in her eyes but ignored it. 'And when you found out that wasn't going to happen *you* had a tantrum—'

'That's not true! Or fair. I hadn't even thought about you giving me a ring.'

It was true—she hadn't. At least she hadn't thought about him doing so with such sensitivity. She'd supposed there would be a ring, but that it would be just a ring.

Remembering the effort he'd made in the restaurant to surprise her, she felt her eyes grow hot. 'How can you accuse me of plotting to keep it?'

He could hear the shake in her voice, and knew he'd hurt her. Knew too, that he was being unfair, unreasonable, cruel. But he wasn't about to start indulging Daisy the way his father had indulged his mother.

It was why he'd arranged this relationship with her in the first place—precisely to avoid that kind of emotional manipulation.

'I find that hard to believe. You could hardly take your eyes off it in the car.'

Fighting tears, Daisy shook her head. Did he really think so little of her? Had it not occurred to him that she might have another, innocent, less self-serving motive for admiring the ring?

'Not because I thought it was mine—'

Suddenly she couldn't speak. How could she explain it to Rollo? A man who was indifferent, brutally dismissive of anything romantic. A man who dealt solely in facts. Who reduced everything to assets and liabilities. A man who was happy to fake his own marriage solely to con a business rival.

How could she expect him to understand that she hadn't been acting?

That just for a moment, when he'd slid the ring onto her finger, everything had felt real and perfect. Just like she'd imagined it would in her fantasies of love.

Her eyes blurred.

Only, of course, it was just as phony as the rest of their

relationship. What was more, it had been nothing to do with *her*.

Her heartbeat froze and, remembering how she had squirmed beneath his fingers, her body opening up to his, she felt suddenly sick.

No wonder he had been able to hold himself back. That had all been just an act too. Another way to demonstrate his power over her. Only that time he'd used her greedy body, not her brother, to prove the point.

'Think what you want.' She breathed out shakily. 'I don't care.' Reaching down, she picked up the suitcase. 'Like you said earlier, we have nothing more to say to each other, so if you don't mind, I'm going to see David. I owe him that at least—'

She broke off, her breath catching in her throat, and, staring at her pale face, Rollo felt a dull ache of misery beating beneath his anger.

He'd told her there was nothing left to say.

What he'd really meant was that, trapped in the limo with his anger and his memories, he hadn't known how to say it.

Every time he'd tried to start a sentence it had turned into a minefield—his usual effortless fluency deserting him, every word fraught with possible implications. So he'd done what he always did when faced with doubt and discord. He'd walked away.

Stalking down Madison Avenue towards his offices, he'd tried to clear his mind and focus on the afternoon's agenda. Only he'd been too wound up, his body vibrating with leftover adrenalin, his brain frenziedly trying to work out *how* a pitch-perfect lunch had turned into Armageddon.

And *when* suddenly, incredibly he'd stopped caring about work and started caring about his relationship with Daisy.

He took a step forward.

'You don't need to see David,' he said quietly.

'Yes, I do.' She stared at him wildly, her body shuddering, straining for breath. 'I've let him down and he doesn't even know it.'

The ache in her voice seemed to mirror the ache inside his chest.

'You haven't let him down. You saved him.'

'No, I *tried* to save him—to make everything right, to make this work with you—only now you're going to call the police—'

She was babbling, the words tumbling over each other in a torrent so fast that he had to hold up his hand to stop the flow.

'Wait. *Wait.*' He frowned, her breathless panic driving away the last of his anger. 'I'm not going to call the police. I never was.'

Blood was rushing to his head, joining the clamouring voices telling him not to let her leave.

He took a step closer. 'I know what I said. How it must have sounded. But I was angry. I don't like scenes…'

He hesitated, unnerved by this sudden further breach in his defences. He never confided in anyone, and yet this was the second time he'd done so with Daisy in the space of a couple of hours.

'Look, nothing's changed. I didn't come back to end our relationship. I came back to finish our argument. But that's all it is. An argument. It's what couples do, isn't it?'

His heart gave a jolt. *Couple* was a word he'd consciously avoided his whole adult life. And an argument had always been just something to win. Only winning this time would mean losing Daisy, and he wasn't prepared to let that happen.

Had he been thinking straight that thought would have shocked him. But he was too distracted by Daisy's reaction, or rather the lack of it, to care.

She was staring at him, eyes huge, their brownness lost in the stunned black pupils. Then slowly she shook her head.

'But that's just it. We're not a couple. We're not anything.' She breathed out unsteadily. 'I don't even know who I am half the time, or what's real and what's not.' She met his gaze. 'And it's not just me. Earlier, I was upset—'

He opened his mouth to speak, but she held up her hand to stop him. 'I know it wasn't rational or fair. But I *was*. Only you didn't realise. You thought I was acting.'

A silence fell over the room.

'And that bothers you?'

His question caught her off guard. She stared up at him wearily.

'Yes. Maybe it shouldn't, but it does.' Her mouth twisted. 'I thought the boundaries would be clearer. That I'd feel different when I was being me without you. But it's all merging and—'

She stopped.

Now it's even more complicated, she finished the sentence inside her head.

Thinking back to how he'd touched her, her frantic response, she felt her cheeks start to burn. She'd had other lovers but it had never been like that—so urgent, so feverish. In the space of a few heated moments Rollo had blotted out the past and obliterated every sexual experience she'd had.

But she would rather run down Madison Avenue naked than let him know how strongly he affected her.

Swallowing hard, she reached down, picked up the ring and held it out to him. 'Here. This is yours.'

Rollo stared at her outstretched hand and then slowly took the small gold hoop.

The limpid brown of her eyes heightened the flush of colour on her cheeks. She had never looked more beautiful. But it wasn't her beauty that was making his heart pound.

It was her bravery. He knew how much it would take for him even to admit weakness, let alone reveal his deepest fears. He glanced down at the ring, turning it over gently in the palm of his hand. It was such a small thing. Easy to lose and, once lost, almost impossible to find.

Like trust.

He felt her eyes on his face and glanced away, his thoughts converging and then separating like the colours in a kaleidoscope. He'd made a deal with Daisy—and what kind of deal could ever succeed without trust?

Slowly he reached out and took her hand.

'No, it's yours. I chose it for you.' Something shifted in his face, the skin tightening over his cheekbones. 'And I didn't mean to upset you. That's why I came back. To tell you that.'

Daisy stared at him dazedly. It wasn't an apology. But it was the nearest a man like Rollo Fleming would get to one. And whatever it was, he had come after her to say it.

She watched his mouth curve into an almost smile.

'But if you really don't want it, I suppose I could turn it into a tiepin.'

'I do want it.' Her lashes flickered up and, not giving herself a chance to have second thoughts, she said quickly, 'And I want you.'

There was a fraction of a pause and then slowly he slid the ring onto her finger. And then, breathing out, he drew her close to him so she could feel his heart beating in time to hers.

'And I want you too.'

For a moment they stood together in silence, and then she felt him shift against her and, looking up, she saw he was frowning.

'What is it?'

'I'm late for a meeting.' His eyes met hers.

'So go,' she said lightly. 'I'll be here when you get back. I'm not going anywhere.'

She felt his arm tighten around her waist, the muscles in his chest growing rigid.

'No, you're not. But *we* are.'

She stared at him, confused. 'We are?'

'Let's get out of here.' He glanced around the apartment, his face creasing. 'Out of Manhattan. Go somewhere we don't have to pretend.'

Her pulse shivered with excitement. 'Where do you have in mind?'

He smiled slowly and her heart contracted sharply with pity for any poor woman who might truly love Rollo. With beauty and charm like his, it was easy to forget his ruthless determination. But, looking up into his smooth, handsome face, she knew he would always be one step ahead of her. And she would be exactly where he wanted her to be.

'I have a small cabin upstate—in the Adirondacks. It's a bit rough and ready, but what do you think? You and me in the wilderness together?'

It sounded like a question, except she knew he didn't expect or need a reply. But as heat uncoiled inside her, she lifted her mouth to his and gave him her answer.

'I should warn you there are bears in the woods. Black bears. They're a lot smaller than grizzlies, and they rarely bother humans, but you should be careful just the same.'

Leaning forward, Rollo picked up his coffee cup. Having arrived at Mohawk Lodge just twenty minutes earlier, they were relaxing in front of a panoramic view of the lake and the Adirondack Mountains beyond. In the distance the forest looked like the setting for a fairy tale but Daisy barely noticed the view.

She was still reeling from the trip in his private helicopter. Or rather, the way Rollo had held her hand during the entire flight, his leg pressing against hers, his mouth temptingly close as he pointed out landmarks and filled her in on the history of the region.

She nodded, then frowned. 'Did you say bears?'

He put his cup down carefully, his eyes narrowing.

'What's up?'

'Nothing.' She met his gaze, then sighed. 'I just didn't realise your whole life was like this.'

'Like what?'

'Like… So amazing.'

He shrugged. 'I don't really think about it.'

'I suppose you get used to it,' she said slowly.

But somehow she couldn't imagine a life in which owning a helicopter and a lakeside cabin would ever be anything other than incredible. It was another reminder of the differences between them.

But right now she needed to concentrate on what they shared, not on what they didn't, and, putting her cup down, she said brightly, 'So how about that guided tour you promised me?'

The cabin was delightful. Set in seventy-five acres of unspoilt meadows and forest, it was built of timber and stone but it shared the same high-spec luxury as the penthouse. And letting Rollo show her around had been the right decision. As they walked outside onto the deck, where a swing bed swayed gently in the warm breeze, her stomach tumbled over with happiness as she felt his hand close around hers.

'So, do you fancy a swim?'

She frowned. 'I don't know. What's the water like?' she said cautiously.

'Probably quite mild.'

Glancing up at his face, she rolled her eyes. 'I might need a second opinion before I whip out my bikini. I'm not entirely sure I trust your judgement.'

Lifting her hand, he tipped it sideways so that the stones in the ring caught the light.

'I thought you liked your ring.'

'I do.' She pinched his fingers playfully. 'I was talking about this place. You said it was a "small cabin."' Glancing inside at the huge stone fireplace and vaulted, beamed ceiling, she shook her head. "'A bit rough and ready," you said. I was expecting bare floors and no electricity.'

Not a soaking tub and a French chef.

Looking up, she fell silent. He was staring at her steadily, eyes dark and unblinking, and then he tugged her towards him and she clutched at his arms as her legs seemed to slide away.

'I can do rough,' he murmured and, lowering his head, he brushed his mouth across hers. Fingers splaying around her waist, he pulled her closer, his breath warm against her throat. 'And I'm certainly ready.'

Her head was spinning… Her body melting like wax near a flame.

Only not with longing but with shame.

Picturing the way he'd pulled away from her, knowing how impossible it would have been for her to do the same, she felt a flicker of doubt and fear.

He felt it too and, lifting his head, his gaze focused steadily on her face.

'What is it?'

She hesitated, her eyes shying away from his. She wanted him so badly. But she couldn't give herself to him. Not now she knew his desire was motivated by power, not passion.

'Daisy? *Daisy?*'

His voice was insistent, inexorable. It was a voice she could not refuse.

'Yesterday when we… When you—'

She frowned. There was a tremor in her voice and she knew that her eyes were bright with tears.

'I know you wanted sex. But I also know that you didn't want *me*.'

It had been a guess—a theory. But as he gazed down at her in silence she felt a rush of misery so intense that she couldn't bear to look at him. Pushing against his chest, she edged away, fixing her gaze on the shimmering mass of water.

'You're wrong.'

She lifted her face to his, her heart leaden in her chest.

'So why did you stop?'

How could you stop? she wanted to ask, remembering the strength and the violence of her longing for him. How could he have been so coolly detached?

But, glancing at his handsome face, she thought he looked anything but detached now. Instead he looked strained and unsure.

He shook his head, the skin tightening across his cheekbones.

'Short answer—I'm an idiot. I wanted to prove to myself you were *optional*. That demonstrating my willpower was more satisfying than you could ever be. But I was wrong. On both counts.' He grimaced. 'The last twenty-four hours have been the most uncomfortable of my entire life. And all I managed to prove is that I can't actually function because I want you so badly.'

She breathed out, her heart pounding with a mix of shock and relief and a stunned, helpless happiness.

But she wasn't going to make it easy for him. He had hurt her. And, yes, she knew it was because he hated losing control. But he had to understand that although that might be a reason for his behaviour it didn't excuse it.

'How do I know that's true? That you want me? You might be pretending.'

His eyes narrowed and then her heart rate seemed to double as he pulled her firmly against him and she felt the hard length of his erection pressing against her.

'Trust me, Daisy. This is real. And it's for you. Just you.'

Reaching out, he touched her face gently and the warmth of his fingertips sent a tremor through her body.

'You're all I think about. All I've been thinking about since I kissed you in my office. It's like I'm living from one moment to the next. But if you won't believe what I say then maybe I'll just have to show you instead.'

And, lowering his mouth, he kissed her. It was a kiss like no other. Hotter, deeper. And his mouth possessed her with a ferocity that wiped out all conscious thought.

As his hands moved lightly over her back and shoulders and neck she shivered beneath their touch, head swimming, body swaying against his as he nudged her backwards. She bumped into the swing, felt wood scraping her bare legs, and then, slipping his hands around her waist, he lifted her up onto the mattress.

His hands were urgent against her skin, pulling off her boots, her T-shirt, and somehow her jeans came off too and she was suddenly naked except for her underwear.

Her breath caught in her throat as he leaned over her, his face tensed with passion and something softer, less guarded. And she knew that he wanted her to see what he was feeling, to know it was real.

In a heartbeat, her doubts were forgotten. His hunger was her hunger. Only it was more than hunger. It was like being consumed by fire—total and complete surrender to the flame of passion that burned between them.

She stared up into his face. 'Kiss me,' she whispered.

His eyes on hers were the dark green of the forest across the water and, leaning forward, he kissed her slowly, his tongue probing between her lips, delicate and deliberate, so that heat stabbed inside her.

'Open your mouth,' he muttered. 'I want to taste you.'

He was barely breathing, his head empty and hollow of anything except the pulse beating in his groin.

As the late afternoon sun spread over the deck, liquid gold spilled over her skin and he felt his last atom of self-control dissolve.

He dipped his head, dipped and licked inside her mouth, his teeth nipping, tugging her swollen lips. And, moaning softly, she kissed him back, her fingers digging into his scalp, pulling him closer and deeper until he broke away panting, his eyes blunt and unfocused.

For a moment he stared at her in silence, dazed, dry-mouthed, almost drunk on her beauty, then slowly he cupped her breast in his hand, his thumb brushing against the tip of her nipple, and the blood gathered thickly inside him as he watched her face soften.

Daisy shuddered. A thread of heat was stretching out inside her and suddenly she was arching upwards, her thighs trembling. She felt him push aside the flimsy fabric of her bra, felt his mouth closing over her breast and then his fingers were slipping over her body, across her stomach and hips and between her legs, clasping the pulsing ache against the palm of his hand.

Her breath thickened in her throat. Suddenly she was clawing at his belt, her nails scraping against the denim of his jeans, tugging the zip down, her whole body vibrating with need as her fingers found the smooth hardness of his erection.

At the touch of her hand his body jerked involuntarily and groaning, he lifted his mouth and shifted against her, reaching into his pocket for a condom, fingers tearing clumsily at the wrapper. And then he was smoothing it on, feeling himself grow thicker and harder.

Maddened, she clutched at him frantically, her back curving upwards, seeking more of his mouth and his hands, as he tugged her underwear to one side. The weight of his body was pressing down on her and into her and she rocked against him, her face buried in his shoulder, the pulse inside her beating wildly.

He shifted his hips and she felt a sharp sting of ecstasy and tensing, she shuddered against him. And then his mouth found hers and, groaning her name against her lips, he pushed up, driving into her hard and fast while her body still contracted around his.

Later, bodies still entwined, they watched a rose-coloured sun sink behind the mountains. Breathing out softly, Daisy ran her hand lightly over his stomach.

'This place is so remote. How did you come across it?'

'I did a deal a few years ago with a guy called Tim Buchanan. He and I enjoyed the same kind of activities, so he invited me up here for a weekend.'

She raised an eyebrow. 'Activities! Sounds intriguing!' She gave him a small teasing smile. 'You're not one of those role play fanatics, are you? You know—the kind who re-enact the Civil War. I won't come out of the shower and find you dressed as Abraham Lincoln, will I?'

His eyes gleamed. 'I meant shooting and fishing. But I'm always up for a bit of role play.'

His fingers tiptoed over the curve of her hip and a hot shiver slid over her skin, her body responding both to his touch and the teasing note in his voice. 'Well, let me know and I'll unpack my crinoline,' she said lightly.

Glancing back across the lake, she sighed.

'You're so lucky it was for sale.'

'It wasn't. But I liked it, so I made him an offer and he accepted.'

She nodded, as though she too was in the habit of purchasing lakeside mansions on a whim.

'Your family must love it.'

Even before she heard the edge in his voice she could feel a slight tensing in his shoulders.

'I'm sure they would have done. But both my parents are gone.'

How had she not known that? He knew all about her family. But somehow his past had never come up for discussion. Or maybe he had chosen to keep it to himself.

'Oh, I'm sorry.'

And she was. The thought of losing one of her parents filled her with dread—to lose both seemed intolerable.

'But they must have been so proud of you and everything you've achieved.'

This time his hesitation was unmistakable. For a minute she thought he wasn't going to answer. Finally, though, he gave her a perfunctory smile.

'Isn't every parent?'

He didn't move, but she could almost feel him retreating from her. Nodding mechanically, she decided it was time to change the subject.

'Do you think we could sleep out here tonight?'

She felt him relax.

'I guess so.' His gaze locked on to hers. 'Won't you be scared though? Like I said, there are wild animals out here.'

'They don't scare me,' she said huskily. 'I know how to tame them.' And, wriggling closer, she climbed on top of him, catching his wrists with her hands.

'Are you sure?'

His voice was hoarse, his eyes dark and fierce, and she could feel the pulse beating beneath his skin.

'Yes,' she murmured. 'Only I might need a bit more practice.'

'Good idea. Practice makes—'

But he broke off on a gasp as, lowering her mouth, she ran her tongue lightly over the smooth muscles of his chest, then lower, down the line of soft golden hair on his stomach, and then lower still…

Afterwards, she lay in his arms, watching him sleep. She felt drowsy but she didn't want to close her eyes. Or for the moment to end.

All her life she'd been searching for passion. Looking for that intensity of feeling, that intimacy of knowing somebody inside out.

Only she'd never imagined finding it with Rollo.

At best, she'd assumed that being with him would offer a respite from the heartbreak of another failed romance. What she hadn't expected was this incredible sexual chemistry—a physical attraction that filled her with wonder and yearning.

It might not be love.

It might not be permanent.

But right now she was living in the moment.

And she was going to make the most of it.

As the warmth of his body seeped into her she curled her arm more tightly over his chest and, closing her eyes, fell instantly asleep.

CHAPTER EIGHT

IGNORING THE BURNING ache in his lungs, Rollo sprinted up the hill. Only another couple of metres to go and—

A small but intrusive alarm broke through the pounding of his heart and, slowing to a jog, he headed towards the wooden jetty that stretched out into the lake. His arms were shaking, the T-shirt he was wearing was damp with sweat, but the heat and chaos of his body felt inconsequential beside the turmoil inside his head.

He had woken early, eyes straining against the first sliver of light slicing through the blinds. There was nothing unusual about that. The business world was always awake somewhere in the world, and he routinely made property deals at all hours of the day and night. Normally, he found it easy to get up early.

But this time he'd been oddly reluctant to move. He'd felt warm and comfortable and it had been easy to lie there, drowsily listening to the sound of the waves lapping against the deck.

Only beneath his lethargy and the comforting rhythm of the water there had been a nagging sense of something being different.

It had taken him a moment to realise that the difference was Daisy.

Or, more particularly, the fact that at some point during the night her soft body had curled against his. And he hadn't pushed her away.

For a moment his mind had stalled. He had felt wrongfooted by the sudden, new and unsettling state of affairs. As a red-blooded male, wanting sex was hot-wired into his

DNA. But waking up beside a woman was something he'd taken extreme care to avoid throughout his adult life.

Yet there she'd been, legs tangled between his, her hand curling over his waist—

From somewhere in the forest the sharp cry of a bird jolted his mind back into real time. Leaning forward against the railing, he stared dazedly across the water, trying to make sense of his behaviour.

It took several minutes for him to concede that it might have something to do with Daisy. Or rather sex with Daisy.

His skin tightened and he felt an almost unbearable tug of sexual anticipation, just as he had during the night, when it had been impossible not to reach over and pull her into his arms.

It had been wild, heated, mind-blowing, and she had made him want more, give more, feel more than any woman he had known before. Her feverish demands had matched his, her hands, lips, body had been like quicksilver. Even now, with the cool breeze blowing across the water, he could feel the white-hot imprint of her touch on his skin—

But nothing had really changed, he reassured himself. Daisy might look like a sleeping princess, with her long, blonde hair spread out over the pillows, but there would be no fairy-tale ending to their relationship.

Yes, he would marry her. But only because he needed a wife to persuade Dunmore to sell to him. Although after last night, she felt more like a compulsion than a necessity.

Remembering her smooth, naked body, and his own speechless, almost savage exultation at the way she had melted into him, he felt himself grow instantly and painfully hard.

Breathing out slowly, he frowned. There it was again: that same nagging uneasiness that had woken him. The sense that Daisy was different.

That he was different when he was with her.

But why? It wasn't as though he'd lived a life of celibacy. He'd had many women. All beautiful and sexually eager, and at the time he had wanted them—some of them badly. But never like this. Never with this relentless, excruciating hunger. And never once that hunger had been sated. Walking away had always been easy. Only not this time. Not with Daisy.

His mouth twisted. He'd had to force himself to get up this morning. And he'd only done it to prove to himself that she was an indulgence he could resist.

But instead her absence was like an actual physical pain. Every nerve, every sense focusing in on it, like a toothache.

He frowned. Sex with Daisy was supposed to cure his sexual frustration, not exacerbate it. Only it appeared that instead of having his appetite sated he had grown instantly and intensely addicted to her.

Probably it was because he'd never gone without sex for so long, or had to deal with so much intimacy. And so what if it was taking longer than usual to work her out of his system? He had a whole year to wear her out in his bed.

In the meantime, however, he needed to be careful. Disciplined. Pragmatic. It would be easy to lose himself in his desire for Daisy, but he must not lose sight of the real reason she was in his bed. Or the fact that once Dunmore signed over that building to him she would be gone from his life for ever.

And turning away from the lake, he began a leisurely jog back along the jetty towards the lodge.

'What's this?'

Gazing up at Rollo, Daisy stifled a yawn. 'What's what?' she asked sleepily.

He never seemed to tire of touching her, and now he was caressing her leg, his hand moving slowly down from her hip.

After he'd returned from his run he'd showered and woken her impatiently and they had made love for most of the morning. Now they were lying in bed together, their skin hot and damp, their bodies exhausted. Or rather *she* was exhausted. Rollo seemed energised by the morning's activities.

'What's what?' she said again.

'This.'

She felt his fingers stop and slowly trace a figure of eight on the skin above her knee, and instantly she forgot her question, forgot his answer, forgot who and where she was. Her whole body was trembling, nipples tightening, a soft, liquid heat spreading inside her so that she could hardly breathe, could barely control the longing spilling over her skin.

She stared at him dazedly, hardly daring to believe he was there beside her, all sleek, warm muscle and smooth, golden limbs. He was just so gorgeous, and he made her feel gorgeous too.

Not just gorgeous, but somehow freer and truer to herself.

With other boyfriends—with everyone, really, except David sometimes—she felt as though she was always pretending to be someone else. Someone she didn't want to be—happy-go-lucky, ditsy Daisy, who never quite pulled it off, whether 'it' was a relationship or her career.

But with Rollo, it was different.

She felt different.

Unsurprisingly, she thought grimly. Even aside from his being one of the richest men in the country, it wasn't exactly a run-of-the-mill relationship. Her other boyfriends might have been lazy and thoughtless and immature, but none had blackmailed her into playing their wife.

But it wasn't just the framework of their relationship that was making her feel so blindsided. It was Rollo himself—or rather the way he demanded a truthfulness, an honesty, that other men did not. Not just with facts but with herself.

With him there was nowhere to hide. He wanted all of her. The good, the bad and the pretend-it-never-happened. No one had ever got under her skin and turned her inside out like that.

It made her feel helpless, off balance, and yet in his arms she felt warm and secure, all her old fears and doubts about herself kept at bay by the steady beat of his heart.

She felt her own heartbeat stumble as a flush of heat crept over her cheeks.

That was the trouble with sex.

She'd been there before, and each time it had been the same old story. Sex felt so *intimate*. And it was—physically. Only really it was nothing but bodies wrapping round one another.

She frowned. It sounded if not bleak, then mechanical, and not at all like the way she had felt with Rollo. But then sex with him had been beyond anything she'd ever imagined. She'd never responded to any man like that—so fiercely, so freely. It was exhilarating—and terrifying. At times she couldn't even recognise herself. Who was this woman who initiated and demanded so much? But it had felt good to be that woman. To be herself—the Daisy she had wanted to be for so many years.

Her thoughts slowed.

Being with Rollo felt right in other ways too. Maybe it was because they shared a secret. But it felt as though they knew other well. Almost as though they had been reunited after a long separation. Which was not only untrue, she admitted ruefully, but also made no sense whatsoever.

She felt his gaze on her face and, pushing aside her thoughts, she glanced to where his fingers were still doodling over her skin.

'Oh, that.' It was a small cut just above her knee. She felt a flush of heat rise over her face. 'That's where I banged into that board thing in your office.'

Beside her, Rollo tilted his head back, her words acting like an emergency brake on his runaway desire. His office! His hand trembled slightly against the scar on her leg.

How could he have forgotten how they met? Or the real reason she was here in his bed. He felt a flicker of irritation that he'd let his libido get in the way of business.

'That reminds me—James Dunmore rang. He's invited us to lunch. Apparently he very much wants to meet you.'

Daisy stared at him in silence. There was an expression on his face she didn't quite recognise, and momentarily she thought it might be regret.

But his next statement instantly dispelled that idea.

'Holiday's over,' he said casually. 'Time to go back to work.'

His words echoed inside her head.

It hadn't felt like a holiday. It had felt like a honeymoon. Either way, though, it was over.

Forcing herself to smile, she met his gaze.

'That's great,' she said quickly. 'I'll go and get dressed. We don't want to keep him waiting.'

As the helicopter rose upwards, Daisy glanced furtively at the time on her phone. Her heart was beating nervously. Now that she was actually about to meet him, she would have liked more time to get to know the man for whom this charade was happening.

Damping down her panic, she cleared her throat. 'Is there anything I should know about Mr Dunmore? I mean, I know the basics, but—'

Turning, Rollo stared at her, his cool expression a clear indication that the relaxed lover of the past few days had been replaced by the dispassionate property tycoon.

'The basics will do just fine.'

He glanced back out the window.

Beneath them, the soft green of the forest was growing

sparser. Roads were starting to crisscross the landscape. Soon he would be shaking hands with Dunmore, Daisy by his side. It was the moment he'd been working towards all his life—the moment when his goal switched from impossible dream to possible reality.

So why, then, did he want nothing more than to turn back time? To go back to the lodge and it be just be the two of them.

It was nerves, he told himself quickly, his gaze tugging towards where Daisy sat, wearing a navy pencil skirt, a gold chain belt accentuating the waistline of her fitted grey blouse. Nerves and a raging, unassailable lust for the tempting body that lay beneath that demure outfit.

Pushing aside his desire, he cleared his throat.

'Dunmore's been married to the same woman since he was nineteen. He's a romantic.'

He smiled, but Daisy couldn't bring herself to smile back. The dismissive tone in his voice, his barely masked incredulity that a man could truly love a woman, let alone choose to stay with her, for life tasted bitter in her mouth.

But it wasn't her problem, she reminded herself quickly. Maybe if theirs was a real relationship, his emotional disconnect would matter. But thankfully she would never have to endure the pain of loving Rollo. What she felt for him was just simple and shallow: lust.

Perhaps he registered the effect of his words, for when he spoke again she saw that the mockery in his eyes had faded.

'You'll be fine. He's a nice man who just wants to hear about you—about us. All you have to do is pretend you're madly in love with me.'

He shifted closer, his hand tightening on hers, and suddenly her mouth was dry, her heart hammering, her entire body so aware of him and only him that for a moment the noise of the helicopter faded away and it was as though they were flying through the air alone together.

'Is that all?' Their eyes met and she managed to smile. 'In that case, no problem. You can be Romeo and I'll just channel my inner Juliet.'

He laughed softly and she felt a rush of pleasure. Not just because she had made him laugh, but at the way his body was sprawled against hers. There was a take-it-for-granted intimacy to it that would have been impossible only a few days before.

'Both of us dying over lunch seems a little extreme.'

'That's where you're wrong,' she said lightly, glancing out of the window at the skyscrapers below. 'It can't be true love unless someone dies or ends up alone and heartbroken.'

Turning back, she expected him still to be smiling. But instead his eyes were fixed on her face, his expression serious and oddly intense.

'I thought you believed in happy-ever-after,' he said quietly.

The stillness in the cabin seemed to press against her so that suddenly she was painfully aware of her own breathing.

'I did. I do—'

A pulse of tension was beating beneath her skin. Staring at him in confusion, she rewound their conversation, searching for an explanation for this abrupt change of mood.

Then from somewhere behind her head the intercom crackled and the voice of the pilot split the silence.

'Just to let you know we'll be landing in about five minutes, sir. There's a slight breeze, but other than that it looks like it's going to be a beautiful day.'

Moments later the helicopter touched down on the roof of one of Manhattan's many skyscrapers, and then they were walking across the concrete, her heels tapping like castanets.

'This way, Mr Fleming… Ms Maddox.'

A bodyguard in a dark suit stepped forward, gesturing towards the lift. Watching the numbers change as the lift descended, Daisy felt her stomach tighten. It was almost the moment of truth. The moment she found out if all that preparation had paid off and the audience believed her performance.

She breathed out silently.

Everything should be all right. She knew his back story the way she knew her own life, and her body still pulsed with the aftershock of his lovemaking.

And yet something was wrong.

Beside her, Rollo was silent, his face expressionless. But something in the way he was holding his body made her instantly forget her own nerves.

'Rollo—'

He didn't answer and she held her breath, feeling almost as she had when she'd broken into his office. Only this time it was clear she was intruding on something deeper. She felt a sudden slippery panic slither over her skin. If she felt like an intruder, how were they ever going to convince Dunmore that their relationship was real?

'Rollo. It's going to be okay.'

'I know.'

The distance in his voice caught her off guard. But before she could respond, the lift doors opened and she felt his hand on her arm. And then he was guiding her forward, past another bodyguard into a large, open-plan living space where two men stood talking casually by the window.

She stopped abruptly. 'Rollo—'

Behind them she felt the bodyguard discreetly retreat as Rollo turned to face her.

A muscle flickered in his jaw. 'Are you trying to make us late?'

It was an accusation dressed up as a question. But with a sting of shock, she realised it was more than that. It was a justification—a reason to be angry. But why did Rollo need to be *angry*?

And then, looking into his eyes, she felt a sudden painful tightening in her chest as she realised that it wasn't anger he was feeling. It was fear. He was afraid of blowing the deal.

Instinctively she stepped forward and, taking his hand, squeezed it between her fingers.

'I know how much this matters to you. It matters to me too, and together we can make it work. So please don't push me away.'

As the silence stretched between them she thought he might do just that. But he didn't. Instead, after a brief hesitation, his fingers tightened around hers.

'I'm sorry,' he said quietly.

She breathed out sharply.

'Good.' Her eyes flared. 'You should be. From now on it's you and me against the world, right?'

As he nodded, she leaned forward and kissed him fiercely. When finally she drew back, some of the tension had left his face.

'Was that for luck?' he said softly.

She shook her head. 'We don't need luck. I just wanted to kiss you. And now I want you to take me to lunch.'

Halfway through her starter of *burrata pugliese* and wild strawberries, Daisy decided that James Dunmore was one of the nicest men she had ever met. Tall, with greying red hair, he was reassuringly unpretentious and far less intimidating than she'd expected given his wealth and status.

As they'd walked across the living room, he had greeted them warmly, thanked them both for joining him, and then immediately apologised for his wife's absence.

'Emily was so looking forward to seeing you again, Rollo, and, of course, to meeting you, Daisy. Unfortunately her sister was taken ill at the weekend, so she flew up to Vermont to be with her.'

He'd turned to the red-haired man standing next to him.

'But on the plus side, I've managed to coerce my nephew, Jack, into joining us. He heads up my East Coast legal department.'

Jack stepped forward. 'Hey, Rollo, good to meet you.'

'And this is Daisy.'

Dunmore's blue eyes had gleamed. 'I must admit to having an ulterior motive for inviting Jack to join us today. When I heard that Rollo had got engaged I wanted a witness to the transformation. And, of course, to meet the woman who finally tamed him.'

Rollo had smiled coolly. 'I think my reputation may have been somewhat exaggerated by the media.'

'Well, I like mine,' Daisy had said softly. 'The woman who tamed Rollo Fleming! That would look great on a T-shirt, don't you think?'

Dunmore had laughed. 'It certainly would. Now, why don't we eat? I hope you're hungry, Daisy. I'm supposed to be watching my weight, but my chef, Jordi, makes it extremely difficult.'

The food was delicious. But after spending so much time around reserved Manhattan socialites, it was James Dunmore's company that Daisy enjoyed most. He was warm and relaxed and, although he was the CEO of a property empire, it was clear he saw himself as a husband and father first.

'So, Jack is your brother's son?' Leaning back to let the waiter clear her plate, Daisy glanced critically from Dunmore to his nephew. 'He looks just like you. Except—'

'He's got all his own teeth.'

She laughed. 'I was going to say that he's got a different jawline.'

Dunmore frowned. 'That's true. Not many people notice that. They just see the hair—or what's left of it. You're very perceptive, Daisy.'

Smiling, she shrugged. 'I'm an actress. Sometimes the right jawline gets you the part.'

The older man ran a hand through his hair. 'Being red-headed runs in the family. Jack's father and I used to get mistaken for one another a lot when we were younger.'

Daisy looked up curiously. 'But you're not twins?'

He shook his head. 'Oddly enough, we actually have different mothers. But we both take after our dad.'

Leaning forward, Rollo laid his hand over hers. 'Daisy has a twin. Her brother, David.'

'A twin brother!' Dunmore beamed. 'You must have a very intuitive understanding of men.' He glanced pointedly across the table at Rollo. 'That must come in handy.'

Daisy smiled. 'I wish it did. But David is nothing like Rollo.'

Or was he?

Not so long ago likening her uptight, sensitive brother to Rollo Fleming would have seemed utterly far-fetched. Now, though, it didn't seem nearly as implausible. Rollo might appear autocratic and ruthless, but she had seen another side to him. Nervous, less guarded and kind too—particularly to her brother.

Pushing aside that disconcerting train of thought, she lifted up her glass. 'He's nothing like me either.'

'But you're close?'

'Very.' She nodded. 'We were inseparable when we were little. We still are. But we're very different. Not just in looks but personality, interests. I don't know what I'd do without him. He's like my conscience—always there inside my head.'

'Sorry to butt in.'

It was Jack. He smiled at Daisy and then turned towards his uncle.

'That was a message from Tom Krantz.'

Dunmore frowned. 'Sorry, Daisy, would you excuse me? I wouldn't normally let business interrupt, but—'

'You don't need to explain.'

Taking a sip of water, she smiled. But inside, her heart beat out a percussive rhythm of guilt.

David.

Her brother.

Her twin, who was always inside her head.

Once upon a time that might have been true. But she'd barely given David a thought over the last few days. Instead all fraternal concern had been blotted out by lust and self-absorption.

Lowering her glass she was suddenly conscious of the silence across the table.

Looking up, she met Rollo's gaze.

'I know you miss David. And I know you're worried about him,' he said softly, letting his fingers close around hers.

He envied the closeness she shared with her brother. The absolute trust and dependence. It was pure and powerful and unbreakable.

His chest grew tight. Or it was supposed to be anyway. He forced a smile.

'But he's going to be okay. I'll make sure of that.'

Daisy nodded. His hand felt warm. But it was the warmth and the certainty in his voice that eased the pain in her heart as Dunmore turned back towards her.

After coffee, they sat and chatted easily, until finally Rollo glanced at his watch.

'We really ought to be getting back.'

'Of course.' Standing up, Dunmore patted Rollo on the shoulder. 'But on one condition. I insist that you both come up to Swan Creek for the weekend. We'll have lunch, and then maybe, Rollo, we can have another look at that proposal of yours.'

CHAPTER NINE

BACK AT THE PENTHOUSE, they tumbled into bed. It was fast and urgent, both of them gripped by the same hot desperation, furiously goading each other with their hands and mouths and bodies, until finally they shuddered to an explosive climax together.

Afterwards, Rollo gathered her against his damp body and, breathing out softly, drifted instantly into sleep.

Beside him though, Daisy lay wide awake. Beneath the beating of her heart Dunmore's offer was playing on a loop inside her head.

'Maybe, Rollo, we can have another look at that proposal of yours.'

Rollo had played it cool. He had shown no hint of triumph. But she knew that the older man's words were exactly what he had been hoping to hear. What she too should have been pleased to hear. After all, the quicker Dunmore agreed to sell to Rollo, the sooner she would be free of him.

Only she didn't feel pleased. In fact, being one step closer to Rollo achieving his goal, and thus to her freedom, was making her nerves twitch so that being still was suddenly an impossibility.

What she needed was an anaesthetic—a way to numb her brain. A few rigorous laps of the rooftop pool should do the trick.

Gently lifting Rollo's arm, she slid off the bed and padded towards the dressing room.

Ten minutes later, she was sliding through the clear blue water, her mind so focused on the rhythm of her stroke that soon her anxieties faded away. Finally she could swim no more and, heart pounding, she pulled herself out onto the deck.

As she wiped the water from her eyes her heart did a backflip. Rollo was sitting on one of the loungers, wearing jeans, his feet and chest bare, a towel dangling from his hand.

She smiled. 'I thought you were asleep.'

'I was. But I woke up and you were gone.'

There was a tension in his voice she might have missed had she not grown so attuned to the subtleties of his manner.

'I was a bit wound up,' she said lightly. 'So I went for a swim.'

His eyes rested on her face. 'What's up? Are you still worrying about David?'

She was about to nod automatically, but with shock she realised that she wasn't. She had spoken to her parents and her brother on the way back to the apartment, and they'd been surprised—particularly David—by the news of her engagement. But as she'd expected their happiness had outweighed any misgivings. She felt calmer about everything except—

She shook her head. 'It's not David. It's James. Mr Dunmore.'

His gaze searched her face with a hint of impatience.

'What about him?'

She shrugged. 'I don't know. I suppose he wasn't real before. Now he is. And I liked him,' she said simply.

'And that's a problem?' His fingers tapped irritably against the arm of the chair.

She caught her breath, his impatience stirring irritation of her own. 'Yes. I don't like lying to someone I like and respect.'

His eyes narrowed. 'I'm sure you'll still "like and respect" him when he agrees to sell to me.'

She stared at him, her heart banging against her ribs. He was missing the point. Or choosing to miss it.

'It just makes me feel shabby. He's a nice man. He doesn't deserve—'

'Deserve what?' His face was set, the tension in his body now a tangible presence. 'The large sum of money I'm going to pay him? Dunmore's a businessman. If he sells to me, it will be a business decision, not a favour or a charitable bequest.'

She shivered. His whole manner had changed, his face hardening to a mask so that it was all she could do to meet his gaze.

'That's not what you said before,' she said hoarsely. 'You said he'd only sell to someone with the right values. That's why we have to marry, isn't it? So he'll believe you've found love and happiness with the right woman?'

He flinched at her words—or maybe it was the sunlight catching her eye, for when she looked at him again he seemed as poised and cold as before.

'I'm not responsible for what Dunmore believes or feels.'

'What about what you feel?' The blood was humming in her head, a nub of dread chafing beneath her heart. 'I thought you liked him.'

A muscle flickered in his cheek.

'It would make no difference to my decision if I didn't. This is business, and feelings have nothing to do with business.' He stood up abruptly. 'But, more important, neither do you. In case you've forgotten, you're just here to clear a debt.'

Her breath seemed to fray in her chest. *Just here to clear a debt.* It sounded like an epitaph. And in a way it was—an epitaph for her naivety.

Had she really thought having sex with Rollo would change their relationship? She'd been wrong.

They were back to being strangers.

She wanted to rail against her stupid, gullible self for the way she had lain in his arms, opened her body to his, felt—

Her hands started to shake and, balling them into fists, she directed her fury at Rollo instead.

'No, that's *your* reason, Rollo, not mine. I'm here because I love my brother. But do you know something? I'd stay now even if you *weren't* blackmailing me, because I know how much this deal means to you. Perhaps if you cared about anything other than your business and that building, you might understand that. Oh, and you might not have to blackmail a stranger into playing your wife. You might actually be the man you're pretending to be!'

His face was blank, but she could tell he was fighting for control…at the edge of losing his temper.

'You know nothing about me. Or what I care about.'

There was a clear note of warning in his voice and she was glad, for it meant that she had struck a nerve.

'Why? Because I'm just a woman clearing a debt?'

But even as she spoke she knew that it wasn't about her. This was about *him*. About his anger and his arrogance and the mask that came down every time he thought she was getting too close.

'You're wrong, Rollo. I do know what you care about. You care about honesty. Only you're not being honest now about why you're upset with me.'

There was a long, quivering silence. Finally, he breathed out unsteadily. 'Did you mean it? What you said about staying with me?'

She blinked. She hadn't planned on saying those words; they'd sprung from somewhere deep inside. She felt suddenly vulnerable, hearing them repeated back to her. But even if it meant looking foolish and weak, she wasn't going to lie to him.

She nodded. 'But I don't suppose that matters to you any more than I do.'

'You *do* matter...'

'I know.' She spoke coldly, her eyes blazing. 'Without me you won't get your building—'

'No, not because of that...' He hesitated, a tremor moving across his face. 'What I said yesterday—it was true. You're all I think about and—' The skin across his cheekbones was stretched taut; his shoulders rising and falling. 'You're right. I am upset.'

'Because I said I didn't like lying to Dunmore?'

'Yes—no.' His mouth twisted, his fingers curling around the towel. 'It just seemed like you were worried about him and David and *their* feelings and not about me.'

'That's not true.' She breathed out shakily. 'I do care about you. But you don't want me to.'

His hands stilled and for a moment he stared at her in silence. Then he said flatly, 'You're a good person.'

She stared at him uncertainly. 'Not really. It's easy to do the right thing for love.'

'Love?' He frowned, his gaze suddenly intent.

She felt her face grow warmer. 'I meant for David. I love my brother.' She bit her lip. 'I'd do anything for him. For any of my family. That's what matters to me.'

Not that Rollo would ever understand that, she thought wearily. Other than a few offhand remarks, he'd barely discussed his childhood, and his careless exploitation of her relationship with David suggested that family meant nothing to him.

But, glancing over at his face, she felt her heart start to pound. She had expected derision or incomprehension, coldness or anger. But instead he looked stricken.

And suddenly she understood.

'It matters to you too.'

His head jerked up, his eyes widening like an animal's, poised for fight or flight, and instinctively she lowered her voice.

'That's why you want that building, isn't it?'

Her breath caught in her throat as his gaze fixed past her, at some unseen point in the distance. But she knew where he was looking. She'd seen the picture on his desk.

He nodded slowly but didn't reply, and for a moment they stood in silence like actors in the wings, waiting for their cue.

Then finally, he nodded again. 'I used to live there. A long time ago.'

It sounded like the beginning of a fairy tale. But she knew from the strain in his voice that his story would have no happy ending.

'With your parents?' she prompted gently.

He nodded. 'My father wasn't a practical man, but he had ideas. And passion. That's how he met my mother. He was working at a country club as a groundsman and he saw her with her parents. And just like that he knew she was the one. So he cut all the roses he could find and when he gave them to her he asked her to marry him.'

He gave Daisy a small, tight smile.

'He lost his job. But he didn't care because she said yes.'

She nodded, wondering how a smile could be so sad. 'That's so romantic. They must have been very happy.'

His smile tightened. 'He was.' He paused, his eyes bleak. 'My mother not so much. After they got married, they moved to the city. It was hard. My father didn't earn much, and his "ideas" used up all her trust fund. She hated not having money—hated living from day to day. But then when I was about ten, and my sister Rosamund was four, he got a really good job.'

Daisy stared at him in shock. *Sister!* She had thought he was an only child. But now that he was finally talking so openly she dared not interrupt.

'It was good money, and he rented an apartment for us. It wasn't huge, or fancy. But for the first time my mother was happy. We all were. There was even a playground, with swings and slides, and I used to take Rosamund there all the time. My mom would cook and we'd have dinner as a family and then we'd play cards. It was perfect.'

Her heart contracted at the wonder in his voice. 'What happened?'

He shrugged. 'I don't know. She'd be okay for maybe a month or two, and then she'd start coming home late. Missing meals. Then she'd pack her bags. Threaten to leave.'

Remembering his face when he'd found her with her suitcase, Daisy felt a pang of misery. No wonder he'd reacted so furiously. It must have reminded him of other times—other suitcases.

'And did she?' she said in a small voice.

'No. My father would buy her some gift, or take her out to dinner, and she'd be happy again. He spent so much money trying to make her happy. And then one day they came to the apartment.'

'Who came?' She held her breath, waiting for the answer, even though she knew what it would be.

'The bailiffs.' His face was harder than stone. 'It turned out my father had lost his job months earlier, only he hadn't wanted to tell her. We had to move out. There and then. In front of all the neighbours.'

She swallowed. Her eyes were burning, but not with anger. 'I'm so sorry, Rollo.'

His shoulders were rigid. 'The first time was the worst. Like everything else, it got easier with practice.'

His matter-of-fact tone as much as the implication of his words made her stomach clench painfully, and she had to grit her teeth to stop the tears in her eyes from falling.

'My mother couldn't bear it. She left the week before my thirteenth birthday.'

This time the effort in his smile was too painful to witness and she glanced away, feeling slightly sick.

'There was a note. She blamed my father for being fired, wasting their money, losing the apartment. For ruining her life. I'd heard it all before. But seeing it written down was a lot worse.'

He frowned.

'My dad took it very badly. He felt completely responsible, and he became obsessed with getting the apartment back. He thought if he did, that she'd come home. So he worked and worked. And then one day he collapsed. He was in hospital for a couple of weeks. And then he died.'

His mouth twisted, and without thinking she stepped forward and gripped his hands with hers.

He glanced down at her with a sort of angry bewilderment. 'He made me promise I'd get the apartment back. You see, he still loved her.'

'And you will,' she said firmly. '*We* will.'

His eyes searched her face. 'After everything I've done and said, you still mean that?'

She nodded. 'I do.'

I do.

Her words danced inside her head and she stared past him dazedly. Behind the skyscrapers the sun was shining like a golden orb. But it was dull and shadowy in comparison to the sudden blazing realisation that burst into her head like a comet.

She loved him.

Her chest felt hot and tight. Surely she must be mistaken. But no matter how many ways she tried to deny or dispute it she knew she was right. She loved him. Why else would she care so much about his happiness? His dreams. His future.

Only she couldn't think about that now—much less share it with Rollo.

Stepping forward, she slid her arms around him, and after a moment he pulled her close, gripping her tightly. She felt his lips brush against her hair.

'I'm sorry. For what I said and what I didn't say.'

Tipping her head back, she met his gaze. 'It doesn't matter. So what happened afterwards? To your mother?'

She saw the reluctance in his eyes, felt the sudden rigidity in his arms, but after a moment, his muscles loosened.

'I haven't seen or spoken to her for seventeen years. She writes to me, but I don't read the letters. There's no point. Nothing she can say would change what she did.'

Daisy nodded. His words were an echo of what he'd said to her in the limo. He'd been lying then and she knew he was lying now. Only it didn't seem like the right time to point that out.

'But wouldn't your father have wanted her to know about the apartment?' she said carefully. 'For her to know how much he loved her?'

'She knew,' he said tersely. 'My mother left because she was having an affair. She didn't care about my father. She didn't care about me. And she didn't care about the apartment. When she walked out she took what she wanted and left everything else behind. Including me.'

Something shifted in his expression and just for a second she could see the hurt defiance of the boy who'd been abandoned. Helplessly she squeezed his arm. As an actress, she knew how powerful words could be. But what words were there that could undo this kind of damage?

'Maybe she was going to come back later, when she was settled somewhere,' she said haltingly. 'Nobody would want to take a child away from its home.'

'That might depend on the child.' His face was contorted; he sounded drained, defeated.

'She took my sister, so maybe she only really wanted a daughter.'

Daisy breathed in sharply. Suddenly it all made sense.

Thinking back to their first meeting in his office, she felt her stomach clench. He'd been angry—rightfully so, considering he'd just caught her breaking into his office—and she'd assumed his fury would dissipate. But she'd been wrong. Instead it had stayed constant, dark and churning beneath the surface, swift to rise up. And accompanied by a resistance—a refusal to let slip the mask he wore…that hard, smooth golden mask of absolute control.

And now she understood why.

He didn't trust anyone. He didn't believe in love or believe he was worthy of loving. That was why he was scared to commit and care—and why he'd arranged to marry a stranger.

Pain skewered her heart. She stared at him in silence, knowing, feeling, *loving* him. All of him. Especially his angry teenage self. She loved that Rollo as much as, if not more than, the gilded billionaire.

Desperately she searched for something to say—some words that would take the pain from his eyes and the aching misery from his voice. Words that would explain his mother's actions and make him feel better about himself.

But sometimes actions spoke louder than words. And, wrapping her arms around his neck, she kissed him gently.

CHAPTER TEN

SHIFTING BACK IN his seat, Rollo gazed down at his desk, his green eyes narrowing as they focused on the dossier in front of him. Pictured on the smooth, laminated cover was the building of his dreams. It had always been out of his reach, either through lack of finance or lately because of James Dunmore's persistent and frustrating refusal to sell. But, undeterred by the obstacles in his path, he had pursued it relentlessly. And now, the final hurdle was in sight.

Leaning forward, he ran his hand over his company's logo and breathed out softly. Tomorrow he would meet with Dunmore at his Hamptons home to discuss the sale. It was nothing short of a miracle.

And it was all down to Daisy.

Without her he would still be struggling with his image as a serial philanderer. But now his legendary lack of commitment had been rebooted—rebranded as merely the symptom of a man desperately seeking that one special woman with whom to share his life.

As far as everyone was concerned—particularly Dunmore—that woman was Daisy.

Only he knew better.

He knew it was a sham.

Or that was what it was supposed to be.

Lately though, the distinction between reality and pretence felt increasingly hazy and obscure.

He frowned. At first he'd assumed it was a consequence of cohabitation. Now though, his assumption that he could enforce any kind of boundary seemed naive, laughable. Not only had Daisy sneaked past every barrier he'd built between himself and the world, but the devastating sexual attraction they shared had effectively eroded the line between their private and public relationship.

A muscle twitched in his jaw. And now he was losing control of more than just his body. He'd never discussed his private life with anyone before, much less his past. Yet yesterday, with Daisy, he'd turned into some kind of talk-show guest. He'd told her everything—every humiliating little detail.

And she'd listened to each and every word as though it mattered. As though he mattered. And the fact that she'd done that blew his mind almost as much as her admission that he no longer needed to blackmail her into staying. Given how he'd treated her, it was more than he deserved.

He shifted uncomfortably in his seat. He'd been so ruthless—callously exploiting her love for David to get his own way. What kind of man would do that? And how would he feel if someone treated Rosamund with such contempt and disregard?

His chest grew tight.

He'd buried the pain of the past for so many years, but now all of a sudden he couldn't stop thinking about his mother and sister. Picturing Rosamund, her eyes widening with delight as he pushed her on the swing, he gritted his teeth. His anger had made it easy to concentrate on the bad but it was much harder to brush aside happy memories.

However thinking about the past was pointless. There was nothing he could do to change it. The only change that mattered right now was the fact that finally Dunmore was willing to talk terms.

Pushing back his chair, he picked up the dossier and walked purposefully across his office. Every step was bringing him closer to keeping his promise. He should be feeling excited…elated.

And yet all he could think about was what would happen afterwards.

When the contracts were signed.

And when Daisy was extraneous to his life.

Stepping out of the limousine onto the smooth paved driveway in front of Swan Creek, Daisy stopped dead. Rollo's apartment had been a shocking and awe-inspiring revelation of how the other half lived. The Dunmores' Hamptons home took that shock and awe and magnified it tenfold. It was so immense, so impressive, so imposing, that for a moment she wondered if she was actually dreaming.

But then Rollo's hand slid over hers and she knew she was awake.

'I know it doesn't look like it,' he said softly, glancing up to where James Dunmore and his wife, Emily, stood smiling on the steps. 'But to them it's home. Like the penthouse is our home.'

The warmth of his hand matched the warmth in his voice—and the warmth in her heart when he'd said 'our home.'

Since Rollo had confided in her about his past she had found it almost impossible to stop thinking about his mother's behaviour and its devastating impact on her son.

She had thought he wanted the building for profit, or simply to satisfy some baffling masculine need to conquer a business rival. Instead it was all about keeping a promise to his father.

Her throat swelled. Finally she was beginning to understand what had made him the way he was, and everything looked different now. His reticence was no longer a flaw but a teenage boy's perfectly understandable response to being abandoned by his mother. And beneath his ruthless exterior there was a man who was capable of loyalty and love. A man she wanted to get to know so much better.

But she still hadn't told him that her feelings had changed. So many times over the last few days she'd been on the verge of saying something—words had jostled inside her head, eloquent and clumsy, euphoric and tentative, all jumbling together so that it had been an effort to speak normally at all.

And an impossibility to declare her love.

But maybe that was for the best.

She knew how hard it had been for Rollo to reveal his past. Right now, faced with the chance to make a deal with Dunmore and make good on his promise, what he needed to do was focus on the present.

So, smiling up at him, she gripped his hand more tightly and together they walked up the steps towards their hosts.

Emily Dunmore was as delightful as her husband, and Daisy quickly forgot the grandeur of her surroundings.

'James tells me that you met Rollo at his office?'

They were having coffee in the sun-soaked garden behind the main house.

'I did.' Daisy smiled at the older woman. 'I was waitressing at one of his parties.'

'I was working as a hotel receptionist when I met James. He was a guest, and I thought he was the most handsome man I'd ever seen.' Emily glanced across at her husband, her eyes gleaming. '*And* the most objectionable!'

Everyone burst out laughing.

'He kept extending his stay. Every day, another night. Only he wouldn't look me in the eye when he talked to me. And he was so officious. I was spitting mad.'

Shaking his head, James leaned over and took his wife's hand. 'I was only supposed to stay one night, but I couldn't take my eyes off her. I knew she was the one. Only I'd hardly even spoken to a woman outside of my family, and this goddess at the front desk clearly thought I was repulsive. So I thought I'd try and impress her with my natural authority.'

He groaned.

Daisy laughed. 'What happened?'

'I made a complete fool of myself for ten days and then I left.'

'What?' Daisy frowned. 'Why didn't you ask her out?'

James shook his head. 'I was too scared. I walked out of that hotel and got on a bus and went two thousand miles across the country to San Francisco.'

'That's so far away...' Daisy said slowly.

His face creased. 'I didn't have a choice. My dad had got me a job working for a friend in the construction business. It was all set up.'

Emily's fingers tightened around her husband's hand. 'I thought I hated him. But I'd got used to having him around, and every time I looked up I thought he'd be there—only he wasn't.' The older woman glanced across at Daisy, sadness clouding her eyes. 'I must have cried for a week.'

James stared affectionately at his wife. 'I didn't cry. I did something far worse. I resigned after five weeks. I got another bus and went all the way back across the country and walked into that hotel and got down on one knee. I couldn't speak, I was so choked up—'

'But I knew what he was asking, and I was so happy I burst into tears.'

There were tears in Daisy's eyes too. But, glancing over at Rollo, she felt her body stiffen. He alone was dry-eyed, and there was a strange expression on his face she couldn't interpret.

Later, after lunch, the Dunmores retired, claiming tiredness and old age. But Daisy suspected it was their way of giving their young guests some space. Or maybe they still liked spending time alone, she thought wistfully as she and Rollo stretched out on the pristine white sand of the estate's private beach.

'It's so beautiful, isn't it?' she said softly.

A light breeze was blowing in across the ocean, and behind them clumps of grass quivered on the dunes beneath the hot afternoon sun.

He shrugged. 'It's not as beautiful as you.'

Daisy punched him lightly on the arm. 'We're alone now. You don't have to say that,' she said teasingly.

'I know,' he said quietly. 'But I mean it. You *are* beautiful.'

She looked up at him uncertainly. With the sun's dazzle illuminating the bones beneath his smooth golden skin, *he* was the beautiful one. But it wasn't his beauty that was occupying her thoughts. It was the slight distance in his manner. Remembering how he'd been before their lunch with James Dunmore, she nudged his arm again.

'And you're clever.' She gave him a quick reassuring smile. 'That's why tomorrow you're going to be the new owner of a prime piece of Manhattan real estate. And you'll have kept your promise to your father.'

His gaze was fixed on the ocean and her eyes fluttered anxiously over his face.

'You don't seem very happy.'

He turned to look at her, his mouth twisting into a smile. 'Of course I am. It's everything I want.'

Daisy nodded, her lips curving automatically into an answering smile. But inside a splinter of misery seemed to split her in two.

It's everything I want.

His words reverberated dully inside her head, blocking out the sound of the waves and the sudden swift beating of her heart.

It was just a throwaway remark. He probably hadn't given it a thought. But did that make it less or more true? And what had she expected him to say? That he had everything he wanted but *her*?

As casually as she could, she glanced past him out to sea. Really though, she was furtively watching his face. Since he'd confided in her she'd been doing that a lot, her eyes involuntarily searching for some change to reflect what felt like an incredible turning point in their relationship.

But what had really changed between them?

Sighing, she sifted through her memories, trying to be objective. It was true he'd shared a painful and personal fragment of his life, and for a short while at least he had seemed to need her. Not as an actress. Not for sex. But for herself.

And it had felt incredible at the time—a tiny but significant step towards trust, as though a tiger had momentarily allowed itself to be stroked.

Picking up a smooth white pebble, she sighed and laid it gently on the sand.

Of course, that was only her perception of what had happened. As far as Rollo was concerned he'd probably filed it away under 'momentary weaknesses, never to be repeated.' Certainly he'd given her no reason to think it had changed his view of either her or their relationship. Nor had he made any reference to their conversation or attempted to confide in her further.

She picked up another pebble. Whatever she thought had happened had most likely only taken place inside her head.

She sighed again.

'That's it. You're out!'

Startled, she glanced up as his fingers caught hers and firmly unclenched her hand, tipping the pebble onto the sand.

'Out of what?'

'The game. You had three strikes.' He frowned, his eyes picking over her face. 'Or in your case, three sighs! So come on—what's bothering you?'

It was the perfect opportunity to tell him the truth. That she loved him with a love that was rooted so deeply nothing could cause it to wither. That she would always have his back and would willingly go into battle for him.

But before she could reply he said quickly, 'Is it coming here? Meeting Emily?'

His eyes were startlingly green in the sunlight, his voice brusque with that anger again, and she felt her spine stiffen and the words dry in her mouth. For a moment there was no sound but the surf and the crooning cry of a distant gull, and then his fingers tightened on hers.

'Sorry.' He shook his head. 'I'm sorry. I didn't mean that to sound so forceful.' His mouth twisted. 'I know this is hard for you. James and Emily are good people, and I know how much you like them.'

Reaching into the sand, he picked up a pebble and handed it to her.

She nodded. 'They're so generous and humble. And so in love still.' Her heart gave a thump as he handed her another pebble. 'I suppose they remind me of my mum and dad.'

Shifting in the sand, she glanced over her shoulder to where the mansion could just be seen behind the sand dunes.

'Although Swan Creek is slightly bigger than the Love Shack.'

'More Love Chateau?' he said softly.

She smiled, responding to the teasing note in his voice. 'That's good. Perhaps you should try running a business.'

'I would love to run my own business, but I have this girlfriend. She takes up all my time.' Abruptly his face shifted, grew serious. 'How are they like your parents?'

His question pulled her up short. She frowned. 'I suppose they have the same sort of closeness…like they're always aware of each other.'

She bit her lip. It was the sort of closeness she'd dreamed about for years. A closeness born of trust and honesty.

'That's a *good* thing, isn't it?'

He sounded so unsure that she burst out laughing. 'I think it is.'

He nodded. 'Only you sounded like it might not be.'

His eyes searched her face so intently that suddenly she felt shy, self-conscious.

She shrugged. 'It's what I've always wanted.' She gave him a swift, tight smile. 'But you can't always get what you want—'

'Just what you need?'

Their eyes met.

I need you, she thought helplessly.

Instead she nodded. 'Which is why you can buy chocolate and stationery everywhere.'

He groaned. 'Chocolate, I get. But stationery?'

She laughed. 'I love notebooks. And pens.'

'That stops as soon as we're married.'

'Is that your version of a prenup?' She raised an eyebrow. 'Then you're going to need a lawyer, because stationery is non-negotiable.'

His eyes gleamed. 'In that case I might have a few non-negotiables of my own.'

Watching his expression grow blunt and tight, she shook her head. 'You have a one-track mind, Rollo Fleming.'

'Only with you. And if we weren't being forced into a state of celibacy—'

'It's only been a couple of hours.'

Glancing at his watch, he grinned. 'Five hours and seventeen minutes.'

It was stupid, but the fact that he was counting the minutes made her feel ridiculously happy. The urge to tell him so was almost overwhelming. But instead she shook her head.

'Only another day to go and then we'll be back at the apartment and we can do whatever we want, wherever we want.'

He ran his finger slowly down her arm. 'I thought *I* was the cold-blooded one,' he said softly.

She hesitated, and then took a breath, fear and hope tangling inside her. 'Of course, you could just tell James the truth. About why you want the building.'

He didn't reply—just stared past her at the tumbling waves so that she thought he hadn't heard her.

Finally he turned and gave her a small, polite smile. 'I don't think that will work.'

'Why not?' There was a knot in her stomach. Biting her lip, she tried to keep her voice steady. 'He wants to sell to someone with family values. You only want that building to keep a promise to your father.'

He was still smiling, but his fingers felt suddenly rigid against her skin. 'And how do I explain us? What "family values" does our sham engagement represent?'

There was no easy way to answer that.

She drew in a deep breath. 'It was just an idea.'

'Are you having second thoughts?'

His eyes on hers were dark and tormented. She shook her head, bewildered by the sudden shift in his manner. 'Of course not. I like the Dunmores, and I don't like lying to them. But my loyalty's with you, Rollo. It will always be.'

He nodded, and some of the tension in him eased. '*Always* as in *for ever*?'

She nodded. 'I know how much this deal means to you.'

She stared at him, blindsided by longing and hope and fear, wanting to speak, to go further, to risk everything. But instead she wrapped her fingers more tightly around his and squeezed.

'It means a lot to me too.'

She swallowed; her voice was shaking, and the beating of her heart was drowning out the sound of the waves. Only it didn't matter. All that mattered was finding the words to reach him. To make him understand. Even if that meant making herself vulnerable.

'I care about you and I want you to be happy.'

His face was blank and unsmiling. She held her breath as he stared at her in silence, and then finally he said quietly, 'I want you to be happy too.'

She could hear the struggle in his voice. But she knew how far they had come for him to admit even that much. And right now it was enough. Glancing down at the heart of pebbles she'd made in the sand, she breathed out softly. She had enough love for both of them.

'In that case let's go back to our room. We've got at least an hour before dinner.'

His dark, hungry gaze fixed on her face, tugging at her like a fish hook, so that suddenly she was breathless with desire, her body impossibly hot and tight. And then, without warning, he pulled her to her feet and hand in hand they ran towards the dunes.

The following morning, James Dunmore invited Rollo to his study to go over the proposal, and Daisy joined Emily on a guided tour of the estate's lavish gardens.

'So is this the actual creek?'

They were standing on a small wooden bridge above a grass-edged stream.

Emily smiled. 'It is. And those are the swans.'

As Daisy turned two immaculate swans glided across the water, their curving necks as delicate as white bone china cup handles.

'They were here when we bought the land. Just the two of them and a tiny run-down fisherman's hut.'

'How do you know they're the same pair?' Daisy asked curiously.

'The local wildfowl centre keeps track of the birds. And, of course, swans mate for life.'

Daisy nodded, a pang of guilt clutching at her stomach. It felt wrong to deceive such good people. But she had promised to be loyal to Rollo and she would keep her promise.

They had lunch behind the house, beneath a beautiful canopy of the palest purple wisteria.

'Emily and I thought we should have champagne.' James smiled at his wife. 'To celebrate your engagement.'

'How lovely!' Daisy managed to say. But she couldn't keep her eyes from sliding towards Rollo.

'That's very kind of you both.' His smile was dazzling and irresistible, and she forced her lips upwards into a smile of her own.

'I wonder, James, would it be premature to celebrate another forthcoming union?' Rollo spoke easily, master of the situation. 'Between our two companies?'

There was a short silence, and then James nodded slowly. 'Yes. Let's make it a double celebration.'

So that was it, then, Daisy thought dully. Everything she and Rollo had worked so hard to make happen had happened. Why, then, did she feel as though it was over before it had begun?

Suddenly she wanted to cry. But instead she smiled and laughed and drank champagne and ate her meal, focusing on every mouthful until finally it was over.

She lay down her spoon and looked up at her hostess. 'That was delicious, Emily. Thank you.'

Emily smiled. 'I think we'll take coffee in the gazebo. It's so hot, and there's always a lovely light breeze there.'

Five minutes later, James handed Daisy a cup of coffee, a smile creasing his face. 'You must come and stay with us after the wedding.'

They had moved to the gazebo and, as Emily had predicted, it was cooler and more comfortable to sit there, with the breeze coming in from the ocean.

'Rollo's looked at buying a property out here before, and New York's no place to bring up a family.'

A family!

Daisy nodded mechanically. But her mind was blank. They had never discussed a family, and she had no idea of the correct response.

But rolling her eyes at her husband, Emily leaned forward and said quickly, 'James! They're not even married yet!' She turned to Daisy. 'I'm sure you and Rollo will want to enjoy some time together in the city.'

James frowned. 'Of course.' He glanced apologetically at Daisy. 'I'm sorry. Forgive me, I'm an old man, I work on a different time scale to you and Rollo.'

Daisy nodded. The effort of smiling was making her face ache. 'P-please don't apologise. It's just we've never talked about children. We didn't have to… I mean, we won't be—'

She glanced across at Rollo, expecting him to smooth over her confusion. But he said nothing—just stared at her, an expression on his face she couldn't fathom.

There was a short, strained silence, and then Rollo cleared his throat.

Daisy's eyes were pleading with him. She needed his help—needed him to step up and save the day. Save the deal that was the culmination of years of hard work.

He'd never wanted anything more.

But now that it was within his grasp he realised that it wasn't worth the sacrifice. Wasn't worth the lies and deceit. And the compromise.

'We haven't discussed children.'

'Of course not. Couples these days tend to wait—' Emily began.

But he shook his head. 'I wish that were the reason, Emily.' He paused, his face like stone. 'But it's not. Daisy and I didn't discuss children because it's not you, James, who's working on a different time scale. It's me.'

His eyes met Daisy's and suddenly she knew what he was about to do.

'No, Rollo—'

Reaching over, he took her hand and squeezed it, his eyes greener and brighter than she had ever seen them.

'It never would have worked.'

Abruptly he dropped her hand and, standing up, he turned towards James, his face fierce.

'It's not her fault. I made her do it.'

'I don't understand, Rollo.' The older man stood up too. 'What time scale? And what did you make Daisy do?'

But he *did* understand, Daisy thought miserably. She could see it in the way his jaw was tightening, and in the hardening of his eyes.

'It's a fake. *We're* a fake.'

Even though she'd known what he was about to say, Daisy flinched at Rollo's choice of words. But it wasn't just what he said that hurt. The relief in his voice was so painful to hear that she had to grip the arms of her chair to stop herself from crying out loud.

'You'd do this? You'd lie about a marriage? About being in love?' James shook his head, anger vying with disbelief.

Rollo shrugged. 'You wouldn't sell to me so I became someone else. And I needed Daisy to help me. To be my wife.'

She swallowed, the sound echoing inside her head. His eyes were staring at hers directly, as though they were alone, and the intimacy of his gaze was so at odds with the brutality of what he was saying that she thought she might throw up.

'How long were you going to carry on with this charade?' James asked coldly.

Rollo stared past him. 'A year,' he said finally. 'But I see now that a year was too long. Even a month has been too big a sacrifice to make.'

She breathed in sharply. It felt as if she'd been stabbed.

'You've gone too far, Rollo.'

James looked shocked, and for some reason that made everything so much worse.

'The deal is off. Over.'

Rollo nodded. For what felt like a lifetime he stood and stared at her, his gaze clear and calm, with the same acceptance of a gladiator stepping into the Colosseum. Then, turning, he walked away, his footsteps swift and light against the stone slabs.

'Please…' Daisy turned towards the Dunmores. 'You have to stop him. I know we did a bad thing, but he did it for the right reasons.'

James Dunmore stared at her in bewilderment. 'I don't understand. He made you a part of this, and yet you want to help him.'

'Yes, I do.' Her voice was filling with tears.

'But why?'

'I know why.'

Stepping forward, Emily Dunmore took Daisy's hand.

'It's because you love him, isn't it?'

'Yes, I do. But it doesn't matter anymore, does it?'

And as Emily pulled her into her arms she gave in to the misery and the pain and wept.

CHAPTER ELEVEN

FOUR WEEKS LATER, Daisy was still not entirely sure how she'd got back to New York. After Rollo had walked out, the Dunmores had refused to blame her for her part in the deception, and she had managed to stay calm while James had teased the whole story from her.

But in the face of their kindness, she hadn't been able to stop herself from bursting into tears again.

And it had been a relief to cry.

To grieve for what might have been.

But it had been more of a relief to get home.

For the first few days—a week, even—she had wept just like Emily Dunmore had. Then finally the tears had stopped.

Maybe she had no more tears left, she thought as she wiped down the tables in her parents' restaurant with swift, automatic efficiency. Or, more likely, the time for crying was over.

Now it was time to start living again. That was pretty much what David had said to her. She had visited him in rehab and told him the truth. And, just as she had done when he'd admitted his gambling problem, he'd pulled her into his arms and told her he'd be there for her.

Back at home, her father had handed her an apron and suggested she take a few shifts at the restaurant. Neither he nor her mother had pressed her for details. They'd simply welcomed her home and offered comfort and support.

And, of course, a job.

Glancing across the restaurant, Daisy almost smiled. Unbelievably, and for the first time in her life, she was actually enjoying waitressing. There was something comforting in the repetition of clearing tables, taking orders and making small talk with people. Better still it was nothing like her life in Manhattan.

It was a month since James Dunmore's limousine had dropped her at her parents' house. A month since she had last seen or spoken to Rollo. Not that she'd expected to hear from him. She'd known the minute he'd turned and walked away that she would be deleted from his life. And so she'd done the same, ruthlessly weeding out everything he'd ever given her.

Her heartbeat leapfrogged. She had given her ring to James and he had promised to return it to Rollo. Given their history, she hadn't wanted there to be any risk of confusion. Or even the slightest possibility that she might have to see him again.

Although there was no chance of that happening. In his own words, the month they'd spent together had been a month too long.

The pain caught her off guard and, lifting up the condiments, she ran her cloth over the mustard and ketchup bottles, grateful for the distraction of physical activity.

Not that she was going to give in to the pain. She was stronger now. Sadder too. But determined to make her life matter. Which was why, when she'd saved up enough money, she was going to university to study English. She'd always wanted to go to university but had never thought she was good enough, and being an actress had been a legitimate way to disguise that self-doubt.

But she was done with being other people. Now she was going to be herself, and if that meant failing and facing up to her fears, then so be it. There was no shame in trying hard or finding something a challenge. Only in lying to others and oneself.

Her lips curved upwards. It wasn't quite a smile—she wasn't there yet—but maybe when David came home tomorrow she'd be ready. Although, knowing her twin, he'd probably already guessed. After all, he knew her better than anyone. As well as he knew himself.

And just like that, her head began to spin, her words raising a memory of another restaurant, a pair of green eyes, and a deeper voice than her own saying softly, *'You're different. I know you as well as I know myself.'*

'Are we done here, Daisy?'

She jerked her head up, heart pounding. Her dad was standing in the doorway.

Outside in the street, the traffic lights had changed to green and cars were streaming over the crossroads and somehow it soothed her. Life carried on; her life too, and it was a good life. She had a loving family, a job and now she had a future.

Turning towards her father, she nodded. 'Yeah, I'm done. Let's go home.'

'What time is David getting here again?'

Daisy groaned. 'I told you, Mom. He doesn't need a lift. He wants to get a cab.'

Her mom frowned. 'And you think that's okay?'

'Of course. He caught a train from New York. I think he can manage a ten-minute cab ride.'

Her mother's face cleared. 'In that case I'm going to nip across to Sarah's to borrow her square tin. Then I can make the cake and you can ice it.'

Two hours later, Daisy was sitting at the table in her parents' backyard, trying to ice a message onto the top of her brother's favourite triple-layered chocolate-mousse cake.

He wasn't due home for at least an hour. Which was lucky, she thought seconds later as, glancing down, she saw that she'd made the letters far too big, so there was only room to fit 'Welcome Ho' across the top of the cake.

She sighed. Why was she doing the icing anyway? Her skill set in the kitchen was pretty much limited to peeling and slicing.

Dropping the icing bag, she looked up towards the kitchen window. 'Mom! *Mom!*' she yelled. 'I think you should do this. Otherwise it's just going to be a mess!'

From somewhere inside the house, she heard the doorbell ring and, rolling her eyes, she cursed softly. *Great!* It was probably Sarah. Now her mom would chat for hours and then it would be all Daisy's fault when the cake looked as if it had been iced by a hyperactive five-year-old.

Except it wasn't a woman speaking. It was a man. Her body stilled. And, judging by the excitement in her mother's voice, it was not just *any* man. It was her brother. Damn, David! It was so typical of him to arrive early.

But suddenly she was grinning, her face splitting from ear to ear, and, jumping to her feet, she ran up the steps towards the house.

And stopped.

It wasn't David walking slowly across the deck.

It was Rollo.

Time had numbed her pain. But now it returned, more acute and intense than ever, together with a panic that seeped over her like melted tar, gluing her body to the spot.

'Hi.'

At the sound of his voice her skin seemed to shrivel over her bones. It was the voice she heard at night when she slept, and in daytime whenever her mind was idle.

It was a voice she'd learnt to love. A voice that made her want to run and never stop running.

'How did you find out where I lived?'

Her heart was turning over and over in her chest like one of those mechanical toy monkeys. She wanted to touch him so badly it hurt. To reach out and caress that beautiful face. To hold him close and listen to him breathe. Only she couldn't. He wasn't hers to touch or caress or hold. He never had been.

'I asked David.'

His eyes were fixed on hers, and the expression on his face was nothing like his usual cool self-assurance. He looked hesitant, uncertain, like a man dying of thirst who thought he was seeing water for the first time in days.

She shook her head in shock. 'I don't believe you.' The thought of David betraying her hurt almost as much as Rollo's sudden reappearance in her life. 'He wouldn't do that.'

'I didn't give him a choice.'

Anger surged through, washing away the hurt and fear. She stepped towards him, fists curling. 'What did you do? Did you threaten him?'

'No. Of course not.'

'Why "of course"? That's what you *do*, isn't it?'

He ran a hand over his face and for the first time she noticed the dark shadows under his eyes, the slight hollowness in his cheeks. But she stonewalled the flicker of concern, watching in silence as he struggled for control.

'I just told him I needed to see you,' he said finally.

She stared at him, eyes widening with disbelief. 'You're joking, right? He knows what you did. He knows you blackmailed and humiliated and abandoned me. He wouldn't want you anywhere near me.'

Tears filled her throat and for a moment she couldn't speak, couldn't even look at him. But, no matter how hurt she was inside, she wasn't going to let herself fall apart in front of Rollo Fleming.

'Get out of this yard and stay away from me. And stay away from my family.'

'Daisy, please. I want—'

She flinched at the rawness in his voice. But as he took a step towards her she backed away, her hand raised up like a shield.

'It doesn't matter what you want, Rollo. I can't give it to you. Don't you understand? There's nothing left. Before I met you, I had a home and a job. It was only a room in my brother's apartment and a job I hated, but it was mine. It was *my* life. And you forced me to give it all up.'

She was fighting to breathe and, despite the heat of the day, she felt cold—icy cold. And so alone. Just seeing him again reminded her of the pain of his absence. Of how badly she missed him.

She stared at his face. His beauty broke her heart.

Or it would have done if he hadn't already broken it.

Crossing her arms in front of her chest, trying to contain the pain and the misery, she lifted her chin. 'I gave you my loyalty and you told me it was worthless. You said being with me was a sacrifice you weren't prepared to make.'

'That's not what I meant.' He shook his head, his eyes suddenly too bright, his voice strained. 'I wasn't talking about my sacrifice. I was talking about yours.'

His shoulders rose and fell.

'What do you mean?' she said shakily.

'When you told me at the apartment that I didn't need to blackmail you…that you would help me get the building… I knew you meant it. I knew you'd be there for me.'

'So why did you throw it all away, then?' she stormed at him. 'We were drinking champagne. Celebrating our engagement and your deal. And then you told James it was all a sham.'

She bit her lip. Even though fury burned like fire beneath her skin, she couldn't stop herself from caring about him. About the promise he'd made and now irretrievably broken.

Some of her anger faded. 'I'm sorry you lost the building.'

'You're *sorry*?' He frowned, his mouth twisting. 'How? Why?'

She looked past him, trying to sift through the tangle of her emotions to something neutral.

'I know how much it meant to you.'

He nodded, his face distant and shadowed. 'It's what I wanted my whole life. But it doesn't matter anymore.'

With an effort, she forced herself to sound cool, pragmatic. 'You did your best.'

His head jerked up, and the air seemed to tremble around him.

'You don't understand. I don't care about the deal. I don't care about the building or about the promise I made. I care about *you*.'

Her heart lurched, and beneath her feet the ground seemed to lurch too.

'No. You don't get to say that. Not here, not now.'

The tears she had been trying to hold back began to fall and angrily she wiped her face.

'I'm not crying because I care,' she managed finally. 'So don't think I am. I'm crying because I'm angry. With you.'

'I know. And you have every right to be angry. I treated you so badly.' His voice cracked and he breathed out raggedly. 'I wish I could go back and stop myself behaving like that.'

'You hurt me,' she raged at him. 'Humiliated me. Discarded me like I was last year's overcoat. You didn't just walk out on your deal. You walked out on me. You left me—'

Suddenly she couldn't bear it any more. She wanted him gone.

'Just go, Rollo, please.'

He shook his head. 'I can't.'

'Why not? Why did you even come here, anyway?'

He reached into his pocket, fumbling inside, and then suddenly she blinked, a flash of gold and green momentarily blinding her.

'Where did you get that?

It was the ring he had given her. The ring she had returned.

'From James. He came to see me. He gave it to me. He also gave me a pretty hard time. Told me a few home truths.' His face was drawn. 'I deserved them.' He drew a steadying breath. 'He told me I was a fool for letting you go. That you stood up for me after I left.'

Her cheeks grew warm, and she looked away. 'I did. Which makes *me* the fool, not you.'

'Daisy…'

He spoke quietly, but something in his voice tugged at her heart and she turned reluctantly, her pulse leaping frantically in her throat.

'He said you loved me.'

There was a moment of silence.

'Was that true?'

His skin was stretched tight across his cheekbones.

A shiver passed through her, but she couldn't lie to Rollo—no matter how much it hurt to tell the truth.

She nodded mutely.

'And what about now? Is it still true now?'

His eyes bored into her, reaching inside so there was nowhere to hide.

She nodded again.

His chest heaved, and he breathed out shakily. 'Then marry me.'

His voice was so quiet she could barely hear him. But his words punctured her skin like nails.

She stared at him numbly, her brain frozen. 'You don't want to marry me, Rollo. You never did. I was just a means to an end.'

'At the start.'

His eyes were feverish and she could see that he was trembling, his whole body shaking like a marathon runner.

'But then it changed. *I* changed. Only I didn't know how to tell you.'

His face was tight with emotion.

'Tell me what?' she whispered.

'That I love you,' he said hoarsely.

And the last of her grief and pain was forgotten.

'I don't deserve you, Daisy. But I love you. And I want you to be my wife. For real, this time. That's why I had to leave. I knew you hated lying to the Dunmores. But you would have kept doing it—for me. And I couldn't bear that, so I had no choice. Or rather, I *had* a choice. And I chose you.'

Her heart tumbled over in her chest and a wild, dizzying happiness that was tinged with sadness swelled inside her.

'It was your dream. You gave up your dream for me.'

He shook his head.

'My dream's right here.'

Reaching out, he took her hands.

'And I have a confession. You were right. After I told James about my father he agreed to sell to me. We signed the contracts this morning. That's why I couldn't come before. I wanted there to be no confusion about why I want you to be my wife.'

His expression was so earnest, so eager, that Daisy couldn't decide if she wanted to laugh or cry. 'So I'm just a bonus?'

He laughed unsteadily. 'I'd say yes, but that icing bag looks dangerous!'

She smiled. 'In my hands it's a lethal weapon. Take a look at the cake if you don't believe me.'

His face shifted, grew serious. 'You're not a bonus,

Daisy. You're the jackpot. I love you so much. I'll always love you.'

'*Always* as in *for ever*?' she said shakily.

Nodding, he gently lifted up her hand and slid the ring onto her finger.

For a moment they stared at one another in silence, like survivors from a storm. Then, fiercely, he pulled her against him, burying his face in her hair, his breath warm and shaky against her throat.

'I was so scared,' he whispered.

Gently, she stroked his cheek.

'Of what?'

'That James had got it wrong. That maybe you wouldn't forgive me.'

Her heart swelled protectively. 'I was scared too. Scared I'd lost you.'

'That won't happen. It can't. You're part of me. The truest part.'

He held her gaze. The emotion in his eyes was raw, naked, unguarded; and she loved him more than ever for being able to show his vulnerability and need for her.

She rested her cheek against his, soaking in his love. Finally, she sighed.

'We should probably tell my parents what's going on. They must be freaking out by now.' She frowned. 'I wonder why they haven't come outside…'

Rollo screwed up his face. 'That might be my fault. I may have been a little…*impassioned* when I was trying to explain myself. I haven't really done the whole parent thing in a long time.'

She bit her lip, a question forming in her mind. Only before she could ask it he pulled her close—so close that she could feel the beating of his heart.

'I've been so angry for so long. With my past. With

my mother. You made me face that anger and face my fears. But—'

'You need to see your mother,' she said gently. 'And Rosamund.'

He nodded. 'Yes.'

'I'm glad.' Watching his beautiful mouth curve upwards, she smiled teasingly. 'I always wanted a sister.' Her fingers curled into his shirt. 'But nowhere near as much as I want you.'

And then she pulled him closer and they kissed, losing themselves in each other, in desire, and in longing and need and love.

EPILOGUE

'YOU ARE KEEPING an eye on the time, aren't you, Dad?' Taking one last look at her reflection in the full-length mirror, Daisy glanced anxiously at her father's face. 'I don't want to be late.'

Her father shook his head. 'You're not late.' He paused, his eyes softening. 'But even if you were, you'd be more than worth the wait. You look beautiful, Daisy. Truly lovely.'

She smiled. 'You're my *dad*, Dad! You're supposed to think that.'

'Yes, I am.' Leaning back against the sofa, her father smiled back at her. 'But that doesn't make it any less true. And if you don't believe me, wait until Rollo sees you.'

Picturing her husband-to-be's reaction, Daisy felt her skin grown warm. She knew just how he would look at her...the way his green eyes would narrow and darken. Her heart contracted. Last night he had stayed in Manhattan, and she had travelled to the Hamptons with the rest of the wedding party. And even though it had been less than a day she missed him.

As though reading her thoughts, her father reached out and squeezed her hand. 'Not long to go,' he said quietly.

Daisy nodded. Her dad was right. In less than an hour, and exactly one year after they'd met in his office, she would become Mrs Daisy Fleming.

They had decided on a small, intimate ceremony on the beach at Swan Creek. Daisy had always loved the idea of being married barefoot, with just the sound of waves instead of music, but she'd expected Rollo to want some huge high-profile society wedding.

He'd been adamant. The wedding was not for show. Only

those nearest and dearest to them would be invited: her parents and David, his mother and Rosamund, and, of course, the Dunmores. And now it was really happening.

She shivered with nervous excitement.

'Are you cold?' It was her father's turn to look anxious. 'Do you need a cardigan or something?'

Dropping her gaze to her elegant white silk slip dress, Daisy laughed. 'Honestly, Dad! I'm about to get married. I'm not going to wear a cardigan.' She rolled her eyes. 'It's not even cold.'

It wasn't. A light breeze was blowing in from the ocean, and even though it was early evening the air was pleasantly warm.

'Must be wedding nerves, then.' Her father spoke lightly, but there was a glimmer of concern in his eyes.

She shook her head. 'I've never been more certain of anything, Dad.'

And with good reason.

A lot had happened over the last year. In collaboration with James Dunmore, Rollo had renovated his old apartment block into modern but affordable family homes, and Daisy had successfully completed her first year at university. More important, though, he had worked hard to forgive his mother, and together he and Daisy had spent time getting to know her and Rosamund. They weren't quite a family yet, but there was love and the beginnings of trust.

Her father cleared his throat. 'You really love him,' he said quietly. 'And it is real, isn't it?'

She nodded. 'I do. And it is.'

As part of her resolution to live her life as honestly as possible, she had told her parents everything that had happened with Rollo. David too had admitted his gambling problems, and it had been hard for her mother and father to hear the truth. But after their initial shock their love and support had remained unchanged.

'Of course, I'm just your dad, so I've never believed anyone could deserve you.' He smiled. 'But I don't think I've ever a seen a man so in love.'

She nodded, her heart pounding, suddenly overwhelmed by emotion.

'Right, then!' Her dad stood up and held out the simple posy of white daisies she'd chosen as a bridal bouquet. 'Are you ready?'

In reply, she slipped her arm through his.

Outside, the sun was starting to set, lighting the sky with a pinkish-gold haze.

Rosamund, her bridesmaid, was waiting at the edge of the beach, eyes bright with tears. 'Oh, Daisy, you look beautiful.'

But there was only time for a quick hug and then they were walking over the dunes towards the sea.

And there Daisy stopped, covering her mouth with her hand.

In front of her, all across the sand, lanterns glowed in the fading light. Lanterns arranged in the shape of a daisy. And standing beside the minister, in the centre of the petals, was Rollo—so golden and handsome in his white shirt and cream linen trousers that she could hardly breathe with loving him so much.

As she walked towards him he stepped forward, and she saw the love in the eyes.

'You made it.'

His voice was hoarse with emotion, and as he took her hand, she realised he was shaking as much as she was.

'*We* made it,' she said softly.

Later, after they'd exchanged their vows and mingled with their guests, he took her by the hand and led her away. As they stood beside the ocean, his eyes fixed on hers so intently that suddenly her pulse was leaping like the waves.

'Are you happy?'

His hand brushed against her bare shoulder, and a surge of desire rippled inside her.

'I've never been happier,' she said truthfully.

He stepped closer, his other hand curving around her waist. 'I love you, Daisy.'

'I love you too,' she whispered. 'I always will.'

'*Always* as in *for ever*,' he said fiercely, and as she nodded he wrapped his arms around her and kissed her as the sun set slowly behind them.

* * * * *

HIS MERCILESS
MARRIAGE BARGAIN

JANE PORTER

CHAPTER ONE

RACHEL BERN STOOD outside the imposing doors of the Palazzo Marcello shivering, the wind grabbing at her black coat and ponytail, sending both flying.

Overhead, thick gray clouds blanketed the sky and the rising tides sent water surging over the banks of the lagoon, wetting the streets of Venice, but the stormy weather wasn't so different from her weather in Seattle. She'd grown up with rain and damp. This morning she wasn't shivering from cold, but nerves.

This could go so very wrong. It could blow up in her face, leaving her and Michael in an even worse situation, but she was at her wit's end. If this didn't get Giovanni Marcello's attention, nothing would. She'd tried everything else, tried every other form of communication, but every attempt resulted in silence and the silence was destructive. Crushing. She was taking a huge risk, but what else could she do?

Giovanni Marcello, an Italian billionaire, was also one of the most reclusive businessmen in Italy. He rarely socialized. He had no direct email or phone, and when Rachel finally reached Signor Marcello's front office management, they were noncommittal about relaying messages to the CEO of the holding company, Marcello SpA. And so she was here, at the Palazzo Marcello in Venice, the family's home for the past two hundred years. Until the turn of the twentieth century, the Marcellos had been a shrewd, successful manufacturing family that had earned its place in society through hard work and wealth, but in the past forty years, the family had expanded from manufacturing and construction into real estate and, under the helm of Giovanni Marcello, investing in world markets. The Marcello fortune had quadrupled through Giovanni's management, and they had become one of the most powerful and influential families in Italy.

Thirty-eight-year-old Giovanni continued to head up the holding company based in Rome, but she'd just discovered through her hired investigator that he rarely put in an appearance at the office, choosing instead to work from Venice. Which was why she was now here on his doorstep, exhausted and jet-lagged from traveling with a six-month-old baby, but determined. He couldn't ignore her any longer. There would be no more shutting her out, or more importantly, Michael.

Heart aching, eyes stinging, she glanced down at the bundle in her arms, the baby thankfully finally sleeping, and silently apologized for what she was about to do. "It's for your sake," she whispered, bringing him close to her chest and giving a light squeeze. "And I'm not going far, I promise."

Even in his sleep, the baby wriggled in protest. She smiled ruefully, easing her hold, but she couldn't ease the guilt. She hadn't slept since they left Seattle, but then, she hadn't slept in months, not since she'd become his full-time caregiver. At six months he should be ready to sleep through the night, but maybe he felt how unsettled she was, or maybe he was missing his mother...

Rachel's eyes stung and her heart smarted. If only she'd done more for Juliet after Michael's birth, if only she'd understood how distraught she had been...

But Rachel couldn't turn back time, and so she was here, about to hand him over to his father's family. Not forever, of course, just for a few minutes, but to make a point. They needed help. She was broke and about to lose her job, and it wasn't right, not when his father's family could, and should, help.

Swallowing, she raised her hand and knocked firmly

on the door, and then, in case the knock couldn't be heard inside, she pressed the button for the doorbell mounted on the wall. Did the bell even work, she wondered? Had anyone heard her?

Between the wind and the lapping of water and the voices of tourists and travelers on the lagoon, she wasn't sure if anyone was stirring within the palazzo. She knew she was being watched, though, and not from within the building, but from the photographers stationed outside. There was one across the lagoon and another on a balcony of an adjacent building, as well as another parked in a tethered gondola. She'd seen the cameras as she stepped off the water taxi and was glad to see them as she'd been the one to tip them off, teasing the various media outlets that something significant was happening today, something to do with a Marcello baby.

It was easy enough to accomplish when one's job hinged on publicity, marketing and customer relations for Aero-Dynamics, one of the largest airline manufacturers in the world. Normally her PR efforts were to attract new, affluent customers—sheikhs, tycoons, sports figures, celebrities—by showcasing AeroDynamics sleek jet designs and luxurious interiors, but today she needed the media because they could apply pressure for her. Their photos would draw attention, and subsequent public scrutiny, and Giovanni Marcello would not like it. He valued his privacy and would take immediate steps to curtail the attention. But before he did that, she needed to make sure that she got the right action and the proper results. She didn't want to shame the Marcellos, or alienate them. She needed them on her side—correction, on Michael's side—but her actions now might do the opposite and push them further away—

No, she couldn't go there. She wouldn't think that way. Giovanni Marcello had to accept Michael, and he would, once he saw how much his nephew looked like his brother.

Rachel lifted her hand to knock again, but the door swung open before she could rap a second time. A tall thin elderly man stood in the doorway. Shadows stretched behind him. From the doorstep, the space appeared cavernous, with a glinting of an ornate chandelier high overhead.

She looked from the grand light fixture to the elderly man. He wore a plain dark suit, a very simple suit, and she suspected he wasn't family, but someone who worked for the Marcellos. "Signor Marcello, *per favore*," she said calmly, crisply, praying her Italian would be understood. She'd practiced the phrase on the flight, repeating the simple request over and over to ensure she could deliver the words with the right note of authority.

"*Signor Marcello non è disponibile*," he answered flatly.

Her brows furrowed as she tried to decipher what he'd said. *Non* was not. *Disponibile* could mean just about anything but she sensed it was a negative, either way.

"*È lui non a casa?*" she stumbled, struggling to remember the words, not at all sure she was getting the tense right, or the correct words, never mind the words in the proper order. Her little phrase book only gave her so many options.

"*No. Addio.*"

She understood those words. *No,* and *goodbye.*

She moved forward swiftly before he could close the door on her, using her low-heeled boot to keep the door ajar.

"*Il bambino Michael Marcello*," she said in Italian, before switching to English as she thrust the infant into the old man's arms. "Please tell Signor Marcello that Michael will need a bottle when he wakes."

She drew the diaper bag strap from her shoulder and set the bulging bag down on the doorstep at the man's feet. "He will also need a diaper change, probably before the bottle," she added, fighting to keep her voice even, almost impossible when her heart raced and she already itched to reach out and wrench the baby back. "Everything he needs is in the bag, including his schedule to help him adjust. If there are questions, my hotel information is in the bag, along with my cell number."

And then her voice did break and her throat sealed closed and she turned away, walking quickly before the tears could fall.

It's for Michael, she told herself, swiping tears as she hurried toward the canal. *Be brave. Be strong. You're doing this for him.*

The baby wouldn't be away from her for more than a few minutes because she fully expected Giovanni Marcello to come after her. If not now, then surely at her hotel, which was less than five minutes away by water taxi, as she'd left all her contact details in the diaper bag.

And yet, every step she took carried her farther from the palazzo and closer to the water taxi waiting for her, and now with Michael out of her arms, she felt hollow and empty, every instinct in her screaming for her to turn around and go back and have this out with Giovanni, face-to-face.

But what if Giovanni refused to come to the door? How was she to force Giovanni out for the necessary conversation?

The old man shouted something, his voice thin and sharp. She didn't understand, but one word did stand out. *Polizia.* Was he threatening to call the police? She wasn't surprised if he was. It's what she'd do if someone just abandoned a six-month-old infant to her care. Numb and heartsick, she kept her focus on the water taxi tethered in the canal. The driver was watching her and she waved, signaling that she was ready to go.

Seconds later, a hand seized her upper arm. The fingers gripped her tightly, the hold painful. "Ouch!" Rachel winced at the painful hold. "Let go."

"Stop running," the deep male voice ground out, the

voice as hard as the punishing grip, his English perfect with just the slightest accent.

She turned around, the persistent wind having loosened dark strands from her ponytail, making it hard to see him through the tangle of hair. "I'm not running," she said fiercely, trying to free herself, but he stood close, his grip unrelenting. "Can you give me some space, please?"

"Not a chance, Miss Bern."

She knew then who this tall man was, and a shiver raced through her as she pushed long strands of hair behind her ears. Giovanni Marcello wasn't just tall, he was impressively broad through the shoulders, with thick black hair, light eyes and high cheekbones above a firm, unsmiling mouth. She'd seen pictures of him on the internet. There weren't many, as he didn't attend a lot of social events like his brother Antonio had, but in every photo he was elegantly dressed, impeccably groomed. Polished. Gleaming. Hard.

He looked even harder in person. His light eyes—an icy blue—glittered down at her and his strong, chiseled features were set. Grim.

She felt a flutter of fear. It crossed her mind that beneath the groomed exterior was something dark and brooding, something that struck her as not entirely civilized.

Rachel took a step back, needing her distance even more now.

"You said you weren't running," he growled.

"I'm not going anywhere, and there's no need for you to be on top of me."

"Are you unwell, Miss Bern? Are you having a breakdown?"

"Why would you ask that?"

"Because you've just abandoned a child on my doorstep."

"He's not being abandoned. You're his uncle."

"I strongly suggest you retrieve the child before the police arrive."

"Let the police come. At least then the world will know the truth."

He arched a black brow. "So you *are* unwell."

"I'm perfectly well. In fact, I couldn't be better. You have no idea how difficult it has been to locate you. Months of investigation, not to mention money I couldn't afford to spend on a private investigator, but at least we are here now, face-to-face, ready to discuss new responsibilities."

"The only thing I have to say to you is collect the child—"

"Your nephew."

"And return home before this becomes unpleasant for everybody."

"It's already unpleasant for me. Your help is desperately needed."

"You, and he, are not my problem."

"Michael is a Marcello. He's your late brother's only child, and he should be protected and provided for by his family."

"That is not going to happen."

"I think it will."

His eyes narrowed, the icy blue irises partially hidden by dense black lashes. "You are deliberately trying to provoke me."

"And why not? You've done nothing but irritate and provoke me for the past few months. You had many opportunities to reply to my emails and phone calls, but you couldn't be bothered to reach out, so now I'm returning to you what is yours." Which wasn't actually true—she wasn't leaving Michael here, but she didn't have to let him know that.

"You're definitely not sound if you're abandoning your sister's son—"

"And Antonio's," she interrupted tautly. "If you recall

your lessons in biology, conception requires a sperm and an egg, and in this instance it's Juliet's and Antonio's—" She paused, grinding down to hold back the rest of the hot painful words, words that ached and kept her from sleeping and eating. Juliet had always been foolish and impractical, her dreams littered with hearts, flowers, expensive sports cars and wealthy boyfriends. "The DNA paperwork is inside his diaper bag," she continued. "You'll find his medical records and everything you need to know about his routine in there, too. I've done my part. Now it's your turn." She gave him a brittle nod and turned away, grateful for the water taxi that still waited for her.

He caught her once more, this time by the nape, warm fingers sliding beneath her ponytail to wrap around her neck. "You're going nowhere, Miss Bern, at least not without that child." His voice had dropped, deepening, and she shuddered at the sensation burning through her.

His grip was in no way painful but her skin tingled from head to toe. It was almost as if he'd plugged her into an electric socket. As he turned her to face him, goose bumps covered her arms, and every part of her felt unbearably sensitive.

She looked up into his cool blue eyes and went hot, then cold, feeling a frisson of awareness streak through her. She wasn't afraid, but the sensation was too sharp, too intense to be pleasurable. "And you really must stop manhandling me, Signor Marcello," she answered faintly, her heart thudding violently.

"Why is that, Miss Bern?"

She stared up into his face, her gaze locking with his. There was nothing icy about his eyes now. No, they glowed with intelligence and heat and power. There was a physicality about him that stole her breath, knocking her off balance. She tried to gather her thoughts but his energy was so strong she felt it hum through her, lighting her up, making her feel as if he'd somehow stripped her bare.

Gulping for air, she looked down at his strong straight nose and the brackets on either side of his mouth. His face was not a boy's but a man's, with creases and lines, and if she didn't dislike him so much, she would have found the creases beautiful. "You are giving the paparazzi quite a show, you know," she whispered.

His strong black brows pulled.

"All the manhandling won't look well in tomorrow's papers. I'm afraid there are too many incriminating photos."

"Incriminating photos—" He broke off abruptly, understanding dawning.

His hand dropped even as his gaze scanned the wide canal and the narrow pavement fronting the water and old buildings. She saw the moment he spotted the first of the cameras, and then others. His dark head turned, his gaze raking her, the blue fire blistering her. "What have you done?"

His voice was deep and rough, his accent more pronounced. Her pulse drummed and her insides churned. She'd scored her first hit, and it scared her. She wasn't accustomed to battling anyone, much less a powerful man. In her work, she assisted, providing support and information. She didn't challenge or contradict.

"I did what needed to be done," she said hoarsely. "You refused to acknowledge your nephew. Your family falls in step with whatever you say, and so I've pressed the issue. Now the whole world knows that your brother's son has been returned to your family."

Giovanni Marcello drew a slow deep breath and then another. He was shocked as well as livid. He'd been played. *Played.* By a manipulative, money-hungry American no less. He despised gold diggers. Greedy, selfish, soulless. "You contacted the media, inviting them here today?"

"I did."

Rachel was no different from her sister. His fingers curled a little, the only sign that he was seething inwardly. "You're pleased with yourself."

"I'm pleased that you've been forced out of hiding—"

"I was never hiding. Everyone knows this is my home. It's common knowledge that I work here, as well."

"Then why is this the first time I've had a conversation with you? I've reached out to your company staff again and again, and you've never bothered to respond to anything!"

Who was she to demand anything from him? From the start her family had only wanted one thing: to milk the Marcellos. Her sister, Juliet Bern, wasn't in love with his brother, rather she wanted Antonio's money. And once she could no longer blackmail Antonio, Juliet turned on his family, and then once Juliet was gone, it was Rachel's turn. Disgusting. "I owe you nothing, and my family owes you nothing. Your sister is gone. Well, my brother is gone, too. Such is life—"

"Juliet said you had a heart of ice."

"Do you really think you're the first woman to try to entrap Antonio?" *Or me?* Gio silently added, as he'd been played for a fool once, but he'd learned. He knew better than to trust a pretty face.

"I didn't entrap anyone. I didn't sleep with anyone. I find no pleasure in this, Signor Marcello. If anything, I'm horrified. I am not reckless. I do not fall in love with strangers, or make love to handsome wealthy Italian men. I have scruples and morals, and you are not someone I admire, and your wealth doesn't make you appealing. Your wealth, though, can help a little boy who needs support."

"So I'm to applaud you?"

"*No.* Just have a conscience, please."

From the corner of his eye, Giovanni saw a photographer move, crouching as he crept forward, snapping away. His gut tightened, his chest hot with barely leashed anger.

He couldn't believe she'd managed to draw him out of the palazzo and into this scene, a very public scene with witnesses everywhere.

With his position at the helm of the family business, he'd worked hard to keep personal affairs out of the news. It'd taken nearly a decade to restore his family's fortune and his family's reputation, but finally the Marcellos were a name to be proud of and a brand that garnered respect. It hadn't been easy to redeem their name, but he'd managed it through consistent, focused effort. Now, in one reckless moment, this American was about to turn the Marcellos into tabloid fodder once more.

He wasn't ready. He was still struggling to come to terms with his brother's death and refused to have Antonio's memory darkened, his name besmirched, by those consumed with greed. "This isn't a conversation I intend to continue on the streets of Venice," he ground out. He was usually so good at avoiding confrontations. He knew how to manage conflict. And yet here they were, staging an epic soap opera, just a block off the Grand Canal. It couldn't be more public. "Nor am I about to let you abuse my family. If there is to be a story, I shall provide the story, not you."

"It's a little late for that, Signor Marcello. The story has been captured on a half-dozen different cameras. I guarantee within the hour you'll find those images online. Tabloids pay—"

"I'm fully aware of how the paparazzi works."

"Then you're also aware of what they have to work with—me handing the baby to your employee, you chasing after me and now us arguing in front of my water taxi." She paused. "Wouldn't it have been so much easier to have just taken my phone call?"

His gaze swept her face. He felt an uneasy memory of another woman who looked very much like this American Rachel Bern…

Another beautiful brunette who had been exquisitely confident…

He pushed the memory of his fiancée, Adelisa, from mind, but her memory served a purpose. It reminded him of his vow that he'd never let a woman have the upper hand again. Fortunately, he knew that stories could be massaged, and facts weren't always objective. Rachel had come to give the photographers a fantastic shot, something they could take to every newspaper and magazine, and Gio could help her with that. He could ensure the paparazzi photographers with their telephoto lenses had something significant to capture, something that would derail her strategy.

Giovanni pulled her to him, one arm locking around her waist, the other hand free to lift her face. Holding her captive, he cupped her chin and jaw, angling her face up to his. He saw a flare of panic in her eyes, the brown irises shot with flecks of green and gold, before he dropped his head, capturing her mouth with his.

She stiffened, her lips still, her breath bottling. He could feel her fear and tension and he instantly gentled the kiss. Although he'd reached for her in anger, he wasn't in the habit of kissing a woman in anger.

Her mouth was soft and warm. Despite her tension, she was soft and warm and he pulled her closer, tipping her head farther back to tease her lips. He stroked the seam with the tip of his tongue, her mouth generous and pliant. A quiver raced through her, her body shuddering against him and he stroked the seam again, playing with the full upper lip, catching the bow gently in his teeth.

She made a hoarse sound, not in pain, but pleasure, and a lance of hot desire streaked through him, making him hard all over.

He deepened the kiss, her lips parting for him, giving him access to the sweet heat of her mouth. It had been months since he'd enjoyed a kiss half so much, and he took his time, the kiss an exploration of taste and texture and response. His tongue traced the edge of her upper lip and he felt her shudder, her mouth opening wider.

She tasted sweet and hot, but also surprisingly innocent, and his body throbbed, blood drumming in his veins. With his arm in the small of her back, he pulled her even closer, stroking her mouth, over her lower lip, and then finding her tongue, making her shiver again.

Her breathless sighs and little shivers whetted his appetite. It'd been a long time since he felt hunger like this. It had been a year and a half since he'd broken things off with his last mistress, and he'd spent evenings with different women since, but he hadn't slept with any of them. How could he when there was no desire? Antonio's death had numbed him to everything, until now.

Abruptly Gio released Rachel and took a step back, his pulse thudding hard and heavy, echoing the hot ache in his groin. She stood dazed and motionless, her brown eyes cloudy and bemused.

"That should give your photographer friends something intriguing to sell." His voice sounded harsh even to his own ears. "It will be interesting to see what story the papers run with the addition of these news shots. Is it really about the baby? Or is this more? A lover's quarrel, their passionate encounter, an emotional goodbye?"

She exhaled, her cheeks flushed with color, her eyes overly bright. "Why?" she choked.

"Because this is my city and my home, and you are the outsider here. If there is to be a story, it's going to be *my* story, not yours."

"And what is that story, Signor Marcello?"

"Let's make this easier. It's always best to keep the

story simple. I am Giovanni—close friends and family call me Gio, and you may call me Gio—and I shall call you Rachel."

"I prefer the formal."

"But it rings false," he answered, reaching out to lift a dark glossy tendril of hair from her cheek and carefully smooth it back from her face. Her skin was soft and so very warm and he was reminded of the kiss, and the heat and the sweetness of her mouth. Such a mouth. The things he could do to her mouth. He still felt carnal and hungry. Desire still ran hot in his veins. It was a novelty after so many months of grief and emptiness. "We are no longer strangers. We have a history. A story. And the media, I think, will be enamored with our story."

"The only story is the truth. You have a nephew you refuse to acknowledge, never mind support."

"But is he my nephew?"

"Yes, you know he is. I've sent you the birth certificate and we can do a DNA test while I'm here—"

"Proving what?" he retorted. Before she could answer, he reached for her again, his hand coiling in her long dark hair, tilting her head back to take her mouth in a long, searing kiss.

She didn't stiffen or resist. If anything, she leaned into him and he wrapped an arm around her slender frame holding her against him as he deepened the kiss, his tongue sweeping her mouth, tasting her, weakening her defenses. By the time he lifted his head, she was silent, no fight left in her. Her wide brown eyes looked up into his.

"You should never underestimate your opponent, Rachel," he said quietly, running his thumb lightly across her soft flushed cheek. "And you most definitely shouldn't have underestimated me."

CHAPTER TWO

RACHEL COULDN'T THINK. Her brain was foggy, and her body had gone to mush. She could barely control her limbs much less her wild emotions. What had just happened? And how had she lost power so quickly?

It was the kiss. The kiss had been her undoing. It was that good. *He* was that good. And if Antonio had kissed Juliet this way, Rachel almost understood why Juliet lost her head.

"Now you're going to wrap your arm about my waist," Giovanni said, his hand settling low on her back, hand warm against the base of her spine, "and we're going to retrace our steps and we'll return to my house together."

"I'm not going to—"

He captured her face, kissing her again, deeply, teasing, stroking her lips and the inside of her mouth, setting her body on fire, destroying her resistance. She reached for his sweater, clinging to the softness, needing support, but the cashmere stretched, yielding, and she leaned against his chest, unable to stand.

"Stop fighting me, and put your arm around me," he murmured, his deep voice in her ear. "You're making this more difficult than it needs to be."

Her hand turned into a fist and she pressed it against his torso, pushing back at him, angry and off balance, not sure how he'd flipped everything around, seizing control from her. His body was so warm, heat emanated from him, making her want to step closer, not farther away. It was so confusing. She pressed her fist into him, pressing against the lean, hard muscle of his torso. "You're the one playing a game, Giovanni."

"Oh, yes, and it is *my* game."

She licked the swollen fullness of her upper lip. Her mouth still tingled and throbbed from the kisses. "The rules don't make sense."

"That's because you're not thinking clearly. Later it will be clear to you."

"But that could be too late."

He stroked her hot cheek. "Very true."

That light caress made her pulse jump. Her legs still weren't steady. "You need to stop touching me."

His head dipped, his lips against her brow, and then another light kiss high on her cheekbone, his deep voice humming through her. "You shouldn't have started this."

She closed her eyes as his lips brushed her earlobe, the touch warm and light, making her skin tingle. "Stop. This is about Michael, and only Michael," she protested, but her voice was weak and she didn't sound convincing, not even to herself.

He knew, too. She could tell by the glint in his eyes, a bright fierce flash of triumph. He thought he'd won, and maybe he had won this one battle, but it was an isolated battle and he hadn't won the war. At the same time, she couldn't secure Michael's future by remaining outside, bickering.

Or kissing. Because she didn't kiss strangers. She wasn't free with her affections. If anything, she was a little nervous around men, not having a lot of confidence in herself as a woman. It'd been years since she'd been out on a proper date, and Juliet used to say that men would like her better if she'd just relax and not take herself so seriously.

It wasn't that Rachel took herself so seriously, but she didn't know how to flirt, and she wasn't about to resort to flattery just to make a man feel good. Fortunately, in her job she didn't have to flatter and charm, she just needed to know her aircraft, and she did. It was easy to be enthusiastic about luxury planes and all the different ways one could customize an AeroDynamics jet interior.

"Ready to go in?" Giovanni asked, placing a kiss on the top of her head. "Or do we need to give our photographer friends another passionate embrace?"

"No!" Reluctantly she slid her arm around his waist, shuddering as he drew her close to his hip, and then they were walking, but she couldn't even feel her legs.

This was crazy. She couldn't wrap her head around everything that had just happened. Perhaps *he* was crazy. Perhaps she'd just thrown herself from the fire into the frying pan. Was that the expression? In her dazed state, she couldn't be sure of anything right now. His kisses… They'd wrecked her. His touch absolutely baffled her.

No one touched her. No one wanted to kiss her. And she knew he didn't really want to kiss her, but he'd done it to shift the power, seize control. It had been a shocking move but surprisingly effective. That's the part she didn't understand. When had kissing someone become the way to handle a situation? And why had it worked so well on her? She should have been able to resist him. She should have been outraged and offended and not melted.

And she had melted. Into a puddle of boneless, spineless sensation.

But now she needed to gather herself and focus and think. *Think.* She needed a new plan, and quickly.

They were crossing the pavement, approaching the palazzo, and while she dreaded entering Giovanni's home, she'd at least have Michael back.

Rachel suddenly stumbled, tripping over her own feet. His arm tightened around her, and he drew her firmly against his side. "Too close," she protested.

"I can feel you trembling. If I let you go, you'll fall."

"Blame yourself. You had no business kissing me."

"Has it been that long since you've been properly kissed?"

"I wouldn't call it a *proper* kiss. In America we don't manhandle women."

"Yes, I've heard that American men don't know how to handle women. Such a shame." They paused several feet from the door. He tilted her face up, stared into her eyes. "You look better now that you've been kissed, though. Less pale and pinched." He smiled into her eyes but there was a predatory gleam in the blue depths. "Do you want to thank me now, or later?"

She knew what he was doing, striking a pose, giving the photographers more pictures with different angles for a wide variety of shots, but it infuriated her that he'd taken her big moment and turned it into his. "This is going to end badly," she said tightly.

The corner of his mouth lifted, and he stared down into her face for a long, tense moment, before laughing shortly. "Are you just now figuring that out?"

The front door suddenly swung open, and he kept her close as they entered the palazzo, passing through the high wooden doors and into the cavernous central hall lit by an enormous Murano chandelier, at least seven feet tall, a masterpiece of sparkling glass leaves, flowers and fruits all set amongst intricate, delicate glass rods and fanciful, fragile arabesques.

A member of his staff had obviously been at the front door watching and waiting for them, as the front door opened before Giovanni could touch it, and then closed quietly behind them. Rachel turned her head, craning to see if it was the old man who'd answered the door earlier, but Giovanni was urging her forward, moving her toward the stairs.

Think, she told herself. She needed to clear her head and follow a thought all the way through instead of this—this capitulation of reason and control.

"You can let me go now," she said, shrugging to free herself. "There are no cameras here."

His arm fell away but his fingers remained low on her spine, creating insistent pressure as he marched her up the sweeping marble stairs to a formal salon on the second floor. The doors again magically closed behind them and only then did Giovanni's hand leave her.

She felt more than a little lost as she glanced around a room that could only be described as magnificent. More glittering chandeliers lined the ceiling, with matching sconces on the wall. Tall windows overlooked the canal while massive framed mirrors covered portions of the walls, the antique mirrors reflecting the gray light outside, highlighting the frescoed and plasterwork ceiling.

Rachel was out of her element but she'd never let him know. It was bad enough that he thought she'd enjoyed his kiss.

"Who has Michael?" she asked, standing stiffly in the center of the room. "Can you send for him?"

"No." Giovanni gestured for her to sit. "We have quite a lot to discuss before he joins us."

"We can talk once he's back with me."

"You left him here. I'm not about to just hand him over as if he were a lost wallet or umbrella."

"You know why I did that."

"I know you're an impulsive woman—"

"You could *not* be more wrong. I am a very calm person—" She went quiet as she saw the lift on his eyebrow. "You're making me upset. You've been impossible from the start."

"We've only just met, and it was not an auspicious first meeting, with you abandoning an infant on my doorstep, and then running from the scene."

Rachel clamped her jaw tight to keep from speaking too quickly, aware that every word could and would be used against her. She fought to control the pitch and tone of her voice. "I did not abandon him. I would not *ever* abandon him. I love him."

"Odd way of showing it, don't you think?"

"I was trying to get your attention."

"And now you have it." He gestured again toward the silk upholstered chair and sofa. "May I help you with your coat?"

"No, thank you. I won't be staying long."

He gave her an odd look, his lips twisting as if amused. "Are you sure you won't be more comfortable?"

"I'll be more comfortable when I have the baby."

"He's in good hands at the moment, and we have a great deal to discuss before he joins us. So I do suggest you try to be comfortable, since the conversation probably won't be." Gio's gaze rested intently on her face before dropping to study the rest of her. "It's been an unusually eventful morning. I'm sending for a coffee. Would you like one?"

She shook her head, and then changed her mind. "Yes, please."

He reached for his phone from a pocket and shot off a message. "Coffee should be here soon," he said, sitting down in the pale blue silk armchair facing the upholstered sofa. He stretched his legs before him, looking at ease. "Are you quite certain you wish to stand for the rest of the day?"

His tone was lazy, almost indulgent, and it provoked her more than if he'd spoken to her sternly. She felt her face flush and her body warm. "I certainly have no intention of being here more than a half hour at most."

"You think we can sort out Michael's future in thirty minutes or less?"

He sounded pleasant and reasonable, too reasonable, and it put her on guard, hands clenching at her sides, knuckles aching with the tightness of the grip. He was easier to fight when he was defensive and angry. Now she felt as if she were the difficult one.

It wasn't fair but clearly he didn't play by any rules but his own.

Drawing a quick breath, she sat down on the edge of the small wood framed sofa, the elegant and delicate shape popular hundreds of years ago, the silver silk fabric gleaming with bits of red and pale blue threads.

She folded her hands in her lap, waiting for him to speak. It was a tactic that worked well with her wealthy clients. They preferred being in control, and they felt most in control when they could dictate the conversation. She'd let Gio direct the conversation. He'd think he was in charge that way and she could use the time to regroup and plan.

But Giovanni was in no hurry to speak. He leaned back in his chair, legs extended, and watched her.

There was no sound in the grand room. No ticking clock. No creaking of any sort. Just silence, and the silence was excruciating.

Her pulse quickened as time stretched, lengthening, testing her patience. Her nerves felt wound to a breaking point. She exhaled hard. "If we don't speak it will definitely take longer than a half hour to sort out Michael's future," she said shortly, irritated beyond reason with Giovanni. He was playing a game with her even now, and it made her impossibly angry.

"I was giving you time to compose yourself," he answered with a faint smile. "You were trembling so much earlier I thought you could use a bit of time for rest and reflection."

"It was cold and damp and windy outside. I was freezing, thus the shivers. It's a natural reaction when chilled."

"Are you cold now?"

"No, this room is heated. It's quite nice in here."

One of his black brows lifted ever so slightly but he didn't speak, and her stomach did a nervous flip-flop.

He was toying with her deliberately. She was certain he wanted to make her uneasy. But why? Did he think she'd collapse into tears? She didn't like the silence but it was preferable to being held and touched. She had an excellent head for business and had proven herself remarkably good at establishing and maintaining professional relationships, but personal relationships, those were problematic.

She hadn't dated enough when she was younger. Although it'd be tempting to blame the opposite sex for failing to notice her, it wasn't entirely true. She lacked confidence and had failed to put herself out there. Dating seemed to require too much energy and effort, with too many ups and downs to make the dashed dreams and rejection worthwhile.

Instead she focused on work, pouring herself into the job, earning promotions and bonuses as well as praise from senior management. While other young women her age were busy falling in love and needing time off for romantic weekends and holidays, she closed deals and made Aero-Dynamics money and found tremendous satisfaction in being the one everyone could count on for being there and doing what needed to be done.

Which was all very good and well at the corporate office, but sitting here in this enormous room, facing a tall, handsome, charismatic Italian, she was secretly terrified. She could sell a man a thirty-million-dollar airplane, but she fell apart when kissed, especially if the kiss was dark and sexual, destroying all rational thought.

"The silence is soothing, is it not?" she asked, struggling to sound as relaxed as he appeared.

He seemed to check a smile, grooves bracketing his firm mouth. "Indeed."

"I hope we can drink our coffee in silence. Silence

makes everything better," she added, frustration growing. "Especially when it's in such an impressive room." She glanced around the salon, the proportions alone overwhelming, never mind the grand paintings and light fixtures. "I suppose you hoped to intimidate me by bringing me here to your grand salon."

"This is not by any means my most impressive room. It's actually one of the smaller salons on this floor, considered by most to be intimate and welcoming." His lashes dropped, concealing the intense blue of his eyes. "It's my mother's favorite. If she were here, she'd serve you coffee here."

Embarrassed, Rachel bit her lip and glanced away, more self-conscious and resentful than ever. Two weeks ago, when her private investigator gave her Giovanni's address and she realized she'd have to come to Venice to get him to meet with her, she'd pictured meeting him somewhere neutral and public, perhaps at her hotel in one of the cheerful pleasant rooms downstairs, or maybe a quiet restaurant tucked away off the more public thoroughfares.

She'd imagined he'd be proud and arrogant, possibly grim and unsmiling. It hadn't once crossed her mind that he'd kiss her, and then walk her into his home and shut the door and create this awful air of privacy. Intimacy. She swallowed hard and struggled to think of something to say. "Does your mother live here?"

"Part of the year. During the winter she likes to go to her sister's in Sorrento." He rose from his chair and walked toward the wall of tall windows, pausing before one window, his gaze fixed intently on a distant point.

She wondered if he was looking for the photographers, or if there was something else happening on the lagoon. She used the opportunity to study him. He was easily six-two, maybe taller, and his shoulders were broad, his spine long, tapering to a lean waist and powerful legs. Even from the back he crackled with authority and power. He was not the recluse she'd imagined.

Still staring out, Gio added, "I confess, I'm surprised you never reached out to her. I would have thought that in your desperation you would have approached her. Who to better love and accept a bambino than the grandmother?"

She folded her hands in her lap. "I did reach out."

He turned to look at her. "And?"

"She wasn't interested."

"Is that what she said?"

"No. She never responded."

"She probably didn't get your messages then."

"I didn't just call. I wrote letters, too."

"All sent to the Marcello corporate office in Rome?"

Rachel nodded.

His shoulders shifted. "Then that is why she didn't receive them. Anything to my mother would go to my assistant, and my assistant wouldn't forward."

"Why not? It was important correspondence."

"My assistant was under strict instructions to not disturb my mother with anything troubling, or upsetting. My mother hasn't been well for a while."

"I would imagine that she'd be delighted to discover that Antonio had left a piece of him behind."

"I can't—and won't—get her hopes up, not if she is being used, or manipulated."

"I wouldn't do that to her."

"No? You wouldn't have asked her for money if she'd responded? You wouldn't have demanded support?" He saw her expression and smiled grimly. "You would have, and you know it. I do, too, which is why I had to protect her, and shield her from stress."

"I would think that having a beautiful grandson—Antonio's son—in her arms would help her heal."

"If the child in question really was Antonio's…maybe."

"Michael *is* Antonio's."

"I don't know that."

"I have proof."

"DNA tests?" he mocked, walking again, now prowling the perimeter of the room. "I'll do my own, thank you."

"*Good*. Do them. I've been waiting for you to do your own!"

He paused, arms crossing over his chest. "And if he is Antonio's, what then?"

"You accept him," she said.

His dark head tipped as he considered her. "Accept him. What does that even mean?"

She opened her mouth to answer, and then closed it without making a sound. Her heart did an uneven thump and suddenly it hurt to breathe. Michael needed support—not just financial, but emotional. She wanted to be sure Michael wasn't forgotten, not by her family, or Antonio's.

It was bad enough that Michael had been left an orphan within months of his birth, but the way Juliet died… It was wrong, and it continued to eat at Rachel because she hadn't understood how badly Juliet was doing. She'd been oblivious to the depth of Juliet's despair. Rachel could now write an entire pamphlet on postpartum depression, but back in November and December she hadn't understood it, and she hadn't been properly sympathetic. Instead of getting Juliet medical help, she'd given her sister tough love, and it was absolutely the wrong thing to do.

It had only made everything so much worse. It was without exaggeration, the beginning of the end. And it was all Rachel's fault.

Rachel had failed Juliet when her sister needed her most.

CHAPTER THREE

GIOVANNI WATCHED RACHEL'S eyes fill with tears and her lips part, then seal shut, her teeth biting down into the soft lower lip as though she was fighting to stay in control.

He didn't buy the act, as it was an act.

Adelisa had been the same. Beautiful, bright and spirited, she'd captured his heart from the start. He'd proposed before the end of the first year, and delighted in buying her the pretty—but expensive—trinkets her heart desired.

Her heart desired many.

Diamonds and rubies, emeralds and sapphires—jewels she ended up liquidating almost as quickly as he gave them to her. Not that he knew what happened to them until much later.

His family warned him that Adelisa was using him. His mother came to him privately on three different occasions, sharing her fears, and then reporting on rumors that Adelisa had been seen with other men, but he didn't believe it. He was sure Adelisa loved him. She wore his engagement ring. She was eagerly planning their wedding. Why would she betray him?

Six months later he heard about a pair of stunning diamond earrings for sale, a pair rumored to come from the Marcello family. He tracked down the earrings and the jeweler, and they were a pair of a set he'd given Adelisa the night of their engagement party. They were worth millions of dollars, but more than that, they were family heirlooms and something he gave with his heart.

He was stunned, and worse, humiliated. His mother had been right. He'd been duped. And everyone seemed to have known the truth but him.

It'd been ten years since that humiliation, but Gio still avoided love and emotional entanglements. Far better to enjoy a purely physical relationship than be played for a fool. And now his narrowed gaze swept over Rachel, from the classic oval shape of her pretty face to the glossy length of her ponytail with the windswept tendrils. She was neither tall nor petite, but average height and an average build, although in her dark coat, which hit just above her black knee-high leather boots, she looked polished and pretty.

He didn't want her to be pretty, though. He didn't want to find anything about her attractive or desirable, and yet he was aware of her, just as he was aware that beneath her winter coat, there were curves, generous curves, because he'd felt them when he'd drawn her against him, her body pressed to his. "So what is your plan?" he asked tautly. "Have you sorted out how you intend to get us to accept the child? Because a family is not just DNA. A family is nurture, and relationships, and those develop over years. You can't simply force one to accept an outsider—"

"Michael is not an outsider. He's Antonio's son." She'd gone pale, her expression strained. "And my sister's son," she added after a half beat, "and I know you have no love for my sister, but she cared for your brother, deeply—"

"We're in private now. You can drop the script. There's no need for theatrics."

"You don't even know the facts."

"I know enough."

"Well, I thought I did, too, but I was wrong, and Juliet's no longer here because I got it wrong. Michael has no one but us and you can think what you want of Juliet, and me, but I insist you give him a chance—" She broke off as the door opened and a young, slim, dark-haired woman entered carrying a huge, ornate silver tray filled with silver pots and smaller sterling silver dishes along with a pair of china cups and saucers.

Rachel was grateful for the interruption. She needed a moment to compose herself. She still felt so rattled by his kisses. There had been nothing light or friendly in the way he took her mouth, claiming her as if she belonged to him, shaping her to his frame. She did not belong to him, and to have his tongue stroke the inside of her mouth, creating the dark seductive rhythm that made her body ache—

The sound of Giovanni speaking to the maid broke her train of thought. Heart thudding, Rachel knotted her hands in her lap, realizing she hadn't just gotten Giovanni's attention, she'd given him control. She'd wanted his assistance, but clearly help would be on his terms, not hers.

The young maid placed the silver tray on a table next to the couch, not far from where Rachel was sitting, before leaving.

Giovanni crossed to take one espresso and handed her the other.

Rachel took the small cup and saucer. "When will you permit Michael to join us?"

"As soon as he's finished his bottle."

"He's awake then?"

"Yes."

"And he's okay?"

"Apparently my staff is already besotted with him. Anna said the girls are fighting over who is to hold him next."

"Allow me to resolve the argument. Send for him, and I'll hold him."

"You haven't had your coffee yet."

"I can multitask."

"And deprive my staff of the opportunity to kiss and cuddle a baby?"

"But by keeping him from me, you deprive me."

"Is it such a deprivation?" Gio's voice was pitched low. "I would think it's a relief. Your letters made it sound as if you were at your wit's end—exhausted, and overwhelmed, close to breaking."

She flushed. "You read my letters."

"As did my attorneys."

Heat rushed down her neck, flooding her limbs. "So you were stonewalling me."

"I had my own investigation to do."

"You took your time."

"I don't respond well to threats."

"I never threatened you!"

"Your letters demanded I act before I was prepared to—"

"This isn't about you! It's about a child who has lost both his parents. It's selfish to deny him a chance at a better life."

"We've returned to the material demands, haven't we?"

"Material is only part of it. There is the cultural aspect, as well. The baby might have been born in Seattle but he is only half-American, and he needs to know you, his father's family. He needs to be part of you."

"Why aren't you enough?"

"I'm not Italian, or Venetian."

"And you think that's important?"

"Yes."

His lips compressed, his jaw firming "I doubt you value his Venetian ancestry and heritage as much as you value the Marcellos' wealth and clout."

"Can't I want both for him?"

"But I don't think you really want both."

"That's not true. I've worked hard to get to where I am now, but even with an excellent job, I barely make ends meet. And as a single woman, not yet twenty-nine, I'm in no position to raise a child on my own, much less a Marcello—"

"What does that even mean to you? A Marcello?"

"Your family is old, and respected. Your history goes back hundreds of years. The Marcellos have contributed significantly to modern Italy, but you personally have done so much for Italy's economy that just last year you were awarded the Order of Merit for Labor." She saw his black eyebrow arch, his expression almost mocking. "And yes," she added defiantly. "I did my homework. I had to in order to find you."

"Fourteen years ago the Marcello holding company was on the verge of bankruptcy. No one wanted to do business with us. No one trusted us. I have poured myself into the company to rebuild it, sacrificing a personal life in order to make the business my focus. And so, yes, I know manufacturing, construction and real estate, but I'm not interested in expanding the family."

"But the family has been expanded," she said quietly. "With or without your consent."

"You're revealing your hand," he replied. "I see where you're going with this. How we all owe him, because he is my brother's son. His heir."

"That's not where I'm going."

"No? You're not about to play the Marcello heir card?"

She dampened her lips, trying to hide her sudden flurry of nerves because she had played that card, and she'd played it with the press. "I'm not asking for a piece of your company. I'm not wanting Michael to inherit Marcello shares or stock, but I do believe you can, and should, give Michael a proper education and the advantages I could not provide for him."

Giovanni's lip curled. "You didn't ever want to leave Michael here. In fact, you never intended to actually let him go. How could you? You wouldn't be able to justify the child support you feel you deserve."

"This isn't about me."

"Isn't it? Because let's be honest, a six-month-old has very few material needs. Milk, a dry diaper, clean clothes—"

"Time, love, attention."

"Which you want to be compensated for."

"*No*," she said sharply, before holding her breath and counting to ten. She had to stay calm. She couldn't get into a fight, not now, not before anything was settled, and certainly not before Michael had been returned to her. "I wish I didn't need your money. I'd love it if I didn't need help. I'd love to be able to tell you to go fly a kite—" She hesitated as she saw him arch a brow. "It's an expression."

"I'm familiar with it."

"I was trying to be polite."

"Of course."

His sarcasm made her want to take a poker iron from the fireplace and beat him with it, which was something, considering the fact that she was not a violent person, and did not go through life wanting to hit things, much less human beings. "I don't want to be compensated. But I can't work and care for Michael at the same time, nor does AeroDynamics provide an on-site nursery. The fact is, there is no solution for child care for someone in my position."

"That problem disappears, though, if you claim Antonio's assets in the Marcello holding company, allowing you to retire from your job and raise the child in the comfort and style he deserves." Giovanni's blue gaze held hers, his mocking tone matching his cynical expression. "Have I got it right?"

Offended, she stiffened. "You've created a fascinating story, but it's not true."

"Do you share the same father and mother as your sister?"

"Yes."

"So you were raised in the same…struggling…blue-collar household?"

She heard the way he emphasized *struggling* and winced.

"We were not a blue-collar household. My father was a re-spected engineer for Boeing. He was brilliant. And my mother managed the front office of a successful Seattle dental practice."

"Not Seattle, but Burien."

So he had done some research, and he'd found her family wanting.

She battled her temper, not wanting to lose control again. It was one thing to become muddled by a kiss, but another to allow his words to stir her up. "Yes, Burien, just a few miles south of downtown Seattle. Living in a suburb was a lifestyle choice. That way my mother could work and be available to see us to the school bus before school, and then meet our bus afterward. She juggled a lot, especially after our father died."

"Money was an issue."

Her smile was gracious. She would be gracious and se-rene. "Being middle class is not a crime, nor does it reflect badly on my family. Wealth doesn't make one superior."

"It does give one advantages...physically, socially, psy-chologically."

"But not morally." She held her smile, hiding her fury. She'd met many arrogant, condescending men at AeroDy-namics but they'd never shamed her for having less. "Mor-ally you are not superior in any way. In fact, I'd say morally you are inferior because you've refused so far to do what is right. You're more concerned about protecting your cor-poration than your nephew—"

"We were discussing wealth and its advantages, and you've turned it into an attack."

"Not *attacking*, just stating my position."

"That you are morally superior because you're of the working class?"

"If I'm morally superior it's because I didn't turn my back on my nephew like you!" She drew a shallow breath, stomach churning. "I knew your brother. He was my client and he'd be devastated that you've rejected his son—"

"I haven't rejected my nephew, and you could not have known my brother well if you thought he was pleased in any way about your sister's pregnancy. Her pregnancy devastated him. It hastened his death, so before you lecture me about moral superiority, why don't you look at your own family?"

Her lips opened and closed but she couldn't make a sound.

Giovanni rose. "Your sister is a classic gold digger. She wanted a rich man and she found one in Antonio. She didn't care that he was ill and dying. She didn't care that she was making excessive demands. All she wanted was her way, and she got it. So save your speeches, Rachel. I know just who you and your sister are. Master manipulators, but I won't be played. Good day. *Addio*."

He walked out, leaving the door open behind him.

Giovanni climbed the staircase two steps at a time, anger rolling through him, anger and outrage that a stranger would try to tell him who his brother was and what his brother wanted.

Growing up, Antonio had been Giovanni's best friend. They'd had a younger sister but she'd died at six, which had only brought Antonio and Gio closer together. Antonio and Gio were so close that Gio, an introvert, didn't feel the need to have a lot of other friends.

They ended up attending the same boarding school in England, and then the same university. Antonio loved business and finance while Giovanni preferred engineering and construction, which made them a good pair, and they both looked forward to working together at the Marcello corporate office, which is what Gio did right after graduating from university. But Antonio went on to graduate school, earning an MBA from Harvard. Giovanni had been the one to convince their father that it was a smart investment, sending Antonio to America for the prestigious program, as he'd be able to bring his knowledge back to Marcello corporate office afterward.

It didn't work out that way, though. While at Harvard, Antonio was introduced to a big financial firm on Wall Street and they were impressed with his mind and his linguistic ability—Antonio, like Giovanni, spoke five languages fluently. The firm courted him, wanting him to work for them in their Manhattan office. Antonio accepted the offer as it was extremely lucrative and involved a great deal of travel and perks that he wouldn't get working for the family business.

Giovanni was shocked by his younger brother's decision. It'd felt like a betrayal. Marcello Enterprises was in trouble. Their father had made years of bad decisions, and Giovanni, the practical, pragmatic engineer, needed his brother to help save the company. Without Antonio they could lose everything. But Antonio wasn't eager to work for a company that was floundering—even if it was his family's.

Gio met Adelisa right after Antonio accepted the position in Manhattan, and he'd shared with her his disappointment, and his frustration. She'd been a good listener. Too good a listener, actually, as she would later share company secrets with others, undermining everything Gio had worked so hard to accomplish.

Of course, not all women were like Adelisa. But when you were one of the wealthiest men in Italy, it was hard to trust any woman's motives.

CHAPTER FOUR

For a long moment after Giovanni walked out, Rachel sat frozen on the couch, thoughts blank, heart on fire, Gio's sharp words ringing in her head preventing her from thinking or feeling anything other than pain and shame.

Gio was right, and wrong. But more right than wrong. Juliet *had* wanted a wealthy boyfriend. She'd wanted to marry a very rich man and it had been her goal since she was in junior high school.

Juliet felt she deserved better than everyone else. She wasn't ordinary like Rachel. She was beautiful. She'd been a pretty baby and had grown into a little girl who turned heads. Juliet knew it, too, and from the time she was small she dazzled everyone she met.

It started with their parents, and then Juliet turned her charm onto her teachers, and she went through life wrapping everyone around her little finger.

It seemed to Rachel that she was the only one Juliet couldn't manipulate, and over the years it created tension between them and friction in the family. Juliet would have a tantrum when Rachel refused to capitulate to her demands, and then Mother would intercede, and inevitably she took Juliet's side. Mother had been firmly on Juliet's side last spring when Juliet began dating Antonio and needed loans to buy new clothes and pay for expensive hair and skin appointments.

Rachel had refused to give her sister money for a new wardrobe, telling Juliet to do what everyone else did and look for employment so she could buy new clothes with money she'd earned. "She'd have more self-respect," Rachel told their mother when Juliet had the expected melt-down. "It's not right to give Juliet everything she wants."

"Why are you so hard on her?" Mother answered. "She's not cut out for business the way you are."

"That's not true. She's smart, Mom. She's just really lazy."

"You're so grumpy all the time, Rachel. Where's your sense of humor?"

"I *have* a sense of humor, but it's hard to feel like laughing when Juliet can't hold down a job. She lives off loans from you and me."

"It's been months since we've floated her any money. She's getting better at managing her funds."

"Because her bills are getting paid for by one boyfriend or another."

"At least she has a boyfriend."

"Wanting a boyfriend isn't exactly aspirational!"

"Oh, yes, that's right, Rach. You're far too intelligent to fall in love."

"No, Mom. I'm not too intelligent to fall in love. But I'm too intelligent to turn a man into a meal ticket." She paused but her mother was silent now and Rachel pressed on. "I should think you'd be uncomfortable with Juliet always trying to cash in from her looks. She doesn't think she should have to work because she's beautiful but good looks can only take one so far—"

"You're jealous."

"Mom, I'm too old for this. I might have been jealous when I was fourteen and she was twelve and Juliet stole my first boyfriend, but I'm twenty-eight and I have great friends, a job I love and a life I enjoy."

"Then why care that Juliet is doing life her way? Don't resent her happiness. She's sure she's found the one, and I fully expect an engagement announcement any day now."

But Mrs. Bern was wrong. There was no engagement,

but there was an announcement. Juliet was pregnant and her rich boyfriend, Italian businessman, Antonio Marcello, had broken things off with Juliet and returned to Italy without her.

It had been a terrible time in Seattle afterward. Juliet had been heartbroken, and then not even two months later, Mother died. They hadn't known she was unwell. Mother hadn't even known. If there was a blessing, it was that Mother went quickly, without months of suffering. She was there one day and then gone the next.

Not even three weeks later, they learned through a newspaper article that Antonio Marcello had died in Rome, at home, with his family at his side.

Juliet never really recovered after that. First Mother, then Antonio, and Juliet still had the third trimester to get through, but there had been too many hits and shocks. She went into labor depressed and didn't bounce back after delivery.

Rachel had been impatient with Juliet in the months following Michael's birth. She'd tried to hide her irritation, and she'd given her pep talks, perhaps more vigorous than necessary, but Rachel was overwhelmed by Juliet's depression and her sister's inability to care for the baby. Work was stressful with rounds of layoffs due to the economic downturn, and God knows, they needed Rachel to be employed. She was the only one keeping the family afloat.

But Rachel was barely coping herself. Mom was gone, Juliet wouldn't get out of bed, the baby needed looking after and Rachel didn't know what had happened to her life.

It wasn't her life anymore.

A light knock sounded on the open door. Rachel looked up to see the young maid, Anna, standing in the doorway.

"Please, follow me," Anna said in stilted English.

"Where?" Rachel asked, unable to move.

"I am to…walk you…to the door."

"Where is my baby?"

Anna frowned.

"Michael. The bambino," Rachel said, setting the cup down. "I cannot leave without him."

"Sorry. Signor, he said the bambino he stays here. You... go." She gestured to the door. "You come with me, please?"

"No. Absolutely not. I'm not leaving Michael here. Bring me the baby. *Now*."

"I am sorry. I cannot. Signor will telephone you later, yes?"

Rachel was on her feet, crossing the room. "Where is he? Where is Signor Marcello?"

"He has gone to his office. I will show you to...down the stairs. Please come—" Anna broke off as Rachel brushed past her, stepping into the hall.

"Where is his office? Which direction?" Rachel demanded.

"No. Sorry."

Rachel's gaze swept the hall, certain that there were only more formal rooms on this floor. She glanced right, to the marble stairs they'd climbed earlier. The wide gleaming steps continued up at least another two floors.

She headed for the stairs and quickly climbed up. Anna chased after her, speaking in a stream of broken English and Italian.

Rachel ignored the girl. "Giovanni," she called, her voice echoing in the stairwell. "Gio! Where are you?"

Her voice bounced off the marble and the high ceiling, but she wouldn't stop until she found him. "I'm not leaving here, not without Michael. So if you want me to go, Gio, give me Michael and I'll go, but there is no way I'd leave—"

"Enough." A door at the end of the hall opened abruptly, and Giovanni appeared, expression dark. "You've done nothing but create a circus since you arrived this morning. My staff is not accustomed to screaming and shouting."

"They are Italian. I seriously doubt they are shocked by genuine emotion," she retorted, marching down the hall toward him. "And you… How could you just go and leave me there like that?"

"I said goodbye. You were the one who refused to leave."

"You knew I wouldn't go without Michael."

"You didn't seem to have a problem leaving him here earlier." He stared down at her, blue eyes snapping fire. "Are you sure you and your sister are not twins?"

He couldn't have said anything more hurtful if he'd tried. Her eyes smarted and her throat sealed closed.

Giovanni was arrogant and condescending and lacked even the smallest shred of human compassion. Thank God he didn't intimidate her. She'd worked with dozens of powerful men over the past five years, men who had incredible power and staggering fortunes and egos to match. They all liked to be flattered. They all felt entitled. They all needed to be right. Giovanni was no different. She'd never get what she wanted if she fought him. If she angered him. If she continued to alienate him.

Alienating him would just hurt Michael, and that wouldn't be fair or right. Juliet had made mistakes. Her life had become such a mess. But Michael wasn't a mess. Michael was pure and innocent, and that innocence had to be protected. Yes, she'd failed Juliet, but there was no way she'd fail Michael.

And so, even though a dozen different things came to mind, protests and rebukes, in the end her feelings didn't matter. *She* didn't matter. This was about her nephew, who'd been left without a mother or a father and needed someone to champion him. And that someone was her.

"I don't care what you think of me," she said unsteadily, "but I do care what you think about Michael. He did not ask to be born. He is innocent in all this. And whether you like it or not, he carries your brother's name, and DNA, and if I have to go to your court to get him proper child support, I will."

"I don't doubt you would, but you'd find that our courts move at a snail's pace compared to your courts. You could be waiting for six or eight, or even ten years, for any type of legal decision."

That knocked her back, thoughts scattering, but then she managed a careless shrug and found her voice. "You're happy to wage a public war for that long? It seems so unlike you, considering how much you value your privacy."

He shot her a look she couldn't quite decipher. "So let's put our cards on the table. Let's stop with the games. How much are you asking for him?"

"How much child support?" she asked, needing to clarify his question.

"No. How much do you want for him? How much will it cost to take him off your hands permanently?"

CHAPTER FIVE

For a second Rachel couldn't breathe. The air bottled in her lungs until they ached, and her head felt light and dizzy. She exhaled on a gasp. "You...*want*...him?"

"That is probably stretching the truth."

"Then why are you even asking?"

"Maybe I'm curious as to what it would take to get you out of my life."

"So you don't really want him—you just want to be rid of me."

"I want the problem to disappear, yes."

"But the problem would be living in your palazzo. Unless you sent him elsewhere. Boarding school for infants, maybe?"

He gave her a long, hard look. "He would not be mistreated."

"Would he be loved?"

"My family is not in the habit of abusing children."

"That's not the same thing as being cherished and adored—"

"He would be raised the way Antonio and I were raised. With equal parts love and discipline."

"And would you be the one to raise him?"

"That's something to still be sorted out."

"I couldn't give you an answer then, not without knowing who'd raise him. Financial support is important but his care...the affection he receives...is everything and will determine not just his health but his happiness."

"I wasn't raised in the Dark Ages. I know children need affection."

"Would you be able to give him a mother, or would you hire a nanny?"

"I am not about to find a wife just to give him a mother. I'd hire a nanny."

"Would you be able to spend significant time with him?"

"I am a bachelor. I work long hours. But I would ensure that my nephew had the best care money could buy."

That sounded awful. She suppressed a shiver.

One of his black brows lifted. "What's wrong? You don't look happy."

"He deserves more than an expensive nanny."

"She'd be well-trained and dedicated—"

"I think I've heard enough. You've painted a dreadful picture. There is no way I could leave Michael to your care."

"But you were so insistent that Michael be raised as a Marcello!"

"Is that how you were raised? With the best nanny money could buy?"

"Yes, and the best boarding schools, before attending the best universities."

"You didn't grow up here at home?"

"No. And I turned out well, wouldn't you say?"

"You turned out heartless."

"I'm practical, not heartless. There is a difference."

"Well, I want him loved, and protected, so no, you can't buy me off. I'm not going to abandon him."

"But isn't that what you did earlier? You handed him to my steward and walked away without a backward glance."

"It was a desperate ploy to get your attention, and it worked."

"Desperate people have a price. I know you have yours."

"I'm not that desperate."

"Then go back to Seattle, Rachel, and stop wasting my time." He turned around and walked away from her, entering the room with the open door.

The sharpness in his voice made her chest tighten and her stomach fall. Was he really so cold and callous or was he testing her? Either way, she was here, and she was not about to be scared off.

She followed him into the room. "Life is not black or white, Gio, and I don't believe in all or nothing. I believe in discussion and compromise—even when it's uncomfortable. We need to find a middle ground—" She stopped as she noticed the soaring stone arches that divided the large room into two. On one side of the beige arches was a massive desk and chair, and on the other was a wall of windows framed in stained wood, topped by clear leaded glass and Palladian style arches. The high ceiling was paneled in dark wood and beams. The marble floor was the color of vanilla and matched the warm plaster walls, while the white slipcovered furniture in the sitting area looked effortlessly chic. This, she thought, was what people meant when they said Italians had style.

She worked with designers on a daily basis, creating custom plane interiors, but this took her breath away. It was visually stunning. History reimagined. Luxury reinvented. "Incredible," she murmured. She didn't know what she loved more—the soaring stone arches that looked as if they'd been lifted from ancient ruins, or the magnificent leaded glass windows that allowed the light to deeply penetrate the room.

"Your office?" she asked, still marveling over the elegant simplicity. No mirrors or gilded surfaces here. No Murano glass. No shimmering sconces. Just dark wood, stone pediments over tall doorways, marble slab floors and windows that allowed light to spill everywhere, brightening surfaces and reflecting off the white furniture.

"Yes." He'd taken a seat on the edge of his dark desk and watched her do a slow turn in the middle of the room.

"It's beautiful."

"Thank you."

She approached one of the arches and ran her hand across the surface. "How much of this is original?"

"All of it. This floor was private, built for the family, not for entertaining. I asked my designer to make a few modifications, but the building dates back to the late fifteenth century and we protected the architecture."

"What did she change?"

"The marble floor is new. The plaster has been patched and repaired. We stripped off the coat of paint that had been applied to the windows and then stained the wood to match the beams."

"I can see why you want to work here. I would want to work here."

"With technology one can work from anywhere, and I can accomplish far more here than in a noisy office with endless interruptions." He exhaled, expression shuttering. "You were saying about a middle ground?"

She hesitated. "Can we find one?" When he didn't immediately reply, she added, "I don't expect us to become friends. But if we could try to become…allies, just for our nephew's sake, I think it would help him. He doesn't have a lot of family anymore, which is why it would be nice if his surviving family could be cordial."

Giovanni didn't know how to answer her. He'd been furious when he'd walked out of the silver salon earlier, insulted that she'd lecture him on how his own brother would have felt. She had no idea how close he and his brother had been, or how much he'd grieved for Antonio this past year.

He turned away, faced the window, biting back the sharp words he wanted to say. "The baby. He is healthy?"

"Yes. Michael's meeting all his milestones, and more." She drew a breath. "Would it be possible to please send for him now? I realize that I must appear indifferent to you with regards to Michael—"

"You do not appear indifferent at all."

"But perhaps not as attached as I am. I am very attached." She drew another quick breath, her voice thickening. "I've been in his life since his birth, and I've taken care of him from the beginning when Juliet wasn't able to. And then once she was gone, it was just him and me."

He said nothing, letting her talk, because he'd been curious about this very thing. What had Michael's early months been like? Who had been part of his life?

She continued, filling the uncomfortable silence. "So you can see why I'm anxious to have him back in my arms, and why I find this all so very difficult. We've spent a great deal of time together these past few months…in fact, we've spent all our time together these past few months, and I'm missing him. Terribly, as a matter of fact."

Giovanni did not want to like her, or care about her in any way, but it was impossible to not feel anything when tears clung to her lashes and her voice was hoarse with emotion. She was either an incredible actress or she deeply cared for the child.

"Would you please send for him now?" she asked, her gaze meeting his and holding it. "Please?"

He wasn't ready to return the child to a woman who'd abandon him to a stranger, but her husky, tearful request softened his resistance. She sounded sincere, as well as anxious, and Giovanni reached into his pocket and drew out his phone to send a text message to his housekeeper, requesting that the child be brought in. "There," he said quietly, "He should be here soon."

"Thank you," she said gratefully, shooting him a smile.

Her smile knocked him off balance. It shaped her generous mouth, tilting the corners up, rounding her cheeks and warming her dark brown eyes. She was an attractive woman, but when she smiled she was positively beautiful.

He frowned, irritated with himself for noticing. He didn't

want to find her beautiful. Nor did he want to remember how she'd felt outside by the canal, her slim body pressed to his, all curves and soft warmth. Just because she was soft and warm, didn't mean her heart was pure or her intentions good.

A light knock sounded on the open office door and Anna entered carrying the child, who was now awake and squirming, making fretful cries. Anna glanced at him, and he nodded at Rachel.

Rachel moved forward, meeting the maid partway, eagerly taking the infant, cuddling him close to her breast. She kissed the top of his head, and then his temple, and crooned something in his ear. The baby stopped crying. She kissed him again, gently rocking him and he lifted his head after a moment and looked up into her eyes and smiled.

A knot formed in Giovanni's chest. He glanced away, uncomfortable. Here, supposedly, was his brother's son, and yet Gio was an outsider.

It crossed his mind that maybe he had waited too long to become acquainted with his nephew. In trying to be cautious and thorough with his investigation, he'd allowed Rachel to bond with the child. If he wasn't careful, she might run and disappear with Michael. He couldn't allow that to happen. He'd lost Antonio. He couldn't lose Antonio's only child.

Giovanni stepped around to the front of his desk, and moved a pile of papers to a different corner, and then closed a file on his lap. "Michael likes you," he said casually.

Rachel froze. For a second she'd forgotten all about Gio, which seemed impossible now that she was looking up at him. Giovanni Marcello was not a man you'd ever forget. His energy was intense, and at times, overwhelming. "I love him," she answered.

"You really didn't have any intention of leaving him here, did you?"

"I prayed I wouldn't have to get into the water taxi, and I didn't."

"But what if I hadn't come out? Would you have gone?"

"I would have returned to my hotel and waited for you there." She kissed one of Michael's small fists, his skin soft and damp. The small hand had been in his mouth just moments ago. She wrinkled her nose, which made Michael laugh. "I would have waited for maybe twenty, thirty minutes, but if you hadn't come by then, I would have returned here."

"And done what?"

"Broken down your door. Screamed bloody murder."

"It didn't make you uneasy, leaving him here?"

Her heart did a painful beat as guilt assailed her. "It terrified me." She nuzzled Michael's cheek, breathing in his sweet baby scent. "But the future was equally terrifying, and so I did what I thought I had to do, believing that ultimately, you would emerge, and you would help, and you'd make sure that your brother's son would be raised by those who loved him."

Giovanni sat down in his desk chair and leaned back. "How could you have so much faith in a stranger, when you knew I'd rejected all your other attempts to see me?

"Because Antonio had such faith in you." She saw his expression darken and she felt a pang of anxiety, but she'd started down this path and had to finish. Fighting the flurry of nerves, she lightly patted the baby's back, as much to soothe him as to calm herself. "He said you were the best of the best and absolutely trustworthy. He'd said more than once that the Marcellos would not have what they do today if it wasn't for you and your sacrifices."

"It's never a sacrifice when you're helping your family."

"But you still gave up your needs for theirs."

"Just what did Antonio tell you?" he asked. "I'm interested in knowing. It would help keep his memory alive."

She shot him a look over the baby's head. It was obviously that Giovanni wasn't asking so much as commanding her to share. She smiled faintly, thinking how nice it must be to have so much power over others. He wasn't just accustomed to people doing *what* he wanted, but *when* he wanted it and exactly the *way* he wanted it.

He must have caught the curve of her lips. "You're smiling," he said.

Her shoulders twisted. "I was just thinking we're so different, and our expectations are so different. I arrived here in Venice, shaking and nervous, so nervous that I hadn't slept in days and couldn't eat. I was so worried about the outcome. I was certain you'd refuse me, certain you wouldn't see us, but hoping, praying, you might." She was talking too much, practically babbling, but she couldn't stop herself now that she'd begun. "You see, I came prepared to plead and beg, fight and cry. I came determined to get on my knees if need be—"

"You are aware that is not how you presented yourself this morning at my front door? There was no begging or pleading. You showed up armed and dangerous."

"We both know that first impressions matter. If I started out weak, you wouldn't have respected me or taken my request seriously. And I need you to respect me, not because it will change me, or the outcome of my life, but because it will change Michael's."

Giovanni looked at her from beneath his lashes, his blue gaze piercing, assessing, his firm mouth pressed into an uncompromising line. But something *had* changed. The very air felt different, charged somehow with an energy and emotion she couldn't decipher. Her stomach cramped from exhaustion and far too many nerves. "I think this is our cue to leave. I have rooms booked at the Hotel Arcadia, and we'll return there now so Michael can be changed and have another bottle before taking his afternoon nap."

For a long moment there was silence, and then Gio leaned forward. "I think you should stay here."

She blinked, confused. "Here? Why?"

He rose and walked toward her. "You've started something, calling the paparazzi and inviting them here. You unleashed the wolves, and once they're out, they don't go away. They're circling, waiting for you—"

"You make it sound as if they're going to attack!"

"Because they will. And you're not going to be able to control them." He stopped in front of her, his gaze raking her first, and then the baby, who was contentedly gumming his fist. "It's not safe for you out there anymore."

Rachel's heart was racing, and not because he was frightening her, but standing this close she could feel his incredible physical energy as strongly as when he'd held her and kissed her outside in front of the cameras and anybody else watching. "They are photographers, not assassins."

"They might as well be assassins. They're not your friends. They'll want a piece of you, again and again."

"I'll keep that in mind."

"Then I'll send for your things from the Arcadia and we'll get you settled here—"

"No!"

He ignored her protest. "It's not safe for you out there. You can't be running around Venice, hopping in and out of water taxis with my nephew, and there is no need, either, when we can accomplish everything we need here, in privacy."

"I'm not…comfortable…staying here."

One of his black eyebrows lifted.

"It's your home, not mine," she said too quickly. "I'm not suggesting you'd be a poor host, but I would be a poor guest. I don't sleep well and I spend half the night pacing, unable to relax."

"But you will be able to relax here. You'll have help with the child—"

"Can you please stop calling him the child? His name is Michael. Michael Marcello."

"Michael Marcello Bern," he corrected. "I've seen the birth certificate. Your sister and my brother were not married, which is why Marcello has become a middle name instead of a surname."

"*This* is why I don't want to stay here," she said, looking away and biting down hard on her lower lip.

Instead of trying to meet her halfway, he was sharp and negative, offering nothing but criticisms. He didn't want to see Michael as a real person. He didn't want to acknowledge Michael as someone of value. No, far better to make him a problem. Something to be discussed the way you'd discuss a bad business deal.

"He's a gorgeous boy, and he's inherited the Marcello coloring. I don't know if he looks like Antonio. I don't know what Antonio looked like as a baby, but he's lovely—"

"No one is criticizing him, and no one is locking you up, or taking your freedom away. But you need help—you've said so many times—and you'll get that help here."

She looked down into Michael's face. His big dark eyes looked up at her, his expression trusting and adoring. Her heart squeezed. She loved him. She'd become so attached to him and couldn't imagine life without him. "I don't want my old life back. He's…mine…now. But yes, help, would be nice. The *right* help that is."

"Then stay here where Michael can get lots of attention and you can rest."

Rachel drew a breath. "I really would be free to come and go? I could go for walks, or shopping?"

"As long as you don't take Michael, yes, as I am going to insist that he stays here, hidden and secure. I want to keep him from the cameras. What we discuss, and the decisions we make, should not be dictated by the media." He reached into his pocket and drew out his phone. "I'll send for Anna. She'll show you the way to the guest rooms on the fourth floor."

CHAPTER SIX

SHE'D BEEN TO Venice once before, and she'd loved the city then. It had been like a fantasy, an implausible city built on water with twisting streets and secret courtyards, whimsical arched bridges and mysterious exteriors that hid fairytale interiors.

She'd spent her entire visit wishing she could get lost inside one of the grand private homes lining the canals, exploring the historic palazzos, discovering the Venice that tourists never got to see. Four years later, she was back, a guest in one of the finest Venetian palazzos, and her guest suite took her breath away.

"Your room, Signorina Bern," Anna said, opening the tall wood shutters, allowing light to pour in.

Despite the gray gloomy day outside, the room glowed with color. The thick wood moldings and beamed ceiling were a lustrous gold, and the walls were covered in a fine blue silk the color of aquamarine above a teal and ivory marble wainscoting. A plush carpet in a brilliant blue with a gold and cream border nearly hid the dark hardwood floor, while the soaring four-poster canopy bed dominated the middle of the room, the posts completely hidden by opulent silk curtains and swags of fringed valances in the same gleaming aquamarine hue as the walls. The effect was dazzling, and would have been overwhelming if not for the crisp white bed coverlet and line of plump pillows against the blue painted headboard.

Anna pointed to the tall antique wardrobe with the mirrored doors. *"Il vostro guardaroba."* She struggled to remember her English. "For your clothes, yes?"

Rachel nodded, patting Michael's back. "Yes, thank you."

Then Anna crossed the room, moving to the center of the far wall, and opened the tall door, showing her through to a connected room where a gentleman was putting together a crib. "For the bambino."

It was another bedroom, smaller and far less opulent, the walls a pale shade of green, and the bed was smaller as well, anchored to the wall and featuring a cornice with green brocade fabric. The room was pretty and fresh with a pair of armchairs flanking the marble fireplace, but nothing like the grandeur of her room.

"Very nice," Rachel said, thinking it a lovely room, the colors reminding her of a nursery, but she didn't need Michael in a separate room. "But he could sleep in my room. His crib can be set up in mine."

Anna frowned. *"Non so quella parola."*

Rachel had no idea what the maid was saying and was too worn-out to try to make herself clear, when really, Michael's crib was not all that far, especially if she kept the door open between the rooms. She nodded, giving in.

Anna's gaze skimmed the baby's room and then the blue bedroom. She seemed satisfied with what she saw. *"Vorresti pranzo?"* she asked.

Rachel hated how stupid she felt. *"Pranzo?"*

Anna made the motion of feeding herself. "Eat. Lunch? *Pranzo*, yes?"

Actually Rachel was suddenly quite hungry. "Yes, please. Thank you."

As the door closed behind the maid, Rachel sat down with Michael in the blue velvet upholstered chair, and sighed, flattened. It had been quite the morning. Her head was spinning. She closed her eyes, and didn't open them until the knock at her door woke her.

Glancing down at Michael, she saw that he, too, was

sleeping. She smiled a little and carefully rose, opening the door for Anna, who had brought her a lunch tray.

Anna positioned the tray on the small table next to the blue chair, shifting the small plates of crostini topped with truffle-laced cheese, prosciutto and whipped salted cod forward, leaving the bowl of salad behind, before opening the bottle of fizzy water and filling a glass for Rachel. "Thank you," Rachel said gratefully.

Gio entered the room as Anna slipped out. He was carrying Michael's diaper bag and he placed it on the foot of the bed.

Rachel was between bites. She slowly set the toast down and just looked at Gio, who seemed impossibly tall and imposing.

"Do you need anything?" he asked gruffly.

"I'm fine," she answered, giving a strained smile. "I've gotten quite adept at eating one-handed." But just then Michael shifted, stretching, and slid across her chest. She readjusted him and grimaced. "Perhaps adept isn't the right word, but we get by."

Giovanni's forehead creased. "Have you really had no help?"

"Friends will sometimes pop by, and when they do, I practically shove Michael into their arms before dashing off to shower and shampoo my hair."

"If I was one of your friends, I don't think I'd stop by very often."

She grinned ruefully. "They don't, not anymore. I think they've all realized I'll just put them to work…and then I'll disappear."

He stood in front of her, looking down at her, a crease between his strong black brows. "He looks very much like Antonio," he said after a long moment.

"I wondered," she answered.

Another uncomfortable beat of silence passed. "Hand him to me. My arms work, and you can eat."

Giovanni didn't have a lot of experience with babies. He hadn't thought about being a father since he ended his engagement to Adelisa. But seeing Michael nestle against Rachel's breast stirred something within him.

Love. Longing. Pain.

Not for his own children, but for this baby. Antonio's son.

He missed Antonio. He missed his best friend. Antonio had been warmth and humor, wit and charm. He'd balanced Gio and provided perspective. Just seeing the baby—Antonio's baby—made the grief more acute. Maybe it was because the baby also made Antonio real again.

In Michael, Antonio still lived.

Gio took the baby from Rachel and awkwardly settled him on his shoulder. Michael fussed a little, and then relaxed, back asleep.

The small body was warm. The infant's hand flexed and relaxed against Gio's neck. The feel of Michael's tiny fingers made the air trap in his lungs. His chest tightened—more sensation, more uncomfortable sensation.

Even without a DNA test, Giovanni was increasingly certain that Michael was Antonio's. There was definitely something in the baby boy's face that reminded him of the Marcellos, and not just because the infant had a thatch of jet-black hair and the dark bright eyes. The six-month-old had a habit of pulling his brows, frowning in concentration, making himself look like a world-weary old man. It was something Antonio had always done, even as a very young child. He'd focus intently, thinking whatever he was thinking, and then when satisfied he'd smile.

The smile was Antonio.

The frown was Antonio.

Which meant, Michael belonged here in Venice. The Marcellos were Venetian. They didn't grow up in America, much less on the West Coast in a city like Seattle.

"Won't you miss him if you return to work?" Gio asked quietly.

"Yes," she answered, looking unhappy.

"Then stay home with him."

"But I have bills—"

"You've come to me for help. Let me help."

"How?"

"You wanted financial help. I'll give it."

"You'd pay my rent? And make my car payment? And give me an allowance for food and incidentals?" Her brows pulled. "I don't think so. I couldn't accept that. I don't want to be that dependent on anyone."

"Don't think of it that way. Think of it as earning a salary. Instead of paying for a nanny, I'd pay you."

"Which would make you my employer." Her cheeks flushed a dark pink. "No, thank you."

"But you need an employer."

"I have one. And it's a job I like very much, too. I need help paying for a nanny, that's all."

"But that's not all you need. You've made it clear that you want my family to be part of his life. You want us to ease some of the responsibility. So let us do that. Let me do that."

She pushed the tray back and rose. "I can take him now. I'm finished."

"No need. I have him. Why don't you relax?"

Her jaw tensed. She tried to smile but it was strained. "I'm sure you have things to do, whereas I have nothing."

"You could rest. Take a nap—"

"Can't. I don't really sleep anymore." But she did sit down again, and her hands folded in her lap. She was still smiling, but the smile was brittle. He saw for the first time the tension at her mouth and the shadows under her eyes.

"Is Michael sleeping?" Gio asked.

"He still wakes up at least once each night."

No wonder she was exhausted. "At what point do babies sleep through the night?"

"He should be able to sleep through the night now. I'm afraid it's a habit he's developed. He doesn't drink much when he wakes up. He likes to socialize." Her lips pressed into a line. "I'm trying to convince him that daytime is much better for play."

"Perhaps I should hire a night nurse while you're here—"

"No! Don't do that. He'd be frightened. It's hard enough not being in his own bed, in his own room. Having a stranger care for him would surely confuse him."

"But what about you? Couldn't you use a night of uninterrupted sleep?"

"Yes, but I would feel guilty, and then I wouldn't sleep and it'd be a pointless exercise all the way around."

Gio glanced down into Michael's face and then at Rachel. "But if you hope to return to work, you need to get used to help. Soon you'll be away from him for eight hours or more a day."

He could see the misery in her eyes. She wasn't happy about that, either.

Gio gave her a long thoughtful look. "I'm glad you're here. It's time I did my part." He carefully eased the baby back into her arms. "We'll discuss this tonight. Let's meet for drinks in the library at seven. Signora Fabbro will stay with Michael."

"Mrs. Fabbro?" she repeated.

He nodded once and walked out.

Heart pounding, Rachel watched Gio leave, her insides a jittery mess.

Everything was changing. She could feel it. Once again her life was being upended.

But before she could sort out why she felt so uneasy, Anna arrived with Rachel's luggage. The maid wheeled in the large suitcase, and then removed the lunch tray.

Suddenly everything felt different—not just precarious, but overwhelming, and she didn't even understand what was changing.

While Anna insisted on unpacking the suitcase, Rachel placed Michael in the crib, and then she didn't know what to do with herself.

Jet lag didn't help anxiety, and right now her anxiety was at an all-time high. Sleep would help. Sleep always helped, but instead she paced the luxurious suite on the fourth floor of the palazzo, a fist pressed to her mouth as she chewed mindlessly on a knuckle, trying to ease the sick, heavy panicked sensation filling her middle.

She understood why Giovanni wanted her in his family palace. Notoriously private, he was trying to limit the media's access to Rachel and the baby. He was trying to protect his family name, and he wanted security and safeguards in place, but for her, it was suffocating. It was hard giving up her personal space, and she couldn't help feeling as if she'd lost her independence and control. Control was important in this instance because she needed room to move and think.

Before lunch she would have said that she didn't think Gio knew the first thing about babies, and she'd thought his coldness had been due to inexperience with small children, but when he'd taken Michael from her, he'd handled his nephew with an easy confidence and almost affection.

What if Giovanni wanted to do more than provide financial assistance? What if Gio wanted Michael to stay in Venice?

The thought turned her insides into ice. She wasn't just accustomed to caring for Michael now, he was part of her. She loved him. She never used the words out loud, but she was his mother now. He was her son. If Giovanni challenged her for custody, Rachel would be in trouble. Juliet didn't have a living will. There had been no instructions for Michael, nothing to indicate her preference for guardianship.

Gio had a legitimate claim if he wanted to sue for custody.

She prayed he didn't want to be guardian. She prayed he didn't want to be responsible for a baby, because truthfully, she didn't want him making decisions about Michael's life or physical care. She just needed Giovanni's financial support so that once she and Michael were back in Seattle, she could hire a good sitter or nanny, buy the basic things a small person needed and move on with her life, a life as a single mother.

Mrs. Fabbro arrived at Rachel's door promptly at six-forty-five, announcing herself with a firm, loud knock.

Small and sturdy-looking, Mrs. Fabbro had steel-colored hair, shrewd dark eyes and a firm mouth that didn't seem likely to smile as she marched into the room. Introductions were awkward as her English was worse than Anna's and Rachel struggled in her limited Italian, but conversation was no longer an issue once Mrs. Fabbro spotted Michael in his fleecy pajamas on his blanket on the floor.

Rachel had placed him there so he wouldn't fall or get hurt while she dressed for dinner, and he seemed perfectly happy playing with his hands and kicking his legs in the air and just enjoying his freedom. But from Mrs. Fabbro's rapid Italian, the older woman didn't seem pleased to find her charge on the floor. She walked across the room and scooped him up from his blanket, crooning to him in Italian as if they were long-lost friends.

For a long moment Michael stared at Mrs. Fabbro, not sure whether she was friend or foe, but then his eyes crinkled and he grinned and put a wet fist on her chin.

"Bello raggazo," she said approvingly.

Michael chortled, and Mrs. Fabbro put him on her hip for the tour of the rooms. "His bed is in here," Rachel said, walking into the adjoining room that had obviously been a sitting room before someone added the crib.

"His bottle is here," she added, pointing to the sideboard, where she'd laid out his bottles and formula. "One bottle before bed, and then I burp him and put him down. He sleeps on his back, no covers, or toys with him."

She'd already made a bottle so it would be ready, but she made a second one up, just so the woman could see how they were made. "Do you have any questions?" Rachel asked.

Mrs. Fabbro shook her head and took Michael's hand and helped him wave bye-bye before taking him on a walk around his room.

Rachel was now free to finish preparing for dinner but she stood a moment in the doorway watching the older woman talk to Michael and point things out, giving him his first lessons in Italian.

Rachel's eyes stung, and she blinked back the prickle of tears. She wasn't sure why she suddenly felt so emotional. She ought to be happy that Mrs. Fabbro was efficient and quick to take charge of Michael, but Michael had been her responsibility long enough that without him, she felt painfully empty.

Things had been chaotic and stressful for months, and it was only recently that she'd begun to feel more settled and comfortable as Michael's mom. They'd begun to find a rhythm, and they'd created a schedule that helped them both, and she understood that it was her and Michael together now. She understood that it would probably always be just the two of them, at least in terms of them as a nuclear family.

If only she could take Michael with her to drinks and

dinner. She'd feel better. Safer. Michael was a good distraction. Whenever she'd felt too much earlier, she'd patted Michael's back and kissed his sweet soft cheek, and he'd helped calm her. But tonight she wouldn't have Michael as a buffer. It would just be Giovanni and her. Alone.

Rachel returned to the tall painted wardrobe where she'd hung up the two dresses she'd brought. The rest were trousers and sweaters and coats, winter wear appropriate for Venice's chilly wet weather. The dresses were ones she might have worn to a business dinner, a long-sleeved black velvet sheath dress with a V-neckline, or a chocolate-colored lace dress with cap sleeves and a tiered skirt that went from high to low, with the shortest ruffle at her knees and then the longest touching the ground.

She'd brought the dresses thinking that maybe there would be a dinner with Giovanni Marcello, imagining he might invite her and Michael to his home one evening, or maybe to meet at a local restaurant, but being here was nothing like she'd imagined. She felt so unsettled, so nervous.

Aware that she'd soon be late, she quickly slipped into her black velvet dress and pulled her hair back into a loose chignon before slipping into heels and reaching for a dark gray velvet wrap with a pretty black and silver beaded fringe. It had been her great-grandmother's, and even though it was a vintage nineteen-twenties shawl, it still looked exquisite and just a little bit well-loved, but perfect for a night like tonight when Rachel needed confidence.

The elderly butler from the morning was waiting on the third landing for Rachel and he walked her slowly down the hall. The butler gravely opened the door and stepped back, and Rachel entered the Marcello library, a windowless room where the walls were covered in antique ruby brocade paper and narrow gilded bookshelves rivaled massive oil paintings. The center of the room was filled with oversize crimson sofas and thickly padded upholstered armchairs, pieces promising comfort and not just style.

Rachel spotted Gio across the room, dressed in a dark suit and white dress shirt. He looked immaculate and handsome—far, far too handsome—and it suddenly struck her as odd that he hadn't ever married. He was a man who had everything. Why was he still a bachelor in his late thirties?

Giovanni turned at the sound of the door quietly closing. He'd been pouring a drink and he straightened when he spotted Rachel hesitating on the threshold. She looked different this evening. Younger, softer, a little less sure of herself.

Earlier today she'd reminded him of Adelisa, but tonight she was just Rachel, and he didn't know if it was due to the simplicity of her black velvet dress, or perhaps the way she'd styled her hair, the long thick strands twisted and pinned at the back of her neck in a style that struck him as Edwardian. Even her dress and shawl had a hint of old-world elegance. Maybe that was the difference. She looked pretty and fresh without being overdone.

"I'm sorry for being late," she said a little breathlessly.

He shook his head. "Not late."

"I think I am, by about ten minutes."

"It's just an *aperitivo*, a predinner drink. Our schedule is not set in stone." He nodded at the tray with the crystal decanters and glasses. "What can I pour for you?"

"Do you have any wine, or is that not a suitable *aperitivo*?"

He smiled faintly. "Sparkling wine is definitely suitable. Would you prefer Prosecco, Fragolino, or perhaps Brachetto?"

She moved slowly toward him, expression shy. "Are they all wine? Will you think me terribly gauche when I say I don't know the difference?"

"They're all wine with bubbles. And does my opinion matter? Earlier today you said you didn't care what I thought of you."

Her shoulders twisted. "I was feeling defensive earlier."

"And you aren't now?"

"I've had a chance to nap and relax, and gain a little more perspective."

"And what is that?"

"If we're to be allies, not adversaries, we need to get along, right?"

For a long moment he just looked at her. "We shall see what you have to say after I show you the papers."

"What's in the papers?"

"Let's have that drink first." He saw her quick glance, and the worry in her brown eyes. She wouldn't like what she saw. He wasn't surprised at the newspapers. It's what he'd intended, but it changed everything. For him. For her. For all of them.

"It sounds as if a quick lesson is in order," he said casually. "Prosecco is Italian, it's a sparkling wine made here in Veneto from Glera grapes. Fragolino is a sparkling red wine, also made in the Veneto, from the Isabella grape, while Brachetto, also a sparkling red, comes from the Piedmont region." He looked at her. "What sounds good?"

She wrinkled her nose. "Too many choices."

"Let us simplify. Red or white?"

"White, please."

"Prosecco it is." He opened a bottle and filled a flute for her. "I think you made a good choice. This comes from the Marcello vineyard."

"You have a winery?"

"It's a small one, but I'm proud of it. The wines are beginning to win awards and receive international recognition."

"Are you very involved?"

"I bought the ailing vineyard six years ago. We're just starting to turn a profit. Winemaking is a labor of love. You don't do it to get rich."

"Is the Marcello vineyard your labor of love?"

"More than I expected."

"Now I'm even more embarrassed that I knew nothing about Italian wine."

"I don't pretend to be a vintner. I'm an engineer. I build things."

She took the flute from him, and then looked up into his eyes. "I'd like to see the papers. You have me worried now."

He walked her to the long table behind the couch. He'd cleared the table of everything but the newspapers and pages he'd printed from various digital media sites.

Every story ran with one or more photos, and every story had a shot of Rachel with Michael, but there were far more photographs of Rachel in Giovanni's arms than of Michael himself. The baby was a secondary story to Giovanni Marcello passionately kissing the mother of his child.

He watched Rachel lean over the table to get a better look at the different pages, her lashes lowering as she scanned the headlines, and then glanced over the photos. As she studied the papers, color suffused her cheeks, turning her pale ivory skin to a hot pink.

"I can't read the headlines since they seem to be in every language but English," she said quietly. "Can you please translate for me?"

"'Marcello's Love-Child! Gio Marcello's Secret Affair! Mystery Mistress and Mother to His Child! Is This the Marcello Heir?'"

As he read the translated headlines to her, the pink color receded, leaving her face pale. "Is there no mention of Antonio? Do they all think that the baby is yours?"

"They all seem to think that Michael is ours."

"But I told them the baby was the Marcello heir—" She

broke off, lips tightening. She gave her dark head a shake, the coiled knot at her nape glossy in the soft lighting. "The kiss. That changed everything, didn't it?" She looked up at him, frustration etched on her face. "You said it would, and you were right."

"I had to control the story."

"But we're not a couple, and he's not our child, which makes every bit of this a lie!"

"The tabloids don't care. They just want to sell copies and increase their advertising."

She began to quickly stack the pages. "Thankfully these are not stories on the front page of the papers," she said, irritably. "And these are not serious newspapers—"

"Well, two of the papers are national newspapers. The story and photos are not on the front page, but placed inside the lifestyle and society pages."

Papers stacked, she folded them in half, and then folded them again, hiding all the headlines and incriminating photos. Once she'd finished hiding the headlines, she reached for her flute and gulped the fizzy white wine as if she, too, could disappear into the crisp bubbles. "No one will take me seriously at work if this story gets traction." She shot him a desperate look. "You must smash this story, before I no longer have a job."

"You were the one that contacted the media. You started this."

"I didn't start this, I shared the truth. Facts—"

"Facts that could wreck the Marcello name and reputation. I couldn't have that."

"But my name and reputation doesn't matter?"

"One's reputation always matters, but you've far less invested in your name and brand than I do."

"No, I'm not a billionaire. No, I don't head up a huge corporation. But my name is also very important. Maybe not to you, but it is to me." She exhaled hard. "I'm going to correct them."

"We're not going to correct them. This is what I wanted."

"Even though the stories are false?"

"We know that, but the public doesn't, and in this instance, fiction is preferable, because these are headlines we can shape and control."

CHAPTER SEVEN

RACHEL SET HER half-empty flute down and walked away. She'd only had a couple of sips but the wine was going to her head, making her emotional, which of course didn't make it easier to think.

It was also easier to be logical when she wasn't standing close to Giovanni. He was too beautiful, too much like a model she might have admired in the pages of a glossy magazine with his high cheekbones and strong chin and firm mouth that kissed far too well. He had a face that made her melt, but unlike Antonio who was laid-back and friendly, Giovanni was hard and reserved. Shuttered. He exuded intensity, confidence and power, things she could handle when sitting at a conference table or on the phone in a long-distance call, but not close to her, not when Giovanni made the power feel physical, masculine, sensual.

Even now, standing across the room, she could still feel him, his energy hot and simmering, electrifying the room. Electrifying her.

She didn't think she'd ever met a man who'd filled a room the way he did, owning the air and space, swallowing all the oxygen so that she couldn't breathe.

Most troubling of all was that a small part of her had almost enjoyed the intensity, and that same part of her was humming with awareness. She'd never admit it to anyone but she'd been drawn to his energy and the shimmering heat surrounding him—even though the heat and energy could obliterate her.

Her brain was warning her off, telling her that he was too much for her. Too hard, too confident, too dangerous. Her practical side understood that he didn't care for her, and that he wouldn't protect her, that nothing good would come of allowing herself to be intrigued by him.

But she was already intrigued. She was fascinated and curious and drawn to him…

Standing next to him moments ago, she wanted him to touch her again. She'd wanted him to reach for her and cover her mouth with his and make her feel what she'd felt earlier.

If that wasn't crazy, she didn't know what was.

No, crazy was the fact that she didn't like him, or admire him, and yet she still wanted him to touch her again. She wanted to feel more. Even now, with sofas and tables and armchairs between them, she was still responding to him, the very thought of him kissing her again making her shiver inwardly, making her ache.

"Why do you want the paparazzi to think the baby is ours?" she asked, her voice low and husky.

"It's simpler."

"It's actually not. It is going to be far more work trying to convince people that we were a couple and we had a baby—"

"They already believe it."

"But I don't like that story!" Heat rushed through her, the heat so strong that her skin prickled and burned.

"I don't like it, either, but given our choices, it's the better one."

"Why? *How?*"

"This version deflects attention away from Antonio and Juliet. We can protect and preserve their memory, allowing the mistakes of the past to fade—"

"Antonio and Juliet had a baby. Why is that such a travesty?"

"They weren't married, or even serious. It was a brief affair, a sexual fling—"

"I disagree. Juliet loved your brother, deeply."

"I'm sure she wanted to be convincing."

"She really did care, Giovanni."

He shrugged. "Maybe as much as she could care, but either way, she was ultimately selfish and destructive and not someone I want associated with my family."

Rachel recoiled. "That is incredibly harsh," she breathed, putting a hand to her middle, trying to calm herself, not easy when her stomach did wild flips. Juliet hadn't been an angel. She didn't have many altruistic bones in her body, and yet she wasn't the devil incarnate. She'd been complicated and had had aspirations—aspirations Rachel didn't understand—but when all was said and done, she was her sister, her younger sister, and it was painful to hear Giovanni's brutal denouncement. "You met her then?" she asked.

"No. But I know a great deal about her, and women like her."

His scathing tone made her see red. Her chin jerked up. "Juliet loved him—"

"There was no love. I can promise you that." Gio's light blue eyes narrowed, his full mouth firming. He looked hard and darkly handsome, arrogant and utterly unapproachable. "Your sister saw her opportunity to make a fortune and took advantage of the situation."

"I am absolutely certain Juliet didn't know he was ill. *I* didn't know he was ill, and I was the one that introduced them."

"*You're* responsible."

She thought for a moment he was joking, or teasing, but there was no softening of his features, or flicker of warmth in his eyes. "Do you need to blame someone? If so, yes, blame me. It's all my fault. I did it. The love affair, the pregnancy, the tragic loss of two beautiful people—"

"You're not helping."

"I'm not helping? What about you? Have you no responsibility at all, to anything other than your business, and your name, and protecting your brand? You say my sister was selfish—well, you are every bit as calculating and self-serving. It's a shame you didn't meet her. You and Juliet would have been a perfect match!"

"You are not that innocent, Rachel. You have played a significant part in this drama."

"Did I? How fascinating."

"I'd use the word despicable, rather than fascinating, and it makes me wonder how many other men did you introduce her to? How many of your clients did she date?"

"That has no bearing on Juliet and Antonio's relationship."

"I think it does. You were her matchmaker, weren't you? You'd introduce her to your wealthy clients, helping her to land a rich husband."

"I never played matchmaker. Not once. Antonio and Juliet met because your brother and I were out discussing the plane delivery schedule over a drink and she walked in, and so yes, I introduced them, but it wasn't planned."

"So she never dated any other of your clients? And think carefully about your answer, as your credibility is on the line. You weren't the only one to hire a private investigator. I know all about her *dating* history."

Rachel drew a rough breath, shaken. "What do you mean?"

"She'd been on the hunt for a rich man for years, and she used you fairly frequently for introductions—"

"It may have happened once or twice, but it was by chance. I never set out to introduce her to any of my customers. It was always by accident."

"You expect me to believe that?" He crossed the room, closing the distance in long livid strides. "Come on. Be serious. Tell me how it really worked. Did you get a percentage? Were you ever offered a piece of the action?"

She backed up into a bookshelf, and then could go no farther. "How can you say such a thing? What is wrong with you?"

"It struck me just now that you are part of the game. I suspected it—"

"You're wrong. I'm not playing a game. There is no game. There is just a baby boy that needs our help." She drew a short sharp breath, face hot, her heart hammering so hard she felt like throwing up. He was awful. Beyond awful. "Good night," she choked, putting down her glass and racing from the room to climb the white Carrera marble stairs as quickly as she could.

She heard Gio's oath as he followed.

She ran faster, but his legs were longer and he reached her just before she reached the next floor, his hand circling her wrist, stopping her progress. She teetered on her heels.

He put his hand on her waist, turning her around. "Where are you going? What are you doing?" he growled.

She was out of breath and close to tears. "I'm not going to stand there and listen to you make ugly accusations. You have a twisted view of the world, and I refuse to be dragged into—"

His head dropped, his mouth covering hers, silencing the words. She stiffened, but he pulled her closer. Her lips parted to protest and she tasted the warm sweet wine on his breath and could smell his fragrance and the mixture was delicious. He smelled delicious.

Funny how she disliked Giovanni so much and yet she loved his kisses…

He made her feel beautiful and desirable, and in his arms, with his mouth on hers, his body pressed against her, she felt wonderfully alive. Almost too alive. Fire streaked through her veins, making her hum.

She'd always felt this way on the inside, deep down, but

no one had ever brought it out in her, or seen her as anything but practical and pragmatic. And cold.

But she wasn't cold. Her feelings were strong and they went so deep. She'd spent her life trying to hide the intensity of those emotions, but Giovanni had somehow discovered them and he knew just how to use them against her.

She didn't know if he felt her shudder, but he drew her even closer, his lips parting hers, his tongue caressing the softness of her lower lip, and then stroking deeper, sweeping her mouth, electrifying her nerve endings, making them dance.

Was it terrible that she liked the way he touched her? That she welcomed his arm around her waist and his hand sliding low on her hip?

She welcomed the crush of his chest and the sinewy strength of his legs. He was hard and commanding, and nothing had ever felt so exciting, or quite so right.

No kiss had ever felt so good. She felt good. Brilliant, and beautiful, and fiercely alive, tingling everywhere. It wasn't real; it couldn't be real. Men loved Juliet, not her. Juliet fascinated men with her physical perfection. And Rachel was so far from perfect...

The thought stopped her, ending the magic, reminding her of who she was, and who he was, and why he was here.

She pulled back, breathing heavily, body still exquisitely sensitive, to look up at Gio. "We shouldn't do this." She struggled to speak, her voice low and hoarse. "It won't help."

He stared down at her, his brilliant eyes studying her intently, taking in every inch of her face before reaching out to trace one of her eyebrows and then the other. *"Bella donna."*

She blinked, unable to think of anything but the stroke

of his finger along the arch of her brow. It felt good to be touched. Everything inside her was warm and aching, tingling with need. She'd forgotten that she could feel need. And desire.

Maybe that's why the desire was so strong. Maybe she'd gone too long without feeling anything, and now she was feeling, and it was intense. Her entire body trembled. Her lashes closed as he caressed her jaw, his thumb stroking along the jawbone and then over the fullness of her mouth. Waves of pleasure rippled through her and she couldn't suppress the shudders. It was embarrassing, feeling so much, wanting to be kissed and touched and pleasured.

She swallowed hard and opened her eyes, her gaze locking with Gio's. His eyes were hot, bright, and the intensity in the depths burned her. He wanted her, too.

It was a heady realization and it rocked her, bumping up against her confidence, or lack of. She could maybe pass as a decent kisser but she wasn't experienced, and she didn't have the first idea how to please a man.

Furthermore, she shouldn't be thinking of how to please a man if that man was Michael's uncle, billionaire Giovanni Marcello.

"We'll both regret this tomorrow," she said, keeping a hand on his arm because she didn't trust her legs, or her balance. "It'll make the discussions more difficult."

"You were the one that said it would be better if we liked each other."

"I didn't mean physically."

"You can love a child, and still be a beautiful woman."

"I don't have affairs and flings, Gio. I'm not looking for a relationship, either."

"But you don't have a boyfriend."

"Heavens, no," she choked, face hot. "I'd never kiss you if I did, and I haven't had a relationship in years." It was more than that. She hadn't ever had a serious boyfriend or a first lover, but she wouldn't confess the entire truth. It'd be too mortifying if he knew.

"Why not?"

"For the same reason you prefer to live here, instead of Rome. I'm a solitary creature. I like my space."

"Even though I barely know you, I have to say I don't believe you." He ran a fingertip over her cheekbone and then around her ear. "You strike me as someone who very much needs people. Provided they are the right people."

She was lost, looking into his eyes. He was right. She did need people, good people. It was hard being responsible for everyone and everything. Hard having to be the grown-up, from a very young age. But she'd rather be the grown-up and do the right thing, than be impulsive and hurt Michael and the need for stability in his future. "I agree with you," she said, drawing away. "But I also know that you aren't one of those people for me."

He gave her a look she couldn't decipher. "I'm not in the habit of arguing with women."

"Good."

"But I'm going to prove you wrong."

Her heart did a funny little flutter that made her breathless and hurt all at the same time. "Please don't. I'm only here for a few days. Let's focus on Michael. He's what's important." She climbed one step and then another until she reached the landing, and then paused to look down at Giovanni. Her heart did another painful beat. "Tomorrow let's sort this out for his sake, please. I need to return to Seattle."

"Is that the best thing for Michael? Or the best thing for you?"

She frowned. "It's the best thing for both of us."

"I'm not sure anymore that it is."

Her heart fell. She was right. He was changing his mind.

He wanted Michael to stay here. He wanted Michael in Venice. Her eyes stung and her throat ached.

Before she broke down in tears, or said something she'd regret, Rachel fled.

Gio stood on the marble stair and watched Rachel disappear down the hallway, her footsteps practically flying in her need to escape.

He exhaled shortly. Tonight had not gone as planned, and what had taken place in the library, that was wrong. He knew he was at fault, too. The entire scene weighed on him. His stomach felt like he'd been chewing on rocks and glass.

He didn't understand how he'd lost control of the situation so fast, and so completely. One minute they were discussing the newspaper headlines, and the next they were battling about ambitious Juliet whom Giovanni loathed, and then somehow Rachel was part of the fight and at the receiving end of his frustration and fury.

He didn't actually believe Rachel was Juliet's matchmaker, and he certainly didn't think she'd benefited in any way from Juliet's schemes, but Juliet was as amoral as they came. To pursue a dying man? To deliberately get pregnant, not caring that you were creating a life where the child would never know his or her own father?

Gio was far from perfect. As Rachel had said, he was driven and ambitious, but there had to be a line one didn't cross. Juliet had no such scruples, and she'd needlessly complicated Antonio's final year, creating pain not just for Antonio, but the whole family.

But tonight his frustration wasn't with Juliet. It was with himself.

Why was he so intent on provoking Rachel? Why did he want to test her, tease her, draw a response from her?

What did he want from her?

But that was actually easy. What *didn't* he want from her?

She'd woken him, and the desire consumed him. It had been far too long since he'd felt emotion, or hunger, and he felt both now.

He wanted her. And he would have her.

CHAPTER EIGHT

HE'D GONE TO bed tense, and then woke in the middle of the night to the sound of a baby crying.

It wasn't an ear-piercing cry, but more fretful and prolonged. Giovanni rolled onto his back, smashing his pillow behind his head, and listened, eyes closed, to the wail coming from down the hall, realizing that he'd heard the crying even in his sleep and had incorporated the sound in his dream.

It hadn't been a pleasant dream, either. He'd been talking with Antonio and they'd argued, and he didn't remember what they were arguing about but it was tense, and Antonio turned around to face him, and as he turned the baby was there in his arms. And then the baby was crying, and Antonio blamed him for upsetting Michael, and Giovanni answered that he'd done nothing and that's when he woke up.

And heard the baby crying down the hall in his room.

Was no one going to the baby? Could Rachel not hear him? Or had something happened to Rachel?

Giovanni flipped the covers back and climbed from the bed, throwing his robe on over his pajama bottoms. The pale green room was dimly lit, illuminated only by a small night-light. In the soft yellow glow he could see Rachel holding Michael and patting his back, crooning in his ear but the baby cried on, miserable.

She was facing the oil landscape on the wall, gently jiggling the baby as she studied the scene, unaware that she was being watched. She really was good with Michael, he thought, very much the mother the baby needed.

They would both stay here with him, he decided. It

was logical. It made sense. Michael needed Rachel, and Giovanni wanted both Michael and Rachel…

"Is this normal?" he asked, approaching them.

She startled, turning quickly to face him. "He's teething. It makes him fretful. But he's not settling down and he feels warm to me. He might be coming down with something, which would explain why he's been not quite himself the past few days."

"He's running a fever?"

"I think so."

"You haven't checked?"

She gave him a look he couldn't decipher. "I didn't bring a thermometer with me, but I'll go buy one in the morning. You must have a pharmacy nearby, and if he's feverish, I'll take him to the doctor and have him checked out, just in case." She pressed her lips to the top of the baby's head. "Sorry to have disturbed you but we're fine."

She turned her back on him as she walked away, pacing back across the room, crooning in the fretful baby's ear. In her pink robe, with her hair loose over her shoulders, she was small and delicate and very, *very* appealing.

His body hardened. He wanted her—in his bed, and out of bed. But she was wary of him, almost skittish. "Do you want me to take a turn with him?" he offered. "Could you use a break?"

"I'm fine."

"You always say that."

"Because I am fine."

"Even when you're desperate, you're fine?"

She laughed softly. "I try very hard not to be hysterical. I don't enjoy the state of desperation."

Rachel blinked when Giovanni laughed, the sound low and husky. It was the first time she'd heard him laugh without mockery, and there was something in his voice, something in his amusement that thrilled her, making her flush with pleasure, her skin tingling, her body responding. It took so little for him to wake her up, make her come alive.

"You have a sense of humor," he said.

"Not according to my mother." But her lips curved wryly. "She thought I needed a sense of humor, at least when it came to Juliet."

"How so?"

"I think she expected me to enjoy Juliet's adventures and triumphs more. Instead I was me. Difficult, prickly porcupine Rachel." She tried to smile again, but it felt tight and uncomfortable. "And to be fair, I wasn't amused by Juliet. She was a lot of work and demanded a lot of Mother's time. Or maybe Mother just preferred to focus on Juliet. Juliet was the beautiful daughter after all, and charming and admired by many. It gave my mother great pleasure to show her off."

"Was your mother beautiful?"

"No. She looked like me."

"You are beautiful."

Rachel sputtered. "Hardly. I'm fairly utilitarian, but that's okay. I've had twenty-eight years to come to terms with my attractiveness, or lack of—"

"Are you being serious?"

"Yes, and I don't want compliments. I don't need them. But I have a mirror, and a phone. I'm on social media. I know what beautiful is, and I know what society likes—"

"Society!" he scoffed. "And social media? You allow such things to influence you?"

"I know what's beautiful. Classical features. High cheekbones. Full, plumped lips. Flawless skin. I don't have any of that. My nose is too long, my mouth is too wide, my jaw is too strong, my eyes are a little too close—" She flushed, appalled that she'd said so much.

"I don't agree with you. Not at all."

"I'm not surprised. We don't agree on almost anything."

She turned away, walking with Michael to the curtained window. She'd pushed the heavy silk drapes open earlier so she could see out. The tall houses across the narrow canal were dark but streetlights illuminated the sidewalk and cast a reflecting glimmer on the water. Venice looked so mysterious at night, with its labyrinth of canals and bridges, arches and hidden squares. It would be fun to explore the city at night, maybe even take one of those touristy ghost tours. Not that she wanted to encounter any ghosts.

"Are you really in danger of losing your job?" he asked, breaking the silence.

Rachel drew a slow breath, and then nodded. "I've used up all my sick days and vacation days, floating days and every unpaid leave day I could take. But management wants me back, or they need to hire someone else."

"Would you really miss work if they let you go?"

She glanced at him over her shoulder. "I love planes. I really like my job. It's exciting to be in the same field as my father. Admittedly, I'm not an aeronautical engineer, but I have his same passion for flight...it's exhilarating."

"So you really don't want me to support you. You don't want to stay home."

She hesitated. "Does that make me a bad woman?"

"Of course not."

"Did your mother work?"

"No." He laughed, a low mocking sound. "Her job was to look beautiful and spend money. She did both, quite well."

"Have any of your girlfriends worked?"

He took his time answering, and when he did, he was brief. "I don't really have girlfriends."

"No? What do you have?"

"Mistresses."

"How does a mistress differ from a girlfriend?"

"There is no emotional entanglement. It's a physical relationship." As if reading her confusion, he added bluntly. "I don't love them. And they don't love me."

"What do they get out of the relationship then, besides sex?"

"Great sex. And gifts."

Her brows arched. "That sounds horrible. Have there been many?"

His mouth curved, a crooked mocking smile. "I'm in my late thirties. So yes, there have been many."

"What are they like? Do you have a type?"

He leaned against the wall, hands buried in the robe pockets. The robe was pulling open, revealing the hard, muscular plane of his chest and a hint of his carved, chiseled torso. "I make it a point not to discuss past relationships."

She forced her attention from his incredibly fit body to his ruggedly handsome face. "I suspect it's not because you're protecting them, but because you don't like remembering. For you, there is no point in remembering. What's done is done. What's gone is gone."

Gio's black brow lifted. "You presume to know me?"

She shrugged. "You're an engineer. I work with engineers every day. You're all excessively practical."

"Next thing I know you'll be saying we lack imagination."

"Not so. You have excellent imaginations. If you didn't, how would you problem-solve? You have to imagine something to be able to build it."

"You fascinate me, *bella*."

"I doubt that very much."

His gaze met hers and held. He looked at her so intently that he made her grow warm all over again.

"I like smart women," he said quietly. "I like successful women. I wouldn't say I have a type but I am drawn to brunettes with interesting faces—mouths that are generous, noses that aren't too short or small, jaws that aren't weak."

Heat rushed through her, even as her stomach turned inside out.

She didn't know where to look, or what to do. Spellbound, she stared across the room at a man who was absolutely larger than life and beyond anything she could have imagined for her. There was no reason he should like her, or be fascinated by her.

When little spots appeared before her eyes she realized she needed to breathe, and she dragged in a breath, dizzy, and dazed.

He couldn't possibly be serious, and yet he didn't seem to be laughing at her, or mocking her. He wasn't even smiling.

No, he looked very hard and very virile and far too self-assured. What she wouldn't give to have that kind of confidence.

Heart hammering, she glanced down at the baby in her arms. Michael had finally fallen asleep, his plump cheek pressed to her breast, his thumb against his mouth. He was so sweet, so beautiful. She loved him so much.

"He's out," she said. "I think he'll sleep the rest of the night without any more tears."

"That's good."

"It is," she agreed, kissing the baby again before crossing to his crib. Bending over, she carefully placed him on his back. In his sleep, Michael sighed and stretched, tiny fingers opening and then relaxing. She watched him a moment, suffused with so many different emotions. Love, tenderness, worry, hope.

Across the room she heard a soft click. Rachel looked up only to discover that Gio was gone.

Rachel woke up to a still dark room that was quiet and cool. Far too quiet and cool. Glancing to the door separating her room from Michael's, she saw that it was closed. Throwing back the covers, she raced from bed to yank the door open. The curtains had been drawn and the room was filled with a watery light. She'd taken several steps into the green room when she spotted Mrs. Fabbro walking past the tall arched windows, talking away to Michael in Italian, while Michael babbled back, as if the two were deep in conversation.

Rachel's pulse still pounded, and yet her lips curved into a faint smile.

Michael seemed to adore the older Italian woman.

Mrs. Fabbro spotted Rachel. *"Buongiorno,"* she said, nodding her gray head.

"Is it very late?" Rachel asked.

Mrs. Fabbro didn't seem to understand the question, but she crossed to the wall, and pressed a button. *"Signor Marcello vi aspetta."*

Rachel didn't understand Mrs. Fabbro, either. She walked over and held her hands out, gesturing that she'd like to take the baby.

Mrs. Fabbro seemed most reluctant to hand Michael over, but after a hesitation, she did.

Rachel nuzzled Michael's warm cheek. He smelled sweet and fresh. He must have had a bath this morning. "Has he eaten?" she asked. "Uh… *Bottiglia di latte?*" she stammered, trying to remember the words for bottle, or milk."

"Si. Due."

"He has." Gio's deep male voice came from behind her. "Two."

"Two?" Rachel said. "He never drinks that much when he wakes up."

"It's nearly noon. He's been up for hours."

Her jaw dropped. "I had no idea. I can't believe I slept that long."

"I told everyone you weren't to be disturbed, and Signora Fabbro has enjoyed her time with Michael. You're going to find it difficult to keep him out of her arms. She loves babies and children. She hates it when they grow up."

"Did she come with good references?"

"The best. She was Antonio's and my nanny." His expression softened as he looked at her. "I didn't tell her Michael was Antonio's until today. But I couldn't deny it when she asked."

"She guessed?"

"She knew he had to be mine, or his. He's very much a Marcello."

"You see the resemblance?"

"I do."

"Are you still going to run another DNA test?"

"It won't change the outcome, will it?"

Rachel shook her head.

"You used a reputable company for the testing. It's a company I've used before—" He frowned, a crease forming between his strong black brows.

"You must be hungry."

His abrupt change of subject made Rachel curious. What else was he going to say? "You've done DNA testing before, then?"

"It's getting close to lunch. We should talk, after we've eaten."

He wasn't going to tell her, was he? Rachel hugged Michael, savoring his sweetness, and the light clean scent from his baby shampoo. "I can't think of food until I have my coffee."

"Are you a big coffee drinker?"

"I live in Seattle. We like our coffee." The baby clearly didn't want to be held so tightly. He wiggled and pushed back against her chest. Smiling, Rachel loosened her hold. "He's feisty this morning. He's definitely feeling better."

Mrs. Fabbro now held her hands out, wanting to take

Michael back. Her thin lips weren't smiling and the expression in her dark eyes was somewhat intimidating.

"She really was your nanny?" Rachel asked, glancing from Mrs. Fabbro to Gio.

Gio grinned. For a split second he looked boyish and young. "She was," he answered, still smiling. "She spoiled us rotten. She's a pussycat. Don't let her stern expression fool you."

Rachel handed the squirming baby over and Mrs. Fabbro triumphantly marched away, putting distance between them. Rachel watched her walk off. "She didn't need to send for you."

"She rang for Anna. I happened to be closer." Gio was also watching Mrs. Fabbro and Michael. "You don't need to worry about him, not with her. She couldn't have children of her own. Antonio and I became hers. She was very close to Antonio, so close that when he opened his own home in Florence, she went to oversee the house for him. She was still in his employ when he died." Gio's expression shifted, hardening. "After his death, I tried to bring her here, but she wouldn't leave his house. She's only here now because we finally closed his Florence villa and there was nowhere else to go."

It was a terribly sad story, Rachel thought, but also reassuring to hear that even as adults, the Marcello brothers had taken such good care of their nanny, and that she loved them so much in return. It was the kind of bond that spoke of affection rather than obligation.

It also made her realize she was going to have to fight Mrs. Fabbro for time with Michael.

"I'll have coffee sent to your room while you change," Gio said. "And then once you're dressed, come to my office for lunch. I can share with you the latest newspapers and headlines, and then we can discuss what we're going to do."

CHAPTER NINE

RACHEL SCANNED THE newspapers spread out on the table in the living room adjoining Gio's study. There were many, too, and in a half-dozen different languages, today, including English.

"Everyone loves scandal," she said under her breath.

He heard her, though. "And sex," he added. "Sex sells."

She glanced across the table, and his expression was bland, but he looked relaxed and perfectly at ease, lounging back in his chair as if they were enjoying a leisurely lunch on a sunny terrace instead of a tense meal on a gloomy winter day.

"We didn't have sex, though," she corrected.

Gio shrugged. "Maybe we should."

She blushed furiously, not expecting that. "Can we stay on topic, please?"

"I am."

"No, that wasn't appropriate."

"It is, if we marry."

Her head jerked up. She stared at him in horror. Why say something like that? Why mock her? "This isn't a game, Gio, and clearly my sense of humor is subpar, because I'm not enjoying your jokes—"

"I'm not playing games, *bella*, and I'm not one for jokes. I suggest marriage because it saves us from scandal, stealing the power from the media and giving it back to us. They don't drive the story—we do."

Rachel's brain couldn't keep up. She couldn't get past the "I suggest marriage" part. "I'm not even listening—"

"But you should," he said, leaning across the table to take her chin, forcing her head up to look her in the eyes.

"Your timing could not be worse. One of Marcello SpA's companies is going public in just a few weeks. We've spent the past year preparing for this. My management team filed to IPO ten weeks ago and we're hoping to be trading in two weeks. It all looked very good, but this…circus you've created will reflect badly on my family, the company and going public."

"I didn't create a circus—"

"You brought the media here," he ground out, cutting her short.

She pulled away and leaned back in her chair, heart thumping, mouth drying. She had brought the media here, but she did it because he'd refused to speak to her or respond to her. She'd done what needed to be done. "I had no idea that you were trying to take a company public," she said quietly. "My coming here now wasn't about you, but trying to get Michael child care so I could return to work before I derail my career. There's nothing left in my checking account. My credit cards can't handle any more debt. I'm here because it's a matter of survival."

He said nothing, his expression grim and unforgiving.

She clasped her hands tightly together in her lap. She hated being weak, hated needing anything from others, having long prided herself on her independence, but Juliet's death had changed everything. "I said this before, and I mean it. If I had the means to take care of Michael on my own, I wouldn't be here. I didn't want to come to you. I would have preferred to raise him on my own, but I don't earn enough to cover a nanny and my bills. Furthermore, I love my job, and if it weren't for the new vice president of marketing, I wouldn't be here now. But he's decided to tighten up my department and he's not interested in excuses or conflicts or personal problems. If I'm not there on Monday, I'm not to return, ever."

The silence was heavy and suffocating. It seemed to stretch forever, too.

Finally, Giovanni broke it. "I wouldn't plan on being there Monday."

His voice was so hard, his tone so ruthless that a shiver raced through her. Rachel pushed back her chair and rose. "Thank you for your hospitality, but it's time I left. Michael and I will be leaving this morning."

She started for the door, and he let her get halfway across the room before he stopped her. "You won't get far without your passports, *cara*."

She froze, stiffening.

"I have the passports, yours and Michael's."

Slowly she turned to face him. "Did you go through my luggage?"

"They weren't in your hotel room. The hotel keeps them, remember? The front desk always takes your passport when you check in, and then returns it when you check out."

He was right. She'd forgotten all about her passport when she'd unpacked. She should have remembered before now. "You can't keep me here against my will. You assured me, promised me, that I was free to come and go." She was shocked that her voice managed to be so calm when her heart was thudding like mad. "But apparently your word means nothing. Apparently you have no integrity."

"Careful, *cara*," he said softly, rising from his chair to walk toward her. "Scandal is one thing. Slander is another."

Her eyes burned, hot and gritty. She drew a quick, furious breath, hands clenched at her sides. "But you did promise. You know you did."

"You are free to leave."

"You'll give me my passport?"

"I'll give you yours, yes. Of course. Do you want it?"

"Yes." Her chin notched up, eyes stinging from unshed tears. "I'll figure out another way. Michael and I don't need a lot. I'll leave my job and look for something else, a job where I can take him with me. Maybe I can be a nanny for another family and they'll let me bring Michael—"

He cut her off with a kiss, a hard, punishing kiss. Rachel's hands moved to his chest to push him away and yet she could feel his warmth through his cashmere sweater and her fingers curled into the softness, clinging to the material and him. She hated him and yet loved his smell and taste.

There was little tenderness in Gio's kiss. His lips parted hers, and he took her mouth with a fierceness that made her head spin. His tongue stroked the inside of her mouth, devastating her senses, sending rivulets of fire through her veins and creating an insistent ache low in her belly, an ache that made her thighs press, trying to stifle the need and how it coiled and curled within her, mocking her self-control.

She'd never felt longing until now.

She'd never wanted anyone as much as she wanted Giovanni.

She was breathless and dazed when he lifted his head. He stroked her flushed cheek, her skin so sensitive that his touch burned all the way through her, breasts tightening, nipples pebbling.

"You can go, *bella*, but my nephew stays," he said, lightly running his thumb over her swollen mouth, making it quiver beneath his touch. "You are an American. I have no claim over you. But Michael is, as you said, a Marcello, and he, as you said, belongs here, with his family."

His head dropped and his lips brushed hers and brushed again before he bit at her soft lower lip, sending a spark of pain through her, the pain immediately followed by pleasure. "But there is no need for you to go," he added. "There is no need for you to worry about anything. You can remain here as my wife and Michael's mother. It would solve many logistical problems, as well as protect the Marcello business and name."

Blinking back furious tears, Rachel gave him a hard shove. He didn't move. He didn't even sway on his feet. She yanked free instead, taking several steps back to put distance between them. "You can't do this," she choked. "You can't. I won't let you."

"And how will you stop me?"

"I'll go to the police—"

"You think they'll take your word over mine?"

"I'll go to the consulate. I'll ask for help."

"And you'll tell them what? That you came here with my nephew and summoned the media and attempted to blackmail me?"

"I never blackmailed you. I never threatened you in any way."

"No? Then you didn't summon the media? You didn't release a press statement?" He must have seen her surprise because he nodded. "I have a copy of the information you sent your media contacts. You have not behaved in an ethical manner. You will not look innocent or sympathetic to anyone."

"You can't take Michael from me!"

"I didn't take him. *You* abandoned him here."

"I never abandoned him!"

"You handed him to my servant and walked away. If I hadn't stopped you, you would have climbed in your water taxi and disappeared."

"You are turning this around. You are making me out to be someone I'm not. I only did what I did because I desperately needed help—"

"Obviously. And you're getting my help, because your desperation is jeopardizing a baby's welfare."

"No—"

"Yes. You knew nothing about me, or my staff, and your impulsiveness put Michael in danger."

Her chest squeezed tight, guilt mixing with fear. "I will not be manipulated."

"But *you* can manipulate *me*?" he retorted so softly that the hair rose on her nape and an adrenaline rush made her knees shake.

She couldn't speak. Her heart hammered double time. She stared at his chin and mouth to keep from looking into his eyes, afraid of what she'd see there. "Marriage is out of the question. You don't love me. You don't even like me. I refuse to sacrifice myself to further your business needs."

"But you'll sacrifice me, and my company, for your needs?"

"I haven't done anything. You are Machiavellian, not me."

"Because I am determined to protect my nephew, my company and my employees from a greedy American?"

She stepped forward, her hand lifting, and then she stopped abruptly, horrified that she'd come so close to slapping him. "You are twisting everything, poisoning my intentions. Fibs and lies and half-truths…" She drew a rough breath and then another. "Where does it end?"

"You came here to wage war, and you did, so don't expect sympathy from me, not when you were the aggressor."

"I was trying to help Michael!"

"If you marry me, then you have."

"Your business is not more important than my future."

"And Michael's?" he drawled quietly. When she didn't reply, he added, "You want Michael to be a Marcello, and you tell me that I need to do my part. But then, when I make an offer to you, you refuse it, saying you prefer to return to Seattle. *Cara*, I'm not sure you know what you want."

But that wasn't true. She knew what she wanted. His money. His financial support so she could return to her life in Washington. She didn't want his money by becoming his wife! "You're not playing fair."

"You came here for financial support. I am offering you financial support." He studied her a moment, his lashes down, concealing his eyes, but then his lips curved in a slow heart-stopping smile. "Don't be foolish and proud, *bella*. Don't refuse what you so desperately need."

Rachel grabbed her coat and wallet from her room and left the palazzo, nearly running down the grand marble stairs and across the dramatic entry hall to exit through the house's front door.

She didn't care who saw her. She didn't care if the paparazzi were out with cameras fixed on the door, waiting the newest development in their scandalous story.

To hell with them. All of them, but especially Giovanni Marcello.

The afternoon was cold and the wind whipped the lagoon, sending the high tide sloshing over the canal bank onto the pavement. The sidewalk was wet but not nearly as flooded as yesterday. The tide must be coming down.

Rachel walked blindly down the Grand Canal for a block before turning at the corner and heading away from the busy street along a narrower canal. In her head she went through the last confrontation she'd had with Gio, pausing now and then to focus on something he'd said that was particularly infuriating.

Like the passport situation.

She'd forgotten all about the passports when she'd unpacked, but it wasn't that surprising as they hadn't been in her possession at the hotel, either. In the United States, the front desk did not retain the passports of international guests, but it seemed that it was the practice in Italy to collect them and keep them safe, and normally it wouldn't be a big deal, but she was outraged that the hotel would return them to Gio, and not her. And even more outraged that he had the audacity to keep them. Gio knew she wouldn't leave

Italy without Michael. Gio knew he'd trapped her, and he wasn't at all remorseful. Rather, he was proud. *Pleased.* Giovanni the Conqueror. Giovanni the Villain.

She kicked hard at a deep puddle, sending water flying in every direction, drenching her legs. She shuddered at the cold, the damp chill doing nothing to improve her mood.

She wanted to leave Venice so badly. She hated being trapped and cornered. She hated that Giovanni had forced her to move into his home, and then he made it impossible for her to leave.

This visit to Venice had become a nightmare. She'd lost control the moment she rapped on the Marcello's front door. Why had she thought she could manage Giovanni? Why had she thought this could turn out any other way but unhappy?

Rachel didn't want to marry Giovanni. She didn't want a pretend engagement, much less a real one, never mind a wedding ring. She didn't want to live in Italy. But at the same time, she wasn't going to walk away from Michael.

What she wanted was to go home with Michael and hire a sitter and return to work and have some order in her life. She was tired of the chaos, tired of the stress, tired of things she didn't know and understand.

When Juliet got pregnant, it changed Rachel's life, too. Juliet wasn't the only one who became a mother, Rachel became the backup caregiver, and then after Juliet died, the surrogate mother. It hadn't been an easy transition for her. Rachael hadn't planned on becoming a mother for years. A decade or more. She'd planned on working until her midthirties at least, wanting to focus on career and the opportunity to save her money so that she'd have a proper nest egg, resources to sustain her in case of emergency, because God knew, life was full of emergencies. When one had spent one's life struggling and scrimping, budgeting and worrying, the idea of financial security was huge.

Being financially independent would be life changing, and her plan was to do it for herself. She'd never dreamed that she'd wait for someone to take care of her. The idea of looking outward for support made her almost ill. No, she wanted to be strong and capable. She wanted to respect herself, and she would if she could provide for herself and any children she had.

Money, finances—those were such sensitive topics. Her mother certainly found it impossible to discuss financial topics with Rachel. She'd become emotional and cry, tearfully repeating that she was doing her best.

Rachel didn't want her mother crying or becoming defensive. She wasn't trying to criticize her mom; she just wanted to understand and help. How could she make things better for the family? How could she help ease some of the worry? It was a large burden. Mom was good at so many things, but managing money wasn't one of them.

Money, money, money…

Rachel wandered down streets until she approached St. Mark's Square. The famous piazza was lined with raised boards as the water was deeper here, flooding the entire square. She balled her hands inside her pockets and lowered her head to watch her steps.

How was she going to do this? How was she going to protect Michael and placate Giovanni? Because she wasn't about to marry a man she didn't love, and she most definitely wouldn't marry a man who didn't love her.

Rachel was many things—loyal, hardworking, determined—and those traits were evident. But she had a secret few people knew. She was privately, secretly terribly romantic.

She wanted love, big passionate love. She wanted the happy-ever-after and the lovemaking that resulted in fireworks and maybe even a few tears of joy.

She'd held out all these years for someone special, someone extraordinary. And she was determined to continue to hold out for the right one.

And the right one meant love, not lust. A small part of her—maybe a big part of her—desired Giovanni Marcello, but desire wasn't the answer and she was ashamed that she responded to him so easily. From now on, she would keep her distance. She had to. Otherwise Giovanni would have her in his bed, taking her virginity and the last shred of her self-respect.

Giovanni saw Rachel leave. He'd been at the window when she left the house, walking down the front of the Grand Canal to turn the corner and continue down the block. She disappeared for a few moments, and then reappeared as she cut down a narrow street.

She walked with her head bent and her hands buried deep inside her coat pockets until she entered an arched tunnel. If she kept going along that street, she'd eventually arrive close to St. Mark's square.

He wondered if that was where she was going.

He stood another moment looking out at the window before going to change into knee-high waterproof boots and his heavy winter coat.

He didn't know why he was going after her. She'd eventually return. She had no choice but to return, and he knew she'd never leave Michael. He'd seen her with the infant and she was as attached as a mother. She'd taken the little boy into her heart and was determined to provide the best possible life for him. He knew all that, and he didn't question her intentions, not anymore.

He didn't question her values, either. He understood what she wanted and it was the same thing he wanted for Antonio's son. But Michael couldn't have the life he needed, not if he was being juggled between Seattle and Venice, torn between countries and cultures, languages and customs, and Gio wouldn't lose Michael now that he was home.

Gio couldn't look at the infant without thinking of Antonio, and even though it hurt to remember Antonio, it was better than the emptiness of the past year. Gio had grieved for his brother for months, his death overshadowing everything. His brother had been his best friend from the time they were toddlers until they graduated from university as young men.

For the past six months Gio had done his best to avoid Michael. He hadn't wanted to meet this nephew of his, unable to tolerate more anger and more grief. And Gio was still angry, blisteringly angry that his brother decided not to try any of the experimental treatments that might have prolonged his life. He'd also been angry that Antonio spent so much of his last year alive in America instead of being home with his family, angry that his brother failed to take proper precautions and ended up conceiving a child with a shallow, self-serving woman who cared for no one and nothing but herself.

Antonio hadn't just thrown the rest of his life away. He'd crushed it and smashed it into the trash bin. It baffled Gio. Antonio had been among the smartest and the brightest, and he'd been a light in the world. He'd lit up a room with his keen wit and quick mind. He had a razor-sharp intelligence that he never used against another, not because he couldn't, but because he chose to build others up, to encourage them to be better.

Antonio had made Giovanni want to be better. Giovanni might have been the elder brother, but Antonio was his hero. Not because he was perfect, but because he genuinely tried to be good. To make a difference.

Gio's chest ached with bottled air. His hands fisted. Giovanni had lost Antonio but as long as he had Michael under his roof, his nephew was safe.

The high tides had kept all but the most curious and determined tourists out of the flooded neighborhoods, and the streets were mostly empty. Normally Gio liked this Venice, when the streets were wet and he had entire blocks to himself, but today he could take little pleasure in anything until his personal life was settled. He wanted out of the press, out of the tabloid's headlines. It was bad for his corporation to have his personal life become news, particularly when it was featured on the gossip page instead of the business section.

It didn't take much to make investors jittery. It didn't take much to shake the confidence of world markets. He needed to protect the company, and he needed to protect his nephew. That was his focus and his chief concern. Everything else was secondary.

The water grew deeper as he approached Piazza San Marco. His boots sloshed through ankle-deep water as he entered La Piazza, Venice's most famous square, and the only one in Venice called *piazza*. He stepped onto the raised boards that skirted the square, elevating visitors and locals above the flooded area.

It struck him as he eased past a family grouped on the walkway that this was the first time he could remember chasing after anyone since he'd broken off his engagement. He hadn't cared enough about any woman to chase her. It's why he'd taken mistresses. It was a purely sexual relationship, a relationship he controlled, beginning and ending with gifts, leaving his emotions untouched.

He hadn't thought he'd ever feel again but the arrival of Michael unsettled him, and Rachel was waking him up, making him feel. He wasn't comfortable feeling anything. But he didn't seem to have a choice at the moment.

Gio followed the route he was certain Rachel had taken, splashing through water and then following the elevated boards as he approached St. Mark's Square.

Most of the shops and cafés surrounding the square were closed, but a few had remained open, with intrepid storekeepers placing wooden boards across the bottom of their open doors, keeping the water out while allowing customers in.

Gio checked in each open shop and café for Rachel. She wasn't in any of the bigger ones on the piazza, and he exited the square and turned a corner, spotting the small narrow coffee shop preferred by locals who'd stand and drink their espresso, and then leave, not requiring one of the three small tables at the rear.

Opening the door of the café, he stepped inside. There were just a few people at the counter. Beyond the counter were the tables, and two were empty, but at a third sat Rachel. She had a small cup in front of her but she wasn't drinking. Her hands were in her lap and her gaze was fixed on an unknown point in the distance.

She looked troubled. Lost. Gio's chest tightened. He drew a quick breath, surprised by the pang.

He nodded to the staff as he passed and drew out one of the empty chairs at Rachel's table. She looked up at him, the expression in her wide dark eyes a combination of sadness and despair, before her expression firmed, hiding her emotions. "What are you doing here?"

"Hunting you down."

"Why? I don't have a passport. I can't go anywhere."

"I was worried about you."

She exhaled softly, and he could see the sadness again, fear and vulnerability shadowing her eyes.

It made him uncomfortable, seeing her so fragile. His mistresses were strong and confident and needed nothing from him but sex and gifts. They didn't require excessive attention, never mind tenderness or protection.

"I'm tougher than I look," she said, chin jutting up, but

there were tears in her eyes and she looked anything but tough.

Gio struggled with himself. He had been rough on her. He'd frightened her. He took little pleasure in wounding people. Much less women. But he also wasn't afraid of doing what needed to be done. Marrying Rachel would keep Michael in Venice. It was a contract, much like his arrangements with his mistresses. He wasn't doing it out of emotion, but practicality.

Yes, there were other ways to keep Michael in Venice. He could sue for custody. But legal cases of this nature took years, and he didn't want to spend years battling for custody when he could secure it quickly through marriage.

"I do not doubt that," he answered.

"I'm not afraid to fight you," she added.

"Obviously." He waited a moment. "But you won't win."

She searched his eyes, and he let her look, not hiding anything from her, because she needed to see who he was, she needed to understand what he was. Tough, driven, uncompromising. He did what he had to do. Always. And it's why he'd succeeded, because he always did what he had to do, even if it was painful.

"I keep trying to decide if you were teasing or bluffing," she said unsteadily.

"I don't bluff."

She looked hard into his eyes again, and then away. She sat across from him, cradling her cup, expression miserable, and the tension in his chest returned.

Despite the tension, he didn't try to fill the silence. He had learned early in his career to become comfortable with discomfort. He wasn't Antonio; his job wasn't to encourage or inspire. Gio's job was to make money and grow the company and take care of the Marcello employees, and that's what he did. Day in, and day out. Feelings didn't matter. Results mattered. Success. Stability. Financial accountability.

But it was hard to enjoy his single-minded focus when he sat across from a woman like Rachel. She wasn't Adelisa. He wasn't even sure what that meant, only she wasn't his ex-fiancée.

Rachel looked shattered all over again. "You know it's impossible."

"That, *cara*, is an exaggeration. It's not impossible. It's just…difficult."

"I don't want to marry you."

"And that is the difficult part."

CHAPTER TEN

HE WAS CRUEL beyond measure. Rachel's throat ached and her eyes burned. "I am nothing to you," she said quietly. "I am as insignificant as a bug, or a twig on the ground. You have no problem stepping on me, crushing me."

"That is not true."

"But my life and my dreams, they do not matter, not when you compare my needs to yours."

"I am responsible for a huge corporation. My decisions impact hundreds of people, if not thousands."

"You believe what you're saying, don't you? You're a demigod in love with your power." She hoped he heard the scorn in her voice. She hoped he was offended, because she was disgusted and appalled. There was nothing about him she admired.

"You are so consumed with your business. It seems to be the only thing that matters to you."

He leaned forward, narrowing the distance between them. "I have never put business before people. The various Marcello enterprises are made up of people, and not just my family, but hundreds of people, hundreds of loyal employees, and those people matter to me a great deal. The best businesses treat their employees like partners...family. Or, if you come from a seriously dysfunctional family, then hopefully you treat your staff better than family."

He'd inherited his family's business at a point when the company family seemed irreparably broken. The company was losing money, and his father had decided that he'd rather live with his mistress than his wife. Antonio was in America, working for a business that was not their own, determined to get as far from their father as possible.

Gio envied Antonio, because Gio couldn't escape, not as the eldest, and he was surrounded by the family drama, ensnared in it as Father's mistress was none other than his secretary, and the affair had been going on for years, with Father and secretary enjoying numerous "business" getaways and long private lunches behind locked doors.

Italians loved a good drama, especially when it was about sex and a beautiful young woman, a woman young enough to be Giovanni Marcello Senior's daughter.

Gio knew but couldn't convince his father to fire the secretary or end the relationship, nor would his mother divorce his father. Every day was grueling and Gio tried to focus on work, not wanting to be pulled into the middle of the family drama more than necessary. Gio, like his grandfather before him, had a sharp mind and a love for engineering and practical design. He disliked the endless conflict that had marked his childhood and adolescent years, and the only reason he'd agreed to work for Marcello Enterprises was because he loved the construction company his grandfather had founded.

But now, suddenly, the construction company, the Marcello holding company and even the family itself, was teetering on collapse. Gio was livid. He'd had enough, and he put his foot down. Either his father left, or he'd leave. That was all.

His father thought it was a joke, but Gio was furious that the company was being drained dry for selfish purposes when there were hundreds of employees that depended on the Marcellos. He'd never forget that last big battle with his father.

"We owe our employees a solvent company. They shouldn't have to worry if they will have a job tomorrow, or a way to pay their bills. If you don't care about the future of a company that has been around for over one hundred years, get out now before you ruin the Marcello name."

And to Gio's surprise, his father left, abandoning ship, leaving his oldest son to save what he could.

That huge fight had been over fifteen years ago, and Giovanni had headed up the construction division and the holding company ever since. It had been a massive struggle to turn the floundering corporation around, but he had. And so, yes, he was protective of the business, and even more protective of those who worked for him.

"The company is not one thing," he said. "It's not a bank account. It's not an office building. It's not equipment or real estate. It's people, *my* people. And I'm determined to do what is best for them. You see, they all have a vested interest in Marcello's success because each employee is gifted stock each year on the anniversary of their hire date. The longer an employee is with the company, the more stock they hold, which also means they become deeply invested in the company's success. When Borgo Marcello goes public in two weeks, my employees will have the opportunity to make some very good money. We've never done this before. Until now, all our companies have been privately held, but by going public, a number of my employees should make some good money. And that's what I want for them. This isn't about me. It's about rewarding those who have been loyal, when even my own family was not."

She exhaled slowly, staring out past Giovanni to the narrow street.

She didn't know what to say. She didn't know what to do with the information he'd just told her. In some ways she was relieved. But she was also more worried, because if what he said was true, he had very valid reasons for being so protective and proactive about his company.

She didn't want his employees to lose out on an exceptional opportunity. She'd never been offered stock at AeroDynamics, but Rachel did have friends who worked at high-tech companies and owning stock was huge, especially if a company was close to going public.

"There has to be some middle ground, though," she said after a moment. "Something that could protect your company and employees, and also protect me."

He looked at her and waited.

She swallowed hard. "Why does it have to be a real engagement, and a real marriage? Can't we just pretend until your company has gone public?"

"Pretend to be engaged...for an entire year?"

"A year? Why so long?"

"The first year a company goes public is quite volatile. I have no desire to add risk, or damage credibility." He paused, drummed his fingers on the table. "And Michael? What about him? A year from now he'll be eighteen months and walking and starting to talk. Will we want to tear his world apart right when he's becoming confident and secure?"

"He wouldn't know. He won't understand."

"He would if you suddenly left Venice."

Her eyes opened wide. "You expect me to live in Venice for the next year?"

"I expect you to live with me for the rest of your life."

Her lips parted in a silent gasp. Her stomach cramped. He was out of his mind, or far too sure of his power. Seconds passed, and then minutes. Rachel could not bring herself to speak, and Giovanni didn't seem interested in filling the silence, increasing the tension until she wanted to jump up and run. But where could she go? Nowhere. Because Michael was at the Marcello palazzo and she'd never leave Venice without him.

"You want to protect your company," she said carefully after an endless stretch of silence. "And I want to protect Michael. Surely we can both agree on that."

Gio's dark head inclined.

"I understand damage control is needed, especially since the media is fascinated with this fantasy story of ours, but eventually the media will move on to other stories and other scandals, and we can return to our lives, hopefully relatively unscathed."

Gio just waited.

She swallowed and mentally went through her thoughts before speaking them aloud, testing their strength and clarity. "Let's start with the pretend engagement. We can do that. It's not beyond our ability to smile in public and try to behave in a unified manner. It's a role we can manage for a few weeks, or even a few months. But let me be clear, I can't commit to anything longer than that. It's enough for us to take this first step now, implementing damage control, which should prevent the situation from spiraling."

He studied her from across the table, his gaze slowly examining every inch of her face. "So you'll stay here for the duration of the engagement?"

"I have a job, Gio, and I might not be the owner of my company but I have colleagues who count on me, and customers impatiently waiting my return—"

"I don't want you to return to Seattle, not if you're going to take Michael."

"Why not?"

"I don't want him with a stranger all day while you work. You deprive him of you. You deprive him of me. It's not right, not when I'm here, and I want him in my life."

"And what would I do if I stayed here?"

"Be his mother. Be my wife."

"And you'll compensate me, correct? You'll give me an allowance or open a bank account for me." She shuddered. "That is not my idea of a life. There is no independence. There is no freedom."

"Do you have freedom now? Show me your independence. You were on my doorstep begging for help."

Her lips compressed. She averted her head, her hands knotted in her lap.

"I know about your life in Seattle. You had a job, and a two-bedroom apartment—two bedrooms because Juliet often needed a place to crash—and a car with one more year of payments left on it. It's a life, a respectable life," he added quietly, "but it's not fantastic. It's not a dream. There's no reason you can't consider other options, and you need to consider other options, if not for your sake, then for Michael's."

She was so close to crying that she had to bite the inside of her lip hard, brutally hard, to keep the tears from falling. A marriage without love? What kind of future was that?

As if able to read her mind, he added, "Romantic love isn't everything. There is companionship. And passion. I will ensure you're satisfied—"

"Can you please drop this?" she choked, mortified.

"For now."

Leaving the café, they walked in silence for several minutes, pausing to let a group of tourists push past. They were talking loudly and in a hurry, and Rachel stepped back close to the building, glad for the interruption as it had been almost too quiet for the past few minutes.

Another group appeared on the heels of the first, and Rachel pressed her back to the building, letting the next group get by them, too.

"The water is receding," Gio explained. "The tourists have been waiting anxiously in their hotels for the tides to drop, and now that high tide has passed, the tourists are descending on the city again.

"Does it flood this much every winter?" she asked as they started walking once more.

"We usually have a little bit of flooding every winter, but the amount varies. *Acqua alta*, which means high water, can range from just a few centimeters to three or four feet. Last year was a bad year. We had over four feet, and over half the island was covered. It was one of the worst seasons we've had in one hundred and fifty years."

"You sound so pragmatic."

"It can't be stopped, and Venice is never totally submerged. Even when it's bad, half the island is dry, and where we are now is the lowest part of the island. The piazza gets the worst of the high water, creating dramatic photos for tourists, but it doesn't bother residents. We expect *acqua alta*. Venice is an island, crisscrossed with canals. Water is part of our life. We can't escape it, nor would we want to."

"It's true, though, that the flooding has been worse in recent years, and that's due to climate change?"

"Venice has been sinking for hundreds of years, but it's not just because of climate change and the rising seas. The more we develop outlying areas, with the pumping of water and natural gas, the more Venice is negatively impacted. It is serious. It's devastating for those of us who love Venice."

She chewed on her lip, as she looked past him to the wet street beyond. "I think everyone loves Venice," she said after a moment. "How can you not? It's otherworldly. A fairy-tale city."

"So you could be happy here."

She shot him a pensive side glance. "I didn't say that."

"Then I will. You *could* be happy here. It's a fairy-tale city, a place where dreams come true."

Worn out from the emotional day, Rachel had dinner in her room, wanting some quiet and the chance to unwind with Michael.

She held him until after he'd fallen asleep in her arms and continued to hold him for another hour. She loved him so very much. The world was unpredictable and life could be overwhelming, but she was determined to protect him and do what was best for him until he no longer needed her.

He woke in the middle of the night, needing her. She walked him around his green room, and then around her room, making huge loops.

She kept the lights low and tried her best not to engage him, but at the same time she wasn't going to let him cry as he had last night. She didn't want a repeat of last night, where Giovanni was up and worrying about Michael, too.

As she paced, she glanced at the huge oil canvases on the wall, the green silk curtains with the thick gold and green fringe, the high ceiling and the gilt trim. Everything here was so old and valuable, centuries of wealth, and it boggled her mind just how different her world was, and how simple her needs really were.

She didn't need a lot. She didn't want a lot. Comfort was relative.

For Rachel, a comfortable life meant that she didn't have to worry about losing her home, or defaulting on car payments. A comfortable life meant that she could see a specialist when a second opinion was needed, or have a dinner out every now and then. Comfortable meant she could take a vacation once a year, renting a little beach cottage on the Oregon coast, something they'd all done in her family each summer when Dad was alive. She'd loved those annual trips to Cannon Beach and the lazy days where they did nothing but play cards and Scrabble and walk down the long sandy beach.

That had been her ideal life, the one she wanted for her children, when she had children. And now she had a child. She had Michael. She'd become a mother much earlier than she'd expected, and it'd been a shock, losing Juliet and discovering overnight that she was a single mom.

It had been beyond overwhelming. She'd never told anyone, but she'd been angry, too. She'd wanted so badly to have someone to confide in, but she'd worried that women would judge her, saying she was selfish, or lacking. But being a parent was such a huge responsibility and Rachel had wanted to do it right when she did become a mom. She'd wanted to have everything ready, in order. She'd wanted to be mentally prepared, and in a position to be able to be self-sufficient, or as self-sufficient as possible.

Not being able to tell anyone that she was scared and worried and also, yes, a little bit angry—or very much angry—had been isolating. It had left her even more alone because she had all these feelings that weren't socially acceptable, all these feelings where people would judge her for not being a real woman. For not being a good woman.

Rachel's eyes burned and stung. She blinked hard, trying to clear her vision.

All her life she'd struggled with the sense of inadequacy. She knew she was smart, capable, but it didn't seem to be enough. People valued beauty. So many in society placed beauty as the ultimate achievement. And beautiful was the one thing she'd never be, despite her attempts to improve her appearance through makeup and exercise and good hair care.

Throughout junior high and high school she'd pored over teen magazines with their tips on how to bring out one's natural beauty: lip pencil, eyeliner, contour and mascara. She did her face and hair every morning while in college, and continued with the full face routine every morning before work, but the makeup was a mask. It merely served to hide how plain she was beneath, and how fragile her confidence really was.

That was something else no one knew.

She looked polished and professional on the outside, but on the inside, she was filled with self-doubt, and those self-doubts and recriminations had only grown since Juliet died. Like the city of Venice during *acqua alta*, Rachel was drowning.

Gio was surprised to see Rachel appear in the doorway of the breakfast room at a relatively early hour. She was already dressed, wearing charcoal trousers and an oversize sweater, and didn't seem to be wearing any makeup. Her hair had been drawn back into a ponytail high on her head, with just a few shorter wisps loose to frame her face.

She looked pretty, but tired, with lavender shadows beneath her brown eyes.

"Good morning," she said. "I was told this is where breakfast is being served today."

"Yes," he answered, rising and drawing a chair out for her. "Join me."

She sat down, thanking him in a low voice. With her now seated at his side, he could feel her exhaustion.

"Michael had you up again last night, didn't he?" Gio asked.

"It's all right. I'm used to it."

"I don't think it's good for you. I'd like a night nurse to take over in the evenings, at least for the next few weeks. You need your rest, too. It's hard to keep a level head when you're short on sleep, and we have a lot going on right now."

Her brow creased, expression troubled. "So you intend to announce our engagement when?"

Before he could answer, the door opened and the maid appeared. Gio looked at Rachel. "Would you like American coffee or an espresso?"

"Do you have coffee by the pot? I feel like I need gallons of it today."

Gio gave the instructions to his maid and then waited for her to leave. "It's been done," he said as the door closed. "I had my PR firm release the information last night."

Her jaw dropped, horrified. *"What?"*

Gio reached for the stack of folded papers on the seat of the empty chair next to him. He'd read them earlier and saved them to show her. He placed the papers in front of her, with the English version on top to make it easier for her, watching her expression as she scanned the paper's bold headline.

Italian Billionaire Marcello to Marry
American Lover!

"You really did tell them," she whispered.

"I needed to. Media outlets from all over the world have been calling my company, and the company has been trying to send everyone to the PR agency, but it's out of control right now."

She lifted the paper, unfolding it to see the accompanying photo. It was a new one, taken of them yesterday in the coffee shop off the piazza.

For a long moment she said nothing, and then she sighed, the sound that of disappointment and perhaps resignation. "Are they all like this?" she asked, shuffling through the papers to glance at each.

"Yes."

She flipped through the papers again. "How long will this…attention…last?"

"As long as we remain newsworthy."

"I'd like to end the newsworthy element as soon as possible."

"I could not agree more. It's why we're going to push forward quickly, and do a news dump, releasing all the announcements and information at one time so there are no more surprises and no more big headlines."

"How does that work?"

"We're sending out the invitations for our engagement

party today. Once they are in the mail, we'll make an announcement about the party and perhaps do an exclusive interview with one of the bigger tabloids, inviting them into the palazzo and letting them have a look at the party preparations, or even better, plans for our wedding."

"But you're so private. Won't that just whet the paparazzi's appetite for more?"

"I think once I'm more accessible, they'll grow bored."

"You hope," she said.

"I do."

She looked up at him, her eyes bright, her cheeks pink, her emotions right there on the surface. He liked her transparency. He liked that she wasn't the schemer he'd first thought. She was nothing like the kind of women he spent time with, and maybe that was why he was drawn to her. She was fresh and real and emotionally accessible. Her emotions made her more beautiful: the light that shone in her eyes, the quick curve of her lips, the vexed expression when provoked.

She was provoked now. "You expect me to capitulate, don't you? You're expecting me to just acquiesce and marry you."

"Yes."

"You will be disappointed."

"I don't think so. I think you will soon discover that love is overrated, especially when the sex is deeply satisfying."

She flushed and her jaw firmed.

"Or perhaps you've never enjoyed sex—"

"That's enough," she choked. "Nothing about this conversation is appropriate."

"How are we to make love if we can't even discuss it?"

"We're not going to make love, or get married. I have agreed to a pretend engagement. That is all."

She was so flustered, her cheeks were dark pink, her voice breathless. He didn't think she was faking it, either.

Rachel was a different species of woman, and it made him wonder, if she was this emotional and sensitive at the breakfast table, what would she be like in his bed?

The thought made him hard, and a little impatient. He pushed the papers back toward her. "Then what do we do? Have photographers chase you every day? Lie in wait for you and Michael as you run errands? The life you once had is gone, Rachel. This is your life now."

She said nothing, her chin jutting in displeasure.

He could change that expression with a kiss. He was tempted, too, but first, he needed to explain something. She needed to understand his concerns.

Gio searched through the papers until he found the one that had reprinted the photo of her carrying Michael to the doors of the palazzo. The photographer had zoomed in on the baby, taken a close-up of him wrapped in the blanket. The headline was simple. It read, The Billionaire's Baby, but it was enough.

The one photo, coupled with the three words, summed up the dangerous situation Rachel had unwittingly created. Michael was a story, a fascinating story, and people wanted a piece of it. Of him.

Gio placed the Italian paper on top of the English one. He tapped the photo as he read the headline to her, translating it from Italian to English. She looked at him, dark arching brows drawn.

"My grandfather Marcello had an older brother," Gio told her quietly. "He was kidnapped during an outing, taken right from the arms of his mother during a morning walk. The kidnappers demanded a million dollars. My great-grandparents paid the ransom. Their fourteen-month-old was returned to them, in a box."

"Dead?" she whispered.

He nodded. "It was a sensational story, and the three men were eventually arrested, tried and found guilty. But it didn't bring back the child. My grandfather grew up aware that he was the replacement, and equally aware that his birth did nothing to assuage his mother's grief. Money does not always solve problems. Wealth can make one a target. I do not want Michael vulnerable, and yet you, *cara*, have made him so."

Gio could see the effect of his words. Rachel paled and grew still. He almost regretted putting the blame on her shoulders, but she had to understand, the world he inhabited was not like hers. His world was one of power and prestige, but also envy and greed. People could be dangerous. Gio had to protect Michael—and Rachel—from those that would try to destroy them.

The breakfast room was unbearably quiet.

Heartsick, Rachel felt hot and then cold, her stomach plummeting. Last night as she'd paced with the baby, she'd thought about money, and how important it was for her to feel stable and secure. She'd never considered the flip side, and how having a great deal of money could become a trap. "I'm sorry," she said, meaning it. "I'm sorry to have brought Michael to the world's attention. It makes me sick—"

"We just need to be careful from now on. We need to make sure he has the right people around him and be sure he's not exposed to danger."

She nodded jerkily, eyes gritty, trying to wrap her head around Michael's future. He would forever be an heir now: the boy who'd inherit a fortune. It wasn't the life she'd wanted for him. She hadn't wanted to change his life, just improve it. "I wish I could go back… I wish I'd known."

"What's done is done. Now we need to make the best of it."

"But won't a party here invite trouble into your home?"

"I have already vetted the guest list, and there will be security, a great deal of it."

She said nothing and he pressed on.

"The party will be on Saturday, next week. We'll host the event in the grand ballroom. With the invitations going out in today's mail, it will keep the ball from looking like a rushed affair."

"A *ball*? Not a cocktail party? Something simple?"

"It's impossible to host anything in a seventeenth-century ballroom without it looking like a major event. Besides, everyone likes to dance."

"But I don't see how an engagement *ball* will solve any of our problems!"

"It will add legitimacy to our relationship, publicly solidifying us as a couple. People will enjoy helping us celebrate our commitment to each other and Michael."

"Speaking of Michael, when will we tell everyone that Michael is actually Juliet and Antonio's?"

"Never."

"*What*? Why not?"

"There is no need to make an announcement. Those close to us will know the truth. But the rest, why correct them? It's no one's business but ours—" He broke off as Anna returned with coffee and breakfast.

Rachel murmured thanks for her coffee but couldn't even look at the food, far too shaken by the developments. "How many people are you inviting to this party?"

"Two hundred and sixty. I anticipate we will have about two hundred actually attend."

"That's a huge party."

"The ballroom is huge."

"Then put the party in another room, your mother's favorite room, for example. We could have twenty in there and it would be lovely."

"That sounds lovely and intimate, but it won't communicate what we want it to. A large, lavish party doesn't just convey confidence, but excitement, and joy…all the things we want the public to associate with our marriage."

"Our engagement, you mean. A faux engagement, at that."

He shrugged. "The goal is to present a united front to all. Even to those in our inner circle."

"What about your mother?"

"I will tell her what she needs to know."

"The *truth*."

"I am not going to create worry and anxiety for her, not if I don't have to."

"I am not an actress, Gio. I am not good at pretending. I can't even lie well. I don't know why, but if I tell a fib, I immediately blush—"

"That is why you will marry me. Then you won't have to worry that about your acting skills. You won't have to act, or lie. There would be no faux engagement, just a real one, ending in a real wedding. Michael will have his family. You will be able to focus on the baby. I can focus on my business. Everything will be as it should be."

CHAPTER ELEVEN

EVERYTHING WOULD BE as it should—for him.

He would have an heir for his business. He'd have a mother for his nephew. He'd have a warm body for his bed. It was all so easy and convenient for him. She'd made it so easy and convenient.

She inhaled, and then exhaled, face hot, chest on fire. "You don't even regret having a marriage of convenience, do you?"

"I don't romanticize marriage anymore, no."

"But you once did?"

He shrugged. "Once upon a time I was naive."

"What happened?"

"We got engaged, we nearly married, but in the nick of time I discovered she didn't want me. She simply wanted a rich husband."

Rachel went cold, suddenly understanding just why he loathed Juliet so much, and why he'd been so mistrustful of her, too. "I don't want a rich husband," she whispered. "I don't want a husband at all—"

"I understand. But there are consequences in life. We both know that, and we both know marriage would be the best thing for a child that has lost both mother and father before he's even seen his first birthday."

"Everything is suddenly *we* and *us*, but three days ago you wouldn't even say his name!"

"Three days ago I had an attorney working on custody." Giovanni's gaze met hers. "I was preparing to take him from you. And then you showed up on my doorstep with him…and left him. You played right into my hands."

"I don't believe it. You're just saying that. You've never acknowledged him. You've refused to acknowledge him."

"I have spent these past few months researching the legitimacy of your claim, and then considering my options, including suing for sole custody, cutting you out completely. Before I could decide what was the best course of action, you appeared here, forcing my hand." He studied her from across the table. "Suing for custody might still be the best option. That is, if we don't choose to raise him together."

"As a married couple."

He nodded.

She laughed shortly. Why was she not surprised? "You do not play fair."

"Life isn't fair. But I am doing my best to make it as fair as possible for our nephew, whom I believe you care for."

"I love him dearly."

"Then it cannot be such a huge sacrifice to stay here and raise him with me."

She held her breath, heart pounding.

He filled the silence. "You strike me as an extremely capable woman. I have full confidence in you, and that you'll be able to adjust to your new life. Otherwise, I wouldn't marry you. I'm marrying you, I'm making you my wife, a Marcello, because you have the qualities I admire in a woman, and the qualities that would make a good wife and an excellent mother."

"And it doesn't bother you that I don't love you?"

"It would bother me more if you said you did."

Her stomach lurched. "That's horrendous."

"I don't trust romantic love. It's false and changing."

"And I think a loveless marriage is horrific. It makes marriage sound lonely and cold."

"I promise you our marriage won't be cold, not if we're sharing the same bed."

"Sex isn't the answer to everything!"

"Then you haven't had the right partner. Great sex is deeply satisfying."

She couldn't stop blushing. "You are overly confident."

He looked at her for an endless moment, before smiling faintly, looking every bit the confident, arrogant man she'd met her first day here. And when was that? Just two days ago? God, it seemed like a lifetime. Everything was changing, the tides were rising, flooding her world, and she couldn't seem to save herself. "I'll make you a deal then. You come up with a plan that is better. A plan that immediately protects Michael and gives him a family, as well as financial security. Then tell me and we will do that. But if you can't propose anything better, we will marry and move forward with our lives."

He glanced at his watch and grimaced. "I hate to leave on that note, but I have a conference call in a few minutes, and it's one that I can't miss." He pushed back from the table and started from the room, but then stopped before he reached the door. "This is not an easy situation, not for either of us, and I'm sorry."

And then he was gone.

After the conference call finally ended an hour later, Gio remained at his desk, deep in thought. It had been a difficult call, not because of the subject matter, but because he'd found it almost impossible to focus.

Rachel had said she didn't want a cold, passionless, loveless marriage. He agreed with her on that point, but he wasn't worried that they'd have a cold relationship, or passionless, not when he wanted her as much as he did.

He'd been attracted to her from the start, and he'd fought the attraction, just as he'd tried to ignore how much he'd liked kissing her. He loved her mouth, the softness and the fullness, and how she couldn't quite help kissing him back. It made her sexy. Delicious. He wanted to kiss the rest of her. He wanted to strip her and explore those gorgeous curves—hips, breasts, thighs and in between.

In the beginning he hadn't understood why he was so drawn to her. She wasn't like the women he'd dated, and that was her appeal.

But he was tired of all the words. He wasn't a man of words. He was a man of action.

He'd take her to his bed. He'd show her that he could please her. He'd show her that she could be happy with him.

Gio left his desk and walked to the tall arched leaded glass windows that looked over the narrow lagoon. It was another gray day with wisps and tendrils of fog rising from the water. The fog was supposed to get heavier as the day ended, shrouding the streets and water in a cloak of mystery. He loved this Venice, and Rachel would grow to love it, too.

He'd woo her tonight. He'd delight her, pleasure her, and in his bed, she'd become his. There would be no more fighting or protesting. She'd discover she liked being in his bed, and she'd realize she'd liked being *his*.

Gio glanced out at the lagoon once more before returning to his desk. The fog made it the perfect night to go out. They would travel in the Marcello gondola, one of the most elegant boats in the city. It had the patina of age, being well over a hundred years old, and glamorous, the outside lacquered in gleaming black paint while the interior was upholstered in black leather and cream and opulent gold leaf.

He knew where he'd take her for dinner, too. Il Sussurro. It was his favorite restaurant on the island, and without a doubt, the most exclusive. It was incredibly difficult to get a reservation, not just because Il Sussurro had only four tables, but because it was booked out years in advance.

Fortunately, Gio did not have to pull any strings to secure a table, as there was always one waiting for him. Indeed, the fifth-floor table was his, just as the fifth floor was his, which wasn't saying much as the floors of the medieval building were quite narrow, the house built snug, like a ship, each floor consisting of a single room and the central hall with the circular staircase.

Fifteen years ago he helped finance Il Sussurro when no one else would give the chef and restaurateur a loan. The concept of Il Sussurro was like its name—a whisper, a murmur—small enough to be overlooked, maybe even forgotten.

No commercial lender was willing to risk the money on a restaurant that would not even be able to seat twenty-four people each evening. Where was the profit margin in that? While traditional banks questioned the viability of such a venue, Gio immediately grasped the appeal. Privacy. Novelty. Exclusivity.

Intrigued by the vision for the 1384 building, he'd funded the restoration and refurbishment, and Il Sussurro proved to be a huge success.

Gio made a call to Carlo, one of the owners of Il Sussurro, advising his old friend that he'd be dining at his table tonight.

"How many, Gio?" Carlo asked.

"Just two," Giovanni answered. "And it's a special occasion."

"It's always a special occasion when you join us."

"*Grazie, Carlo.* We'll see you later tonight."

Hanging up the phone, he called Allegra Paladin, the founder of Paladin, a Venice-based fashion house founded by a former mistress. When he ended the relationship five years ago he'd given her enough money that she'd been able to open her own business.

On the phone, he told Allegra about the dress he was looking for. It was a couture gown from her September show. The dress was floor-length with a formfitting bodice and long sleeves. There might have been a small collar, he wasn't sure, but the neckline was a deep V, and the color an olive green. Dusty rose flowers were embroidered on the green lace bodice, with larger, looser rose and gold roses scattered on the long sheer skirt.

"I know the one," Allegra answered, amusement in her voice. "But it's not your size, my darling."

"Mmm, funny, but I think you know it's not for me."

She sighed, the sound wistful. "It's true, then? You really are engaged?"

"You'll meet the right man one day, I promise."

"You were the right man."

"I wasn't."

"I should have gotten pregnant," she pouted.

"*Allegra*," he said, a warning in his tone.

"I'm not sure how she managed it. You were always so zealous about protection with me."

"I don't want to have this conversation. But I do want the dress. I need it today, and it will have to be shortened. Can you send a seamstress with it to the house this afternoon?"

Allegra hesitated. "She doesn't seem your type."

"But that's just it," he said quietly. "She *is* my type. She's exactly my type."

"Does that mean you've finally fallen in love, Gio?"

"I'm not sure Rachel would be comfortable with this conversation."

"You are in love," she said, wonder in her voice. "When is the wedding? Have you set the date?"

"We're keeping the details private for now, but it's soon. Very soon."

Rachel was playing with Michael after his afternoon nap when a knock sounded on her door. Opening her door, she discovered Anna in the hall with a middle-aged woman carrying an oversize red garment bag with silver script on it, reading *Paladin*.

"Signor Marcello..." Anna paused, frowning, as if uncertain how to explain.

But then Gio was there to take over. "Has something for you," he said, stepping around the women to enter Rachel's room as if it was his. He crossed to Rachel and took the baby from her, as if the baby was his, too. "The dress is for tonight," he added, holding Michael comfortably against his chest, the baby's diapered bottom resting on his arm. "I hope you'll like it."

Rachel watched as the older woman unzipped the bag and drew out a gleaming green gown, shot with gold threads with pops of rose and light gold flowers. "Oh, it's gorgeous."

"Do you like it?"

"I do. But why wear it tonight? Shouldn't I save it for the engagement party?"

"We're going out tonight. I've booked a reservation somewhere special."

"Won't people see us...or did you want that?"

"It's going to be foggy tonight, a perfect night for us to slip out and not be seen. We'll leave here at eight. Does that work for you?"

"Yes."

"Good. And now the seamstress from Paladin is going to hem the dress for you, and make any other adjustments necessary."

Rachel had never owned a dress like this one before. The bodice hugged her breasts and waist before spilling in a waterfall of silk and lace to her feet. The sheer lace sleeves made her skin gleam and she didn't think she'd ever felt so feminine before. She struggled with her hair, uncertain as to whether she should put it up or leave it down. In the end she drew it into a low side ponytail because she felt too bare wearing it up, and it was so heavy when she left it down.

Rachel was in the great hall right at eight, and yet Gio was already there, waiting for her. "Don't tell me I'm late again," she said, shifting her black wool coat to the other arm.

"No. You're right on time. But you're not going to wear that coat tonight, so give it to me."

"What will I wear instead?"

"A cape."

"Like Batman and Robin?" She laughed.

"Or like a princess from the eighteenth century." He lifted the black velvet cloak from the banister and draped it over her shoulders before loosely tying the braided silk ribbon at her throat to keep it from falling off her shoulders.

The brush of his fingers against her neck sent a shiver of pleasure from her, while the long velvet, fur-lined cloak felt like heaven. It was soft and yet with enough weight to cocoon her in warmth.

"I didn't think I could possibly feel more elegant," she said breathlessly, "and yet I do."

"Wait. I'm not quite done. There is one more small adjustment to make," he said, drawing something from his trouser pocket. "These are not old. Nor are they family pieces. It's something I bought for you today." He opened the small bronze leather pouch and shook out a pair of earrings, the dark green stones spilling into his palm, glimmering with color and light. "I worried that the green might be a little off, but they're such quality stones that I thought it was worth it."

She was almost afraid to touch the earrings, each one made of two emeralds, a large oval at the lobe, with a huge teardrop emerald beneath. "They're real?" she whispered.

"Yes."

"They're so big."

"They are dramatic, but they'll suit you."

"I hope you're not spending money on me. I don't want you to—"

"Don't deprive me of the pleasure of treating you." He tilted her chin up and slipped the slim gold post through the hole in her earlobe before attaching the back, holding the decadent earring in place. "Now the other ear."

"This isn't a treat. It's called spoiling. The dress, the cape, the earrings."

"Hasn't anyone ever spoiled you before?"

"No."

"That's criminal. You deserve to be draped in jewels."

Rachel couldn't help laughing. "As if I were a courtesan in a Turkish harem?"

"Or a young bride, anticipating her wedding day."

She flushed, blood surging to her cheeks, making her face feel hot and sensitive. "Now you're making me nervous."

"No need to be nervous. Enjoy being spoiled."

She dipped her head to hide her blush. "Thank you for the gifts…for all of them."

"My pleasure. You look beautiful."

She glanced up, her smile unsteady. "I think, though, I know what you are doing."

"And what is that?"

"You're trying to break down my resistance. You want to win me over."

Deep grooves bracketed his mouth. His bright blue eyes glowed down at her. "I've already won you over. You just haven't admitted it yet." His head dropped, and his lips brushed hers, lightly, fleetingly, sending a sharp tingle up and down her spine. "But you will, soon."

The boat slid through the lagoon, the gondolier standing at the back, eyes sharp, seeing what they couldn't, steering with hardly a splash. The night was so quiet and still with the fog. The streetlamps looked like distant balls of light. The stillness created a magic, and Rachel found herself holding her breath again and again, senses heightened and delighted.

They soundlessly slipped from one canal to another, turning corners she didn't even see, easing under bridges that popped out of nowhere. She was grateful the gondolier knew the city so well because she was completely lost, and yet it felt good to give up control. It was almost a relief. She'd been fighting so hard to keep everything together and tonight she could control nothing—not the dark, or the fog, or the direction they were to go. She could only sit and feel, exquisitely aware of Giovanni next to her, his tall, imposing frame hard, his muscular body warm.

She couldn't see far. Sometimes she saw nothing, but there were other moments when she could just make out the shape of a building, or the shadow of a person walking on the pavement, footsteps muffled by the fog. Every now and then the gondolier's oar splashed, or they'd pass another gondola and the drivers would murmur a greeting as the boats slid by.

It was all a fantasy, she thought, a seductive dream that was lulling her, relaxing her so that she found herself leaning against Gio, letting him support her weight. She could feel his thigh against hers, and her shoulder against his chest. His arm was around her, his palm flat against her waist, his fingers just brushing her tummy, and it shouldn't be anything, but it was. It was intense. It all felt dizzying and overwhelming and she was feeling things she had never felt before, and imagining his hand on her bare skin, his fingers caressing her, stroking her, finding the curve of her breast and the hollow between her legs.

She wanted him to touch her and explore her—

"You're cold?" he said, his voice near her ear, feeling her shiver.

"Just a little," she lied, almost boneless with need, before drawing a tremulous breath. He'd been right earlier. She *was* starting to fall for him. She wanted him and was teased by the idea of a life with him. No one had ever taken care of her before. No one had ever spoiled her or desired her, either…

But desire wasn't love, and the risk was huge. She was falling for him; she could have her heart broken.

"We're nearly there." He held her tighter, closer, his fingers so very close to the apex of her thighs that she was stunned she hadn't burst into flames.

She didn't understand the attraction, or the emotions sweeping through her. She didn't understand how she could be falling for someone who was also such a threat. Maybe the problem was that she had never felt this kind of intense physical attraction before. Maybe the problem was that she had never felt this way about *anyone* before. Her feelings were not intellectual, nor were they rational. Her feelings really weren't feelings but hope and desire, fear and need. It began as a baffling, carnal desire that had bypassed her head to fill her body, humming in her veins, and had turned into a curiosity and hunger that made her want him to want her—not just her body, but her mind, and her heart—all of her.

She turned her head and looked at his darkly handsome profile and felt everything inside her tighten and flip.

He was beautiful. There was no denying it. But that wasn't a good thing, not in this instance, because honestly, he was too beautiful for her. And he wasn't just ridiculously handsome, he was also brilliant and successful. Wealthy beyond belief. Women like her didn't get men like him. No, Gio was the kind of man Juliet snagged, the kind of man who wanted perfection on his arm. Even dressed in an expensive gown and draped in velvet and fur and jewels, she wasn't perfection. She wasn't even close.

He would not be happy being married to her. He would resent her, and that would be intolerable… It would break her heart.

Gio didn't know what happened, but something did. One moment Rachel was happy and relaxed, leaning into him, and then the next she'd become stiff, her slim shoulders hunched, head bowed.

"What's wrong?" he asked.

"Nothing," she answered.

"Something has upset you. You're sad."

She lifted her head but couldn't quite look him in the eyes. "This is a mistake, you know. All of this."

"The boat ride? The earrings? What?"

"The gifts, the date, the proposal." Her voice cracked. "The marriage. You would hate it, and I would hate it, and we'd be miserable, trapped together, and I can't do more misery. I've had enough misery and enough guilt to last a lifetime."

"What do you feel guilty about?"

"What *don't* I feel guilty about?" He saw her lift a hand to the gentle sway of her emerald earring. "And then you buy me these beautiful things as if I deserve them, but I don't. I am not who you think I am, and I am not someone you will be happy with. Please, just let me take Michael home. Please—"

He silenced her anguished words with a kiss, not to stifle her, but to try to comfort her. He kissed her deeply, melting her resistance, kissing her until she was no longer stiff and chilled, but warmly pliant, her body pressed to his.

Aware that they were no longer moving, he lifted his head. Her dark eyes still glittered with a hint of tears, but something else, too. "I don't know what you've done, or why you feel guilty, but I don't believe it's as bad as you think," he said quietly.

She struggled to smile but failed. "Your fiancée...why did you fall in love with her?"

"She was beautiful and glamorous and exciting."

"I'm none of those things."

"Thank God you are not shallow or superficial. We wouldn't be marrying if you were."

"Not even for Michael's sake?"

"No. I'd take him from you. I'd sue for custody and be done with you."

"Without a hint of remorse?"

"With absolutely none."

His candor surprised her. She blinked at him, her dark eyes wide, expression bemused, and then the confusion lifted and she laughed. "You sound like a dreadful man."

"I am." And then he kissed her lightly before releasing her. He rose and stepped from the gondola and extended his hand to her. "But if anyone can manage me, it's you."

She'd felt distraught just a few minutes ago and yet he'd somehow turned the moment around, dispelling the shadows, first with his kiss, and then with his words.

She didn't know how he did it, but she was grateful. Rachel gathered the billowing cape and put her hand into his, and stepped from the gondola onto the pavement. However, as she stepped out, her high heel caught in the hem of her long lace gown and she lurched forward, losing her balance.

Gio was there, though, his hands circling her waist, preventing her from falling.

He used the momentum to draw her against him and hold her there. She exhaled hard. One moment she was tumbling through space, and the next she was in his arms, pressed to his hard frame, feeling every bit of his sinewy strength.

She ought to pull away, and yet for the first time in ages she felt safe. She felt supported. She wasn't alone.

It crossed her mind that she didn't want or need the jewels and gowns, but she wanted *him*. She very much wanted him: heart, mind, body and soul, and she was ready to be seduced, ready to feel more, and have more, and be more. And so she stood there, letting his warmth penetrate her long black cloak, penetrate her tingling skin, piercing all the way to the marrow of her bones.

If he kissed her now, she'd kiss him back. If he kissed her now, she would reach out and clasp his nape, her fingers slipping into his dark crisp hair. She'd stand on tiptoe and savor the feel of his lips on hers. She'd taste him and explore his mouth the way he explored hers. She would take advantage of the opportunity to feel, wanting to feel every nuance possible.

His arm tightened around her waist, and his lips brushed her temple. "I'm afraid to let you go," he said. "The last thing I need is you falling into the lagoon."

His lips sent the most delicious shivery sensation through her and she couldn't quite hide her smile. "Don't worry," she murmured. "I can swim."

His lips brushed over her eyebrow. "Yes, but a gentleman wouldn't just stand there and watch a lady splash about. I'd have to come in after you and be heroic. It would be most annoying."

She laughed a low husky laugh. It was hard to think straight; her pulse was racing and her head felt light, making her giddy. "Indeed, because then we would both be cold and wet. Far better for me to be the only wet one."

"But of course once we reached the palazzo, I would have to be sure you were all right. I would have to send you to a hot bath, and then make sure you were towel dried properly, and then wrapped in a robe. I would insist you were seated before a fire with a glass of warm brandy in your hands, and that you stayed there until there was no chill left and you were warm inside and out. I would have to stay close and be sure you were following directions. It would require considerable time and energy on my part, and I am quite sure you would find my ministrations tedious."

"It does sound awful," she murmured unsteadily, leaning against him, her breasts pressed to his chest.

"It would be awful," he agreed, his head dropping, dipping, his mouth brushing the shell of her ear. She shuddered at the warmth of his breath and the way her nerves danced with awareness.

"See? You are shivering with distaste," he added, sliding a hand over her throat, slipping up to outline her chin and then the delicate bones of her jaw. "Imagine how unhappy you would be, locked in my room, naked before my fire."

She shivered again, with anticipation and nerves. "I think it's time to feed you dinner. You sound hungry, and a little bit barbaric."

"I am hungry, but it's you, *cara,* I want."

CHAPTER TWELVE

RACHEL HAD NEVER enjoyed a meal in a private dining room before, let alone served by their own waiter, with a crackling fire in a massive stone fireplace keeping them warm.

The food had been amazing, course after course, with far too much wine, and now that all the dishes had been cleared for coffee, she couldn't help sighing with pleasure. What an incredible restaurant, what a special meal. The company, though, was the best part. Giovanni Marcello had to be the ultimate dream date.

"I don't want you worrying anymore," Gio said, breaking the comfortable silence. "There is no reason for you to struggle and juggle and feel desperate about anything. I can provide for you, easily."

Rachel stared into his darkly handsome face. He wasn't the stranger he'd been when she arrived at the beginning of the week. She didn't know him well, but there was an undeniable attraction, as well as a connection between them, that hadn't been there days ago. "I'm afraid if I married you, I'd lose myself."

"I'm not going to own you, no more than you'd own me."

"I don't think anyone could ever own you. You are far too strong, too independent."

"You're every bit as strong as me."

She gave her head a small shake. "I'm not, though. If you really knew me, you wouldn't be impressed."

"Maybe it's time you explained. Why do you feel so guilty?"

She shook her head, not just unwilling to tell him, but unable. She knew the words would horrify him. They horrified her. "I can hardly admit the truth to myself. I can't imagine what you would think."

"Tell me." He reached across the table and stroked her cheek. "*Cara, bella*, I promise you it isn't as bad as you think."

She didn't agree, but she was tired of all the emotions bottled inside of her, and truthfully, she wanted him to know, especially since he was so determined to marry her. It might change his mind. "I didn't want to be a single mother. I didn't want to do it this way. I wanted to wait until I was ready and I could be a good mom, and I'm not… I'm not…and I hate myself for being like Juliet. Selfish and self-absorbed—" She bit ruthlessly into her lower lip to keep the words from spilling out. Because even now, she could feel how black the truth was, and how ugly it made her.

Rachel had deliberately set the bar high for herself. She'd done it because she was different from Juliet. Stronger. Smarter. *Better*.

"How are you like her?" he demanded. "What have you done that is so selfish and self-absorbed?"

"I've resented that I was needed to help manage Juliet's life…sorting her problems, fixing her mistakes. And then when Juliet fell in love with Antonio, and ended up pregnant, I was livid, because it's one thing to overdraw your checking account, but it's another to have a baby." She pushed at the lone spoon still on the tablecloth. Her eyes burned but she could not cry. "Juliet never had to stand on her own feet. She'd always had Mother, and then when Mother was gone, Juliet couldn't cope anymore, and she died, and I inherited her son."

Rachel let her lashes fall, and she held her breath, wondering when Gio would speak, wondering what he'd say, but he was silent.

After a moment she forced herself to continue. "I wasn't happy about how my life changed. I resented a three-month-old baby. I resented my own nephew…" She bit down into her bottom lip. "How could I do that to Michael? How could I hate him when he did nothing wrong?"

"You didn't hate him."

"No, but I wasn't happy. And when Juliet died, I didn't feel love. I just felt anger. And mostly anger with her because I felt like she took my choices away from me."

"Those are normal emotions," Gio said quietly. "Anyone would feel that way."

Rachel swallowed with difficulty. "I lived so much of my life in Juliet's shadow…and then once she was gone, I still lived in her shadow." Her head lifted and she looked at Gio. "Being a single mom was not my plan. It was really important to me that I could be self-sufficient and financially independent before I married and had children. Instead, look at me. I show up, begging on your doorstep."

"You weren't begging. You were fierce and very defiant."

She wished she could smile but couldn't. "I can't forgive myself for being angry with Juliet, and I can't forgive myself for resenting my orphaned nephew, and I can't forgive myself for not being a better sister to Juliet when she needed more of me, not less."

"Which is why you need to forgive yourself. If you can't forgive yourself for being real and human, you'll never be happy."

"I don't deserve to be happy—"

"Of course you do. And I don't know why you feel inadequate, or if you were made to feel inferior as a child, but it's a lie, and a travesty. You are a beautiful, intelligent woman, a passionate loyal woman, and that is rarer and more valuable than the emeralds on your ears."

The gondola ride was quiet on the return home. Gio said no more than two words during the trip and despite the warmth of her cape, Rachel felt chilled to the core, regretting what she'd told him, wishing she hadn't revealed so much.

Gio took her hand, assisted her from the gondola onto the embankment fronting the palazzo, but didn't let it go, as he walked her inside. As the door shut behind them, he turned her to face him. "Your sister died tragically, and unexpectedly, but you are not to blame for that."

She pushed the hood back on her cape. "She was suffering from postpartum depression—"

"I understand you are grieving for her, but you were not responsible for her—"

"But I *was*—"

"No, and that's the lie. I don't presume to understand all your family dynamics, but you were not put on earth to be your sister's caregiver. You're here to be you, and live your life, and find happiness in your life."

"Maybe. I don't know. But I do know that I can't fail Michael."

For a moment there was just silence, and then Giovanni untied the silk cords on her cape. "You mean, *we*," he corrected. "*We* can't fail him, and *we* have to do better."

He held out his hand to her. "Why don't we go up and check on him together?"

Reaching the third floor they discovered Michael was asleep in his crib, and Mrs. Fabbro resting in a chair not far away, her hands folded across her middle, her steel-gray head tipped back, eyes closed.

The elderly woman opened her eyes when they approached. Gio spoke quietly to her, and Mrs. Fabbro answered, then with a brief nod and briefer smile in Rachel's direction, she left.

"It was a good night," Gio said to Rachel. "No problems. No fussing. She said he's settling in well here, but thinks we need to think about giving him a proper room."

"I feel badly that we were out so late. Mrs. Fabbro is not a young woman."

"Mrs. Fabbro is delighted to be needed. She would take Michael home and keep him all to herself if she could."

"But I hated seeing her sleeping in a chair."

"If she'd wanted to, she could have slept on the bed. She used to do that with us when we were small and had nightmares."

"Your mother didn't come to you?" she whispered, leaning over the crib to check on Michael.

The baby was fast asleep, his round cheeks rosy. She smiled down at him, thinking he looked like an angel.

Gio reached into the crib and lightly stroked a wisp of Michael's black hair. "If my mother was home, yes. But sometimes she'd travel with my father."

Rachel felt a pang as she saw how gently Giovanni touched their nephew. From the beginning he'd been comfortable holding Michael, and she wondered if he'd had a lot of experience with children, or if he was just a natural. Either way, it was reassuring to see.

Giovanni sighed. "Speaking of Madre, I need to tell you something."

"Is she on her way back home?" she whispered.

"Not exactly." He hesitated. "Come, let's go to my room, and I'll explain all."

It turned out that "Come to my room" didn't mean Gio's office suite, but his bedroom. Rachel felt a flutter of nerves as they entered the high-ceilinged room covered in dark beams with gold stencil, the walls a rustic pumpkin-hued plaster, the bed surprisingly modern and austere with a white linen cover. Two white slipcovered chairs flanked the stone fireplace. Books covered a farmhouse table, with more books stacked on the nightstand next to the low bed.

"Would you like a glass of port?" Gio asked, peeling off his coat.

"I'm good, thank you," she answered, sitting down in one of the chairs by the empty hearth.

"Do you mind if I have one?"

"Of course not."

He went to the long wooden table that nearly ran the length of the wall and drew the stopper out of the glass decanter and filled a small glass. He turned to face her, his expression shuttered. "Madre doesn't live here anymore. And she's not visiting her sister in Sorrento. She's in a home in Sorrento. I had to make that decision earlier in the year. She has dementia, and it had become too dangerous for her here. I tried my best to keep her here, but there are so many stairs and halls and empty rooms…as well as windows and water." He looked down into his glass. "I did have to fish her out of the lagoon more than once. It was awful. And then she didn't know me."

"I'm sorry."

"She doesn't know about Michael. She doesn't even know that Antonio is gone. She doesn't know any of us anymore—" He broke off, brow furrowing. "I go see her once a month. I know it's not enough, but it is incredibly painful to sit at her side and listen to her ask me over and over who I am." His jaw jutted. "I don't like feeling helpless. And every time I see her, I do."

"I understand," Rachel said softly, and she did.

"I, too, wrestle with guilt. I feel guilty that I am not there with her more, guilty that I wasn't able to keep her here, in her own home. But it hasn't been an easy year. Antonio's death was impossible. It was like a dance step…quick, quick, slow. The diagnosis was quick, and then he was gone to travel and have his last big adventure, and he only returned when he was ready to die, while the actual dying part was brutal and slow." He began unbuttoning his dark shirt. "Once he began dying, it took forever."

"Were you there with him?" Rachel asked, watching his hands work, tackling one button after another.

"Yes. He wanted to die at home—his home, the one in Florence. I was there for the last thirty-five days. I haven't been back in the house since. At some point I need to do something with it, but I have no desire to return anytime soon. Too many memories. Too much suffering."

She felt his pain and it ached within her. "We've both had so much to deal with this year. I feel badly that I judged you—"

"Don't go there. We were both doing the best we could. It wasn't perfect but it was our best. One can't do more than that."

"Yet I always feel as if I *should*."

Shirt unbuttoned, Gio looked at her, his blue gaze intense, the irises bright and hot.

"You set impossible standards for yourself," he said.

"I do," she said softly, thinking she'd never met anyone half so handsome. His cheekbones were high, his eyebrows were straight and black, his jaw was now shadowed, his mouth beautiful.

Her heart thumped as he crossed the room, his shirt open, exposing his broad chest and hard torso, to sit down in the chair opposite her. He was so close now that if she leaned forward she could touch his thigh. Her mouth went dry. She felt positively parched.

"Can I have a sip of your port?" she asked.

He handed her his glass, his fingers brushing hers. She felt a frisson of pleasure all the way through her.

She sipped the warm rich sweet liquor, and then again, welcoming the burst of flavor on her tongue and then the heat that followed, down her throat to seep through her limbs.

She handed the glass back, and then immediately wished she hadn't.

"Come here," he said, gesturing for her. "You're so far away."

"Not that far." Rachel's heart did another painful little beat. "And I think it's safer here."

"There's no canal to fall in. Nothing to hurt you should you lose your balance."

She tried to smile but her throat constricted, her hands balling at her sides, hidden by the gleaming folds of her gorgeous gown. If she let him, he would be her first. And if they married, her first and her last. He would be everything.

"You could hurt me," she said, the words popping out before she could stop them.

He looked relaxed, sitting on the arm of the chair, and yet there was something watchful in his manner. "Why would I do that?"

"We're so different." Her mouth felt dry. "And our dreams are so different."

"I don't know if we are that different. We both value family. We work hard, and try to think of others. We want Michael to be safe, and loved. And we both want to be happy, as well." He smiled a little, but the smile didn't reach his eyes. If anything it emphasized the shadows in the blue depths, the shadows a testament to his grief over losing Antonio.

"Have I missed anything?" he asked quietly.

The fact that he was still grieving for his brother rendered him human, and vulnerable. Yes, he was still impossibly beautiful but he was a man, and he'd hurt, just as she'd hurt. She wanted to comfort him now, but wasn't sure how.

She drew a shallow breath. "Can we both be happy?"

"You mean, together?" he asked.

She nodded.

"If we can move forward together and let the past go."

"It's not easy to let it go, though," she said, nails pressing into her tender palms. "Because you couldn't have saved

Antonio, but I could have saved Juliet—" She broke off, chest squeezing, throat tightening, the air trapped in her lungs. She blinked, trying to clear the sting of tears.

"How?" Gio asked, covering her clenched hands with one of his.

"If I'd found all the pills ahead of time. If I'd known she was stockpiling them. If I'd known she was suffering from depression…"

"But you didn't. How could you?"

Rachel's shoulders twisted. "I should have realized she wasn't coping well. In the weeks leading up to her death, she needed more and more help from me, and near the end I had become an almost full-time caregiver." She chewed her lower lip. "I wasn't happy about it. I told her so, too."

"Ah." His hand squeezed hers. "That's why you feel guilty."

"I wish I could go back and do it differently. You have no idea how much I regret those pep talks and lectures. I was trying to help, but I am quite certain they just made her feel worse…they just isolated her further. Rather than giving her tough love, I should have driven her to a doctor."

He tugged her from her chair and pulled her toward him, settling her on his lap. "Hindsight is always clearer," he said gruffly, tilting her chin up to look into her eyes. "But at the time, you didn't know, and you were doing your best."

Rachel bit harder into her lip, fighting to hold back the tears. She hated remembering, and most of all she hated remembering that last night, because every time she thought about that final evening, she thought of everything she should have said or done. "I'm not disappointed in Juliet," she whispered brokenly. "I'm disappointed in *me*."

He kissed her then, his mouth covering hers, his tongue stroking the seam of her lips, until her mouth opened for him. He kissed her with hunger and need and something else she couldn't articulate, and her hands came up to press against his warm, bare chest. He felt good, his skin like satin over dense, hard muscle, and she was torn between pushing him away to preserve her sanity and pulling him closer.

She was sick and tired of fighting herself. Sick and tired of fighting him, and her desire for him. Everything had been so difficult for so long, and she was ready for something else, something new. Could they be happy together? Was it possible that out of all the terrible loss and grief they could create something new?

"I think it's time to take you to bed to stop you from thinking too much," he murmured.

"I am thinking too much," she agreed hoarsely.

"I know the perfect solution for that," he answered, hands sliding into her hair, tilting her head back to give him access to her mouth. He kissed her hard, his tongue first lightly stroking her lips, before finding the roof of her mouth and then the tip of her tongue.

Her pulse jumped and her legs shook as heat flooded her.

The kiss deepened, his tongue taking her mouth, making her melt. Hot sensation rushed through her and her thighs pressed, trying to deny the ache inside her and the way desire coiled within her.

She shuddered as he urged her closer, his strong hand low on her hip, holding her firmly against him, letting her feel his erection. She blushed, and hated herself for blushing. She felt like such a child. It would be a relief to know what to do, to feel confident about herself. Her inexperience had become a problem.

"You're still thinking," he growled in her ear.

"I'm sorry. It's a problem. I'll try to stop—" She broke off as he reached behind her neck and found her zipper.

With practiced ease, he drew the zipper down and slipped the dress off her shoulders. It puddled to her waist.

And then he stood, rising with her in his arms as if she weighed nothing and carried her across the room.

Panic rushed through her, heightening her emotions, making her pulse race even faster. She wanted him and was glad he would be her first, and yet she also worried she'd disappoint him. Should she tell him that she was still a virgin? Did a man want to know something like that? Or would it put too much pressure on him?

He placed her on the bed and her gown slid all the way down, in a pool of shimmering green and gold.

Giovanni's gaze swept over her as she lay before him in her delicate lace bra and matching thong panties. His lashes dropped and his firm lips curved in appreciation. "The things I want to do to you," he said, his voice low.

She exhaled breathlessly, heart pumping so hard she could barely think straight.

Gio joined her on the bed, stretching out over her, his weight braced on his elbows to keep from crushing her. Gazing down into her flushed face, he thought she'd never looked more beautiful. Her dark eyes shone and her soft mouth looked swollen and so incredibly kissable, so kissable that he lowered his head and took her mouth again.

"And Michael? What if he wakes?" Rachel gasped, as he shifted to her neck, kissing down the column to the rise of her collarbone.

He didn't try to answer her immediately, too intent on claiming one lace-covered nipple, his teeth finding the sensitive tip and tugging ever so gently. She gasped again, her body shifting restlessly beneath his.

"Mrs. Fabbro is with him," he answered at length, licking the taut peak, the damp lace imprinting on her tender skin. "She returned to the room after we left, and is sleeping in there with him tonight."

"You didn't say that earlier," she choked, and then arched up as he covered the nipple, sucking again in firm tugs that had her panting, her hands going to his back, her nails pressing against him.

Gio welcomed her sighs of pleasure, just as he welcomed the edge of pleasure and pain as her nails bit into his back. He hadn't wanted to be with anyone this past year. He hadn't wanted intimacy or sex. He hadn't felt desire... He hadn't felt anything, but now he was feeling hunger, desire, need, and he was impatient to have her, impatient to bury himself in Rachel's soft, wet heat.

"Are you on birth control?" he asked, lifting his head.

She shook her head.

"You're not protected?" he repeated, struggling to hold back when all he wanted to do was bury himself inside her.

"No." She drew an unsteady breath. "I've never needed it."

"You leave it to your partner?"

"Yes. No. I mean—" She drew another quick breath, her breasts rising and falling, the dark pink nipples tight buds against the pale creamy skin. "I'm a virgin. I've never needed protection before."

Giovanni stilled, stunned. Was she serious? She was twenty-eight years old, nearly twenty-nine. Were there twenty-nine-year-old virgins out there?

He felt her draw a breath, her rib cage rising and falling. Her voice was tremulous when she spoke. "I realize it's a bit odd, and probably uncomfortable." She inhaled sharply and exhaled, the sound half laugh, half sob. "It's uncomfortable, even for me. I never meant to be this...but here I am. Sexless. Emotionless." Her hand reached out, searching for something to cover herself with.

He rose up, careful not to crush her. "You are not without emotions. You just lack experience. There is a difference."

She said nothing. Her gaze was fixed on a point past his shoulder but he could see the shadows in her eyes, and then came the silent film of tears.

"What happened?" he asked, head dipping to kiss just beneath her jaw, and then another kiss to the tender skin of her throat. "Did someone hurt you? Who broke your heart?"

Her slim shoulder twisted. "No broken heart. I was just holding out for true love. It didn't happen."

"You've never been in love?"

"I think I've come close, but it always ended before I was convinced it was a forever love."

He placed a kiss along her collarbone, and then lower. She shivered and sighed, as he cupped her breast. He eased his hand back and forth over the taut nipple. She inhaled with each stroke, her breathing increasingly shallow.

"And yet you're so sensitive," he murmured, stroking down, his hand caressing the length of her, from her full breast, over her flat stomach to reach the soft mound between her thighs.

"You make me sensitive," she whispered huskily, squirming as he caressed her lightly through the lace panty, light deft touches that made her thighs clench.

"Or maybe you've never given someone the chance to please you." He leaned over and kissed one of her pelvic bones. Her hips rocked against him. He kissed the other and her breath caught in her throat.

"If someone can't please my brain," she choked, "he's not about to get close to my body."

He smiled as his teeth found the edge of elastic bordering her lace thong. "How do you explain us then?"

"You didn't waste time. You went straight for my mind."

He nuzzled her between her thighs, and then traced her with the tip of his tongue. He heard her broken cry as his tongue followed the cleft, the soft shape of her, and then between, where she was so very responsive.

She cried out again when he pushed the scrap of lace aside and touched her with his fingers and tongue, parting her to taste her and tease her. She was tense, nerves wound tight, and trembling as he licked her, slow long flicks of his tongue that had her gasping for air.

Her hips ground up, and he pressed a hand to her tummy, holding her down, holding her still, while he flicked and sucked on her delicate nub, the tender hood hard against his tongue.

"Gio," she choked, her hand reaching for his shoulder, then sliding into his hair.

He could feel her tighten beneath him, feel her struggling, not wanting to lose control. He eased a finger inside of her, caressing that spot inside her warm slick body and sucked again on her, before gently sliding in another finger, working the inside of her while he matched the pressure on her clit.

She cried out his name as she climaxed, her body tensing, convulsing with pleasure. He held her after, her supple body so warm in his arms.

"That," she whispered, awed, "was amazing."

"Good. But that, *bella*, was just the beginning."

CHAPTER THIRTEEN

RACHEL DIDN'T REMEMBER falling asleep, but when she woke up, she was astonished to discover she was still in Gio's bed, in his room. Morning light streamed through a break in the curtains, streaking the carpeted floor. Memories of last night returned in a rush.

Rachel sat up swiftly, covers clutched to her breasts.

Giovanni reached out and drew her back down. "Where are you going?" he asked, sleepily.

"Michael," she protested, even as Gio pulled her toward him.

"He's with Mrs. Fabbro, remember? I am sure they will be fine for a little bit longer." Gio rolled her onto her back and kissed her, his body hard and warm.

She shivered with pleasure, feeling the thickness of his erection press between her thighs. He'd made her climax twice last night and yet he hadn't taken her virginity. She was ready to lose it. Ready to be his.

"Make love to me," she said, locking her hands around his neck.

"Don't you want to wait for our wedding night?"

"No. It puts too much pressure on the evening. I already feel so much pressure."

"Why?"

She wasn't sure how to explain it to him, but her inexperience was an issue, at least for her. She wanted him, and was glad he would be her first, and yet she was also so very nervous and worried that she'd disappoint him. It was one thing to be a virgin at eighteen, but another at twenty-eight. "What if I'm not any good?" she asked, her voice cracking ever so slightly. "What if you're sorry—"

"You worry far too much about everything. Stop thinking," he said. "Stop analyzing. It's time to live."

"I agree. I want to live. Make love to me. Now. Please."

He rolled her over, so that he was now on the bottom, and she was lying naked on top of him. His hand swept down her bare back, over her hip to tease her bottom. He caressed her like that, once, twice, his touch so light on the curve of her backside, and each brush made more of her nerve endings come to life.

He slid his hands over the curve of her butt again, finding the sensitive crease where her cheeks ended and her leg began. He played with the crease and then the tops of her thighs, stroking out and then in again, melting her from the inside out.

"Please, Gio," she whispered, pressing her pelvis to his, her belly knotting, her womb feeling so empty it made her frantic. She'd waited so long for this, and she was ready. She didn't need more foreplay. She didn't need him to be gentle. She wanted to be taken.

His hand slipped between her thighs, finding her slit. She was hot and wet, and his fingers slipped easily into her, stroking, teasing, before sliding out to spread the moisture over her nub, making her buck.

"Gio," she gritted, arching up as he caressed her again.

He rolled her back over, his knees parting her thighs, holding her open for him. She looked up into his hard, handsome face as she felt the head of his shaft at her entrance. He was smooth and warm and she rubbed herself against him, enjoying the way he felt, and how deliciously sensitive she was with him against her.

He lowered himself to kiss her. "I don't want to hurt you," he said against her mouth.

"It will only hurt the first time, so let's get the first time over."

"My pragmatist," he murmured, smiling. "I appreciate your candor, but it doesn't sound sexy."

"I'm not sexy," she said hoarsely as he shifted, adjusting himself so that the tip of his shaft was pressing at her entrance.

She exhaled slowly as he pushed in. He was large and she felt tight, but he kept pressing forward, and she drew a deep breath, trying to focus on his warmth and how he felt like satin, but it was snug, as he pushed in, and it began to sting.

Her eyes burned and she blinked, surprised by the pain. She really was too old to be a virgin, she thought blinking back tears.

"I'm hurting you," he said, growing still.

"It's okay," she whispered, her hands sliding around his back, savoring the warmth of his skin and the dense muscle in his back. He did feel good, and she wanted this, and it would only hurt the first time. "Don't stop."

"*Bella*, darling—"

"Please. Don't stop."

He thrust deeply, burying himself in her. Gio kissed her, giving her time to get used to him, and as she responded, kissing him back, he began to move, hips rocking, withdrawing to sink back into her. She felt a sensation that made her sigh, not quite a tickle or tingle, but something almost delicious. He thrust into her again, and she felt the same pleasure. She relaxed, welcoming the press of his body and the way he sank deeply into her. Her pulse quickened as his tempo increased, and she began to breathe more deeply, feeling her body tighten around him. He was driving her toward another orgasm, and she gripped his shoulders, her body lifting to meet his, wanting the pressure and pleasure, wanting him, wanting more of this sensation of them together.

They felt like one. They felt the way she'd thought love

would feel. Bright and intense and stunning and so deeply satisfying.

And just like that, she knew two things—she loved him, and she couldn't hold back anymore. She gave in to both then, her heart opening to love him even as her body yielded to the pleasure. She shattered beneath him and kept shattering, and then he, too, must have been climaxing, as he stiffened and his hands buried in her hair, his hard body filling her completely.

For long moments afterward, her heart pumped, and her skin felt hot and flushed. She closed her eyes, savoring the feel of Giovanni and the weight of him on her and in her. It was wonderful. Being with him was wonderful. She knew he didn't love her, and would probably never love her, but in that moment she was happy, genuinely happy, and she laughed out loud, a bright quick gurgle of sound.

Gio lifted his head, looked down at her. "You're laughing?"

"Yes." She smiled up at him, feeling impossibly good, and so very relaxed. "I'm not a virgin anymore, am I?"

"No. Sorry, *bella*, you've been deflowered."

"Thank God! It was about time."

His expression turned wry. "I hope you mean thank God it was with me."

"Well, of course. That, too."

"Hmm."

She snuggled close. "It was amazing, Gio. You were amazing. Thank you."

Later, after their bodies had cooled, Gio kissed her, and then climbed from bed.

"I'll send for coffee," he said.

"Thank you," she said, snuggling down under the covers. "I take it you'll be in your office the rest of the day, doing your usual calls and meetings?"

He paused in the bathroom door, his body beautifully

hard and muscular. "In meetings, yes, but these are meetings with you."

"With me?" She propped herself up on one elbow. "Why are we having meetings?"

"I should say appointments. Today is the day we're meeting with the journalist from the big UK magazine, the one that is doing the story on our wedding."

Rachel's smile began to fade. "Gio, not today. Not yet. We haven't even discussed our wedding. We haven't even really planned the engagement party."

"That's just it. I think we should combine them. Why have two events? Why not turn the engagement party into a surprise wedding reception?"

She no longer felt like smiling at all. The big bubble of happiness inside her had popped, as well. "You're serious, aren't you?"

"There's no reason to drag it out. Let's wed and be done with it—"

"How charming."

"It will be. We can make it fun and today will be fun at any rate. We have a florist coming, and a baker who specializes in wedding cakes."

"I'm surprised you don't have my wedding gown picked out for me."

"I do have a designer coming. She'll have some dresses and sketches."

"Gio, this isn't how a wedding is supposed to work."

"Rachel, we agreed we were going to do what was right for Michael. This is the right thing for him."

She ground her teeth together, holding back tears of frustration.

"*Cara*, darling, we will be happy."

She said nothing, battling the lump filling her throat.

He sighed. "I don't have time to coddle you now. The journalist and her photographer will be here in less than two hours. Do you want me to call in a hair stylist and have someone do your hair for the pictures?"

"I can do it myself."

"Very well. Coffee is on the way. I'm going to shower and shave. Today is about looking happy. Do try to look happy, *bella*, okay?"

Rachel showered and washed her hair, and then while it dried, she spent a half hour with Michael, walking him around the house, showing him all the beautiful things there were to see—chandeliers and Venetian mirrors, gilded frames and oil masterpieces. "This is all your house, too," she told him, struggling to smile, struggling to keep her tone light when her heart felt unbearably heavy because she felt tricked.

Gio had seduced her last night to further his agenda.

It hadn't been a night of mad passion. He hadn't been overcome by emotion. He'd known the reporter was coming today to get their "story" for the magazine, the story being important because it protected Gio's business and all his valuable investors.

She was not important. She was just a means to an end.

Rachel returned Michael to Mrs. Fabbro, and then dressed in her brown lace dress and styled her hair, twisting it up and letting a few tendrils fall free to frame her face.

She could barely stand to look at her reflection. She was too upset, too hurt. Turning from the mirror she headed downstairs, arriving just as the journalist and the photography crew stepped through the front door.

Giovanni made the introductions and ushered everyone into the rose salon with the famous frescoes by Gregorio Lazzarini. The photographer set up his equipment while his assistant arranged the lights and white screen. The English journalist, Heidi Parker, immediately began asking questions, and Gio answered everything she asked with an easy, sexy smile. He looked incredibly comfortable, and when Rachel remained quiet, he slid his arm around her and kissed her on the brow, and then the lips, playing the part of the besotted lover.

"Where will the wedding reception be?" Heidi asked.

"The ballroom," Gio said. "Would you like to see it?"

Heidi nodded and the photographer joined them. Gio opened the doors and stepped back. He didn't need to say or do more. The room spoke for itself, appearing to stretch the length of the house, but that might have been an illusion due to the soaring ceiling with the Baroque frescoes and lavish gold paint.

It wasn't hard to imagine it glittering at nighttime, all five of the lavish chandeliers lit, the crystals gleaming and reflecting light while guests mingled and danced below.

Rachel's heart ached as Gio shared some of the wedding details. It would be without a doubt the most beautiful and fashionable event of the year. The reception would be extravagant, and Giovanni would serve the Marcello wine from his vineyard. But it wasn't the kind of wedding she wanted. She didn't want a show. She didn't want fuss and extravagance. She wanted something intimate and warm and full of love.

They left the ballroom and headed for the dining room, which had been turned into a floristry. Flowers were everywhere, in buckets and vases, in hand-tied bouquets and elegant boutonnieres. The bouquets were lush and wildly romantic and Rachel found herself lifting one and smelling it, and then froze when she realized the photographer was clicking away, capturing her with the pink roses and peonies and lilies.

"Beautiful," the photographer said, giving her a smile.

It was all she could do not to cry when Gio pulled her into his arms and kissed her, giving the photographer another "candid" shot, and then Gio was sharing more details about their guest list and who had been invited. They were all society people, and Heidi scribbled away, murmuring about what a spectacular event it would be, such an A-list party.

The very description sent a chill through Rachel. She was not an A-lister herself. She was not even close to a B-or C-list.

Gio was right. She was firmly middle class. A woman from Burien, Washington who had to struggle for everything in life.

"How does it feel knowing that you will have the wedding of the year?" Heidi asked Rachel. "Is it at all intimidating?"

"Very much so," Rachel answered, voice wobbling. "Giovanni's friends are powerful and influential…aristocrats, millionaires and billionaires, race car drivers, fashion designers, models, actors and socialites…" Her voice faded, the stream of words ending. "Not my sort of people at all," she concluded unsteadily, aware that Heidi and the photographer had just exchanged curious glances.

Giovanni didn't seem disturbed. He kissed the top of her head. "My sweet bride."

Heidi scribbled something. "And the baby?" she asked. "Will we meet him? Do say yes. We are so hoping for a picture of the three of you."

"No. We're determined to protect his privacy," Gio answered firmly. "It was the one condition we had about the interview. The focus would be Rachel and me. It's not fair to Michael to put him in the limelight."

Heidi nodded. "Of course. And I did know. But what kind of journalist would I be if I didn't try?"

Gio gestured toward the door. "I believe our chef is here. Shall we go discuss our wedding cake?"

While Heidi stayed back with the photographer, helping hold one temperamental light, Rachel moved close to Gio, whispering to him as they exited the dining room. "You seem to be quite enjoying the fuss."

"It's for the cameras."

She shot him a dubious glance. "I don't believe you."

He glanced back at Heidi, who was now bustling toward them. His broad shoulders shifted. "I want a wedding to remember."

"Funny, but I want a wedding I can forget."

"You've lost your sense of humor, Rachel. Why can't you have fun with this? Why not enjoy planning the wedding?"

"Because it seems like a terrible extravagance!"

"Maybe I see this as the right opportunity to return to society."

"The right opportunity being before the stock offerings," she said under her breath.

But he heard her. He lifted a brow. "My goal is to protect all. The company. The employees. The family. Michael." He reached out and tipped her chin up, his gaze locking with hers. "You."

"I'm not a Marcello."

"Not yet in name, but in body, I've already claimed you."

Her heart hurt and heat washed through her. "You have no idea how much I regret that, too."

He gave her a look. "I don't believe that, and neither do you."

With that, he headed into the palazzo's vast kitchen, a room that might have been medieval at one point, but was a stunning space of light and gleaming white marble.

Like the dining room that had been filled with flowers, the long white marble counters were filled with cakes. Tall, white, layered cakes and large square cakes covered in sugared fruit. There was a cone cake with caramel-covered pastries and puffs of whipped cream and a chocolate something with more whipped cream.

The photographer immediately wanted photos, and Heidi went over to introduce herself to the chef.

Giovanni leaned against a white counter, arms folded across his chest. "You must admit this is an easy way to do an interview," he said as Rachel reluctantly came to stand at his side. "We're giving them a show, but we're not having to tell them very much about us."

"I'd like to give them a show, but it would involve smashing cake in your face."

He laughed softly. "You are determined to be angry."

"You should have told me last night that the reporter was coming this morning. It would have changed things."

"How so?"

I wouldn't have given you my heart, she thought, looking away, jaw grinding to hold back the emotion, *I would have just given you my body.* But Rachel wasn't sure that was true. She didn't think she could have helped falling for him. And maybe that was why she was angry. She'd wanted to hold out for true love. Instead she'd fallen for Gio.

He tipped her chin up. "It wouldn't have changed anything, *cara.* You willingly, happily went to bed with me last night. I kissed every inch of your lovely body, and then this morning, after a good sleep, when you couldn't blame the wine for clouding your judgment, I took your virginity. There was no coercion involved."

"Can you not say *virginity* so loud?" she gritted, face on fire.

"Is that why you're so sensitive this morning? Did you want to lounge around this morning—"

"No."

"Savoring your first time?"

She dug her nails into her palms. "I will slap you if you continue mocking me."

"I am not mocking you."

"Then what are you doing?"

"Teasing you." He leaned forward and kissed her brow. "As new lovers do," he added with another kiss. Gio drew back and smiled into her eyes. "Shall we go select our wedding cake?"

The chef had a speech prepared, and in the palazzo's cavernous kitchen, he shared how cake wasn't just something sweet with which to finish the meal, but the breaking of bread over the bride's head dated to the ancient Romans. The groom would smash the cake—sometimes even throw it at her—as a fertility ritual.

Rachel's lips compressed. "What a lovely thing for a man to do to his bride," she said under her breath. "I'm sure she enjoyed it immensely."

Gio grinned lazily at her. "Is that your sense of humor returning?"

"Oh no. It's gone. I don't think it'll ever be back, either."

He just laughed, and the photographer snapped away, and the chef kept talking as he showed them each of the different types of cake they could choose for their wedding.

"This is the classic Italian white cake," he said, gesturing to a four-tier cake. "It is the one most similar to your American wedding cake style. In Italy, the beautiful white icing represents purity and fidelity, and the bride's faithful devotion to her new husband."

"That sounds like our perfect cake," Gio said.

Rachel shot him a dark glance. "What other choices do we have?"

The chef went on to the next cake. "Many couples choose *millefoglie*, a very traditional cake comprised of very thin, delicate layers of pastry with a light cream mascarpone filling. *Millefoglie* translates to 'a thousand layers' and is finished with powdered sugar and fresh berries. You can also choose a chocolate cream filling instead of mascarpone if you are a chocolate fan." The chef smiled. "The only drawback to such a cake is that it cannot be stacked, so it does not create quite the same centerpiece effect."

"Since my bride is American, I think we should give her a tall cake," Gio said.

The chef moved to the third cake. "There is also the profiterole cake. It is a tower cake, but instead of layers of cake that have been iced and stacked, it is a cone covered in cream-filled pastries. It is a very European cake, popular in France, too, although there it is called *croquembouche*."

The room was silent as everyone looked at her, as if eager for her pronouncement. "I don't care," Rachel whispered, overwhelmed. "Whatever Giovanni wants. This is his big day, too."

Gio's gaze met hers and held. "I think we should go with the traditional layered cake," he said after a moment. "A white layered cake with all white frosting to symbolize my beautiful bride's purity and devotion."

And then it was all over. The photographer and journalist left, and the chef packed up his cakes, and it was just Rachel and Gio with a stack of sketches—the wedding dresses.

Rachel numbly leafed through the illustrations of gorgeous white dresses but they were all just that—formal white gowns that meant nothing to her. She was finding it impossible to wrap her head around the marriage and the wedding and everything else. Finally, she just pushed the sketches across the table to Gio. "You decide," she said. "I don't care. I really don't."

It wasn't the answer Gio wanted, but he smiled lazily, hiding his frustration. But later, when he was in his office, he found himself pausing between conference calls to wonder why he wanted her to care. He wanted her to be enthusiastic; he wanted the wedding ceremony and reception to be something they'd both enjoy, and he wasn't sure why.

They weren't marrying out of love. This was a practical marriage at best. So why should it matter if she was or wasn't excited about the ceremony? Why should he want her to treat this as if it was her dream wedding?

Why did he want her to be happy about marrying him?

Maybe it was because he was actually quite happy with her. He liked her, a great deal as a matter of fact.

He liked looking at her and he thoroughly enjoyed touching her and tasting her and giving her pleasure. He even found himself wanting to hold her, and since Adelisa, he hadn't wanted to hold any woman, not after sex. Usually after his orgasm, he was done. Physically satisfied and ready to move on to the next thing. But with Rachel in his bed, the orgasm was just the beginning. The orgasm was almost incidental. There was something about her warmth and softness that made him want to stay with her, keeping her close, kissing her and exploring her sweet curves, and then making love all over again.

With her in his bed, he felt relaxed and settled. Calm. Peaceful. Yes, that was it. Peaceful. She fit in his life. She fit in his arms and, indeed, in his heart.

He wasn't one to use flowery phrases and spout poetry, and he didn't glorify romantic love, but some part of him believed that marrying might just possibly be the smartest thing he'd ever do, and not simply because it'd keep her and Michael in Venice, but because it'd give him a strong, independent and self-sufficient partner. A partner he could trust.

But she needed to trust him. And be happy with him.

Rachel entered the smaller salon, which had been turned into a dining room for them that evening. In front of the marble hearth, a table had been set for two, with a high chair placed between the two dining chairs.

Seeing the antique wooden high chair at the table put a lump in Rachel's throat. The chair was so ornate, probably a family heirloom, and it made the dining table look cozy and domestic.

Moments later Gio entered the room with Michael in his arms and she had to blink back tears.

"I thought it was time we had a family dinner," Gio said, giving her a smile that made her heart turn over. Michael babbled something and took his fist from his mouth and bounced it on Gio's freshly shaven cheek. Gio grinned and his quick flash of white teeth made everything inside her chest tighten and ache.

Gio looked beyond gorgeous tonight, and his ease with Michael made her want to weep. How was she going to resist a man who loved children?

"You don't mind that I wanted him to join us, do you?" Gio asked, looking from Michael to her.

"No, of course not," she answered quickly, breathlessly. "In Seattle, he's my dinner date every night." She couldn't quite get over Gio's ease with Michael, though. He looked incredibly comfortable and it didn't make sense. He was supposed to be this cold, unfeeling man, and yet he was carting around the six-month-old as if they were lifelong friends. "Have you had a lot of experience with babies and children?"

"None. Does it show?"

"No. You're a natural."

"I think it helps that I like him," he answered, glancing down at the baby, but she heard the way his voice deepened. She heard the rasp of emotion. Gio loved Michael.

"He reminds you of your brother, doesn't he?" she said.

"Yes. It's bittersweet, but definitely more sweet than bitter." He hesitated. "Do you see your sister in him?"

"No. Not at all. He is very much a Marcello."

"So you don't hate all Marcellos."

She felt another pang. "I don't hate you, Gio," she whispered, because she didn't. She couldn't. Not when she'd begun to care so very much. Somehow in the past four days he'd become not just familiar, but *hers*. Her Giovanni Marcello, her impossible Venetian.

Or maybe she felt like his. He was making her his, and she was finding it hard, if not impossible, to resist.

"Good, because Michael and I have a question for you." Shifting the baby, Gio reached into his coat and withdrew a small black ring box.

Her heart did another funny dip. She knew what this was.

He could see that she knew, too, and his lips curved ever so faintly. Gio walked toward her and Michael batted the velvet box. Rachel couldn't move, rooted to the spot.

Reaching her side, he opened the top revealing an enormous, intense yellow, square-cut diamond ring surrounded by smaller white diamonds, but he wasn't looking at the ring. He was looking into her face, his gaze holding hers. "*Bella* Rachel, marry me."

He'd been calling her *bella* for the past few days, and she'd thought she knew what it meant—beautiful—but she wasn't beautiful. Juliet was beautiful. Rachel knew she bordered on plain. "Please don't mock me," she whispered.

"Why can't you be beautiful?" he asked. "Why must you assume I'd want someone like your sister? Yes, she caught Antonio's eye, but she's not the kind of woman I'm drawn to. You are. You are my idea of beautiful."

"You say that because you never met her."

"You don't think I've had my pick of beautiful women? I'm thirty-eight. I'm wealthy. I can support any woman in any lifestyle she wants. Trust me, women are drawn to me, but I want you, *bella*. I'm drawn to *you*."

She swallowed hard. "Do you mind terribly that I'm not interested in your money? And that I am not very interested in having a lifestyle? I just want to be a good mother to Michael, and hopefully, a good wife to you."

"Does that mean you'll accept Michael's and my proposal?"

He hadn't mentioned love, but then, she didn't expect him to. Right now she didn't need the word when she felt his strength and passion and commitment. She believed he would be a good husband. A kind husband. And an honest one, too.

"Yes." She smiled shyly. "Can I put on the ring?"

"If you don't mind that Michael's begun to drool all over it."

"That's his seal of approval, you know," she answered, holding her hand out so that Gio could slide the stunning yellow diamond onto her finger.

"My beautiful funny Rachel," Gio said, putting the ring on her finger, where it glinted with fire and light. He shifted Michael and kissed her, and then again. "I am so glad your sense of humor is back. You make me smile and laugh. It has been such a long time since I did either."

She reached up and touched his jaw, her fingernails lightly raking his jaw. "So you appreciate my brains and beauty."

"All of it. And all of you. I love your eyes and how they show everything you're thinking and feeling. I love your mouth—you have perfect lips—and I love that when I kiss you, you make this little whimper. I find that incredibly sexy."

And then he kissed her and his kiss lit her up like a Christmas tree. "I can't wait until bedtime," she whispered.

"I can't, either, as I intend to show you something new tonight, something guaranteed to give you intense pleasure."

"Don't tease."

"I'm not. It's a promise."

CHAPTER FOURTEEN

RACHEL LOOKED AT herself in the floor-length mirror. Her figure-hugging wedding gown was made of white lace, and the lace hugged her curves before billowing out just above the knees. The lace sleeves were long, reaching the back of her hand, and the fitted lace collar high. Her veil, made of the same lace, covered her from head to toe.

She'd been dressed as if she was still the virgin bride, although she was far from virginal now.

As she put on one of the diamond earrings Gio had given her for an early wedding gift, she told herself she was happy. She was marrying someone whom she was compatible with. Indeed, with him she experienced incredible pleasure. She hadn't even imagined that she could feel so much, never mind the sizzling, dazzling heat that burned in her veins and hummed in her body making her reckless with need.

Of course she wished Gio loved her. She wished he felt for her even half of what she felt for him.

Maybe that's why the sex was so good. It wasn't just sex for her. It was love. When she gave herself to him each night—and morning—she gave herself completely, not just her body, but her soul and heart.

She was lucky to have a good partner, someone to help her raise Michael, someone who would treat Michael as his own son, but still—*still*—it would have been even better, it would have been perfect, if that someone loved *her*.

Earrings in place, she turned away from the mirror and was preparing to leave when a knock sounded at the door, and then her bedroom door opened, and it was Gio.

"What are you doing here?" she said, unable to hide

herself. "It's bad luck for a groom to see the bride on the wedding day."

"I have something for you," he said, entering her room with a large leather box.

"You've already given me these gorgeous earrings."

"This is different."

That's when she saw his expression. Something was wrong. Gio wasn't smiling. He looked somber and hard and impossibly remote. Her heart did a painful little beat.

"What is that box?" she asked. The dark box was the size of a loaf of bread, and the polished surface gleamed, the exterior made of inlaid wood, the wood carved into an intricate design of flowers and fruits and musical instruments. It looked old, hundreds of years old, and valuable. Rachel suspected it'd been designed to hold jewelry or a dagger or something else of value.

"You need to have a look at what's inside."

"Now?"

"Yes."

"Will it take long? We're supposed to be getting married soon."

He carried the box to her bed and placed it on the white coverlet. "I want you to see this before we do. I think it's important…for you. For us."

It was in that moment, when he sounded so distant and grave, that she realized how much she loved him, and how much she wanted to be his wife, and how very much she wanted a happy future with him.

She realized in that moment that she could lose everything, and didn't want to lose everything. Gio didn't love her, but he was good to her, and kind. Fearless and strong.

Deep down she hoped—believed—she could get him to love her one day. That one day they would both be happy, together.

"Why do this now?" she whispered. "You must have a reason."

"I do."

"It can't be good. From your expression, it's not good."

"I just need you to know what I know. And then we will marry, and we will raise Michael together, and all will be well."

But he didn't believe it, she thought. And that was what terrified her.

"Please," Gio said, tapping the box.

Rachel crossed the room and sat down on the bed. As she lifted the box, Gio moved away, going to stand at the windows. She glanced at his rigid back, and then opened the box. The lid was hinged and when lifted, she saw the interior was filled with envelopes and papers.

Rachel carefully lifted the paperwork out and scanned the envelopes and printed emails, shivering as she recognized her sister Juliet's handwriting. The letters and cards and emails were all from Juliet to Antonio.

She took the top envelope. The date on the postmark was December 31. She looked behind that one. The postmark was December 25. The envelope behind that one was postmarked December 18.

The letters went all the way back to May 19, the day Antonio died.

Pulse racing, insides churning, Rachel reached for the letter at the very bottom, the one postmarked May 19, and opened the letter and began to read.

My dearest Antonio,
How dare you leave me? How dare you go? I need you so much. I don't know how to do this without you. I love you too much. I have always loved you too much. We both know it.

It frightens me that I love you more than life itself.

And now you're gone without even a last goodbye and it's not fair. You've never been fair. You swept me off my feet and made me believe in love and miracles. You seemed like a miracle.

You allowed me to dream and hope and believe, and now you tell me that you're sick, and dying, and you should have told me first. You should have told me before I gave you my heart and soul.

Rachel's hands were shaking so hard she couldn't see the next line and she paused, glancing blindly up. "I don't understand," she whispered.

"You will," Gio said.

Gulping a breath, Rachel returned to the letter.

I don't know how to raise this baby without you. I didn't want to be a mother. I wanted to be your wife, your woman, your lover. And now I've a child but not you.

You have broken my heart.

You have broken me.

Yours forever and ever,

Juliet

Rachel's hands shook as she folded the letter back up and slid it into the envelope. A tear fell and she knocked it away as she returned the envelope to the bottom of the pile. She couldn't bring herself to read more.

"Why did you bring these to me?" she choked.

"They are all like that." Giovanni spoke from across the room.

Rachel drew a deep raw breath and then another. "You've read them all?"

"Not all. Maybe a quarter, if that. It didn't feel right to continue reading when they were not meant for me."

"When did you read these? Have you had these all this time?" Rachel struggled to stop the tears but they kept falling.

"Mrs. Fabbro brought the box with her when his Florence home was closed. She used to work for him in Florence, and when the letters arrived from Juliet, she'd put them in this box. She gave me the box several days ago, and I finally had a chance to go through the letters last night." He hesitated. "I couldn't sleep afterward."

"You should have woken me."

"But then you wouldn't be able to sleep, either."

Her eyes continued to burn. She blinked. "She really loved him."

"Yes. I didn't believe her, but I do now."

"She wasn't as shallow as you thought."

Gio was silent. "There is something I haven't told you. I need to tell you." He glanced at her over his shoulder, expression grim. "Antonio loved your sister, too. He didn't leave her because he didn't care. He left her because he didn't want her to see him die. He left her to protect her from the ugliness of his death."

"How do you know?"

"He left her his entire estate. His homes, his assets, his stock in Marcello SpA. All of it."

"What?"

"He didn't leave her penniless. He left her a very wealthy woman, setting her up so that she could raise his son properly, wanting his woman and his child provided for."

Rachel wanted to move but her legs wouldn't stand. She sat, hands clasping the box, heart on fire. "I don't understand. But she received nothing. She didn't know—"

"She was never told."

"How? Why not?"

"I took legal action when his will was revealed, petitioning our courts to investigate the legality of the document."

Gio stood before her, handsome in his tuxedo, but utterly unrepentant. "He had an inoperable tumor in his brain. He was dying. His behavior had become increasingly erratic. I was concerned he was being played, or coerced, and so I asked the courts to intervene—"

"Causing my sister's death," she interrupted hoarsely.

"Your sister didn't want his money, she wanted him."

"How do you know?"

"She refused it. She rejected every bank wire he sent her. Finally, near the end of his life, he simply changed his will."

"And you knew all of this, the entire time?"

"I've learned bits and pieces over time, but yes, I've known since his will was read last June that he left her virtually his entire estate."

Rachel rose, legs and body trembling. She was shaking from her head to the tips of her white silk high-heeled shoes. "You've known since Michael's birth that Antonio wanted to provide for his child, and indeed, tried to provide but you interfered. You withheld support, and not just support, but *love*."

"I did what I thought was right," he answered tersely.

"But it wasn't right, and you…you don't know the first thing about love. You have no idea what love means, or you wouldn't have worried more about your Marcello stock and investments than your late brother's child!"

"I was wrong, Rachel."

"You….you…" She shook her head, eyes burning, chest so tight she couldn't breathe. "You're not just wrong. You're not even the man I thought you were, Giovanni. You're not at all the man—" She turned away to cover her face with her hands. She pressed her fists against her eyes, holding back the scalding tears, and the grief, and the pain.

Gio had lied to her. *Lied.* Nothing about their relationship was true. He was false, and selfish, and incapable of caring for anyone but himself. Incapable of loving.

"Thank God you told me now," she said, choking on a muffled sob. "Thank God I found out before it was too late."

"We're still going to marry, Rachel. We still need to protect Michael."

She nearly lost it then. "You're the last one I'd trust to protect Michael! You've done everything in your power to punish him—"

"I had to be cautious."

"Of course you'd see it that way. I don't. But what I do see is the light, and the truth, and the exit, because I want out. I'm not going to do this. I don't have to do this with you, not anymore. You see, Gio, I don't benefit from marrying you. I don't win anything. I just lose. I lose out on the opportunity to be cherished and loved. And it's not worth it—"

"What about Michael?"

"I love Michael, and will always love him, but we don't need you. We don't need your help. I don't want anything to do with you. Keep your precious Marcello stock. Keep your Marcello name." She glanced down at the huge yellow diamond weighting her hand. She'd thought it absolutely beautiful when he'd put it on her finger but now it symbolized all that she hated. Rachel tugged the ring off and dropped it on the bed, next to the antique wood box. "And your Marcello jewels."

"You don't mean that, *cara*."

"Oh, but I do." Hands shaking, Rachel took off one earring and then the next and tossed them onto the bed, too. "I'll take Michael back to Seattle with me, and I shall raise Michael myself, and he'll be a Bern, and he'll be loved and we might struggle, but at least we'll struggle with love, away from your contempt, and condemnation, and judgment."

Gio crossed the room and caught her by the arm, pulling her toward him. "I understand why you're upset. I was upset last night, too—"

"For different reasons, I imagine."

"No, for the same reasons. My brother loved your sister, and they had a tragic love story, and a tragic ending, but we are not going to continue the tragedy. It ends here. It ends now. Michael was a true love child, and he shall be brought up with love, not fear or shame."

She yanked away and, taking several steps back, began unpinning the veil, not caring that it was tearing at her elegant chignon. "I would never shame him! You're the one that withheld support because you doubted the legitimacy of your brother's love."

"My brother was not himself at the end. The tumor was impacting critical thinking, and he made a number of rash decisions. After his death I was inundated with crises, all requiring my attention as well as that of Marcello's legal team. I wasn't even aware of Michael's existence until my private investigators informed me just before Christmas that your sister had given birth in September and had put my brother's name on the birth certificate."

"So why didn't you reach out to my sister then?" she demanded fiercely.

Gio didn't answer and she swallowed around the lump filling her throat. Her voice was hoarse when she added, "Because you thought she was a gold digger and you were not going to reward her."

"You admit your sister's history was problematic, and I wanted to have a DNA test done to see if the baby was truly my brother's—"

"That was December," she said, balling the long lavish lace veil and throwing it at him. It fell short, though, fluttering to the ground. "This is March. DNA tests do not take three months. And the drag…the excessive amount of time wasn't due to the investigation, it's due to your own blindness because you were duped by a gold digger, and so you assume every woman is a gold digger. This isn't even about Juliet and Antonio…it's about you!"

"Not true."

"Oh, it is true, absolutely."

"Rachel, your sister was not the only one to claim to have borne my brother a child. Your sister was one of dozens."

"I don't believe you."

"Over the years many women have claimed to be pregnant, demanding financial support, or worse, a wedding ring. All were eventually proven false. Until Juliet." He drew a breath, features taut. "Money makes people do stupid things."

"Yes, it does," she shot back, growing angrier, not calmer. "And it's made you selfish and cynical and hard. You think the worst of people, not the best. But once you knew the truth about Juliet, you owed it to her to reach out and do what was right. You *owed* it to her and Antonio to make amends."

"I would have eventually," he answered quietly.

"Eventually," she repeated, voice strangled. "*Eventually* killed her, Gio."

"Money wouldn't have changed her mental state, Rachel. Clearly, she wasn't well if you—who were *there*—couldn't help her. How could I?"

"You accept no blame, do you?"

"My job was to protect my family, including the business, a business that employs thousands of people. To give a quarter of a billion-dollar company to a young woman halfway across the world without doing due diligence, could have meant the end of Marcello Enterprises—"

"It's always about the business, isn't it?"

"I was raised from birth to put the family business first."

"I think you mean from birth you were raised to put the business first. Family appears to be a very distant second."

"I won't apologize for being skeptical. I thought your sister took advantage of a dying man, and I wasn't about to see his estate go to someone who hadn't loved him, but rather saw an opportunity to grow rich at someone else's expense. I will apologize for the lengthiness of the investigation. I insisted it be thorough, but I realize now that my legal team was perhaps too meticulous—"

"You can't even apologize without adding in disqualifiers."

"I'm sorry your sister is dead, but my brother is gone, too." His voice was deep and granite hard, and yet his accent softened the words, taking the truth and pain in them and searing them into her heart. "They're both gone," he added, "but they're not lost to us. They've left us their love child."

"Stop. You don't love, and you don't believe in love."

"That's not true. I love you—"

"*Now* you say it? Now, when it's all over? When it's too late? My goodness, you're desperate—"

He moved while she was speaking, reaching for her, bringing her hard against him. He cupped her face and kissed her, a kiss that was unlike any of the kisses before. This one wasn't hard and fierce, nor was it scalding, blistering with bone-melting desire. This kiss was dark and intense, layered with emotion and raw, undeniable need. He didn't just want her lips and touch. She felt as if he wanted to reach into her and steal her very heart.

"You can't have me," she whispered against his mouth, as tears stung her eyes and filled the back of her throat. "You Marcellos have taken enough." She wrenched away and nearly tripped over her full lace skirt in her need for distance. "It's over, Gio. We're through—"

"Not by half," he ground out. "We have a family."

"You're not part of it anymore."

"It doesn't work that way. You can't cut me out. Your sister didn't leave a will. She didn't indicate that she wanted you to be Michael's guardian. You have no more legal right to him than I do."

"But I want him more."

"That's not true. I want him very much. He's all I have left of my brother, which makes him infinitely dear. Unlike you and Juliet, I didn't have a complicated relationship with Antonio. There was no guilt or anger, no envy or resentment. From the time he was born, he was my brother and best friend. I sat with him as he died, and it killed me watching him suffer and fade. His death wasn't quick, either. It took him weeks to go, and even as great as his suffering was, I grieved terribly when he was gone. I still miss him profoundly."

His words came at her, one after the other, and it was overwhelming his passion and love—love he'd never shown her. She shouldn't be jealous, but she was. Rachel had wanted Gio to love her that much, but he never did.

"No, I didn't rush to Seattle with open arms when I learned of Michael," Gio added. "But I had to be cautious about this claim that he had a son there. A dozen different women claimed they'd had his son or daughter. A dozen different claims to process. A dozen different women who wanted a piece of Antonio's wealth. It was bad enough to lose my brother, but then to deal with all of this desperation and greed?"

Rachel flinched, aware of how desperate she'd been when she'd arrived in Venice on Gio's doorstep. "Desperation doesn't make a person bad!"

"No, but it does make one suspect."

"You should have told me this right away. You should have sat me down on that first day in your mother's favorite salon and laid out the facts—"

"*Buon Dio*, Rachel! You had called the paparazzi. You invited the media to my doorstep. How was I to trust you?"

She shook her head, thoughts muddled, hating that he could tangle her up, make her question everything all over again.

Gio closed the distance, hands settling on her shoulder, his skin so warm through the thin lace of her gown. "We have both made our share of mistakes, but we won't make another one today. We will marry, and we will be a family for Michael. You may feel hurt, and you might be angry with me, but you can't allow your anger to hurt Michael. *Our* baby."

Our baby. The words rippled through her, and she exhaled at the truth in the words. Gio somehow always cut straight to the heart. Maybe it was his engineering mind, or maybe it was his way of problem solving, but it felt as if he'd taken a lance to her, cutting away the garbage and nonsense and revealing what was essential and true.

Michael was theirs. He wasn't Juliet's any longer, nor was he Antonio's.

They were both gone. They would never return.

"We will love him and protect him," Gio said, one hand slipping up over her neck, his fingers spreading across her jawbone, cradling her face as if a jewel or flower. Every place he touched tingled, her skin flushed and sensitive. "We will not be destructive or selfish. We will put aside our differences and do right by our son."

She stared up into Gio's brilliant blue eyes, seeing him, all of him, not just his dark good looks, but his heart. His fierce, hard heart. He was brutal and relentless and he'd smashed her hopes and dreams. "I loved you," she said numbly. "And I gave you my heart, but I've taken it back. It's not yours. It will never be yours again."

His thumb stroked her cheek as it met the edge of her mouth. "We can work through this. And we will, after the wedding."

Her lips quivered at the caress. He stroked down again,

lingering at the curve of her mouth. She didn't know where to look. She certainly couldn't look into his eyes, not any-more, and so she stared at his mouth and chin, her chest filled with rage and pain. Why had she ever come to Italy? Why had she thought that Giovanni would be the help she needed? She closed her eyes to keep tears from forming. "I won't forgive you."

"It's not as bad as that, *il mio amore*."

"It is as bad as that," she corrected, trying to pull away.

He didn't let her. He held her, and then he pressed a kiss to her forehead, the kiss careful, gentle, far too kind. "Our guests are waiting. I will help you put your veil back on, and then let's go finish what we have begun."

CHAPTER FIFTEEN

SHE FELT WOODEN during the twenty-minute ceremony, and then dead during the reception.

It was all a blur. The meal. The toasts. The music. The cake.

She didn't even remember stepping on to the ballroom floor for their dance. She couldn't feel her legs. Couldn't feel anything but Gio's hand on her side, his hand on her back, his hand on her arm as he steered her here and there, from one place to another, keeping her moving, keeping up appearances, keeping it together.

And then finally, finally it was over and she was in her room, but it wasn't her room anymore. During the reception someone had emptied the wardrobe in the blue guest room and taken everything out, taking all of her things out, putting them elsewhere.

Rachel sank onto her bed, the bed that was no longer her bed, her white full skirts pillowing up, and then fluttering down.

She didn't have anything anymore. She wasn't even herself anymore.

The door opened and closed. She knew without looking that it was Gio. She could feel his energy and intensity from across the room.

"This isn't your room anymore," he said quietly.

Hot tears filled her eyes. "You've taken everything from me."

"But I've also given everything to you. My home, my name, my heart—"

"You don't have a heart."

He didn't answer, not right away. He walked around the

perimeter of the room, studying the blue silk wall covering and the enormous gold framed mirror and then the blue painted dresser with the pair of blue vases.

"If that was true, then I wouldn't feel anything right now," he said, lifting one of the blue vases and turning it in his hands. "I wouldn't care so very much that I've hurt you. And I wouldn't mind that you're in here, alone, feeling betrayed and deceived." He set the vase back down and faced her. "But I do mind very much. It wounds me that I've hurt you and ruined your wedding day—"

"Please stop. You're just making it worse. I don't want to talk to you. I don't want to see you. I just want to go home, to Seattle."

"But this is your home now."

"No."

"Yes. And we are a family now."

"Never!"

"And my wife, whom I love."

She covered her ears and squeezed her eyes shut, refusing to listen, unable to endure any more. He'd won. Couldn't he see that he'd won? Did he have to break her completely? "Then prove it," she cried, jumping up. "Prove you love me. Do what's best for me. Let me go."

He stood before her, expression shuttered. "Giving up on you, giving up on us, doesn't prove love. It shows defeat."

"I'm not a challenge. I'm not a business deal."

"I know. You're my wife."

"But I don't want to be your wife, not like this, and for me, this…" She gestured to the room, the house, the city beyond the windows, "This will never be okay."

She had to go. She had to get out of here. She'd leave everything behind. She didn't need her clothes, or her suitcase. She just needed her passport. "I'm leaving," she said hoarsely. "Tonight. I don't want anything from you. I don't want money. I just want my passport so I can go."

"What about Michael's?"

"I'm not taking him with me. He will stay here with you for now, but I'm hiring an attorney. I'm going to sue for custody—"

"It could take years, and I'm not sure you'd win."

"What else am I to do? Stay here and pretend that you didn't lie to me and manipulate me?"

"I'm asking you to forgive me. I'm asking you to understand that I was in a difficult position, too."

"I was not a gold digger!" She threw the words at him, eyes brilliant with unshed tears. "I never wanted your money. I wanted *you*."

"Good. Because I want you. Not just want you. I need you." He hesitated. "I need you with me."

"You don't mean it. You can't even say the words without flinching."

"It's true. I don't speak of love easily, and until tonight, I have never told any woman I loved her. Just as you refused to make love until you had found the right one, I have held out, too. There are only a few people in my life that I can say I truly love. My mother. My brother. Michael. And you." He approached her. "Yes, *you*. I love you, Rachel."

"You're only saying that because you're desperate."

"You're absolutely right. I am desperate. I'm desperate for you to stay. I'm desperate to salvage what's left of our wedding day. Today was horrendous, but we still have the night—"

"No."

"Yes. We have the night, and we have every night from now on. I'm not going to let you go. This is your home now. You belong here, with me." He moved toward her, a slow walk to match his measured words. "Rachel, I didn't have to marry."

"But you did. The media…the company going public… you couldn't have the scandal."

"Money is money. I have plenty of it, but money doesn't buy happiness and I would never, ever marry just to protect my financial interests or investments."

"But you said—"

"It was a tactic." He shrugged, unrepentant. "I wanted you here. I wanted you with me. And yes, I want Michael, but I want you every bit as much. From the moment you appeared on my doorstep, you've been mine. I waited thirty-eight years to find someone like you. You can't think I'm just going to give you up?"

Her head spun. He was saying the right words, all the things she'd wanted him to say, but why did he wait so long? Why hadn't he shared all of this before? "You just don't want me to go."

"You're right. I didn't marry you in an extravagant, romantic wedding to lose my bride before the honeymoon."

She drew a quick, sharp breath. "There will be no honeymoon."

"Of course there will, but there won't be if you leave."

He was trying a new tactic, she thought, and she didn't want to be intrigued but she couldn't help showing a little interest. "Why haven't you mentioned it before?" she asked suspiciously.

"Because it was supposed to be a surprise."

She wished she wasn't curious. She wished she didn't care. But she did care, not about the trip, but about what he might have planned for her. For them. "Where were we going to go?"

"Ravello, on the Amalfi Coast."

Rachel drew a quick, shallow breath, feeling far too many emotions, not the least being regret. "Were we going to take Michael?"

"No. Not on our honeymoon. I wanted time alone with you, my bride, my wife, my heart." He reached for her and drew her toward him, little by little, step by step, ignoring her resistance.

Or maybe it was because she didn't resist very much.

Rachel was exhausted. It had been a roller coaster of a day, up and down, and down and down, and even though she didn't want to care for him, she did. Her love wasn't a flimsy thing, but strong and deep and true.

"You have hurt me so much today," she whispered as he pulled her against him. She rested her cheek on his chest, his arm tight around her.

"I am sorry. I didn't want to bring those letters to you before the wedding, but how could I share them with you after?" He stroked her hair, and then down her back. "That would have been even worse. And so even though the timing was awful, I did what I thought was right. Shared with you everything I knew."

"Even though it meant ruining our day."

"I'd rather we ruin a day than start our marriage with a lie."

Rachel closed her eyes and breathed him in, needing his arms right now, and his warmth. She needed him and loved him, for better or worse. "And what would you do with me on our honeymoon?"

"I would make love to you three or four times a day. I would love you until you felt secure and understood that you're the only woman I have ever wanted to marry. I did not marry you out of obligation or to satisfy the international stock market."

She tipped her head back to look up at him. His bright blue eyes glinted with tenderness and humor.

"It's true," he added, his expression changing, the laughter giving way to a focused intensity. "I married you, *bella*, because I love you. And just in case you need to hear it again, Rachel, *bella, ti amo*. I love you. *I love you*. Do you understand?"

Her heart was beating a mile a minute. "I think so."

"You're not convinced?"

"Not entirely. Not yet."

"What else can I do?"

She touched her tongue to her upper lip, dampening it. "Take me on that honeymoon?"

He grinned, and then his grin faded and he kissed her, a long, searing, bone-melting kiss. "We leave tomorrow," he said. "And we'd better sort out our birth control, or you'll be pregnant before you know it."

EPILOGUE

One year later

IT WAS LATE March and their first anniversary was just a week away. They were scheduled to leave for Ravello in two days to celebrate their first anniversary in style and enjoy a second honeymoon, something both Rachel and Gio were very much looking forward to.

But nothing was going to plan.

Again.

Instead of packing for their seaside villa in Ravello and anticipating their luxurious getaway in the glorious Italian sun, they were zipping along in the Marcello speedboat, heading to the hospital with Rachel tightly, frantically gripping Gio's hand.

She hurt. And she was scared. "He's coming too early," she gasped, as another swift, hard contraction hit.

Gio just held her hand until the contraction subsided. "We're almost to the hospital," he said quietly, leaning over to kiss her. "It won't be long now."

"But what is his hurry?" she cried, looking up into Gio's blue eyes. "He had another month to just hang out and relax. That was all he had to do, too."

Gio's lips quirked, and yet his touch was gentle and calming as he stroked her hair back from her damp brow. "I think he's eager to meet everybody and begin playing with his big brother."

"Well, he should have consulted me about his plans, because *I'm* not ready." Rachel gulped in another breath of air. "But just like a Marcello, he does what he wants and expects everyone to adjust and accommodate his whims."

Gio laughed softly. "Thank goodness you understand your Marcellos."

"You're all a lot of work!"

"And now you'll have one more."

Her tense expression eased, her lips curving. "Thank goodness I love little boys." She looked up into her husband's eyes. "I just want him healthy. I'm scared that he's coming too soon."

"Not all babies go full-term. I was early. He'll be perfect. I promise."

"He doesn't have to be perfect. I will love him however he is."

"I know you will. You are the best mother, the best wife." Gio kissed her again. *"Bella Rachel, ti amo."*

She blinked back tears. "I love you, too." She gripped his hand tighter. "I think the next contraction is starting. They're coming faster and closer." She blinked and exhaled, trying to remember her breathing, trying not to panic. "Oh, I just want to get there. I really don't want to give birth in a motorboat."

He leaned over, kissed her forehead. "We're almost there."

She clenched his hand hard as the contraction made everything tighten. "Oh—oh, Gio. This is serious."

The boat was slowing, the lights of the mainland ahead of them. "I see the ambulance," he said. "We're here. You're going to be fine."

"I don't know if *fine* is the word," she panted, "but as long as I'm not delivering in a speedboat, I won't complain. You know I love Venice, but this is a bit much."

He smiled at her, but didn't answer, too intent on helping her breathe through the pain. "I love you," he whispered as the contraction eased. "And I'm so proud of you. Together we have created the most extraordinary life."

Gio repeated the very same words less than an hour later

as he held his newborn son, a boy they'd already decided to name Antonio after Gio's beloved brother.

Rachel blinked back tears as she watched Giovanni walk around her hospital room, cradling their son, murmuring to their newborn in Italian.

She still wasn't fluent in Italian but she understood what he was saying to baby Antonio.

I love you, my beautiful boy.

Her eyes stung all over again, her heart so very full.

They'd come full circle, she thought, and what an astonishing circle it was. Full of love and hope and the happy-ever-after she'd thought was only found in fairy tales.

Which must mean fairy tales did come true. At least, in Venice they did.

* * * * *

MILLS & BOON

THE HEART OF ROMANCE

A ROMANCE FOR EVERY KIND OF READER

MODERN

Prepare to be swept off your feet by sophisticated, sexy and seductive heroes, in some of the world's most glamourous and romantic locations, where power and passion collide.
8 stories per month.

HISTORICAL

Escape with historical heroes from time gone by. Whether your passion is for wicked Regency Rakes, muscled Vikings or rugged Highlanders, awaken the romance of the past.
6 stories per month.

MEDICAL

Set your pulse racing with dedicated, delectable doctors in the high-pressure world of medicine, where emotions run high and passion, comfort and love are the best medicine.
6 stories per month.

True Love

Celebrate true love with tender stories of heartfelt romance, from the rush of falling in love to the joy a new baby can bring, and a focus on the emotional heart of a relationship.
8 stories per month.

Desire

Indulge in secrets and scandal, intense drama and plenty of sizzling hot action with powerful and passionate heroes who have it all: wealth, status, good looks…everything but the right woman.
6 stories per month.

HEROES

Experience all the excitement of a gripping thriller, with an intense romance at its heart. Resourceful, true-to-life women and strong, fearless men face danger and desire - a killer combination!
8 stories per month.

DARE

Sensual love stories featuring smart, sassy heroines you'd want as a best friend, and compelling intense heroes who are worthy of them.
4 stories per month.

To see which titles are coming soon, please visit

millsandboon.co.uk/nextmonth

MILLS & BOON
MODERN
Power and Passion

Prepare to be swept off your feet by sophisticated, sexy and seductive heroes, in some of the world's most glamourous and romantic locations, where power and passion collide.

MILLS & BOON
Desire

Indulge in secrets and scandal, intense drama and plenty of sizzling hot action with powerful and passionate heroes who have it all: wealth, status, good looks… everything but the right woman.